the
Bachelor's Bargain

the Bachelor's Bargain

CATHERINE PALMER

TYNDALE HOUSE PUBLISHERS, INC.
CAROL STREAM, ILLINOIS

Library of Congress Cataloging-in-Publication Data

Palmer, Catherine, date.
  The bachelor's bargain / Catherine Palmer.
    p. cm.
  ISBN-13: 978-0-8423-1929-4 (pbk.)
  ISBN-10: 0-8423-1929-8 (pbk.)
  I. Title.
  PS3566.A495B33 2006
  813'.54—dc 22   2006011425

Printed in the United States of America

12 11 10 09 08 07 06
 7   6   5   4   3   2   1

For the newest member of our family,
Phyllis Miller Cummins.
I love you, and I'm so grateful God
brought you into my father's heart.
Welcome!

❦

The LORD directs the steps of the godly.
He delights in every detail of their lives.
Though they stumble, they will never fall,
for the LORD holds them by the hand.

Psalm 37:23-24

And we know that God causes everything to
work together for the good of those who love
God and are called according to his purpose
for them.

Romans 8:28

❦

Acknowledgments

MY THANKS to everyone at Tyndale who helped bring Miss Pickworth and her friends to life: Kathy Olson, Ron Beers, Becky Nesbitt, and Karen Watson. Also those in sales, marketing, public relations, author relations, and all who see my books from manuscript to bookshelf. My gratitude also to Anne Goldsmith, who now works elsewhere but is certainly not forgotten. I also thank my husband, Tim Palmer, whose guiding pen is always the first to cross the pages I write. Thank you, honey. Bless you, Andrei and Geoffrey, for loving and supporting good ol' Mom. May God richly bless you all.

And most of all, thank You, Lord, for holding me by the hand.

❧ *One* ❧

Devon, England
1815

Like the finest silk threads twisted and crossed to form a net of gossamer lace, Anne Webster's plan had to be executed perfectly or it would unravel into a thousand strands. The seedcake must be steaming, the ripe quinces baked to perfection, the tea piping hot. The Limoges cup and saucer must gleam in shades of blue and gold on the black lacquer tray. Every facet of the silver teapot must reflect the fire crackling on the grate. Nothing could be out of order, for this afternoon Alexander Chouteau, son of the Duke of Marston, was taking tea alone.

A shaky breath clouded the creamer Anne took down from the Welsh cupboard at the back of the large, dimly lit kitchen. Lifting the hem of her apron, she buffed the silver vessel. She must not tremble when she poured Sir Alexander's milk. Her voice must not quaver when she offered the sugar.

Above all, she must remember to shut the door behind her when she went in. If anyone heard her speaking to him . . . if anyone knew what she had planned . . .

"Anne, do stop your dawdling." Mrs. Smythe slid a dish of baked fruit down the slick boards of the scrubbed pine work-table. The glass clinked as it hit the tea tray. "Sugar those quinces, and be quick about it. I shall not have Mr. Errand screeching at me because the tea was late and His Grace complained at it being tepid. The duchess cannot bear cold toast, and you certainly know how their son demands punctuality."

"Of course, Mrs. Smythe." Anne glanced at the pink-cheeked cook and wondered what the portly woman would do if she knew about the roll of delicate Honiton lace tucked into the pocket of her housemaid's dress.

Mrs. Smythe must never know. If she found out, Anne would be forced to sell her work to the laceman who came out in his chaise every month from London. The long, narrow panel of lace had taken her three months to design, its pattern two months to prick onto parchment, and its silk threads another ten months to weave with her pillow and bobbins.

In France, where it was illegal to own lace, such a panel would be worth a king's ransom. Even in London, the laceman could sell her work for a small fortune, though he would pay her only a fraction of its value. Thus she had designed the pattern for the Chouteau family alone, praying that her plan would succeed. Into this bit of lace she had woven her future.

Quickly Anne took the nippers and broke several lumps from the hard sugar cone. She slipped one lump into her pocket as a treat for Theseus, the duke's mastiff; then she sprinkled a spoonful of sugar crystals across the peeled quinces.

Dear God, she lifted up in a swift and silent prayer, *please let these satisfy Sir Alexander's exacting tastes.*

As she carried the dish across the kitchen, the chill of the black-and-white-tiled floor crept through her thin slippers and around her ankles. Her toes ached. She had been on her feet since before dawn, and she would work at Slocombe House until the last dinner plate was cleared and washed that evening. In between, she must pray that the duke's son would have the temper to listen to an impertinent, headstrong housemaid, that he would have the patience to inspect her length of Honiton, and that he would have the wit to realize the value of the lace.

As she set the dish of quinces on the tea tray, Anne squeezed her eyes shut. *Lord and Father above, this is my only hope*, she reminded Him. God already knew her dire predicament, of course, but she felt it behooved her to call it to His divine attention one more time. If Sir Alexander paid her even half the market value of the Honiton, she would have enough money to quit her position at Slocombe House and return to her family's home in Nottingham. She could hire a barrister to secure her father's release from prison and save her sisters from the mills.

Satan's workshops, her father called the drafty, machine-filled buildings with their deafening clatter and sooty windows. The mills, he had preached in more than one sermon, caused women to sicken and children to die early deaths. As the eldest child in the Webster family, Anne knew that what her father said was true, and she had supported his association with the Luddites even though their activities had landed him in prison.

Now the family's only hope rested in her hands. Could a length of lace, more air than thread, be their salvation? Anne swallowed at the gritty lump in her throat. It had to.

"Head in the clouds, as usual," the cook huffed as she bustled past with a plate of steaming cinnamon and currant scones. "Have you remembered to put tea in the pot, Anne?"

"Yes, Mrs. Smythe."

"She probably put in coffee." Sally Pimm, the first kitchenmaid, eyed Anne as she sifted salt into a copper pot of soup on the stove. In the scullery a cluster of maids giggled at the notion while they scoured stewpans, colanders, and utensils.

"Will not Sir Alexander be surprised," Sally continued, "if he sips up a mouthful of coffee when he is expecting his afternoon oolong?"

"No more than when his oxtail soup tastes as though it were made with water from the English Channel," Anne returned.

Mrs. Smythe's wooden spoon cracked across Sally's knuckles, and she let out a shriek.

"Have mercy!" Sally cried.

"Then stop your chatter and pay heed to the supper, girl! Shall we all be tossed out on our ears thanks to your heavy hand with the salt? Have this as a reminder!"

Forcing herself to turn a deaf ear on Sally's wails as the cook added another whack for good measure, Anne laid a starched cloth over the tray and set the tea things on it. She knew the kitchenmaid was envious of her position. Under normal circumstances, Anne would have joined the staff as a scullery maid. After several years, she might have worked her way up to second kitchenmaid, first kitchenmaid, and then, possibly, cook.

Circumstances were not normal. After the Luddite riots and her father's subsequent imprisonment in Nottingham, Anne had journeyed by coach to the south of England. In London, she had found a position at Trenton House on Cranleigh Crescent in the tony Belgravia district. Hired as a housemaid, she displayed a wit and propriety that soon elevated her to the station of lady's maid to the widowed homeowner's sister, Miss Prudence Watson. Not long afterward, Lady Delacroix had returned from a sea voyage to the Far East. When the young, wealthy baroness took up residence in Trenton House once more, Anne became her trusted assistant and companion.

In that position, Anne had hoped she might earn enough money to pay for a legal defense for her father. But it was not to be. To the shock of London society, Lady Delacroix fell deeply in love with a common tea tradesman. Their winter wedding stripped her of her title—though not her immense fortune—and she was now known simply as Mrs. Charles Locke. Sadly, she had informed Anne that their association could not continue, for she intended to travel with her husband. He had formed a partnership with two men, one of whom was Sir Alexander. Because of this relationship between the two families, Mrs. Locke had penned a glowing referral that led to Anne's joining the staff of Marston House, also on Cranleigh Crescent.

Despite Mrs. Locke's commendation of the clergyman's

daughter, the housekeeper at Marston had intended to put Anne into the kitchen, until Mr. Errand intervened.

"Look at the girl, Mrs. Davies," the butler had intoned, one bushy white eyebrow arching as he inspected the newcomer. "With that face she will be wasted in the kitchen. She has kept all her teeth, her eyes are clear, and though she is no great beauty, she has a certain grace to her carriage. The letter from Mrs. Locke indicates she may have a measure of wit, as well. Put her in the house, and you will please His Grace, for you know the duke despises the fishermen's daughters we normally get."

Anne had been given a position in the grand home, though she was once again a housemaid and earning very little. While most of the *ton* went to London for the spring social season and thence to the beach for the summer, the Duke of Marston preferred Slocombe, his country house in Devon. And in March, he went there with his wife, his younger son, and most of his staff, Anne included.

Not long after their arrival, however, word came that Miss Prudence Watson had fallen prey to a nervous malady and would benefit from a sojourn away from the city. The duke and his wife insisted she be brought to them at Slocombe, and once again, Anne had the pleasure of waiting upon her as a lady's maid. Anne attended solely to Miss Watson's needs except on Saturday afternoons. On that day, Miss Watson kept to her rooms to write letters, the footmen took their leave, and Anne was given the honor of serving tea to Sir Alexander.

A knock sounded on the door. "Now what?" Mrs. Smythe mopped her forehead. "More charity? Sally, see to them."

"I beg your pardon, mum, but I am in the midst of beating

eggs." The kitchenmaid shot a glance at Anne. "Perhaps Anne will do it, if she is not too proud."

"I should be happy to feed the poor if I had the time," Anne said, surveying the hungry men, women, and children who had gathered around the door that led from the kitchen. She could so easily be one of them, and yet she had worked hard to improve her lot. Now she must press forward with her plan.

Touching the lump that was the roll of lace hidden in her pocket, she lifted her chin. "Sir Alexander—"

"Do it now, Anne, and quickly," the cook cut in. "We cannot have them loitering about and gawking at us. The leavings are in a stew pot by the back door."

"But the tea. The duke's son—"

"Ooh, she is in a hurry to be off," Sally Pimm taunted. "Have you an assignation with Sir Alexander today, Miss Webster?"

Anne's cheeks went hot. "He is awaiting his tea."

The cook gave a snort. "Tend the charity first. His Grace's tea has just gone up to the library, where he is meeting with the vicar. The duchess is in the drawing room with two ladies from church, and I am sending theirs now. Sir Alexander's scones will not be ready for five minutes." She pointed her spoon at the door. "See to them, or I shall have to tell Mrs. Davies of your impertinence."

Anne grabbed a ladle. "Yes, Mrs. Smythe."

As she hurried past Sally Pimm, the kitchenmaid smirked. "Do not dirty your apron now, Anne. They say Sir Alexander likes his girls pretty, unsullied, and clean. You must try to please him on at least one count."

"Sir Alexander admires respectful manners and silence," Anne retorted. "That is why his attendant at tea today is I and not some other."

In the scullery, Anne stacked clean bowls and spoons in which to ladle the leavings. She must ignore Sally and hurry. Trying to steady her fingers, she loaded a tray with the dishware and carried it back into the kitchen.

The poor of Tiverton village watched her, eyes shining with hope in their dirt-darkened faces. How could she think only of her own plans when such people were starving around her? Yet she must not let her father go on languishing in prison. And what of her sisters?

"Thank ye kindly, miss." An elderly man tipped his battered hat as she filled a bowl with leavings and handed it to him.

"God bless the duke." A man with no teeth gave her a smile. "And God bless the duchess."

Hurrying down the row of outstretched hands, Anne ladled meat and other scraps from the large pot. *Quickly now, quickly.* In all the months she had served Sir Alexander, this would be his first Saturday to take tea alone. Her only chance to speak with him! If she were late with the tea, he would be in a foul mood and would send her away at once.

"Thanks." A little girl looked up, her tiny face pinched and white as she wrapped one arm around her full bowl. "Be ye an angel from heaven, then?"

"I am but a housemaid, my dear." Unable to resist the child's sweet expression, Anne dug from her pocket the lump of sugar she had saved for Theseus and tucked it into the little one's hand. "There you are. A gift from the duke himself."

The girl turned the lump one way and another. "What is it?"

Anne could hardly imagine she had never seen sugar. "Put it into your mouth."

The child eyed the gift for a moment, then she gingerly placed the small lump on her tongue. "Mmm." Her eyes drifted shut. Long lashes fanned her cheeks. A smile spread across her lips.

The door blew open in the March wind as yet another of Tiverton's needy slipped into the kitchen. Anne took little notice. She knelt before the ragged girl and grasped her sparrow-thin hands.

"For this moment, you are a duchess," she said softly. "In your mouth is the taste of Christmas plum pudding, black currant ice cream, treacle, and Turkish delight. You are dressed in a gown of fine green silk caught up with rosettes of pink ribbon. At your neck is gathered a length of the most exquisite Pointe d'Angleterre lace. Your hair is braided, looped, and curled. Your skin is scented with fragrant heliotrope."

"Now that is a good 'un," a man said with a laugh. "She smells more like coal dust, I should think."

"Hush!" A woman gave him a sharp elbow. "Do not spoil it."

Anne watched the little girl drift in the vision she had created. "White gloves slide up your fingers and over your arms, all the way to your elbows. You have in your possession a lace fan figured with tiny Chinamen trotting across a footbridge. On your feet you wear thin slippers of emerald green kidskin. Pale mint ribbons wind around your ankles. You dance like the wind; your voice sings as high and clear as a bird's; you can draw and stitch and play the pianoforte better than anyone in the realm. In short, my little one, you are the most enchanting duchess in all of England. That is the taste in your mouth. It is dreams."

"Coo!" The little girl's eyes popped open, and everyone chuckled as she threw her grimy arms around Anne's neck. "I almost thought it was true!"

"And well it should be." The man who had just tramped in from the street swept off his dusty hat and gave the child an elegant bow. "The Marquess of Blackthorne, dear little duchess." Then he turned to Anne and repeated the bow. "I am at your service, madam."

Though heavily bearded and scruffy, he possessed a pair of gray eyes that sparkled with fun. What could she do but curtsy in return? "Queen Anne, of course."

"Your Majesty, the pleasure is all mine." Before she could react, he took her hand and lifted her bare fingers to his lips. Warm in spite of the chill outside air, his mouth brushed across her knuckles, lighting a tingle that skittered up her arm. His mustache surprised her in its softness, and she jerked her hand away.

"I beg your pardon!"

"Lavender," he pronounced, straightening. "A clean scent, slightly astringent, with all the promise of spring. Very appropriate."

"I was putting up . . . putting up the linens this afternoon." She shoved her hand beneath her apron. "Tucking lavender among the sheets."

Disconcerted more by her reaction than by the stranger himself, Anne filled a bowl with leavings and handed it to him. Never mind. She must put him aside. He was the last of the charity, and she had not yet heard Sir Alexander's bell.

There was still hope. She started down the row again, this time collecting spoons and bowls.

"If yer going to play at peerage, ye will not want to be Blackthorne," the toothless man said to the tall newcomer. "They say the poor man be dead."

"Dead? Good heavens, how did it happen?"

"Met with an accident while traveling in America. Scalped by them red savages."

"Better him than Sir Alexander," a woman uttered in a low voice. "The marquess was nothing but a rogue, he was. Roved about the country, spent money like water through a sieve, sired babes everywhere he stopped, but could not be bothered to marry here at home and give the duke an heir."

"Good riddance to the blackguard," Anne affirmed. Then she added, "God rest his soul."

"Abominable, was he?" the stranger asked. "Well, the devil take him."

"I should never wish the forces of darkness upon anyone." She set a handful of spoons on her tray. "But an heir apparent has his duties. The Marquess of Blackthorne rightly should have seen to his father's duchy. He was said to wager large sums at cards, and he engaged in more than one duel. He was even known to attend glove matches."

"And bare-knuckle boxing, too," the toothless man confirmed. "If yer bound to play at royalty, man, be the duke. He is well loved by everyone."

"Ah, the Duke of Marston." The tall man turned to the housemaid. "Your Majesty, Queen Anne, be so good as to acquaint me with the health of the master of Slocombe House."

Stacking the used bowls on her tray, Anne tried to suppress her growing irritation with the dusty intruder. She had no time for games. "His Grace is well. He is taking tea in the library."

"And the duchess?"

"With friends in the drawing room." As she approached the man, she realized he was still lounging by the door, his bowl untouched. "You must eat, please. I am to serve Sir Alexander his tea at any moment."

"Is that a royal command, Your Highness?"

Unamused, Anne stared into the man's deep-set gray eyes. In his brown tweed coat with its tarnished brass buttons, though clearly no better off than his companions, he had a demeanor that spoke of some wit. His features were all of angles and planes, and his nose slashed down the middle of his face like an arrow, straight and determined, nostrils flared slightly. Beneath that uncompromising nose, his mouth tilted upward at one corner. Perhaps he was entertained.

"If you will not eat," she told him, "please give me your bowl."

"My dear queen, I have not finished my inquiry. How fare the duke's daughters, the ladies Claire, Lucy, Elizabeth, Charlotte, and Rebecca?"

"I could lose my position at the house," she shot back, her voice low. "Will you eat or not?"

He took a mouthful of mush and grimaced as he chewed. "The ladies?"

"They are fine, of course, all of them married and gone away."

"Even Lady Rebecca?" He raked a hand through his hair.

Coal black, it was a rumple of uncombed curls. "She is young to be wed. What of Alexander, the duke's son?"

"He is to marry in six months' time."

"Is he now? And who is the lucky lady? Not Miss Mary Clark, I hope. She may be a beauty, but she is only the daughter of a baronet. He can do much better."

Anne stared. How did such a beggar know the names and ranks of Society? With his heavy beard, unruly hair, and dark eyebrows, there was an air of wildness about the man. His large hands in their tattered knit gloves appeared so strong as to make him dangerous.

He dipped his spoon into the leavings. "This supper actually grows on one. Not bad at all, in fact. Alexander is not still dallying with Mrs. Kinnard, the actress, is he?"

"Sir Alexander's fiancée is Gabrielle Duchesne, the daughter of the Comte de la Roche."

"Blast! Has he no better sense than to choose a Frenchwoman? With Napoleon restless and France in a muddle, there is no guarantee she can hold onto her fortune."

Anne pressed the tray into her stomach as Sir Alexander's bell began to jangle on the far wall. Absorbed in his own musings, the stranger tapped his spoon against the rim of the bowl. She had to go. But this last of Tiverton's needy was clearly odd, perhaps even a lunatic, and she did not want to irk him. The others began to file out the door as he straightened, focused on Anne's eyes, and gave her a brief nod.

"Is Smythe in?" he asked.

Surprised at his common use of the formidable cook's name, Anne glanced behind her. "She is seeing to the seedcake and—"

"What of Errand? Is he still butler at Slocombe?"

"Excuse me, but please may I have your bowl?" She tried to grab it as he walked past her into the center of the kitchen. "Sir! You must go out the back way! Please, sir!"

"Mrs. Smythe," he called.

The cook lifted her head from sniffing the seedcake and swung around.

"Mrs. Smythe, have you any gingerbread nuts for my tea today?"

"Awwk!" At the first sight of the man, she dropped the plate of seedcake and threw up her hands. "It is . . . it is . . . it is—"

"Ruel Edward Chouteau, Marquess of Blackthorne." He winked at her as he gave his thick beard a tug. "Not quite as hairless as the red savages might have wished me. In fact, I am a little on the bristly side, I fear."

"Lord Blackthorne!" Mrs. Smythe shrieked, her tongue loose at last. "Great ghosts, you are dead!"

"On the contrary. I am quite alive and eager for a cup of your finest oolong. And do send for a barber, will you? I shall speak to Errand on my way up. Perhaps he ought to prepare my father with the news that his elder son has arisen from the grave."

"The marquess is in my kitchen!" As Sir Alexander's bell jangled, the cook stepped over the shattered dish of seedcake and shouted at her kitchenmaids as if they might have some explanation for what had just occurred. "He walked into the kitchen from the back! Where is his carriage? Where are his footmen? Where is the valet? Oh, how could we have known it was Lord Blackthorne? He came in with the charity!"

"Calm yourself, Mrs. Smythe. You know, I always

believed the only place to learn the truth about life at Slocombe House was in the kitchen. Besides, I must have my gingerbread nuts."

"Gingerbread," the cook repeated. "Gingerbread nuts. It is you! Oh, my stars! Oh, help! Mary and Lissy, run to the larder for ginger and treacle! Sally, find Mr. Errand at once. Anne, see to Sir Alexander's tea, for pity's sake. Gingerbread. We must have gingerbread nuts."

Sucking air back into her lungs, Anne slid the tray of used bowls and spoons onto a kitchen table and picked up her skirts. She edged around the room to avoid the tall man in its center, swept up the tea things, and made for the curtained doorway that led into the hall. Her legs felt as though they had been jellied.

That ragged, dusty specimen of charity was the marquess? But the marquess was dead, scalped, and buried in America. And she'd only just wished him good riddance. She had called him a blackguard. Straight to his face!

"Your Majesty," he called out. "Good Queen Anne."

She paused, every limb suddenly rigid. She could not bring herself to look at him. "Yes, my lord?"

"Would Your Royal Highness be so kind as to extend Sir Alexander cordial greetings from his brother?"

"Yes, my lord," she whispered. "Of course, my lord."

The Marquess of Blackthorne was chuckling behind her as she brushed past the green baize curtain and fled into the hall.

⸙

Anne remembered to shut the door. It was the only part of her plan that was not lost. How dare she show Sir Alexander a length of Honiton lace when she had been ordered to tell the man that his brother, the marquess and heir to the duchy, had suddenly returned from the dead? If she failed to carry out her duty, she would be dismissed.

"Set the tea on the table there," the duke's younger son told her as she approached the fireplace. Lounging on a damask-covered chair in the sitting room of his suite, he barely glanced up from the newspaper he was perusing.

Known to enjoy the luxuries of his rank, Sir Alexander cut a fine figure as he drove his gig about Tiverton. In London he was said to shine even more brightly, a veritable star among Society's eligible bachelors. With his tall, slim, well-proportioned physique, thick golden hair, and brilliant blue eyes, he was reputed to have broken many a young lady's delicate heart.

"Sugar, my lord?" Anne asked softly. She had managed to pour his tea without spilling any into the saucer, but she hardly trusted herself with the tiny silver tongs.

"Please." He lifted his head and scrutinized the dish of quinces. "Do pass my compliments to Mrs. Smythe. The fruit appears quite agreeable."

"Yes, my lord." She got the first lump of sugar into his tea without incident. The second landed with a splash. "Milk?" she asked quickly.

"Dare I? I fear it may end in my lap."

"I beg your pardon, sir." Anne glanced up at him. "I shall take the greatest care."

His bright blue eyes greeted hers with a light sparkle. "Pour away, then."

He studied her as she lifted the creamer and tipped it over

his cup. She held her breath. *Please, dear Lord, do not let me spill it. Give me strength. Give me courage.*

"Well done, miss."

"Thank you, my lord." She let out her breath.

"Have you served me in the past?"

"I am lady's maid to Miss Prudence Watson, but she does not require me on Saturdays. Your footmen take leave, and I bring your tea."

"Ah, yes. I begin to recall you." He scrutinized her so intently that she felt a heat creep into her cheeks. "Surely, then, you are familiar with your duties and with the proper decorum required of the duke's staff. Are you aware, madam, that you have shut the door to my sitting room?"

"I am, sir."

"Ahh, I see." He settled back in his chair and stretched out his legs. Deeply set beneath his pale brow, his blue eyes took on a glitter that sent a knot into the pit of Anne's stomach. He did not understand at all, and his shameless advances with the female household staff were common knowledge. She gripped her hands at her waist until the blood drained from her fingers.

If she were to save her father, she must do it now. She must bring out the lace. But if she were to keep her position at Slocombe House, she must tell him about his brother's arrival.

"Pray, what am I to make of this tightly shut door, miss?" Sir Alexander cut into her dilemma. When Anne failed to make an immediate reply, he held up his newspaper, a copy of London's popular daily, *The Tattler.* "Perhaps I should pen a letter to Miss Pickworth and beg her advice in the matter. I might write, 'Dear Miss Pickworth, the housemaid serving my tea today closed the door to my chambers. What shall I do with her?' Indeed, I think a letter is a very good idea. Do bring my pens and inkwell from the—"

"Sir, I beg you will not write to Miss Pickworth," Anne spoke up quickly. The very idea that all London might somehow learn of her indiscretion sent an arrow of fear to her heart. "I closed the door, my lord, because I wished to speak to you in private."

"Privacy between a duke's son and a housemaid? Well now. Have you a certain object in mind?"

Anne watched dark spots dance across her eyes. "Indeed, I do have a purpose, my lord."

"A purpose beyond splashing sugar into my tea and milk onto my lap? This is intriguing. Do you wish to join me in reading Miss Pickworth's latest commentary on Society?" He patted the arm of a nearby chair. "She writes that Miss Prudence Watson's malady has prevented her from returning to London, though her eldest sister and her husband are soon expected home from their travels abroad. 'No doubt Mr. and Mrs. Locke,' writes Miss Pickworth, 'will deeply desire the company of their dear sister, Society's brightest star. But sadly, Miss Watson remains unwell.' Is that not dreadful information? I wonder if you have any notion as to what can be ailing her."

Anne shook her head. She was not about to inform the man that her mistress appeared to be suffering from a deep despondency of spirit and a strangely nervous disposition. Any little thing might prompt a flood of tears or a collapse into hysterics. The smallest events distressed her, and she seemed to find little purpose or hope in life.

"I cannot say what troubles Miss Watson," Anne told him.

"Perhaps we should invite her to come to tea with us today. She is a beautiful young woman and her company might entertain us both. Or do you prefer to have me all to yourself?"

Anne stared at the newspaper. The lump that had been in her throat all afternoon wedged tight. "As Miss Watson's lady's maid, I should be pleased to increase her happiness in any way possible. But she writes letters to her sisters on Saturdays, and I believe she will not wish to be disturbed."

"You know her well, do you?" Ignoring his tea, he set the newspaper down and stood. "Miss Watson's London residence, Trenton House, is very near to my own family's ancestral home on Cranleigh Crescent."

"Yes, sir. I am aware of that." Anne's mouth turned to glue.

Sir Alexander tugged at the hem of his striped waistcoat and loosened the silk cravat at his neck as he took two steps toward her. She lowered her focus, concentrating on the way his narrow-cut trousers came together under the instep of his shiny leather shoes.

"Of what else are you aware, miss?" he asked. "Something more than serving tea in the afternoon?"

She dug her nails into her palm. "Yes, my lord."

"How engaging." He reached out and touched the side of her face. "Your cheeks are aflame. A very pretty pink. Let me see your eyes now. Ah, they are brown. A disappointment, for I am partial to blue-eyed ladies."

"My lord," she managed, "I do not wish to speak of my eyes."

"But you did wish for a tête-à-tête with me, did you not?" He reached around and tugged the white cotton mobcap from her head, and her hair spilled across her shoulders. "Oh, dear, brown again. I have never been fond of brown hair, but your figure is—"

"Sir, it is about lace." Anne shrugged away from the fingers that had reached to touch her hair. "I have come to speak with you about lace. Honiton, to be exact."

"Lace?" He looked up, confusion furrowing his brow.

"I was taught lace design by Mr. Samuel Beacon in Nottingham, and he says I am the finest pattern pricker he has ever seen, and certainly one of the cleverest artists. My execution of lace is said to be exquisite." She gulped down a breath, determined to get it all out before he could say another word or reach for her again. "Thinking only of your future happiness with the Lady Gabrielle Duchesne, the daughter of the Comte de la Roche, I contrived to fashion a design with her wedding gown in mind. I have created a length of the most delicate lace, my lord, using silk threads and more than a thousand bobbins."

Taking a step back from him, Anne dipped her fingers into her pocket and brought out the roll of lace. "As you can see," she hurried on, unwinding its length, "I have carefully created the Chouteau family's lozenge. I centered it just here, believing my lady Gabrielle may wish to use the lace on her bonnet or perhaps at her bodice. Bearing your esteemed heritage in mind, sir, I designed a row of English roses along the edge, while ribbons twined with morning glories loop around the lozenge."

When he said nothing, she gathered her courage, lifted her chin, and continued. "Ferns, of course, have been interwoven throughout the pattern to convey the lush beauty of England.

As I designed this border, I envisioned a garden of the sort that only my lady's future home here at Slocombe House could boast, a profusion of blossoms, vines, and birds. I have given the lace a certain fragility, you see, thinking of the misty air in the south and wishing the fabric to whisper against your bride's skin in a most delicate fashion."

Forcing herself to meet his eyes, she laid the lace in his hands. "I come boldly before you, my lord, only because of my great reverence for your excellent tastes, knowing that you would wish the very best for your future wife. Had I sold this to the laceman, the crest would be meaningless to any other buyer, and so I . . . I would beg you to . . . to consider a fair price—"

"Alex!" The deep voice rang through the cavernous room like a gong. "Alex, old man, how are you?"

Sir Alexander glanced up from the lace, focused on the man who had just burst into his room, and faded to a deathly shade of white. "Ruel?" Anne's lace drifted to the floor. "Can it be?"

She watched in horror as her months of work, her only hope for her father's freedom, came to rest at the edge of the carpet beside the fire. Sir Alexander took a step forward, and the sharp heel of his pump impaled the lace.

"Ruel!" he cried, hurrying across the room with the length of lace trailing behind him. "You are alive. But we thought you were gone! We had heard appalling reports that you were dead. Father has been beside himself, sending out parties of inquiry, posting letters left and right. But you are well. Thank heaven!"

The two men embraced, the one a dark pirate and the

other a golden youth. Anne looked down at her tattered handiwork, remembering her father in prison and the fiendish lace machines that had put him there. Then she covered her hand where, in the kitchen below, a dusty beggar's lips had heated her skin. She decided she agreed with his earlier sentiment.

The devil could take the Marquess of Blackthorne.

∽ Two ∾

"Alex, you are looking capital." Ruel clapped his brother on the back. "How old are you now? Twenty, at least."

"Three-and-twenty, Ruel, and you look abominable. Your skin is as brown as a seaman's. And your hair! Good heavens, where have you been these last months? When did you arrive at Slocombe?"

"Not an hour ago. May I join you for tea? I assume there is plenty."

Ruel glanced at the housemaid. She had backed up against the fireplace, her face as white as chalk and her cheeks a pair of pink roses. This must be the young lady who had served him leavings with the charity in the kitchen, yet she looked different now. Her hair, a rich brown cape around her shoulders, glistened in the red firelight. Her mobcap lay on the floor. Ruel appraised the situation. Alex was still up to his lecherous pranks. Had the maid been a willing partner?

"I shall see to the pouring," he said, aware that the woman would wish to escape and restore her appearance.

"I shall fetch Mr. Errand." Her voice was low. "He will dispatch a footman to serve you, my lord."

"Nonsense." Alex settled into his chair and waved a hand at her. "Pour the tea. My first cup is cold already, and I have no patience to wait for a footman. Seat yourself, brother, and tell me what you have been about. The last intelligence we had of you was from our cousin, Auguste Chouteau. He wrote that you were staying with him in St. Louis in the Missouri Territory."

"The last I heard of myself, I had been scalped by Indians." Ruel looked at the maid again. She was carefully ignoring him. Unable to rescue her cap, which had fallen beneath the tea table, she had tucked her hair behind her ears and bent to pour a second cup of tea. "Fortunately, I have kept the hair on top of my head, and a valet will take a razor to my face."

The maid's attention darted from the teapot to his face. Their eyes met, and the flush spread from her cheeks down her neck. Caught, she shifted her concentration to her tasks again.

How did he appear to a woman, Ruel wondered. Though a common house servant was no judge of aristocratic manliness, it comforted him to see the blush of color that made her fair skin glow. Perhaps he had not lost all his noble bearing during the three months of torment he had spent at sea.

"Before you go out in Society, you must do better than shave," Alexander informed him. "The regent has developed a bit of a tousled mop, but he manages to make it appear rather dashing. You, on the other hand, look a veritable rake. So where have you been, Ruel? No doubt pirating, smuggling, or something else equally illegal."

"Your opinion of my talents has grown since I have been away, Alex. I am flattered." Ruel accepted the warm cup Anne handed him and held it to his lips. Closing his eyes, he took a deep drink. As the steaming liquid seeped into his body, he felt his muscles unknot. He let out a long breath.

"In spite of my appearance," he told his brother, "I have been the perfect gentleman. I departed St. Louis half a year ago and have been traveling homeward since that time. Down the Mississippi River to New Orleans. Around Florida. Across the Atlantic."

"It took you six months to get here?"

"The ship was becalmed at sea for five weeks." He opened his eyes. "We were in danger of starvation. I shall be grateful when sails are put away in favor of steam."

Alex laughed. "Steam! Ruel, you are dreaming again. No one in his right mind would undertake a sea crossing with nothing but steam power. Ridiculous!"

Ruel waved a hand in dismissal. "Never mind. I shall leave that enterprise to the shipyards."

"I should hope so."

"We have other missions to discuss, Alex." He leaned forward, elbows on his knees. He had missed his brother in the years away. Though the younger man's propensity to waylay housemaids and his expensive tastes in food and clothing had never pleased Ruel, he counted on Alex for companionship and counsel. From their boyish exploits exploring the smugglers' tunnels along the coast to their enthusiastic pursuit of London's most enchanting female company, they had been close comrades.

"I have made plans to absolve the duchy from our growing

debt," Ruel announced. "With hard work and determination, we can do it."

Alex raised one golden eyebrow. "Not with steamships, I hope."

"Textiles."

"Textiles?" With a groan of dismay, Alex leaned back and covered his eyes. "We have not the sheep of the Lake District, the mills of the Midlands, or the roads of London, yet we are to build a fortune on fabric?"

Ruel could not suppress a grin. "Your dramatics could be staged in London, Alex. Look at you—a brocade waistcoat, a silk cravat at your throat. Your trousers are so tight it is a wonder you can sit down. You have even managed to impale a bit of lace on your heel."

Reaching across the tea table, he tugged the strip of lace free from his brother's pump. "Dallying with the ladies again, Alex?"

The younger man chuckled. "I am to be married in six months. Gabrielle Duchesne is quite the most sumptuous Frenchwoman I have ever met, and I look forward with great anticipation to our wedding."

Ruel idly wound the lace scrap around his finger. "What is her fortune?"

"Fifty thousand pounds, but you must understand I am deeply in love with the lady. Especially now that I know we shall save the duchy with your textile enterprise. Do apprise me as to how it is to happen."

"A trade triangle. We shall send raw linen and flax from England to St. Louis. The opportunities there are incredible. We shall use our own port, of course, and I hope to acquire ships eventually."

"Steamships, no doubt."

"We shall export our fabric from St. Louis to the United States and France. In France, we shall add to it machine lace from the factory I intend to build in Douai, and *violà*! We shall revitalize French fashion and fill our coffers."

Alex guffawed. "I have missed you indeed, Ruel. Not since you left have I enjoyed such grand entertainment. More tea, please, miss."

"Laugh all you like, Alex, but with only your wife's dowry, you will not be purchasing silk cravats for too many more years." Ruel stuffed the scrap of lace into the pocket of his waistcoat and held out his cup. "I left Devon three years ago for one reason: the duchy was running aground in debt. Father knew it. You knew it. Now I am returned, and I have brought a workable plan. I shall expect your cooperation."

He watched the housemaid pour his teacup full. Too full. The tea edged up to the brim, over the top, and down the sides into his saucer. "Enough!" he said, grabbing her hand and forcing the pot upright.

"I beg your pardon, sir." She dabbed at his saucer with a napkin. "I shall fetch Mr. Errand at once."

"Stay, madam. My brother and I wish to have a private discussion." He glanced up at the woman. Instead of cowering beneath his wrath as she properly should do, she was glaring at him. He frowned.

"Ruel, permit me to understand you," Alex said, setting down his cup. "The duchy grows almost no flax, yet we are somehow to send a grand shipment of it to the Missouri Territory. Are we not at war with the United States, brother?"

"You have been sequestered too long in the countryside.

A peace was signed last December." Ruel took mental note that his brother had not gained any greater interest in world matters than he had evidenced as a boy. "I have calculated our initial investment in raw materials, Alex. The duchy can afford it."

"We have no factory in St. Louis, yet we are somehow to make fabric from this quantity of flax?"

"Exactly. Auguste Chouteau is sixty-nine-years old and a man of vision. Our cousin believes St. Louis will one day become a hub of commerce. He has committed himself to the expansion of the city and her industries. Even as we speak, he is beginning construction of a mill."

"American fabric? French lace? Are you mad?" Alexander leapt to his feet, reached out, and pulled the length of lace from his brother's pocket. "Assume we manage to purchase a quantity of flax," he said, wagging the lace as he spoke. "Assume we manage to ship it all the way to St. Louis. Assume we manage to build a mill there and weave the raw stuff into fabric. Even assume we ship our product all the way to France. That country is in chaos, man!"

"Perfect for our purposes. Did you know Napoleon has just returned to his homeland?"

"You must be joking. He is in exile on Elba."

"No longer. He is free, and by my best guess, all the sovereigns of Europe will unite forces against France. It can mean nothing less than war."

"Wonderful. We are to turn the minds of the French to fashion when their nation is at war. Have you taken leave of your senses, Ruel?"

"Perhaps, but a man cannot depend on logic alone in these times. Without vision, without dreams, the world will overtake us. We must be ready to run with the best of the thinkers, Alex." He stood. "We must not be quick to ridicule the advancements of our age. Factories and mills are springing up everywhere you look. Steam is taking the place of wind and water power. The middle class is getting its hands on the source of money—manufacturing. Money is power. Power in the hands of the middle class spells doom to the aristocracy. And the aristocracy, my dear Alexander, is us."

The younger man stared at his brother. "You are raving."

"I am the sanest man in this society of brainless dandies. If we mean to save our fortune, we must think. Think!" He punched the air with a forefinger. "What does little Tiverton have to offer the world? Agriculture? Mining? Timber?"

"Fishing."

"Fishing? When we can barely supply our own villages?"

"Then what can you be thinking?"

Ruel jerked the scrap of lace from his brother's hand. "Textiles! We are the source of Honiton lace. John Heathcoat has moved his lace machines from Nottingham to Tiverton in order to escape the Luddites and their determination to smash and burn him out of business. We shall take one of Heathcoat's lace machines to France, and there we shall unite their product with our cheaply made fabric to supply every languishing Frenchwoman in the empire."

"How shall we export lace machines to France when you know perfectly well it is illegal to do so? Lace itself has been banned there since the Revolution."

Ruel dropped his voice and leaned close to his brother's ear. "With France in wartime chaos, we shall smuggle our machinery."

"Smuggle it!" Alexander threw up his hands in disbelief.

"Quiet! If we are found out, the plan is dashed. We must arrange a meeting with Heathcoat at once. Do you know him? I understand he is brilliant. I mean to learn all I can about—"

At that moment the chamber door flew open. Ruel clamped his mouth shut as Laurent Chouteau, the Duke of Marston, entered. He was followed close behind by Mr. Errand, the butler, his personal valet, two footmen, and another man.

"Ruel!" The duke's blue eyes shone in his face. He was frail and white-haired, but his bearing was undeniably regal. "So, the intelligence I have had of you is true. You are returned!"

"Father!" A flood of feeling ran through Ruel as he strode across the floor toward the gentleman. Like the little boy who had always adored his father, he threw his arms around the older man and hugged him warmly. "You should not have walked this distance, Father. I fully intended to come to you before dinner."

"I could no more await you than a child anticipating Christmas. These many months, we have had vicious rumors of your death, my boy. But here you are, safe, sound, and hale." He held his son at arms' length and looked him up and down. "Good heavens, what plagues your hair? And have you no better clothes?"

Ruel grinned. "I have just returned from sea, Father. My wardrobe and hair will have to wait. But how are you? Well, sir?"

"Tolerable, tolerable." The duke gestured to a short, round-headed man at the rear of the party. "Do you know our vicar? I was taking tea with him when news of you was brought to me."

Introductions were made, and before Anne could escape she had been ordered to attend to tea for the Duke of Marston, his sons, the Marquess of Blackthorne and Sir Alexander, and the vicar of Tiverton. She nodded quickly, swept up the tea tray with its cold silver pot, and hurried from the room.

ᕫᕫᕫ

"Anne?" Prudence Watson intercepted her lady's maid in the corridor as Anne was rushing back up to Sir Alexander's room. "I am in search of more ink, and . . . Anne, what has possessed you? You are as pale as a ghost, your hair is wild, and you run with a tray full of Slocombe's best silver plate!"

Anne stopped, plunked the tea things on a hall table, and knotted her fingers together. "Oh, Miss Watson, he has taken my lace!"

"Who?"

"Blackthorne, that is who, and I mean to have it back."

"The marquess? He is here?" Prudence Watson clapped her hands to her cheeks in shock. An avid reader of Miss Pickworth's column in *The Tattler*, she well knew the rumors circulating about the fate of the Marquess of Blackthorne. In the past months, Anne had done her best to entertain and amuse the young woman whose golden hair and olive green eyes had tempted many a suitor. But Prudence had an unsettled temperament and a tendency toward histrionics. She had no interest in marriage and could find little to brighten the gloom that had overtaken her. Her lady's maid eventually abandoned all efforts to coddle her and simply became a friend.

"Aye, he is here!" Anne exclaimed, for once unable to calm

her own panic. "After Sir Alexander stomped a hole through my lace, the marquess took it. They snatched it back and forth from each other, waved it about, and abused it in the most abominable fashion. All the while, the marquess went on and on, blathering about lace machines, condemning Luddites, and never knowing he held the finest length of Honiton he shall ever have the good fortune to see."

"Anne!"

"I am going to take it back from him."

"You cannot! He is the marquess."

"He is a blackguard!"

"Oh, Anne!" Prudence took a fan from her pocket and fluttered it nervously before her face. "You know I have admired your lace panel, and I support your plan to sell it, but you cannot confront the duke's son. You will lose your position here, I shall be sent back to London for conspiring with you, and then what is to become of us?"

"You have enough money to live comfortably at Trenton House for the remainder of your life, Miss Watson. As for me, I shall rework the lace as best I can and sell it to the laceman. I mean to pay my way back to Nottingham and hope I never set foot in Devon again."

"What about your father?"

Anne sobered as she picked up the tea tray. "I do not know. Oh, I cannot think." Her voice was almost a whisper. She walked toward the door. "But without my lace, I am lost."

"You cannot go in there!" Prudence caught her arm. "Anne, the duke is inside."

"Aye, and I am to serve them all tea."

"But you have lost your mobcap!"

"Sir Alexander pulled it from my head and threw it to the floor. They are demons, those brothers, the both of them."

"You will dip your hair into the tea!" Prudence tried to stop her as Anne pushed open the door. "Oh, Anne!"

Careful not to spill a drop, Anne walked across the carpeted floor toward the party gathered around the fire. The duke's valet and the butler stood aside to allow her to place the tray on the table at the center of the cluster of chairs and settees. One footman began to pour the tea while the other handed around the cakes, toast, and biscuits. Anne picked up the plate nearest her and turned to the marquess, who stood near the hearth.

"Mrs. Smythe sends gingerbread nuts, Lord Blackthorne," she said, holding the dish before him. "At your request."

He took one of the small baked cakes and met her eyes. His voice was nearly inaudible. "My compliments, Your Majesty."

"You have my lace," she whispered through clenched teeth. "I want it back."

"Ruel, do be so good as to join the vicar and your family at the table," the duke commanded. "We must hear of your adventures."

Lace? He mouthed the word.

"In your pocket. I made it. Please return it to me at once."

"Ruel, what can you tell us of my nephew, Auguste Chouteau?" The duke tapped his cane on the floor. "Did his mother, Madame Marie Therese, welcome you? I understand she is quite prominent in Society in St. Louis. And you must give us to understand her relationship with this gentleman, Pierre Laclede, of whom I have heard so many remarkable things."

Frowning at Anne, the marquess stepped around her and sat down in a chair near the table. "I am sorry to tell you that your sister-in-law passed from this earth last year, Father." He accepted a cup of tea from the footman and turned his attention to the company. "Madame Chouteau was indeed highly esteemed, and with Pierre Laclede she was the mother of four children after Auguste. While in her presence, I found her to be a most charming and cordial hostess."

"She married this Laclede fellow, then?" the vicar asked.

The marquess gave a small smile. "Difficult, given her presence in a Catholic territory and the awkward matter that her husband, my father's brother, René Chouteau, did not die until 1776, well after she had given Monsieur Laclede his four children."

"Harrumph." The duke cleared his throat and took a sip of tea.

"Indeed," the vicar put in, "I have heard it said that Americans are more than a little coarse and unrefined. Rough about the edges, so to speak. Did you discover this to be so, Lord Blackthorne?"

"No more than we," he replied.

Immoral, the whole lot of them, Anne thought as she studied the group of men conversing around their tea. A married woman bearing four children by a man who was not her husband! But how much better was England's *ton*?

Many Sunday mornings she had heard her father denounce immorality from his pulpit. At the family dinner table, he told stories of King George III, who lived at Windsor Castle and had gone utterly mad. His son, the prince regent, had ruled England in his father's place for five years now. And

Anne's own father could not name a more dissolute, contemptible, and immoral man in the entire realm.

She watched the marquess take another gingerbread nut. No better than their regent were these high-born Chouteaus, with their penchant for chasing housemaids about and wooing ladies of Society without benefit of marriage. They were indecent, the whole lot of them. America, for all its wild savagery, could hardly be worse.

"What of your plans now, sir?" the vicar asked during a pause in the duke's inquiry about his son's travels. "Will you settle at Slocombe House for the summer?"

Lord Blackthorne thoughtfully stirred his tea. "Perhaps." He lifted his gaze and fixed it on his father. "Or I may travel again. I am thinking of a tour of pleasure in France."

"France?" The duke rapped his cane on the floor. "Nonsense, boy! We shall be at war with France again in six months' time. You must stay here and take your place. I am not long for this world, and Marston will be wanting a duke."

"Now it is I who must respond with a hearty 'nonsense,' sir. I expect to be taking tea with you well into your hundredth year."

The duke and the others laughed, and Anne could see by the glow in the old man's eyes that he deeply loved his son. The marquess reached out and laid his hand over his father's. Unwilling to witness the mutual tenderness between two men she was determined to despise, she lifted her focus to the fireplace and began counting the statuettes on Sir Alexander's mantelpiece. Blackthorne had her lace, and she hardly cared if he and his father lived to be two hundred. She wanted it back.

"You dare not deprive Society of your presence for another Season," the duke was saying. "Alexander simply cannot bear the press of admiring ladies alone, can you, my boy?"

"I shall warrant my brother's charms have been missed," Sir Alexander conceded.

"I fully expect you to get yourself to London and select a young lady to marry, Ruel," the duke continued, his voice taking on an imperious tone. "Alexander has engaged the lovely daughter of the Comte de la Roche; have you heard?"

"I have given him my congratulations."

"You are the heir apparent," the vicar reminded him. "You must think of the duchy."

"I am thinking of the duchy. Indeed, I think of little else."

The duke sat upright. "Then you have found a woman?"

"No!" Lord Blackthorne gave a laugh and leaned back in his chair. "Father, marriage is the last thing on my mind."

"Surely not! You are a healthy young man with duties clearly spelled out. You will go to town for the remainder of this Season and select a wife. I mean to leave the duchy in good hands, and I fully intend to see your heir before I die."

"Be reasonable, Father. I have been away from England three years, and my own brother tells me I am browner than a sailor. What lady would have me?"

"Any lady with good sense!"

"I have not the slightest inclination to dress myself up as a dandy and parade from one ball to another all Season. Before I left England, it was common intelligence that the Marquess of Blackthorne had the manners and bearing of a rogue. I was considered arrogant, thoughtless, insolent, headstrong, and rude."

"Ruel! You are shocking!"

"Shocking was not the least attribute of my reputation, Father. Ask any lady in London and you will hear the same. I am disagreeable and ill-tempered. I am willful and boorish."

"Bah!"

"I am afraid it is quite true, Father," Sir Alexander put in. "Blackthorne performs with greater success at cards than he will ever do with the ladies. Swoon at his fine physique they will, but marry him they will not."

"I cannot believe it," the vicar of Tiverton said firmly. "Lord Blackthorne is to be a duke. Why, any woman would be—"

"My manners have only grown more coarse with the influence of Americans," Lord Blackthorne interrupted. "I believe even the servants at Slocombe House have labeled me a blackguard."

He lifted his focus to Anne, amusement written in the tilt of his handsome mouth. In perfect agreement with the common assessment of Lord Blackthorne's reputation, she glared at him from her position by the fire. He knew he had toyed with her in the kitchen, he knew he had her lace in his pocket, and he knew he was teasing her even now. She would not be sorry if the marquess found a wife as vain and obnoxious as he.

"You are not a blackguard," the duke cried. "You are my son and my declared heir. Any woman with half the sense of a toad would marry you!"

"Any woman?" Lord Blackthorne rose and stepped from the tea table to the hearth. "Any woman, Father? Shall we put your assertions to the test?"

He dropped to one knee at Anne's feet and seized her hand. She gasped, but before she could jerk her fingers away he placed a firm kiss on them once again. Flourishing one hand in a grand gesture, he looked straight into her eyes.

"My dear Miss . . . what is your surname?"

"Ruel, do not be absurd, I beg you," the duke cut in, chuckling. "Come, come now, my boy."

"Your surname, madam?" Lord Blackthorne repeated.

"Webster, sir," Anne managed.

"My dear Miss Webster, I confess that in the course of our acquaintance I have fallen most violently in love with you. From the moment I took note of your magnificent eyes, I have been bewitched. Never before have I witnessed in any woman such tantalizing almond-shaped eyes. Their upward tilt is charming, and their color . . . the shade of an oak leaf in the autumn . . . the whisper of dark coffee . . . "

"Her eyes are brown," Sir Alexander spoke up. "I have had a look at them myself. Brown eyes."

"My dear Miss Webster, your hair falls about your shoulders like a sheet of molten bronze, a stream of the finest liqueur, a cascade—"

"Brown hair," Sir Alexander pronounced. "Brown, brown, brown. Brown as a mouse's rump."

Lord Blackthorne's eyes softened as he studied Anne. "Chocolate, I think. Hot chocolate laced with cinnamon."

Anne suppressed a gasp. No one—certainly not a man— had ever addressed her in such personal terms. While Lord Blackthorne's description was appealing, she knew he meant it as a joke.

"You have quite terrorized the young lady, Lord Blackthorne," the vicar said. "I should think you have gone far enough with this charade."

"On the contrary." The marquess leaned his arm on his knee and scrutinized Anne. "By heaven, she is a beauty. She actually is truly fascinating."

He turned to the assembled company. A chorus of "Nonsense" and "Absurd" followed his proclamation. Ignoring the comments, Lord Blackthorne gazed at Anne a moment longer. Mortified, she could do nothing but stare back.

"Miss Webster," he said in a low voice, "your cheeks blush with the damask pink of new roses. Your skin is as soft as the velvety down of a petal. Your lips are like ripe peaches in the heat of summer."

"Peaches!" Sir Alexander exclaimed. "Oh, very good, Ruel. You will win her heart with that one."

"Your brow speaks of high intelligence and your speech of good breeding." His eyes narrowed. "I think, perhaps, you can even read books. Is that true, Miss Webster?"

Anne longed to pull her hand away, but the marquess was looking at her with such intensity. His fingers on her wrist were warm and firm. His eyes had melted to rain-cloud gray, and his lips curved with the hint of pleasure. He was making sport of her, of course. She was nothing but a housemaid, the object of everyone's derision.

"The Bible," she said, lifting her chin. "I read it nightly."

"The Bible? Then you are a moral and virtuous woman, two strong qualities that add depth to your engaging beauty." He looked at her a moment longer, then caught himself. "Well, to get on with it. My dear Miss Webster, you cannot be indifferent to the fact that I have come to admire you devotedly. At the hour of our parting this afternoon, I felt that I could not go on. Indeed, I cannot release you now without telling you my heart and asking you if I may have your affection in return. Will you take me, Ruel Chouteau, Marquess of Blackthorne, as your husband and protector through life?"

Anne stared at the man who held her hand. The vicar cleared his throat, but the marquess never took his eyes off her. She knew she could play the blushing housemaid. She could run from the room in horror and leave them laughing in her wake. Or she could play the affronted daughter of a parson and hand Blackthorne a moralizing sermon on the evils of dissimulation. Or she could be herself.

"You have professed your admiration of me, Lord Blackthorne, and I thank you," she said clearly. "Although you intended to ridicule and mock me for the amusement of your company, your false esteem is truly merited. I am, indeed, educated and virtuous. The shape of my eyes and color of my hair are the endowment of my parents, but my skill as a designer of bobbin lace has been honed through my own diligence. Few in Nottingham and none in Tiverton surpass my ability to envision and design lace borders, fans, shawls, caps, and collars. Few can equal the skill with which I am able to prick my designs onto parchment. Some may have similar deftness in the twisting and winding of silk from a thousand bobbins across such a parchment pattern pinned to a pillow, but I am surely one of the most accomplished."

"Gracious," the vicar exclaimed in a somber voice. "Young lady, your impudence is startling."

"Let her continue," Sir Alexander countered. "This is most diverting."

"Miss Webster?" Lord Blackthorne signaled her to go on.

Anne glanced at the duke. He rolled his eyes and nodded. She stared at each of the Chouteaus in turn. Vain, self-important, heedless pagans. Her dismissal was imminent, she realized, and she wanted her lace.

"I descend from a proud line of Britons," she stated, turning her focus on the marquess. "My family are not nobles, but the surname Webster speaks to our profession. We are weavers. We create fabrics, fashion them, stitch them, and mold them to the pleasure of the aristocracy. Without us, Lord Blackthorne, you would appear in Society no better dressed than the legendary pompous emperor whose new clothes were made of invisible thread."

"My goodness." Lord Blackthorne swung around and gave his brother an incredulous look. "Did you ever think of that, Alex? Without this charming young lady and her family, we should all be as naked as eels."

"Bestow a title on them, then," Sir Alexander declared with amusement sparkling in his eyes. "Reward their grand contribution to our cause. Make the Webster family barons or knights."

"You have requested a difficult thing of me, Lord Blackthorne," Anne said to her mocker. "I am a woman who places high value on honesty, charity, and prudence. You have asked for my affection. You do not have it."

"No?" Turning to his father, the marquess held up his hands. "I do not have her affection. What did I tell you?"

Anne squared her shoulders. "Now I should like to ask something of you, Lord Blackthorne. I request the return of my lace panel."

He tugged the lace out of his waistcoat pocket and draped

the fragile masterpiece across his knee. Anne stared down at the craftsmanship that represented more than a year of her labor. Though torn where Sir Alexander's heel had spiked it, the narrow panel was still clean. She could pick out the tattered edges and rework them. Perhaps she could even cut away the central medallion that formed the Chouteau lozenge. She could place a bouquet of roses in its stead and sell it to the laceman for a price, small though it might be.

Lord Blackthorne lifted the border and held it to the firelight. For a terrible instant, she thought him so cruel as to toss it into the flames. She held her breath as he turned the lace one way and then another.

"You designed this, Miss Webster?" he asked.

"Yes, my lord."

The gossamer silk caught the flickering of the blaze and glowed with an inner radiance. "By George, I am mesmerized. This lace is a work of art. Here is our lozenge, Father, depicted in a most accurate and delicate fashion. These roses are . . . well, they are magnificent."

"Thank you, sir." She bent slowly toward the lace as she spoke. "I spent more than a twelvemonth in the border's design, and I should very much like—"

"I am afraid I shall have to keep it," he interrupted her, stuffing the lace into his pocket. "When I have your answer, Miss Webster, the lace will be yours again."

"She told you she could not like you," Sir Alexander said with impatience. "What more can you ask of the wench?"

"Until I know whether or not she intends to accept my proposal of marriage, I fear my father will pressure me relentlessly on that account. I must have Miss Webster's formal rejection, and then His Grace will understand there is not a woman in the land who would willingly yoke herself to me."

"Now, then, Lord Blackthorne," the vicar intoned, "do leave this poor serving girl in peace. You have tormented her beyond reason already."

"Indeed." The duke gave his son a scowl before turning his attention to Anne. "Miss Webster, go and find Mrs. Davies at once. Tell our housekeeper to prepare the chambers of the marquess. They are to be dusted and aired with no little care. Then you may inform Mrs. Smythe to ready an elegant dinner on my son's behalf. Stop at nothing. We shall have the finest from our larder."

"Yes, Your Grace." Tearing her eyes from the marquess's waistcoat pocket, Anne gave the duke a curtsy.

"Prepare the fatted calf," Sir Alexander declared with a grand sweep of his hand. "The prodigal son has returned."

"Let us make merry and rejoice," the vicar quoted from Scripture, "for this brother of yours was dead and has begun to live, and was lost and has been found."

"Amen!" the duke pronounced, as if he were God Himself.

As Ruel watched the dismissed housemaid slip away, three things occurred to him at once.

First, it occurred to him that in Christ's parable of the prodigal son, the dutiful brother had in no wise welcomed home his wandering sibling. In fact, he had been jealous, angry, and resentful. Was Alex as pleased as he seemed at Ruel's return? The turn of events meant Alex had lost the opportunity to be declared heir apparent. All the same, the younger man wore his usual carefree demeanor, and Ruel could not believe his brother had any hostile intent when he alluded to the parable.

Second, it occurred to him that Miss Webster did possess the most intriguing pair of golden brown eyes and the most luxurious mane of chestnut hair he had ever seen. She spoke with fire and wit, and she had shown not the slightest fear in declaring her utter dislike of him. Moreover, she was undoubtedly as talented in the creation of lace as she had asserted.

Finally, it occurred to Lord Blackthorne that he still held that panel of ethereal lace in his possession, and that Miss Webster had not given him her answer.

❦ *Three* ❧

"Whatever can you do?" Miss Prudence Watson whispered. "You cannot steal it back."

Anne studied the shadows creeping across the moonlit ceiling above the narrow bed in the room she shared with Miss Watson. She knew she should count it a privilege to labor in such an elevated position as lady's maid. While she enjoyed the spaciousness and warmth of her mistress's quarters, the other servants slept in small rooms on the top floor of Slocombe House.

Having begun her work there as a housemaid, Anne had seen what that life offered. The rows of beds for the staff were filled with sleeping kitchenmaids, scullery maids, parlor maids, and maids-of-all-work. Dimly lit and musty, the rooms contained nothing more homelike than beds, trunks, hooks for dresses and aprons, washbasins, and chamber pots. Their thin, yellowed walls and bare wood floors contrasted sharply with the opulent lower levels of

Slocombe House, which were outfitted with luxurious carpets, velvet draperies, gilt wallpapers, and cheery fireplaces. The poorly ventilated servants' quarters stayed hot all summer and frigid all winter.

How dare she complain? Yet, in her tenure at Slocombe House, Anne had discovered she was never alone. At mealtimes, the kitchen staff dined together in the kitchen, the household staff ate in the servants' hall, and the upper servants supped in the steward's room. The remainder of her time was spent in tending to the needs of Prudence Watson. Anne bathed, dressed, read her Bible, and worked her lace in the company of the young woman. Even on the rare afternoon off, she was compelled by Miss Watson to attend church or to stroll the grounds with her. Though the two had become friends, the difference in their rank could never be denied. Anne could refuse Miss Watson nothing, and that included talking through the night if her mistress wished.

The tall clock in the corridor outside their room chimed the hour of three in the morning. In two more hours the bell would ring, young ladies would fly out of bed, scrub their faces, pull on dresses, aprons, and mobcaps, and scurry to their posts. Anne would be among them, though she had not been permitted to sleep for a moment.

"You are not actually thinking of stealing the lace from the marquess, are you?" Prudence asked, the note of hope in her voice heavily tinged with dread. "I know your father was among the Nottingham Luddites and upheld their creeds. What were they?"

"Determination. Free liberty."

"Aye, and look what their determination to have freedom

got them, Anne. Look what they received in return for all their sledgehammers and muskets."

Sledgehammers and muskets. Anne wondered if Prudence realized that at first, the Luddites had been a peaceful group—resorting to smashing machines only when their demands for reasonable compensation, acceptable work conditions, and quality control were refused. All that had changed three years ago with a particularly violent attack at a mill in Lancashire. A large body of Luddites, some said more than a thousand, had attacked the mill, which was defended by well-armed guards. Then the government got involved, and many, including Anne's father, were convicted, imprisoned, some even hanged.

For generations—hundreds of years—the beautiful, handmade lace and stockings of Nottinghamshire had dominated the English market. But with the advent of machinery, Anne's father had watched his beloved parishioners endure a drastic decrease in income and prestige. Most had been forced to submit to the regimented and cruel treatment of factory owners just to feed their families.

Prudence was speaking again. "One must know one's place in the world. If you are a stockinger making seven shillings a week, you had better stay a stockinger, no matter how many machines the hosiers bring in. That is your place. Anne, your father may have preached that all people are the same in God's eyes, but I am sorry to tell you he was wrong. There are royalty, nobility, merchants, and laborers. You cannot go from one to the other. I am a tradesman's daughter, and both of my sisters are married to tradesmen. Our wealth and happy connections with Society's elite cannot erase our low position among them. You are a housemaid, and your job is to serve the duke's family. It has been God's hand that put the two of us together again, for if I leave Slocombe, you will not be permitted to go with me."

"You are right," Anne said, though she was unsure how sad this turn of events might be.

"My point is that you are a maid, and you cannot go independently selling lace to Sir Alexander or stealing it from the marquess. You could be put in prison like your father . . . or worse."

Anne rubbed her eyes and focused on the long windows. Where the curtains had been left open, moisture on the glass panes had traced fantastic curls that made her think of a dragon's misty breath. She envisioned the lace she could design of that undulating, magical pattern of swirls and shadows. Of course, no one would purchase a piece of lace so imaginative. The aristocracy wanted their standard roses and bows, perhaps a fern or two, and if they were unusually daring, a cherub or an urn.

"Here is my advice," Prudence said, offering her seventh new stratagem that night. Anne had counted them. "You should forget you ever made that lace panel. It was a foolhardy notion in the first place, thinking you could sell it to Sir Alexander. You are too much the dreamer, Anne. You have no practical sense."

Anne wondered, as she often did, how lace would look dyed in all the colors of the rainbow. At the moment, blonde lace was becoming all the fashion, lavishly trimming dresses, caps, pelisses, and aprons. Only a woman with especially dry hands could make blonde lace. In the summer it must be worked in the out-of-doors, and in winter it could be worked only in special rooms built over cow houses, where the animals' breath warmed the air. The smell in those rooms, as Anne well knew, was pungent, but the soot from any form of flame heat would damage the lace's fine threads.

"This is what you should do, Anne," Prudence said. It was her eighth attempt at dispensing advice. "You should start another piece of lace, this one more marketable, strewn with roses and lilies and such. In one or two years' time, if you save your wages from your work for the duke's family and add to it what you earn from your next lace, you should be able to go back to Nottingham and eventually pay an attorney to defend your father."

One or two years. Anne thought of her father living night and day in the darkness of his small prison cell. How different from the snug parsonage with its quaint library, writing desk, and warm rugs. He had suffered from ill health for many years, and Anne feared he could not live much longer in the confines of a prison.

It was not his physical strength that would suffer so much as his spirit. Mr. Webster considered his books sustenance, his pen and inkstand friends, and his pulpit the very breath of life. His communion with God through prayer and Bible reading were foremost—followed by his determination to serve mankind. He viewed the Luddites and their war against machinery as a cause as noble as the great Crusades, and he was willing to give his life on their behalf. Without Anne to secure his release, he surely would.

She had made it her mission to free the man who had given her breath, taught her to love Christ, and provided the education she valued above all else. Yes, Anne was a Christian, and she did all in her power to honor God. But she had been given a mind and will and strength of her own. She had talent and ambition, and she intended to use it all on her father's behalf. No man would stand in her way. The devil might try to waylay her, but he would not succeed.

"Here is what you should do," Prudence whispered. Suggestion number nine. "You should go down to Tiverton with me for church tomorrow and then take the afternoon off to visit the new mill that Mr. Heathcoat has built. Though I dislike the prospect of losing you, perhaps you might ask for an interview with Mr. Heathcoat himself and show him what you can do with lace. If he has any sense at all, he must put you to work as a designer of embroidery patterns for the machine lace he is manufacturing."

Anne turned her head and frowned at Miss Watson's moonlit profile. "Machine lace?"

"Oh, it cannot be so bad, Anne. Without the embroidery stitched upon it by hand, it is nothing more than boring and tedious net. You must not feel so threatened." In contrast to Anne's straight nose, Miss Watson's tilted upward at the tip, giving her a pert look—though lately Prudence had been anything but pert.

"You must be reasonable, Anne," she continued. "You can remain on the staff here at Slocombe, or you can think of something else rational to do. It is not as though there are many choices."

Anne stroked her fingertips across the hem of the sheet. "I could always be a marchioness."

"There you go again. You will not be logical."

Anne tugged the sheet up to her neck. She knew she needed to sleep, but every time she shut her eyes, she saw the Marquess of Blackthorne winding her lace around his finger and then stuffing it into his pocket. He had known its value at once. He also had recognized the significance of the lozenge, and he understood that the lace had no value to anyone but the Chouteau family. He wanted it for himself, the fiend. *Wicked man. Insufferable lout.*

Clenching her fists, Anne fought the rising tide of helpless anger. He had trapped her. Stealing the lace from him would send her to prison. Begging for its return would be useless. Working another lace border in hopes of freeing her father would take far too long. And she could never betray his ideals by using her skills in the manufacture of machine lace.

"What about taking a husband?" Prudence asked. "The gamekeeper has made his intentions clear. I understand William Green is more than a little put out at your rejection. In spite of his jealous manner, he is not so bad, is he? You would have your own cottage, and you could send your wages to your family in Nottingham."

Anne tilted her head to one side and eyed her friend. "And be subjected to the gamekeeper's brutishness and vanity night and day? Miss Watson, now it is you who will not be reasonable."

"Then look for a soldier to wed. I read in *The Tattler* that Napoleon has escaped from his island exile. Miss Pickworth predicts that England may go to war with France again. Can you imagine? Dreadful thought! Yet, why not make the most of it? As near as we are to France, Tiverton will be full of handsome officers in their regimentals. Soldiers earn solid pay, I should wager. You ought to look for a husband among them as soon as may be."

Anne lifted herself up on one elbow and studied the young woman in the grand canopied bed nearby. "You must try to rest, Miss Watson. You know how important it is to be fresh at breakfast. I am sure the duke will want you to meet his elder son."

"Perish the thought! I abhor introductions and polite, meaningless chatter." Prudence looked at Anne with luminous eyes. "What will you do, dearest friend? Oh, you will not attempt anything foolish, will you?"

Anne let out a deep breath. "Of course not," she replied. "Do try to get some sleep now."

As Prudence's breathing began to slow, Anne studied the curls of mist on the windowpane. Again she thought of the marquess, a man of shadows and darkness. She remembered perfectly the way his fingers had raked through the thick rumple of black curls on his head, the way his cold gray eyes had assessed her, the way his mouth had curved upward in a cynical smile.

She remembered, too, how his hand had felt as it held hers—warm, firm, strong. She recalled the timbre of his voice as he had pronounced her a beauty, had admired her eyes, had called her hair a sheet of bronze, had asked to be her protector.

Protector? There was only one way a man like Blackthorne could protect a woman like Anne Webster.

"You will forget about that lace, will you not, Anne?" Prudence murmured, half asleep. "You will heed my advice?"

Anne watched the sky lighten outside the small window of

her bedroom. The tiny square patch transformed from black to cobalt and finally to a familiar shade of silver gray, the gray of a man's eyes shining in firelight.

❧❧❧

When the Marquess of Blackthorne arrived at church in his chaise-and-four the following morning, not a female in the room failed to take note. The kitchenmaids whispered at how villainously shiny and black his hair appeared in contrast to the blond locks of his younger brother. The housemaids murmured their observations on the massive firmness of his chin, the wondrous breadth of his shoulders, the disdainful expression of his mouth, and the immense height to which he rose as he strode down the aisle toward the family pew.

The merchants' wives and daughters commented among themselves on the fine cut of the marquess's blue coat, its M-notched lapels, shiny brass buttons, flapped pockets, and French cuffs. The mayor's daughter and her friends regarded with admiration his double-breasted waistcoat of striped valencia, his cream-colored trousers, and his fine leather boots.

The landowners' daughters and their mothers took note that the future Duke of Marston had returned to England with his skin scandalously tanned and his attention no more fixed upon them than it ever had been. They observed, however, that in spite of his rakish manners and dangerous air, he had returned all the same and was as eligible as ever.

Anne Webster, seated beside Miss Watson in the second row from the back, saw only one thing. The Marquess of Blackthorne had tied beneath his high, stiff collar a cravat of the finest and most elegant silk Honiton lace.

Almost deaf with fury, she heard little of the vicar's rambling sermon. Instead she watched Blackthorne as he whispered some comment to his brother, chuckled at a tidbit of humor the vicar put forth, and ran his finger around the inside of his collar. Unable to quell it, she had the unchristian wish that her lace would come to life and strangle the man.

After the service, the Chouteau family exited the church first, followed by the inhabitants of their duchy. The duke and duchess departed for Slocombe House in their carriage, while Sir Alexander joined some town friends for a ride on horseback. When Anne emerged into the springtime sunshine, the marquess stood at the bottom of the steps deep in conversation with the vicar.

Miss Watson grabbed Anne's arm. "Do not say a word! I met Lord Blackthorne at breakfast. Despite his wild appearance yesterday and his abominable reputation, he is very noble and will inherit both title and land from his father. No one can speak boldly to him without dire consequences."

"But he is wearing *my* lace. Do you see?"

"You cannot be sure it is yours."

"It is mine, Miss Watson."

"Then let him have it. It bears his crest, and you will never prove you made it."

By the time Anne reached the marquess, it was all she could do to hold her tongue. She crossed her arms, lowered her head to hide her face with her bonnet, and took a deep breath. She was almost past him when he touched her elbow.

"Your Majesty, Queen Anne," he said in a low voice tinged with mock servitude. "How well you look this morning."

"Thank you, my lord," Anne managed through gritted teeth.

"I am happy to see you again today, as well, Miss Watson," he continued. "You cannot mind if I join you."

"No, of course not, Lord Blackthorne," Prudence chirped as the man nodded to the vicar and joined the two women in their walk across the drive toward the road. He slowed his long stride to match theirs and tipped his hat at acquaintances they passed, as though strolling with a tradesman's daughter and a maid were a perfectly acceptable pastime for a marquess. Anne knew Prudence would bolt given half the chance, so she caught her elbow and hung on.

"Your gown is fetching, Your Highness," he remarked, obviously speaking to Anne and ignoring her mistress altogether. "Such a subtle shade of fawn reminds me of the multitude of deer I observed during my time in Missouri. I must tell you it is a color that brings a glow to your lovely eyes."

Anne stared at the road, hardly daring to let herself speak. He was teasing her again, of course, and she had no idea why he found such revolting behavior so amusing. Poor Miss Watson was wilting with shock, her pale skin ashen and her fingers visibly trembling.

"I regret to see," he went on, "that you choose to cover your stunning hair with a straw bonnet. The lavender and crocuses with which you adorned your hat, however, are an exquisite touch. Your Majesty, you could not look more beautiful."

She lifted her chin and fixed him with a glare. "And you could not look more like yourself."

The marquess threw back his head and laughed loudly.

"Ah, I am pleased to find your tongue has lost none of its acidity. Did you note my choice of cravat this morning? I selected a fine length of Queen Anne's lace."

"How witty," she returned. "Yet the lace does not belong to you."

"Do you brand me a thief, Miss Webster?"

Prudence let out a low moan. It was all Anne could do to keep her friend upright. They had left the enclosure of the church and were walking in the lane that led to the main road. Had they turned west, they soon would have entered Tiverton, but they set their direction toward Slocombe House to be in time for the noon meal. In a moment, they would walk onto the road and begin the two-mile journey to the house. As the marquess had left his chaise-and-four at the church, Anne knew his interview could not go on much longer. If only she could keep her wits and forestall Miss Watson's panic.

"I merely speak the truth," she told him. "The lace is mine, and a true gentleman would return it to its owner."

"Unfortunately, I have never been considered a true gentleman," the marquess replied. "I believe you yourself referred to me as a blackguard."

"A reputation you only etch more clearly in mind with your unseemly behavior."

"My reputation is among the least of my concerns, Miss Webster."

"Mine, on the other hand, concerns me greatly, and if you do not return to your chaise at once, Lord Blackthorne, you may damage it irreparably. I hope you do not believe that your brother's pursuit of me yesterday in his chamber was in any way encouraged. I have no interest in becoming a momentary fancy for either of the two sons of the Duke of Marston."

Prudence's groan could have been heard by anyone passing. To Anne's dismay, she realized the road was deserted, all the household staff having hurried ahead. The marquess was showing no sign of returning to the churchyard for his transportation.

"Momentary?" he said. "My dear Miss Webster, my proposition to you yesterday was in no way meant to expire at day's end. If truth be told, you intrigue me more than a little. Where did you come by such pleasant manners?"

"If my manners are seen as pleasant, my lord, you mistake me. I have no pleasant feelings toward you whatsoever."

Again he chuckled and shook his head. "By George, I have not met anyone I could converse with so easily in years. Certainly never a woman. I wonder who you are, Miss Anne Webster, and how you came to be working as a housemaid at Slocombe."

"I was engaged by your father, sir, as you very well know."

"Yet you speak with the words of an educated woman. Your manners are acceptable if not noble, and your wit is delightfully sharp. You do not care for me in the least, and you have not the slightest awe of my rank. In short, you are so refreshing a creature, I have made up my mind to know you better."

"Upon my word, sir!" Anne bristled. "Such a bold address appalls me."

"I concede your evident displeasure, Miss Webster," he told her. "I am deeply wounded, of course."

She shot him a disparaging glance. "My apologies."

"Your father is a schoolmaster," he guessed. "You hail from Tiverton, and your house is filled with books which you delight to read."

"My father's occupations are none of your concern, Lord Blackthorne. We are not under your jurisdiction. Our family dwells in Nottingham."

"You are a long way from home. What brings you to Devon, then? Surely you could find employment in Nottingham."

Anne swallowed. She could never tell this man about her father's imprisonment with the Luddites. As a parson, Mr. Webster had been expected to preach, tend the ill, take tea with his parishioners, but little more.

That he had joined a secret group of men who met in Sherwood Forest and followed the orders of their leader, who called himself General Ludd, had brought utter disgrace to the Webster family. That he had broken into factories and smashed machinery had besmirched his own name forever. He had lost his position with the parish, of course, though the church had allowed his family to go on living in the parsonage until someone could be found to replace him.

Captured and thrown into prison, Mr. Webster had expected the usual sentence for destruction of private property—transportation to Australia. Exile from England for fourteen years would have been bad enough, but during the time he was awaiting trial, the House of Lords passed a bill making such violence a capital offense. Without a skilled attorney to plead his case, he would be hanged.

No, Anne could not have found employment in Nottingham. If Miss Webster's sister had not recommended her to the Duke of Marston, she would have joined her mother and sisters in destitution. As it was, her wages barely kept them alive.

"My presence in Devon can be of no concern to a man such as yourself," she told the marquess. "I am employed to serve your family and guests in the House along with dozens of other young women no different from myself."

"I beg to point out, Miss Webster, that yesterday you stated in no uncertain terms your very great difference from the dozens of other young women in Slocombe House. You claimed to be a better lace designer and pattern pricker than anyone in Tiverton."

"Oh, Anne," Prudence muttered. "Surely you did not say such a thing."

By now there was no hope that he would abandon the two women and return to his chaise. The hilly, wooded property belonging to the Duke of Marston had closed them in on either side, a glorious display of budding trees dressed in pale green. Along the hedgerows at either side of the road sprung bright white snowdrops and purple crocuses. The scent of newly turned earth mingled with the perfume of spring buds. Birds, busy with nest building, chirped and sang and fought over fat worms they pulled from the soft dirt at the side of the road. Anne would have given anything to be able to drink in the morning and dream out a lace pattern to reflect its glory.

Instead she was shackled by *him*. Vile man. She glanced at the marquess from beneath the brim of her straw bonnet. Oh, he was handsome, of course. No woman could deny that. His high-crowned black felt hat added imposing height to his already tall physique. The cut of his clothing, the width of his shoulders, the length of his legs—everything about him was the picture of the manly aristocrat. Only the brownness of his skin gave his face the cast of a pirate. But the twinkle in his gray eyes and the amused angle of his lip showed him for the scoundrel he was.

"As you surely have discovered," Anne said, "by observing my lace panel, which you wear around your neck, I truly am a skilled designer."

"Indeed, Miss Webster, you are talented. In fact, it is this quality about you that intrigues me more than any other. Not only are you lovely, articulate, and mannered, but you possess a skill most remarkable." His fingers touched the crest on the lace. "May I inquire where you learned such technique? Surely no common lace school could teach a young woman how to create a lozenge such as this."

"My training came from the lace school of Nottingham," she said. "What talent I possess is God-given."

"God? Ah, yes, I do recall that you are religious. Nightly Bible readings and—"

The unmistakable, familiar crack of flint striking steel silenced him. An instantaneous report echoed from the hillside.

Gunshot.

❧

Before Ruel could call out a warning, a projectile raked across his left arm at a downward angle. His flesh split wide. The round continued on undeflected. It tore into Anne Webster's thigh, taking with it a piece of her gown, and came out the other side. It ripped a hole near the hem of Miss Prudence Watson's dress before plowing into the dirt at her feet.

Miss Watson screamed. Anne crumpled to the road.

"Down!" Ruel jerked Miss Watson's arm. She shrieked in hysteria, rolled into a ball, and covered her head with her arms. "The hedge," he grunted. "Get to it."

Ruel drew his coat pistol from an inside pocket as he swept Anne up in his arms and ran with her toward the shelter of the thick hedgerow. A puff of smoke, smelling of black powder, drifted across the open road. Still screaming, Miss Watson unwound herself and scrambled for cover.

"Silence," Ruel commanded her. Holding the loaded pistol with one hand, he jerked it from half to full cock and shouted up the hillside. "Show yourself, villain!"

Anne moaned and touched his shoulder where a circle of bright crimson was forming. Oblivious to his wound, Ruel peered through the dense hedge.

"Blast it all; he has gone. Coward." He turned to the women and noted Anne's blood-soaked dress. At the sight of her ashen face, a wave of fear curled through his stomach. A red stain covered the torn hole in her gown, spreading quickly and dripping onto the ground. Biting off a curse, he turned to Miss Watson.

"What about you?" he demanded. "Are you hit?" When he took her shoulder and shook her, the paralyzed young lady let out a cry. "Are you injured, madam?"

"No!" she sobbed. "I am all right."

"Then help me." He shrugged out of his coat, vaguely aware that his shoulder throbbed as though a bee had stung it, and tossed the garment to Miss Watson. "Make a pillow of this. We must stop the bleeding."

He reached for his cravat, realized he had only the bit of flimsy lace, and swore. He grabbed Anne's dress and ripped the hem away with his hands. "Miss Webster, do not flinch. And do not look as if you mean to swoon either. I know you are not the sort."

Anne's eyes fluttered open as he bent over her. He worked at wrapping the length of cloth around her leg.

"Gone clean through," he muttered. "Who could have done this? A highwayman would have come out onto the road after my wallet. Surely Barkham would have challenged me to a duel if he still held a grudge. It has been three years since the incident with his wife. . . . Wimberley cannot still be nursing his anger about that purse I won off him. . . . Of course, there is Droughtmoor. He might still—"

"It was the gamekeeper," Miss Watson croaked. "I saw his brown coat."

"William Green? What have I done to him?"

"Not you. It is her." Miss Watson took Anne's hand and squeezed it. "He wants to marry her. He has asked twice, but she will not have him. I believe he is the man who fired at us."

"Absurd. To kill a woman because she will not marry? Ridiculous."

"She spurned him, my lord."

"But Green is nothing more than a gamekeeper. A peasant. He cannot believe he deserves such a woman as this."

"She is only Anne Webster, sir. Surely you know she is my lady's maid."

Ruel looked down at the woman whose shadowed eyelids had drifted shut. Her face, so animated before, was motionless, her breathing shallow. Only a maid?

"Stay here with her," he ordered Miss Watson, whose large eyes brimmed with tears. "I shall go for my chaise. It awaits me at the church, and I shall send it here at once for both of you. Then I shall go into town and find the doctor. We should return to Slocombe within the hour."

When he started to get up, Miss Watson caught his arm. "No, my lord, please do not go. You are wounded yourself. Your arm . . . "

He glanced at the tattered flesh of his shoulder and frowned. "Dash it all. This is a devilish circumstance."

"Please guard your tongue, Lord Blackthorne, I beg you," Miss Watson whispered. "Anne is a minister's daughter."

Studying the injured woman for a moment, he decided he had no choice. "I must go for the chaise. If she loses more blood—"

"No—that cannot be! I shall go myself. The gamekeeper has no reason to shoot at me. I shall send the chaise to you and fetch the doctor from the village." Miss Watson scrambled to her feet, clapped one hand over her bonnet, and darted away.

"Miss!" He called after her, but she was already flying around a bend in the road, her tattered, blood-spattered skirts dancing at her ankles.

Four

He supposed it had something to do with the way she had woven a royal tale of imagination for the little beggar girl in the kitchen. Or perhaps it was the manner in which she had boldly demanded the return of her lace panel. Maybe it was nothing more than the range of emotions that had flickered across her face during his farcical marriage proposal—indignation, amusement, anger, shy pleasure.

Ruel lifted Anne's shoulders and rested her head against his arm. Whatever the reason that drew him to this woman, she captivated him. He stared in dismay at her pale face. The thick hedge cast blue shadows beneath her cheekbones and over her neck. Though a tiny pulsebeat flickered in her throat and her breath came regularly, she had lost too much blood. Even now, it soaked through the binding on her thigh and seeped onto her bare leg. He rubbed his fingers together, aware that they, too, were stained with her bright blood.

A strange sensation crept over Ruel as he looked at the

woman. He had always viewed his own existence with the cynicism of the rake that he was. Both Ruel and Alexander had been born late in their mother's life. Though the duke clearly loved his elder son, Ruel's mother preferred the younger brother. "That dark, vile little thing," she called Ruel as she chose either to abuse or to ignore him. Yet the duchess doted on Alexander: "My golden gift from God."

Ruel had learned not to care. All women, he had decided while still quite young, were useless except as entertainment. Claire, sixteen years his senior and the eldest of the five lovely Chouteau sisters, had done her best to encourage tenderness in the little boy by playing with him, teaching him songs, bringing him toys from London. But Claire had married the Viscount Eagon the year after Alex was born, so he saw her rarely. His other sisters—busy with fashion and beaux and the goings-on of Society—could hardly be bothered with him.

Ruel touched the tip of his knuckle to Anne Webster's cheek. He had always thought of women rather the way a huntsman views his prey. They were to be admired for their appearance, pursued, and, one hoped, conquered. As many as possible, as often as possible.

A man could be respected for a variety of things—his intellect, his wit, his shooting skill, even his wealth and position in Society. Women focused their whole existence on balls, gowns, and romantic intrigues. They spent their time on such fripperies as playing the pianoforte, stitching fire screens, beading purses. Thus, Ruel had nothing but a passing carnal interest in the female gender.

He had little use for religion either, thinking it a grand collection of gibberish intended to give the weak-minded hope.

He agreed with his friend George Gordon, Lord Byron, on the subject. The poet had commented to him one day, "We are miserable enough in this life, without the absurdity of speculating upon another."

Women. Religion. Balls. Fashion. Grand dinners. The royal court. All of them a great waste of time. Ruel had found his education boring, most of his peers simpering, and his prospects for the future deadly dull. Travel, adventure, and gambling—whether at cards or in speculative exploits—were the only things that interested him.

He cared little for life, his own or that of others. He had wounded two men in duels, several more during a fracas in America, another at the gaming table. He disregarded his own existence, and he had almost lost his life more than once. In fact, he realized as he looked down at the young lady who lay in his lap, a sizable number of men would be happy to see him dead.

Why did the thought of losing this woman send an aching emptiness through his chest? She was only Anne Webster . . . only a maid . . .

He tried to straighten the bonnet that had slipped askew during the shooting. A ribbon of her hair had fallen out and lay across her shoulder. He picked it up and draped it over the back of his hand. As light as silk, it gleamed with golden highlights in the late-morning sunshine. Chocolate laced with cinnamon, he had called the color. No wonder Anne Webster disdained him.

The bonnet refused to go right, so Ruel pulled it off and let her hair spill across his thigh. He traced one finger over each of her eyebrows, marveling at the way they echoed the upward-tilted shape of her almond eyes. She was a housemaid, a minister's daughter, a laceworker. She ought not to have those lips. So full, though pale now, they all but begged to be kissed.

Had any man ever kissed Miss Anne Webster? He thought not. The tone in her voice warned men away. The tilt to her chin instructed them to keep hands off. Even the design of her simple cotton gown spoke of her maidenhood. Where most women enjoyed the current fashion of necklines cut as low as possible and waists cut as high as possible, Anne wore a modest bodice covered by a discreet cotton shawl. She was as untouched and new as that crocus growing beside the hedge.

Swallowing at the hard lump that had somehow lodged in his throat, Ruel stared down at her leg. Slender, firm, and white, it was a sharp contrast to the deeply tanned skin of his own hands. He had seen women's legs, lots of them. But Anne Webster's leg was not meant for his eyes. He tugged at her skirt, yet it was too torn and bloodied to cover her.

"Blast it all." He shut his eyes, searching for answers. In the blackness he saw nothing. Emptiness. Void.

When he lifted his head again, he saw that she was staring at him. Her eyes were a deep shade of brown, the lashes long and black around them. She took a breath, and her face contorted in pain.

"My leg hurts."

"Do not move it."

She bit back tears. "Where is Miss Watson? She is not well."

"Well enough to run for my chaise and the doctor."

"Never mind a doctor," she murmured. "I am prepared to die."

"You are not going to die."

"I believe I shall, sir."

"No." He leaned over her and took her face in both his hands. "No, Anne Webster, you will not. You will get into the chaise and go to Slocombe. You will recover and make lace panels and read your Bible and stand up to the nobility once again. Yes?"

She looked into his gray eyes. "Who are you?" she whispered. "Not . . . not the marquess. He has eyes of cold, hard iron. Yours are soft, kind."

"You may call me Ruel."

"I must tell you . . . Ruel . . . were I to paint your eyes, I should make them the color of a dove's wings."

He clenched his jaw, fighting the emotion that welled in his chest. "Thank you, madam."

"I could make your eyes in lace, I think. I am good with patterns . . . and your hair is all curls . . . like mist on the window. . . . You look very like the marquess, but much more gentle. I must tell you, Ruel . . . I think the marquess was wounded. I saw blood on his shoulder . . . like that on yours."

"I shall look after him, I assure you."

"You are good." Her eyes drifted shut. "Ruel, the marquess asked to be my protector."

"Yes, he did." His voice was ragged.

"I prefer you."

"Thank you, Anne. Thank you very much."

༺ঔৣৡ༻

The doctor predicted Anne Webster would die during the night. She had lost a great quantity of blood. If not that night, she would surely perish within the week. The lead ball had driven bits of dress fabric into her leg, he theorized to Mrs. Davies, the housekeeper. Gangrene was certain to set in. He gave the housekeeper a small bottle of laudanum to dose Anne for the pain, instructed that the vicar be called in the hour of the young lady's death, and hurried up to the rooms of the Marquess of Blackthorne.

There, the doctor blotted, cleaned, and stitched the wound in the shoulder of his very wealthy and very important patient. He then bled the marquess, gave his valet a variety of powders along with a quantity of laudanum, and prescribed bed rest until the injury healed—a month at the least. The marquess was not to use his shoulder in any way during that time, but was to be fed, bathed, dressed, and pampered.

Beatrice Chouteau, the Duchess of Marston, swooned the moment she was told of the dreadful event, and the doctor rushed from the marquess to her bedside. She recovered quickly enough but was confined to her rooms with a headache. She concurred with the intelligence that the gamekeeper was the prime suspect in the shooting incident. Slocombe House rules prohibited female servants from having suitors, she reminded her lady's maids, and such appalling violence was exactly the reason. Romantic liaisons between members of the lower classes always led to trouble.

While the doctor was tending his elder son and wife, the duke stormed up and down the corridors of Slocombe House, rapping his cane on the floor and issuing commands. Footmen flew at his beck and call. He ordered the roadway from Tiverton to Slocombe searched. He demanded that all possible witnesses to the dire event be summoned. He sent for the family's physician from London. He authorized the immediate arrest of William Green. The gamekeeper, to no one's surprise, was not to be found. The duke dispatched a party of footmen to find and detain the villain.

On hearing the report of the shooting, Sir Alexander immediately departed the home of his friends in Tiverton and rode to Slocombe House. He stayed at Ruel's side through the doctor's visit and afterward during the long hours of the night.

Weak from loss of blood and dizzied by the large amount of laudanum he had been given, Ruel found it difficult to recall exactly what had happened on the road leaving the church. He knew his shoulder ached and throbbed, though past experience assured him the injury was not serious. He recalled the uproar when his chaise arrived at the House with him . . . and whom? Two women. He could not place their names. Who were they? There was something about one of them, but he could not . . .

"The ball must have been fired from the south," Alexander was saying when Ruel finally recognized his brother's voice. "A hill rises just beyond the hedgerow where you were shot. It is well-wooded property, and the shooter must have been standing at the top of the knoll in order to have taken such accurate aim. He almost had you through the heart, you know."

Ruel knew. He clenched his jaw against the pain as he straightened his shoulders on the mound of pillows beneath them. Sunlight filtered through tiny slits between the heavy velvet draperies, giving scant light to the dim room. The scent of burning wax mingled with the acrid smell of the powders at his bedside. His mouth tasted of cotton.

"Draw apart those blasted curtains, Alex," he muttered, grabbing the nearest bottle from the bedside table. It was rum. He grimaced and set it down again. "Upon my honor, I shall have the windows opened. Let some air into this room. Where is my valet? Where is Foley?"

His brother laid a hand on Ruel's brow. "Be still. The doctor left strict instructions for your rest. Take some more laudanum, why not? It will calm your nerves."

Ruel scowled at the small container. "Alex, I do not want laudanum. It puts me into a foul humor, and I cannot think clearly. There is something . . . someone . . ."

"You are to take two hundred and fifty drops, enough to relax any man. I confess I have had a little myself just to calm my nerves. Come now."

His hand started toward Ruel's mouth. "No, I said!" Knocking the vial to the floor, Ruel let out a growl. "My head feels like a pumpkin! And my shoulder . . . Where is my valet? I should have eaten breakfast long ago. I have things to do today. I have got to find out where . . . to see . . ."

"If you will not lie down and rest, I shall end up the next Duke of Marston, and by all accounts, that will be a dreadful situation. Father has been ranting all night, storming about the place in high dudgeon."

"Father? Why?"

"No one can find the gamekeeper, of course."

"Gamekeeper . . ." Ruel gripped his sheets in his fists as pieces of the puzzle began to grind into place. If only his head would stop pounding.

Alexander leaned back in his chair and propped a foot on the bed. As if the spike-heeled boots were not enough, the young man wore a blue silk coat and trousers far too tight to be comfortable. Ruel considered tossing out a barb against dandy fashion, but he could not make his befuddled brain or his thick tongue function.

"Personally, I hold it was a highwayman who shot you," Alexander said, fingering the white cravat at his neck. "He must have used a rifle for the ball to have traveled so far and so true. He might have had a blunderbuss, but I understand there was only one ball. Can you recall?"

When Ruel did not answer, he went on. "I shall wager the highwayman knew you would be leaving church Sunday morning, saw that you were afoot, and determined to have your money."

"No one robbed me, Alex."

"Perhaps the highwayman did not expect you to be armed. It was rather rash of you, I think. Do you always carry a coat pistol, Ruel?"

"Since America."

"I should continue the practice if I were you. I have it on good authority that more than one gentleman is displeased at your return to England. Have you considered that the assassin might not have been the gamekeeper or a highwayman at all? It might have been Barkham. When you were exposed in a dalliance with his wife—"

"Fiancée."

"At any rate, I suspect he has not forgiven you. Wimberley, too, has every reason for hostility. You ruined him, you know. He has not been the same since you took his money."

"Won it."

"Fairly? He hardly thinks so, and it would be like him to

travel from London with a rifle that could shoot right through a man's arm and a woman's—"

"Where is she?" Ruel interrupted, remembering suddenly. He tore back the sheets and surged out of bed. "The woman . . . where is she?"

Alexander leapt to his feet and grabbed the bellpull. "Brother, do calm yourself. Foley! Come at once."

Ruel's valet hurried across the carpeted floor, closely followed by two footmen. "My lord, calm yourself," the valet urged. He turned to one of the footmen. "Fetch Mr. Errand."

"Stop!" Ruel commanded. He caught the bedpost for support as the three servants stiffened into obedience. Turning to his brother, he grabbed the man's cravat and pulled Alexander close.

"Where . . . is . . . she?" he repeated slowly, anger burning each word into the silence of the room.

"Who?" Alexander asked. "Please, Ruel, you are making no sense at all. Foley, the laudanum!"

"Two women were with me—where are they now? One of them was wounded."

"I cannot say where they are. Honestly, Ruel, you should return to your bed at once."

Pushing past his brother, Ruel staggered toward the door. The room spun like a child's top. He could hear the mad scramble behind him, the shouted commands. Idiots.

Where was she? He lurched out into the corridor and leaned on a marble bust to catch his breath. *"She is only Anne Webster . . . my lady's maid."* She would be in Miss Prudence Watson's quarters, of course. Upstairs.

"Lord Blackthorne." It was Mr. Errand, the butler. He

approached, gave Ruel a formal bow, and cleared his throat. His bushy eyebrows floated on his face like a pair of matched clouds. "My lord, do be reasonable, I beg you. It is imperative that you follow the doctor's orders and return to your room."

"Hang the doctor! Where are the stairs?"

"His Grace, the Duke of Marston, is below, down the staircase at the end of the second corridor beyond—"

"Not that staircase." Ruel swung away from the wall. The bust he had been leaning on tottered and fell to the floor with a crash. Mr. Errand leapt aside to avoid having his foot crushed. Ruel had rarely been in the women's halls where his sisters had grown up, but their staircases meandered up and down, giving access to every floor. He had played in them as a boy. Now, if he could only remember . . .

"Lord Blackthorne!" Mr. Errand stepped over the fallen bust and hurried down the corridor after him. "Your wound is most grave, my lord. Please do consider your father, I beg you. The duke is beside himself with worry. Quite, quite frantic."

Ruel turned a corner. The walls swayed. He caught a rope to steady himself, then realized it was a bellpull and knew he had probably summoned Mrs. Smythe and half the kitchen staff. Cursing laudanum, he worked his way down the corridor. A green baize curtain hanging at the end of the hall promised a door. A door promised a staircase.

"Ruel, what on earth are you doing? You cannot mean to go up." It was Alexander. "Ruel, do be reasonable. The doctor has ordered you to bed. You must be prudent."

"Prudent? Reasonable?" Ruel mocked as he pushed back the baize and stepped through the doorway. This household was filled with a grand lot of circus clowns. The staircase, narrow and dimly lit, proved almost impossible to navigate. As Ruel struggled upward, the stairs dipped. He braced himself with an arm against each wall and felt a stab of pain in his shoulder. The woman . . . had to find her . . . had promised to protect her.

They scurried up the stairwell after him—his brother, the butler, his valet, the footmen. Like the pied piper, he worked his way up past the third floor, then to the fourth barely ahead of them. He threw open the door at the top and careened out into the narrow corridor.

"Anne!" he bellowed. "Anne Webster!"

Like blank-faced sentinels, an endless row of closed doors lined the hallway. He flung them open one by one. Identical rooms with gilt beds and damask hangings. Was this where they had slept . . . his sisters?

"Anne Webster!" he called again.

A door at the far end of the corridor swung open. The vicar of Tiverton, round-headed, ashen-faced, and perspiring heavily, emerged. He leaned against the doorframe, mopped his face with a white handkerchief, and gaped at the oncoming parade.

"Lord Blackthorne," he uttered. "But you must . . . she is . . . "

"Is she here?" Ruel could not wait for the answer. He shoved his way past the clergyman and through the doorway. "Miss Webster?"

A loud gasp greeted him. "The marquess!" Miss Prudence Watson leapt up from her chair beside a narrow bed and made him an awkward curtsy. "Lord Blackthorne, good morning to you, sir."

Ruel stopped. Anne Webster lay propped on a white pillow, her face as still as death. A thin gray wool blanket covered her fragile body. Her hands, pale and limp, were crossed at her breast.

"Oh no." Ruel covered his eyes. This shared guest room had been her home. This small iron bed her last resting place. *"She is only Anne Webster . . . my lady's maid."* Of course that was true. But she was Anne with the bright brown eyes and the sharp tongue and the keen mind.

"Dear God in heaven," he muttered, turning away and realizing he had not the slightest idea how to pray.

"Ruel?"

At the soft sound, he lifted his head. She was looking at him, her eyes as dark and liquid as ink.

"Anne?"

"Oh, it is you . . . Ruel. You sat with me after I was shot." She smiled. "I remember your eyes. Gentle, dove-gray eyes. You protected me under the hedge."

"Yes, I—"

"Lord Blackthorne!" The butler burst into the room. Sir Alexander rushed to his brother. Footmen swarmed.

"Ruel, you must go back to your chambers," his brother gasped. "This roving about like a madman will never do. The women's floor! Good gracious, man, think what will be said of you."

Ruel stared in confusion as Errand the butler fluttered about the bedroom. Footmen made vain attempts to usher everyone out into the corridor. The vicar slipped back inside and stood trembling against the far wall.

"My Lord Blackthorne. Sir Alexander." The vicar gulped

down a bubble of air as he executed a deep bow in the room. "Gentlemen, I beg of you—"

"Ruel?" Anne's brow narrowed as she looked him up and down. "The marquess?" She glanced at Miss Watson for confirmation. "Oh, but I thought . . . "

"Miss Webster, do you suffer much?" Ruel asked as he stepped to her bed. "Your leg?"

She lifted her chin, and her eyes went cold. "I am well enough, Lord Blackthorne. I had just asked the vicar to hold a private conference with you, but you have chosen to come to me instead."

Confused, Ruel turned to the clergyman. The man was as pale and damp as the handkerchief he dabbed across his forehead. "I beg leave to speak with you in private, my lord," the vicar mumbled. "Away from the young lady. It is a matter . . . a matter of some consequence."

"Do let us go down at once, brother," Alexander concurred. "This maid is clearly delirious, ordering the vicar about and speaking to you in such a way."

Ruel held Alexander back with an outstretched hand. "Miss Webster, on the road you informed me you were prepared to die."

"I am," she said firmly. "My soul rests in the hands of God."

He studied her for a moment and recognized that the peace underlying the pain in her dark eyes meant she had spoken the truth. He could not understand it. The woman had nothing—no wealth, no position, no future. Yet she possessed such calm confidence. Such grace.

"In contrast to you," he told her, "I have no faith in the existence of souls or of God, and I am not at all content to let you die." He turned to the butler. "Errand, send to London for our physician. He must come at once and have a look at Miss Webster's leg."

"My lord, His Grace the duke has already requested the physician to attend you."

"It is this woman, and not I, who needs his attention."

"Brother!" Sir Alexander glowered. "You cannot mean this. It is your shoulder that was wounded, and the woman is nothing to you. Your wits have been dimmed by laudanum. I insist you return to your chambers immediately."

"Upon my word, Alex, this is a scratch. An annoyance."

"But . . . but she is a maid."

"On the contrary." As he spoke, Ruel realized that somewhere in the fog of the past night, his brain had discovered a perfect solution to the problem that had plagued his financial blueprint for the duchy. "She is the key to our future happiness."

⁂

Anne gritted her teeth as the two brothers argued. Her leg hurt much worse this morning, and she felt certain that infection had set in. At some point in the night, a weeping Miss Watson had blurted out the doctor's prognosis: death was inevitable. Anne could only welcome the pronouncement, for she knew it would bring peace from the fever already beginning to rage through her body.

Her only misery came at the realization that she would die without ever helping her father, without ever marrying or bearing children, without designing another scrap of lace, without starting the lace school of which she had dreamed.

She had done nothing of much use to anyone, and her conscience tormented her. Though she knew she ought to pray, she was unable. How could she focus on anything so elusive as God and heaven and the hereafter? God was utterly absent during those dark hours, and she did little but worry and search her mind for reason to hope.

Early that morning as her fever rose, she had arrived at the one solution that might save her family. As soon as Miss Watson was awake, Anne begged her to send for the vicar. But when Anne made her request, his horrified reaction had only made her more despondent. Why now had God chosen to allow the marquess to persecute her? Was she not suffering enough?

"Perhaps you will recall that Miss Webster is the finest lace designer in Nottingham," Lord Blackthorne was telling his brother. His voice mocked her own words. "She is the best pattern pricker in Tiverton, and one of the most skilled laceworkers in England."

Anne weakly lifted a hand and brushed it across her flushed forehead. "Is this your object in coming to my bedside, sir? To ridicule me once again?"

"I have never ridiculed you yet." He squatted on a stool near the bed, his long legs folding up almost to his chin and his great knees spread wide. He propped his arms on them and smiled at her with satisfaction. "Indeed, Miss Webster, I have been altogether serious on every occasion of our acquaintance. And now I shall continue to speak to you with all solemnity. First, I wish you to know I have been given the unwelcome intelligence that William Green the gamekeeper may have been our assailant."

"I saw no one in the forest."

"Nor did I, yet I understand he may have had motive. You rejected his offer of marriage, did you not?"

"I did, sir."

"I wonder at that. Tell me, is our gamekeeper as great a blackguard as I?"

Anne glanced at her mistress. Prudence had covered her face with her hands and seemed to be in ardent prayer.

"Mr. Green is not a man with whom I wish to link my life, though under the current circumstances, I believe that now to be of little consequence," Anne told the marquess. "The gamekeeper is unkind, vain, and rude, but I do not think him capable of murder."

"Why not? Surely your extraordinary beauty and keen wit merit such passion."

"Lord Blackthorne," the vicar cut in, anguish lifting his voice an octave. "I beg you to guard your tongue."

"I shall not. Miss Webster is a promising young lady. Since our fortuitous meeting in the kitchen, I have been considering her situation here at Slocombe House and her obvious skill with lace. Once she is recovered from her injuries, I mean to make good use of her."

"She means to make use of you," the vicar muttered.

"I beg your pardon?" Ruel turned on the stool.

The vicar twisted his hands together. His round head glowed with perspiration. "Lord Blackthorne, I have been requested to tell you . . . to tell you that Miss Anne Webster . . . she accepts your offer of marriage."

"Does she now?" Ruel slowly faced Anne again. "Well, I am dumbfounded."

❦ *Five* ❧

Silence dropped like a thick fleece over the room. Anne
looked at the marquess. Ruel stared at her. Prudence dabbed
her eyes. Alexander shifted from one foot to the other and
glared at the vicar. The footmen held their breath.

"Perhaps I misunderstood you, sir." Addressing the clergyman, Ruel stood slowly. "Please repeat yourself."

"She . . . she accepts." The vicar blotted his chin with the
handkerchief. "I tried to tell her . . . tried to warn her . . . but
I do think she is dying after all, which would remove the
problem, of course. . . . Yet everyone who heard your declara-
tion that afternoon knew it was made in jest."

"I have witnesses," Anne said softly. "The Duke of
Marston, the vicar of Tiverton, and Sir Alexander all heard
your offer, Lord Blackthorne. You proposed marriage to me.
I accept."

"You said you could not like him," Sir Alexander burst out.
"I heard you say you felt no affection for him in the least."

The Bachelor's Bargain

"Surely a nobleman such as yourself, my lord, knows affection is not necessary to marriage."

"Abominable girl. Wicked insubordination. Ruel, say something to the wench!"

The marquess returned his attention to Anne. His gaze traced the narrow outline of her body as she lay in the bed. Her brown eyes never left his face. Again he was struck by her unwavering fortitude.

"Out," he commanded, waving a hand at the assembly. "Everyone, out. I shall speak with her alone."

"Do not harm Anne, I beg you!" Miss Watson stepped out from the corner, her cheeks damp. "She is dying, the doctor said so, and you must not torment her! Sir, she has waited upon me faithfully these many months, and I assure you she is altogether the most kind and affectionate companion a woman could ever hope to find. I am certain that any words misspoken just now can be attributed to—"

"Out!" Ruel pointed at the door.

"Yes, my lord." Prudence ducked her head and hurried away.

When the door shut behind the murmuring, weeping, arguing throng, Ruel turned to Anne and crossed his arms over his chest. "You accept my proposal, do you?"

"I do."

"Are you dying?"

"Yes, sir."

"Then why do you want to marry me, and why on earth should I marry you?"

Anne drew down a deep breath. "Because you know you will not have a wife to burden you more than a day or two.

Because you can extend your mourning a year or longer and stave off your father's demands that you wed in Society. Because as my husband, you will see to the safety of my family in Nottingham. Because I have information about you that would be most useful in the hands of an enemy."

The corners of his mouth tipped up. "My goodness, Miss Webster, you astound me."

"No more than you astound me."

"Let me see if I grasp your logic." He settled into the chair next to the bed where she lay, stretched out his legs, and propped a pillow under his shoulder. "I am to marry you because you will soon die, and I can play the merry widower. My father cannot expect me to wed for more than a year after your passing, and that should keep me quite happy and allow me to fulfill my own goals."

"Aye, sir."

"You wish to marry me because your family is in some sort of financial straits in Nottingham, and you believe that as the son of a duke I could do nothing less than to rescue them."

"I would expect that of you, yes."

He stared at the mist on the windowpane and recalled her confession that his hair reminded her of the curling shadows. For a moment, he could not think beyond it. She had lain just here, looking at this window, thinking of him.

A strange sensation slid through his chest. He turned his head and studied her. Eyes shut, she breathed in a shallow, pained manner. Would she die? Did he care?

How odd that his own mother had fallen so ill at news of the shooting that she had been unable to visit her son. Yet Anne Webster, mortally wounded herself, had managed to concoct a grand plan to save her family. From her deathbed this little woman with the courage of a lion had intimidated the vicar and everyone else into believing she meant exactly what she said. Amazing.

"About this information that would be so useful to my enemies," he said. "Could you expound?"

As she lifted her head, an expression of pain crossed her face. "Lace machines," she said in a ragged whisper. "Smuggling them into France. I heard your plan."

"Good heavens. You were there. Serving tea in Alexander's drawing room."

A little smile tugged at her mouth. "You must learn to be more discreet, my lord."

He studied her for a moment. How could a pair of brown eyes be so entrancing? She was a servant, nothing more. And near death. Yet the intelligence and determination that sparkled in her eyes made him feel he was speaking to an equal.

"And what will you do with your ill-gotten information about my plan to smuggle lace machines into France, Miss Webster?" he asked. "How do you propose to use it against me?"

"Blackmail is a harsh accusation."

"Extortion, then?"

Her shoulders sagged, and she shut her eyes. "I prefer to say we shall strike a bargain of benefit to both of us. A plan that will give us . . . encouragement."

He chuckled. "Exactly how do you mean to encourage me to accept this bargain?"

"If you do not, I shall be compelled to relay your plans to Lady de Winter, the baroness who attended my father's church and supported his cause against the owners of the stocking mills."

Ruel sucked in a breath. The de Winter family held Nottingham's lace industry in the palms of their hands. They were rich and well-connected with English royalty. The baroness—a small, withered old lady who scented herself heavily with rose water—was a close friend and confidante to Queen Charlotte, wife of the mad King George and mother of the regent.

Worse, perhaps, the baroness abhorred the Revolution that had brought an end to the French monarchy. She knew every aristocrat in Paris, she had been personally responsible for smuggling vast quantities of lace into that country, and she would stop at nothing to keep England foremost in the manufacture of handmade lace.

"Trump!" Ruel said, sitting up and leaning across the space that divided them. "Miss Webster, you have played your hand like an expert."

Her brow furrowed, as if she found it difficult to concentrate. "I know nothing of cards, sir. We do not play."

"Ah, yes, the innocent minister's daughter. She reads her Bible every night, wears her pelisse buttoned to the throat, and would never dream of playing at cards. Can she be the same Anne Webster who would hazard her position in order to sell lace to the son of a duke, who would boldly announce that her family's weaving trade was equal to the calling of the nobility, who would dare to coerce a marquess into marriage—"

"You asked me!" she hissed, struggling up onto one elbow. "I had nothing to do with it."

Ruel slid from his chair to the floor, leaned over her, and placed one hand on either side of her head. Her eyes widened.

"You had everything to do with it," he said in a low voice. "You made a beggar child believe she was a duchess. You wove a lace that captured the essence of my homeland in springtime. You faced down my father, my brother, and the vicar of Tiverton. You very sweetly blackmailed me. And, yes, Miss Anne Webster, yes, indeed, you had everything to do with it."

He stared into her face and was surprised to find that a pink flush had suddenly colored her high cheekbones. Though she was scowling at him, he took note that her lips were full and slightly damp. The image of kissing them took him by surprise, but he reminded himself that the prim Miss Webster would in no way welcome the action.

And then he realized that it hardly mattered what happened between them at this moment. Her body was swiftly betraying her into the hands of death, and this woman . . . this very beautiful, very intriguing creature might be lost to him forever.

Before she could speak, he turned his head and shouted at the shut door. "Alexander! Send in the vicar. I am getting married."

Anne clutched the sheets to her neck as the door burst open and people poured into the room. Like angry bees, they swarmed and shoved and shouted, each determined to speak his mind.

Ignoring them, Ruel leaned close to the young woman's ear. "You win this round," he whispered. "But we have only begun our game, Miss Webster. You said our bargain must benefit both parties, and I have a purpose for you as well."

She pressed the heel of her palm against her chest as if trying to steady her heart. "This is no time for games, sir," she replied. "I am dying."

He rose from her bedside and smiled as he shook his head. "I think not."

Sir Alexander reached his brother just as Ruel turned. "Take care of the arrangements between the vicar and our father, will you, Alex? This afternoon should be soon enough for the ceremony. Have the young lady carried down into the front parlor. See that she is bathed, fed, and dressed in something suitable."

"Ruel, you cannot be serious."

"I am always serious." He spread his hands to indicate a path to the door. "You must excuse me now, ladies and gentlemen. There is someone in Tiverton I must see."

Without a backward glance at the woman to whom he had just become betrothed, the Marquess of Blackthorne walked out of the room.

❧

The Duke of Marston studied the huge bed at the far end of the long room he had just entered. The bed's canopy of blue and gold velvet rose almost to the ceiling. At the side of the small bed where Anne rested, Miss Watson rose from a chair of carved walnut and curtsied to her unexpected guests.

Anne was pleased to see that in the past twenty-four hours, her friend had regained a measure of her former fortitude and spirit. The shooting on the roadside had mobilized and enlivened Prudence—almost to the point that Anne saw hope for a complete recovery from the despondence that had plagued the young woman these many months.

"That is her, is it?" the duke murmured to his butler. "That pale creature?"

"That is Miss Prudence Watson, my lord. She has been your guest here at Slocombe House since March."

The duke appeared surprised. "Has she? Well, they do come and go, these guests. Where is the woman in question?"

"I believe the young lady lies abed."

His cane tapping softly on the thick, rose-patterned carpet, the duke approached the canopied bed and scrutinized the mound of white pillows, the spread of heavy blankets, the monogrammed hem of the silk sheets. "I see no one here," he said. "Has she died already?"

"No, my lord. She is still alive. In the maid's bed, over there."

Though Anne could see and hear them perfectly well, the duke continued addressing his butler as if they were alone. Standing at a safe distance across the room, they ignored Miss Watson and peered at Anne as though she were a statue and not a living, breathing soul.

"My son should never have been permitted to ride to Tiverton," the duke said. "His health is not strong."

The butler nodded. "I believe it is of great import that you know Lord Blackthorne was under the influence of laudanum when he confirmed the marriage proposal."

"He is gone off to Tiverton in a cloud of laudanum? This is not to be tolerated. Errand, send someone after him," the duke ordered.

"Yes, Your Grace." The butler signaled to a footman who had taken up his post just inside the bedroom door. "Robbins, see to it at once."

"Now about the girl," the duke continued. "What do we know of her?"

"Your Grace, the doctor has informed me that the young woman is wounded and is likely to perish within the week. Her injury is most grave and infection is setting in. Putrefaction is assured, and not even removal of the limb can ensure her survival."

"Dire news. You are quite certain of this, Errand?"

"Absolutely. If I may be so bold, sir, confining your son to his quarters for a few days will likely solve the problem."

Anne opened her mouth to object to such a cruel suggestion, but the duke resumed speaking.

"This rash impulse to wed is not unlike something Ruel would do. And yet, I should have expected a wiser choice. You tell me she is a housemaid?"

"Indeed, sir. She came highly recommended by Mrs. Charles Locke of Trenton House on Cranleigh Crescent, and she has been in your service less than a year."

"A fisherman's daughter, no doubt."

"A minister's daughter from Nottingham."

"She is no great beauty," the duke observed, taking a step closer to the bed where Anne lay. "I cannot think how my son noticed her in the first place. She is very thin."

"Begging your pardon, Your Grace," Prudence spoke up. Holding her head high, she stepped toward the two men. "Anne . . . Miss Webster, that is . . . she is my lady's maid. I assure you that she is beautiful in every way and utterly without fault. And now, I must kindly beg you to depart my private chambers that she may be permitted to dress for her . . . for her wedding."

The duke scowled. "Her wedding? Bah! That is not to be!"

"You are wrong on that account, sir," Anne said firmly. Ignoring the intense pain, she managed to push herself up and, with effort, to set her feet on the floor. She steadied her voice and said carefully, "I am to wed Lord Blackthorne this afternoon. We have spoken together this morning, and we are agreed on every matter." She took a deep breath as the throbbing in her leg threatened to overtake her, then continued. "Your son and I are firmly attached."

The butler gave a cough. "Your Grace, Laurent Chouteau, Duke of Marston," he intoned, "may I present Miss Anne Webster of Nottingham."

Determined to make a good impression on her future father-in-law, Anne forced herself to her feet, supported herself by clinging to a bedpost, and even wobbled through a semblance of a curtsy. She was thankful for her clearheadedness; knowing she would need to be able to think, she had refused laudanum despite her excruciating pain.

"Your Grace," she said softly, "I beg your pardon for my disruption of your day."

"My day? My life, you mean!" He waved a hand at her. "Sit down, sit down, girl! For heaven's sake, do not perish right in front of me."

Prudence rushed to throw a combing gown around her friend's shoulders as Anne limped to a brocade settee and lowered herself onto it. She could manage the duke better than his son at this moment, Anne decided. Every time she thought of the marquess, she remembered him hovering over her as she lay in her little bed, his mouth so close and his breath so warm.

"Do you plan to die quickly, Miss Webster?" the duke asked, seating himself across from her. "Everyone has assured us you will, and yet I find you looking quite pink at the moment."

"Take comfort, sir, for I am sure I shall not trouble you long," Anne said. "Though I do not wish to die, I understand little can be done."

"My deepest regrets, of course. Now, Miss Webster, it is my understanding that you are the cause of my son's grievous wound."

"It is possible, my lord. I am told that everyone believes the gamekeeper fired upon our party in revenge for my refusal to wed him."

"You may have led to the injury of the marquess," the duke said, leaning forward and pointing at her with his cane, "yet you presume to hold him to his marriage-proposal amusement?"

"I did not find the proposal amusing."

The duke stared at her as though he had not expected such a prompt response. "Indeed. Well, neither did I. But it was clearly a jest, Miss Webster, and you were not to take my son's words to heart."

"My heart holds no place for your son. I merely considered his offer and decided to accept." She lifted her chin. "You yourself stated that *any* woman would have him."

"I beg your pardon," the duke spluttered. "I said no such thing."

Anne glanced at the butler. "Witnesses will confirm my assertion, Your Grace."

"You are a shameful, wicked young lady!"

"I bear no shame for my actions. On the contrary, I consider my behavior exemplary under the circumstances. Your son derided, mocked, and ridiculed me before such esteemed persons as yourself and the vicar. He then appropriated a very dear possession of mine, which he refused to return until I gave him my answer. He further tormented me by walking at my side after church and exposing me to the scrutiny and gossip of all my acquaintances."

"Well!" the duke exclaimed.

"Although the ball that was fired upon us may have been meant for me, Your Grace," Anne continued, unable to hold her tongue, "it just as easily may have been intended for your son. I have the unwelcome intelligence that the marquess has made many enemies, some of whom would take satisfaction in his demise."

"Upon my word, you are quick to voice your opinions!"

"At the hand of the Marquess of Blackthorne I have been ridiculed, robbed, exposed, and mortally wounded." Anne fought back the sudden tears that sprang to her eyes. "I am a godly and moral woman, Your Grace. I was made a proposal of marriage. I accepted that proposal, and I intend to see myself wed. Your son has shown no inclination to withdraw his offer, and to my way of thinking, the matter is settled."

"Good heavens!" The duke stared at the butler. "Mr. Errand, she is eloquent!"

"Indeed, my lord, most articulate."

"Young lady, what do you mean to gain by this marriage?

Surely your motive to wed the Marquess of Blackthorne lies deeper than the redemption of your wounded pride."

"My motive is monetary."

"Aha, I thought so! You may claim to be godly and moral, but greed flows through your veins."

Anne's eyes narrowed. "I am far less greedy, Your Grace, than any more socially suitable mate. You cannot deny that the family of another woman would demand titles, property, retirement of debt, and all manner of other material advantage."

"You do not believe my son capable of a marriage founded on love?"

"I doubt Lord Blackthorne would know the meaning of true mutual affection. I am even more certain that no woman could ever find reason to love him."

"That bad, is he?" The duke dipped his head, attempting to smother a smile. "Well, my dear, if you do not want his affection and you do not expect to live long enough to make use of the social privilege connected to his title, what is it you do want of him?"

Anne squared her shoulders, determined to face this moment with all the poise she could muster. She forced away the agony in her thigh and the feverish heat flowing through her body.

"Your Grace, my father was a Luddite," she said softly. "He is imprisoned in Nottingham for his activities. Had his trial been conducted earlier, he would have been transported for fourteen years. Now he will surely face execution."

"A Luddite. I am all astonishment."

"The Baroness de Winter preferred my father to a small rectory, where he ministered for many years prior to his imprisonment. Now my family is near destitution, and we have no hope of hiring an attorney to speak in my father's defense. Money to speed my father's trial and release is all I would ask of your son, my lord. It is the least I can hope for as the wife of a marquess."

"How very noble." The duke turned to his butler. "She wishes to save her father. Shall we simply give her the funds and be done with it?"

"As you wish, Your Grace."

The duke leaned back in his chair and studied the young woman seated across from him. Anne tried not to stare back. She had recognized the note of sarcasm in his voice and knew where the marquess had learned it. They were a pair, father and son. Clearly each man had confidence in his own power, each acted with little consideration of others' feelings, and each enjoyed manipulating people as though they were pawns in a game of chess.

Circumstances might play with Anne Webster, but people never had. She would not allow it. She knew her own mind and had never felt compelled to hide her thoughts. Her father's sermons had taught her that all men were the same in the eyes of God. His participation in the Luddite movement had illustrated the importance of standing up for right and truth—no matter that one might butt one's head against authority.

"I am inclined not to give you the money," the duke finally said.

"I never asked a donation of you, Your Grace."

"True. You asked a more preposterous thing—the hand of my son."

"Lord Blackthorne asked for my hand, as you well know

because you were in the room when he did so. I would not reject your financial assistance, however, should you find it in your heart to help my family."

"If I were to give you the funds to pay an attorney, Miss Webster, I expect you might willingly expire rather soon. You would have saved your father from execution, and you would lose the will to battle this grievous injury to your leg. In short, you would die, and I should feel most melancholy at having played a part in your demise."

Anne prickled. "If you do not wish to help my family, Your Grace, simply state your position. Your vain attempt to wash your hands of the matter by claiming to want to extend my life is very low."

"Low, am I?" Again the duke turned to the butler. "Errand, do you take note of this girl's insolence?"

"She is brazen, Your Grace."

"Yes, she is." The duke was practically purring like a cat at a bowl of milk when he returned his focus to Anne. "Miss Webster, you are audacious, bold, and impudent. Moreover, you are arrogant."

"I beg your pardon, sir. I intended no offense."

"No, no, I am quite charmed. I should very much dislike to see you die. In fact, I shall have to send the physician to tend you when he comes from London."

"The physician has arrived," the butler said. "He is in the drawing room awaiting your son's return from Tiverton."

"Is he now?"

"Your Grace, the marquess expressed the desire to have the physician examine the young lady. I thought it best to await your wishes in this matter."

"Errand, send for the man at once. In fact, go to him yourself. And you, Miss Watson, please excuse yourself. I will speak to Miss Webster alone."

As Anne's sole supporter hurried out of the room just ahead of the butler, the duke leaned across the top of his cane and peered at Anne. "I am not going to give you any money, Miss Anne Webster," he said in a low voice. "Your father is a Luddite, and I despise all forms of insurrection. For all I care, the authorities can execute your father and spike his head on the town gates."

Anne swallowed. The duke was more a devil than his son. At the thought of her father's death, she blinked back the angry tears that filled her eyes. "You are cruel," she declared.

"I am rational," he retorted. "Luddites seek power, and power in the hands of the masses is a deadly thing. You view the world through the tiny window of your own experience, Miss Webster. I should not mind except that—like my son— you clearly have the wit to see beyond such triviality. Look, please, at life beyond the servants' hall at Slocombe House in Devon, England. Imagine the globe as a great game board spread out before you."

He plunged his cane into the rose-strewn wool carpet and raised himself to a standing position. Anne watched, almost mortified, as he walked toward her. "France, Italy, Spain," he said, stabbing the tip of his cane onto a different bouquet of roses as he called out each nation. "America. India. Africa. China. The entire earth lies at your feet. You, Miss Webster, are England. You are monarchy."

"Yes, sir," she mouthed.

"Are you a great world empire, England? Do you rule all

these small countries—enriching your coffers with their silk, wine, tea, cotton, sugar, precious gems, opium, and gold?"

"No, sir."

"Not yet, but you could. In the strength of the king lies the strength of England. Look what happened to France when the people revolted. Do you wish that a renegade like Napoleon ruled England?"

"No, Your Grace."

"Of course not! Look what happened when the American colonies revolted. Do you wish to live as those savage Americans with their barbarian manners and bizarre politics?"

Anne shook her head. She knew hardly a thing about America, but it must be a dreadful place.

"Look what happened to heaven itself when Lucifer took it upon himself to revolt. Evil was born! Hell was created! Rebellion is a sin, Miss Webster." He hammered his cane on the floor. "The people must stay in their place! Peasants at the bottom. Tradesmen in the middle. The aristocracy at the top. The king to rule them all. And God alone to rule the king! Luddites and their like are a cancer within our nation. They must be eradicated!"

Anne grabbed the arm of the settee. "A cancer, sir?" she said, clenching her jaw as she forced herself to her feet. "Let me tell you what will rot away the core of your precious monarchy and bring death to your dreams of a world empire for England. Machines! Luddites revolted not against the aristocracy but against industrialization. Machines give power to those who own them, Your Grace. Those who own them are the middle class, the merchants. Who suffers? The peasants, of course. But you will suffer, too."

The duke glared at her. "Shall I?"

"The middle class has its hands on the source of money—manufacturing," she said, repeating the Marquess of Blackthorne's own words. To her surprise, they made sense. "Money is power. Power in the hands of the middle class spells doom to the aristocracy. And that aristocracy, Your Grace, is you. You would do well to listen to your elder son."

The duke took a step closer and cocked his head, scrutinizing Anne as though she were an insect under a microscope. Then his frown softened, and one corner of his mouth tilted up.

"By heaven, Miss Anne Webster," he said, "I like you."

She clutched the settee arm to keep from wilting into it. "Thank you, Your Grace."

"You speak this brazenly to my son, do you?"

"I say what is in my heart."

"Yes, well, you have a very good heart and a very upright character, both of which attributes my elder son sorely lacks. You are also articulate, bold, and headstrong, three characteristics absent in most women of this day. Your manners are coarse, but manners can be taught. You are the daughter of a minister, and, in short, I believe we can make you do."

"Make me do what?"

With a wink, the duke turned to the door and called to his butler, who had returned to his post just outside it. "Errand, where is my physician?"

"In the corridor. He awaits your bidding, Your Grace."

"Send him in, send him in." The duke tapped his cane on the settee. "Sit down, Miss Webster. It will never do for you to perish on your wedding day."

❧ *Six* ❧

The two-thousand-degree heat of the forge radiated through the door of the small smithy on the outskirts of Tiverton. Smoke tinged with the sulfurous smell of burning coal drifted out the open windows. Carriage wheels, horseshoes, and plowshares littered the dusty, grassless yard. Wrought-iron pokers, cooking pots, knives, chains, and swords hung from nails driven into the stone wall beneath the overhanging eave.

Just as he had in childhood, Ruel leaned against the smithy's doorframe, lost in rapt fascination. Inside, a tall, muscled man slammed his hammer against a shaft of incandescent orange steel. Each ringing blow against the anvil launched an arcing shower of sparks that lit up the dim, sooty interior.

The blacksmith inspired the same awe he always had, though in the passing years Ruel had grown to nearly equal his size. A large and powerful figure, the smith himself seemed no less forged in a furnace than the implements of war and toil he produced. His straight hair, as black as midnight, hung to the middle of his back in a tight braid. Ruel knew that the rhythm the man hammered out sang of more than a common laborer in a long leather apron, more than a small stone smithy, more than a bleak existence in the south of England.

The beat echoed of drums, battle cries, and prayers chanted in the setting sun. Did the blacksmith still remember the stories he had told the wide-eyed little English boy so long ago? Ruel had hung on his idol's every word—tales of the days when the smith had been known as Walks-in-the-Night, son of an Osage chieftain. He had lived on the banks of a river far away in America, a place he called the Middle Waters.

A warmth filled Ruel's chest as the blacksmith inspected the steel he was shaping into a carriage-wheel spoke. How many times had the young boy watched the dark man scrutinize a piece of his work, eyebrows drawn together, mouth turned down? With a slight nod of satisfaction, the smith buried the metal in the firepot of his hooked forge. His young assistant leapt to pump the bellows, and the mound of coals began to glow.

"Too much heat and the metal burns, Tommy," the man reminded his striker. "Too little heat—"

"Too little, and the metal stock is hard enough to ruin your tools," Ruel finished.

The smith turned at the unexpected voice, and his taut face softened into a smile. "Blackthorne."

"I have come home."

"It was said you had died in America."

"No." Ruel swallowed at the knot that formed in his throat. "It has been a long time, Walker."

"Three years." The blacksmith gazed impassively at the

nobleman for a moment longer, then he held out his arms. "Welcome home, my friend."

Ruel stepped into the warm embrace of the older man and clasped him tightly. The familiar smell of the huge man's sweaty shirt, the heated dampness of his red-brown skin, the fierce strength of his powerful arms transported him to his boyhood. Ruel buried his cheek against the side of his mentor's neck and reveled in the grip of solid hands on his back and the gentle rocking of the smith's body.

"Oh, my boy," Walker whispered, "you have returned."

"Did you doubt I would?"

"They said you were killed by Indians."

Ruel stepped back and took the smith's powerful shoulders. "Your people are good men, Walker, though the settlers they have raided might argue otherwise."

"You saw them? The Little Ones?"

Ruel nodded. "I lived in the home of Auguste Chouteau."

"You stayed in Sho'to To-Wo'n? Chouteau's Town?"

"The settlers call it St. Louis now, and it is no longer a small town, Walker. Auguste has seen his dream grow."

"Your cousin is respected and honored among the Little People. He tries to understand us, and he accepts our religion even though he cannot approve of it. I remember many years ago he spoke on our behalf with the Spaniards."

"And later with the British and the Americans. Did you know that after the war in 1812, he concluded a treaty of peace between the leaders of the Osage and the commissioners of the United States of America? All injuries and hostilities have been mutually forgiven, and there is now a promise of perpetual peace between the United States and the Osage."

"Perpetual peace?" Walker shook his head. "Auguste Chouteau is a good man, but he is a dreamer. So long as settlers keep moving onto our land, building houses, fencing farms, and plowing fields, there can never be peace between us, Blackthorne."

"Perhaps the Osage need a leader who can speak for them. A man like you, Walker."

"Now you dream, Blackthorne. Before you went away, I told you I can never go back. Look at me." He held out his calloused hands. His dark eyes hardened. "Remember? I am no longer a warrior. I am a metal-maker, like the traders and half-breeds. I have not held a bow since I was sent to France. Did you know I have lived in England more than a quarter of a century, Blackthorne? I have forty-five years . . . an old man."

"Nonsense. You are still young and fit. You are the picture of health."

"How little you understand. Why would my people want me to return? Why would they seek my advice? To hear stories of a blacksmith in England? I can hardly remember how to speak their tongue. I have no tribal wisdom to lend the council of Little Old Men who lead the Osage. I have no wife, no daughters to pass along my bloodlines." His mouth grim, he turned back to his forge. "I can do nothing but bend steel."

Ruel studied Walker as the Indian lifted the glowing rod from the furnace with his tongs. He laid the metal on his anvil and began to hammer. How many times had Ruel witnessed this man pouring his rage, his desolation, his agony into the steel? As a child, he had not seen the helpless impotence that bound the blacksmith as securely as the chains he forged. Now he understood it.

"I came to you because you can do more than bend steel, Walker," Ruel said when the pounding ceased. "I need your help."

The blacksmith swung around, his face stony. "You are a grown man now, Blackthorne. Traveling for years at a time, living your own life. What can an old Indian do for you? I cannot make you a wheel to roll, or carry you on my shoulders. I cannot tell you my legends, or take you swimming in the pond, or teach you how to catch a fish as I did when you were a boy. You are a marquess now, and one day people will call you 'duke' and bow to you as though you were a god."

He swung his hammer again, and a cascade of orange sparks lit the room. "Do not come here to tell me of your travels in America or your visits with Auguste Chouteau and the Osage. Do not make me wish for things that can never be. Go away from this place, Blackthorne."

Ruel stood in silence as the blows rained on metal. The small room filled with the deafening sound of the ringing hammer. Walker picked up the carriage-wheel spoke and shoved it back into the furnace.

"Hotter, Tommy," he told his assistant. "Pump the bellows, boy."

"A woman is dying, Walker," Ruel said, his voice almost too low to be heard. "Unless you come, the surgeon will amputate her leg or let her die of gangrene."

"A woman?"

"We are to be married."

Walker fell silent. "Your father will not want me in his house."

"My father will not want a woman to die in his house."

The Indian stared at the glowing coals. "A woman . . . to be your wife and bear your children," he whispered. For a moment he stood unmoving, lost in the fire. Then he lifted his head and tossed the carriage spoke into a trough of cold water. Hot metal hissed. Steam billowed into the room.

"Tommy," he said, "run to the tailor and tell him his carriage wheel will be ready tomorrow."

"Aye, sir."

Lifting his leather apron over his head, Walker nodded at Ruel. "I shall get my bag."

❧

"Amputation might save the young lady's life." The physician regarded Anne through his monocle as he spoke to the Duke of Marston. "First we must transport her to London, bleed her, dose her liberally with opiates, and then remove the limb. I trust she can have no objection."

Anne bit her lip as she tried to reason past the pain swirling through her body. In spite of the heavy dose of laudanum she had been forced to take, her leg felt like a flaming log jerked from a fire. She could hardly move it. Bright red tentacles of infection crept slowly from the seeping wound toward her heart. If the doctor did not take her leg, she would surely die.

She held out her hand. "Miss Watson?"

"I am here, Anne. Rest yourself now." The young woman's gaze lifted to the physician in his fine coat and white cravat. "She is my lady's maid, sir, and my dear friend. Do not cut off her leg, I beg you. The pain would be too great to endure."

"Your friend will certainly die if I do not remove the infected limb." He turned to the duke. "Your Grace, which do you prefer? Shall I perform the amputation, or shall we permit the young lady to perish?"

"Perish?" Ruel strode across the room and pushed past the physician. "Miss Webster, you do not have my permission to die."

Anne studied the face that peered down at her. Gray eyes, curly black hair. Ruel. Or was it? The laudanum made her head swim. She could no longer think clearly at all. Nothing made sense. Permission to die? Did a person need permission to die?

"Walker, please come here at once." Ruel beckoned the man waiting in the shadows near the door. "Have a look at Miss Webster's leg and see what you can do."

Waving Miss Watson to one side, Ruel took her place and bent over the pillow. "Miss Webster," he said in a low voice, "I have brought my friend. I expect you to do exactly as he tells you, and do not—"

"Ruel." The duke's voice was stiff. "This man is not permitted in my home."

Walker's eyes moved between the two men as the marquess straightened. "Your Grace, this is the blacksmith from Tiverton."

"I know who he is. What can you mean by bringing a savage into my house?"

"Mr. Walker knows more about healing than any physician in the area. The townspeople visit him with their ailments. I insist—"

"I shall not have him here." He turned to his butler. "Errand, remove this man."

"Your Grace," Ruel cut in, taking his father's arm. "Be

reasonable. Miss Webster will do us little good without her leg, and no good at all dead. I need her whole and healthy. The physician confesses his lack of skill in this matter, and I am convinced Mr. Walker can heal her."

"Convinced, are you? The Indian is a man of low breeding. A heathen."

"He is the son of an Osage chieftain whose home I visited while staying in St. Louis. Auguste Chouteau hopes to see Mr. Walker returned to America whence he was so ruthlessly exported at the mercy of French officials who—you will recall—held him hostage and used him for the pleasure of their Society until he was able to escape. He fled to us here in England because of his regard for our name."

"The Chouteau family deserves everyone's respect. But why we should reciprocate for an uneducated savage is beyond me."

"Mr. Walker is the most upright gentleman I have the pleasure to know. In honor of Auguste Chouteau, he would be happy to assist us in resolving this medical calamity."

The duke grunted. "You bring a wounded maid into my household and place her in my bed. You make an engagement of marriage with a woman who is so far beneath you as to bring ridicule upon your name. Now you inflict this uncivilized brute upon me. Ruel Chouteau, you wear my name, you claim privileges as my heir, and one day you will own my titles and possess my lands. Have I misplaced my trust?"

Ruel tried to read the message in the duke's eyes. He saw in them a hurt he could not understand. Had he been a disappointment to his father? Was it so wrong to associate with such a man as the blacksmith, simply because Walker had no status in Society?

"Your Grace," Ruel said in a low voice, "I give you my word that I will bring nothing but respect to your name. My primary objective in this life has always been to honor you. With that aim I traveled to America and began to develop a plan to enrich the duchy. I seek nothing more from my existence than security for your properties and your lineage."

"Your associations with commoners do not please me."

"I beg your pardon, Your Grace," Ruel said, his voice flinty, "but I consider neither this woman nor the blacksmith to be common."

He let his focus drift to Anne. Her brown eyes, wide and deeply shadowed, stared out at him from her ashen face. He suppressed the panic that gripped his stomach at the thought of her death. If the duke knew the truth about his son's fascination with a servant . . . about his heir's deep affection for an Indian from the wilderness of America . . .

"Mr. Walker will tend the woman's leg," Ruel told his father, slipping an arm around the duke's shoulder and turning him toward the door. "She, in turn, will assist me in a small venture."

"She plans to marry you, my boy. I hope you know that."

"An alliance of uncertain duration, Your Grace, I assure you."

The duke cast a glance toward the bed. "I rather like the girl. She is a minister's daughter, did you know? Her father is a Luddite, of all things. Imprisoned in Nottingham for smashing lace machines. He has bequeathed her quite a quick tongue. I should think she will be good for you."

Ruel smiled. "I should hope so."

"If you insist on permitting the savage to try his heathen

magic on her, I shall send the physician to tend your mother. The duchess continues to complain of a most tiresome headache."

"Yes, Your Grace." Ruel watched as his father and the others left the room. Once they were gone, he nodded to the Indian.

"Walker, do whatever it takes," he said.

∽◌◌◌◌◌◌◌∾

"You should not disappoint the duke with your behavior, Blackthorne." The tall Osage blacksmith removed a damp white cabbage leaf from Anne's leg and dropped it into a bucket. "He has been more than good to you."

"How does her wound look?" Ruel tried to peer around the tent of sheets Walker had erected over his patient.

"White cabbage leaves absorb pus," the Indian said. "They reduce swelling, too. As soon as the leaf grows hot, I take it away and place another under the bandage. I think the wound is almost clean."

"She seems to be sleeping."

"No, she is awake. The drug they gave her numbed her mind." He placed his palm on Anne's pale brow. "She feels some relief now, as the fever begins to subside. Blackthorne, you must take great care of this woman when she is your wife. You must protect and honor her. There should be no greater love than that between marriage partners. Not even the love between parent and child should be as strong. The duke honors you as his son, but his love for his wife is enduring."

Ruel grimaced at the thought of his self-absorbed, unaffectionate mother and lifted the bucket of cabbage leaves. "I shall take these out."

"Have I not taught you that the bonds of a family must remain unbroken? To the Osage, family ties are as strong as the sinews of the buffalo."

"And yet my mother has not laid eyes on me since my return."

"She is not well. You should leave this woman to me and see to the duchess. With no one to stop him, that London doctor will start some foolishness like filling her stomach with laudanum or draining her veins of her lifeblood."

Ruel held out a fresh cabbage leaf. The Osage waved it away.

"Now it is time for garlic. Put down the bucket." He drew two clusters of cloves from his cloth bag. "The Little People used crushed seeds of the wild columbine to make a drink for fever. For wounds and infections, we use the wild four-o'clock or the butterfly weed. Here, I cannot find such plants, so I make this paste."

Ruel observed as Walker mashed the garlic cloves in a small bowl. The pungent aroma drifted into the room. The Indian spread the paste over the injury to Anne's leg and covered it with a warm flannel bandage. When he had wrapped and tied the cloth around her leg, he lowered the tented sheets and tucked them under the mattress.

"She must rest," Walker said. "Her friend can tend her. You should go to your mother."

Ruel sat in the chair at the edge of the bed for a moment longer and studied his laced fingers. In the passing hours, some of his fears for the housemaid had eased. Now he felt dismayed—almost embarrassed—at the lengths to which he had gone to save her life. Had the laudanum he had been given caused him to take leave of his senses?

"If I am to make this worth the time I have spent on the woman," he said finally, "I have got to finish it. I must marry her."

"Worth the time?" Walker regarded him through narrowed eyes. "Are the lives of some humans worth less than the lives of others?"

"Of course."

"I see. You told me you planned to marry Miss Webster. I assumed you loved her."

"No, nothing like that. The woman is a part of my plan."

"Is Miss Anne Webster only 'the woman' to you, Blackthorne? This marriage sounds like nothing but a sham."

Ruel frowned. "You can be tedious, Walker." He lifted his chin and dismissed his valet with a wave of the hand. "Foley, send for the vicar, and tell my father the wedding will take place within the hour."

"You intend to marry your woman today? She can hardly open her eyes. What is your hurry, Blackthorne?"

Ruel raked a hand through his hair. "Listen, Walker, I mean to make something productive of my life. I shall not spend my time in the company of Society, dancing jigs and penning riddles. I will not give myself to countless hours spent doing as my father does—having the vicar to tea in the drawing room. Riding through the village and lording it over peasants. Hunting foxes, for heaven's sake. Even you, whom I admire, have lived a futile life, have you not, Walker? Hammering steel day after day—sweat pouring down your body, the smell of sulfur in your nostrils. You might as well be living in hell."

The Indian's eyes went as dark as ink. Ruel knew he had

struck a raw place in his friend's heart. Yet he could hardly restrain his tongue. What good was a life so empty?

"My life can mean nothing to you," Walker said, his tone harsh. "What will you make of yours? What is it you really want, Blackthorne?"

"Adventure. Money. Freedom."

"So you will join yourself to this girl as though she were another cog in the machine you are building to glorify and amuse yourself. In all those afternoons we spent together, did I not speak to you of tender affection, Blackthorne? Did I not tell you of the joys of family, of the blessing of a wife and children? Do you not wish for love?"

Ruel shook off the resonating pull of the Indian's questions. "Come now, Walker, it is not like you to speak such pretty words. Family, blessing, tender affection, love? Good heavens, you will drown me in sugar syrup."

"Not pretty words. True words."

"Words have no power, Walker. None. I have never lived with family joy, blessing, or tender affection. Such drivel is the stuff of dreamers. Action has power. A man's own experience is his greatest teacher. I have been taught by my parents' example to value wealth and prestige over love."

"Oh, my boy."

"Enough of your lamenting. Just keep your eye on me, Walker. You will see I am right in the end."

Ruel leaned back in his chair and stretched out his legs. He closed his eyes and gave a deep yawn. Hours of tending the ill did not suit him. He needed to be up and about, paying a visit to Mr. Heathcoat, the lacemaker, investigating the shooting incident, calling on old friends, making preparations for his trip to France.

He opened his eyes. Anne was staring at him. The dark brown-gold of her gaze ran through him like a shower of sparks. In spite of himself, he leaned forward, elbows on his knees.

Heavens, she was a beauty. Even this close to death, the young woman shone with a strange inner light. Her skin was luminous alabaster. Her cheeks glowed a soft pink. The outer corners of her eyes tilted up, so she seemed to be smiling at him even though her lips were still.

"Miss Webster," he said, unable to hide the concern in his voice, "are you still quite content to die?"

❧❧❧

The Duke of Marston marched into the chamber, his cane fairly piercing holes in the carpet as he hurried toward the bed where Anne Webster lay. "Now then, Ruel," he sputtered. "What is this news I am told? Can you really mean to wed the girl this very afternoon?"

He paused before his son and glanced at the young woman. With a gasp of shock, he turned to his butler. "What have you done to the girl, Errand? Not an hour ago, she was plain! Now look at her!"

The butler regarded Anne. "I believe she has been improved upon, Your Grace."

Ruel understood the men's astonishment. The moment he had stepped into the room late that afternoon, surprise tumbled down him like a spray of icy water. "Come, Father, admit it," he now addressed the duke. "She is an angel."

Catherine Palmer

Disconcerted, Anne touched her hair. Artfully curled and pinned into the latest fashion, it shone a deep bronze in the candlelight. Ruel realized that although one of the maids had performed this magic, Anne had no idea how she looked. The dress that her mistress, Miss Watson, had selected from her own wardrobe was positively entrancing. The gathered skirt fell to her ankles in a whisper of sapphire blue silk. Soft puffed sleeves hung halfway to her elbows, and were met by white gloves that covered her hands and forearms.

"But . . . but . . ." The duke fumbled for a moment. "Altered though she is, Ruel, you cannot mean to marry the woman today."

"You can hardly be troubled at my failure to publish the banns, Father," Ruel said as the duke approached. "I should imagine we must keep the wedding as quiet as the regent's secret marriage that preceded his alliance to our current queen. Two wives at the same time. Imagine that."

"Do not speak of such things, boy! As it is, your mother can hardly move without smelling salts to rouse her. She cannot believe you intend to marry a housemaid. Dire, dire misfortune, she assures me. I informed her the lady was a minister's daughter and not entirely unacceptable, but the duchess is not to be swayed. A minister has no money, she reminded me. I certainly cannot acquaint her with the uncomfortable news that this particular girl's father is doomed to execution. The daughter of a criminal, no less! No dowry, no money, no grand wedding at St. James's in London. Your mother is beside herself. Quite, quite distraught."

Ruel drew back from Anne and crossed his arms over his chest. "My mother will not attend the wedding, then?"

115

"No, of course not. She is predicting the stars will fall from the sky."

"May I have the pleasure of your blessing, Your Grace?"

The duke waved his son away. "Is the young lady expected to live?"

"Indeed."

"Then how can you think of actually marrying her today? I understood you hoped to spend at least a year in mourning to escape my constant pressure for you to wed in Society."

"No indeed. I plan to make good use of my wife."

"And then? What will you do with her when she has served her purpose? Cast her aside?"

"I shall see to her welfare, of course. I am an honorable man. To my way of thinking, this situation is hardly uncommon. You asked me not to speak of the regent, but I believe he has set a fine example. Thirty years ago he married a commoner, Mrs. Maria Anne Fitzherbert, a Roman Catholic widow. Ten years later, without benefit of divorce or annulment, he married Caroline Amelia Elizabeth of Brunswick. The future king of England—a bigamist. No one is troubled by it."

"Nonsense! You would never do such a thing. Besides, the regent had a friend deny the first marriage in the House of Commons."

"Would it be so difficult to deny a marriage made under these circumstances?" Ruel gestured to Anne. "A dying woman. A deathbed wedding. A marquess and a housemaid. When I elect to terminate the arrangement, surely the good vicar will be able to come up with some rule or regulation we have violated here."

"Upon my word, Ruel, would it not be simpler just to take Miss Webster as your mistress? If you want royal example to follow, why not emulate the regent's brother, Prince William, Duke of Clarence? He has spent twenty years with that actress."

"Dorothea Bland?"

"Ah, yes. She is known as Mrs. Jordan, you know. Prince William's mistress has given birth to ten children by him, and certainly no one has condemned him. Should he accede to the throne, I suspect he will ennoble every one of his illegitimate offspring. So why not take Miss Webster as a paramour?"

"The daughter of a minister? I hardly think Miss Webster would agree to that. You have met the woman, sir. She has a mind of her own and a barbed tongue to match it."

"Ah, yes. So she does." The duke turned his attention to Anne. He tilted forward on his cane and ran his gaze up and down her. "Going to live, are you, young lady? Well, I hope you have kept your wits through this ordeal. You will speak to the marquess as you spoke to me earlier, will you not?"

Anne managed a nod.

The duke chuckled. "Very good. Then I shall give your union my blessing, though one cannot deny this is dreadfully irregular. Dreadfully. Ruel, in spite of your ill-conceived marriage and common wife, you must promise that after you inherit, you will behave in a manner befitting your title."

"Of course, Your Grace. I shall do my utmost to honor your name and bring fortune to your property."

The duke glanced at Walker, who had warily backed into a corner and stood half hidden in shadow. "The Indian is responsible for Miss Webster's improved health, is he?"

"Indeed. We owe him our gratitude."

"Gratitude?" He pointed his cane at the blacksmith, but at that moment the vicar entered the room. As Walker quickly exited, a cluster of curious gentlemen hurried in. Ruel recognized various church and town officials, as well as several of the duke's comrades who had been summoned earlier in the day to observe the momentous occasion of the wedding of a marquess.

Amid the hubbub, Mr. Errand called for order. Footmen rushed to bring chairs into the bedroom for the guests. Housemaids folded away blankets and put out urns of fresh flowers they had snatched from other rooms in Slocombe House. Kitchenmaids brought in silver trays laden with sweets, which Mrs. Smythe had managed to prepare upon hearing the shocking news. A lady's maid slipped a fresh rose blossom into Anne's hair. Another dusted scented powder on her neck. A third arranged her dress as two footmen lifted her from the bed.

"I declare it smells of garlic in here!" The Duchess of Marston waved a silk handkerchief across her nose as her younger son escorted her into the room. "Someone fetch my smelling salts lest I swoon again."

"Mother." Ruel stepped away from his valet, who was attempting to tie on a fresh cravat. He could hardly believe she had come. Like a child surprised by an unexpected pat on the head, he took the woman's arm. "May I show you to a chair, Your Grace?"

"Leave me be, Ruel." She swatted his hand with her fan. "Alex, do tell your brother to attend to the matter at hand. I understand he has come up with yet another way to vex me."

Ruel's jaw tightened as Alexander led their mother to a

wide settee. She patted her hair, waved her fan beneath her chin, and fussed at the maid who was arranging her skirt. Nothing had changed. Ruel covered the familiar hurt with grim determination and turned away.

"Let us begin." He strode to the settee where Anne had been seated and took his place at her side.

⸎⸎⸎

Leaning back against the velvet cushions, Anne tried to make sense of the unreality before her eyes. Somehow she had gotten herself into a private bedroom with the Duke and Duchess of Marston, their two sons, the vicar of Tiverton, and at least a dozen other people. Gentlemen sipped from delicate glasses and nibbled at cakes. The sweet scent of perfume mingled with the pungent smell of garlic—and both seemed to be emanating from her own body.

It was worse than a nightmare. Most confusing of all had been the snippets of conversation that now played a game of chase inside her head:

"Miss Webster will do us little good without her leg, and no good at all dead. If I am to make use of her, I shall need her whole and healthy. . . ."

"You make an engagement of marriage with this woman who is so far beneath you as to bring ridicule upon your name. . . ."

"I actually like the woman. She is a minister's daughter, did you know? He has bequeathed her quite a wicked tongue. . . ."

"There should be no greater love than that between marriage partners. . . ."

"I do not believe in such drivel. I have been taught by my parents' example to desire wealth and prestige, not love."

Anne searched the room for the source of the words she remembered. The duke, there by the fire. The duchess, fanning herself on a settee. The healer, gone.

"Dearly beloved . . . ," the vicar of Tiverton began.

A wedding. Her own wedding.

A tall man with dark, curly hair took her hand. She shut her eyes, confused. For what seemed like hours, she had listened to the Marquess of Blackthorne hold forth. The man was full of himself, vain and obnoxious. He had not the slightest concern for others. Could not believe in love. Enjoyed using people. Cogs in a machine.

"Anne?" That deep voice again. So near. So gentle and warm.

She opened her eyes. Ruel. Sitting beside her, his black hair in a tumble over his brow. How kind he was. Protecting her. Bringing that dark-eyed physician to heal her. Ruel had saved her life. Just as he had promised.

"Ruel . . ." She looked into his gray eyes. She thought . . . hoped . . . prayed . . . the man she was marrying was Ruel . . . but she had the terrible feeling he might be the Marquess of Blackthorne after all.

☙ *Seven* ❧

Whatever the name of the man Anne had married, he did
not show himself again after the wedding. She was told he
had gone to London on business. In place of a husband,
the black-haired physician came every morning to the large,
drafty bedroom to tend her. He changed the garlic poultice—
which sent Prudence Watson and all the other attendants
scampering from the room—bathed the bullet wound with
calendula lotion and sage tea, and then replaced the bandage
with a clean garlic-paste poultice.

Within a week, the man—who called himself Walker and
claimed to be an Indian from America—began washing
Anne's injury with diluted calendula tincture and peach-pit
tea. He made a fresh goldenseal, plantain, and comfrey oint-
ment and packed the wound. By the end of the second week,
the wounds where the ball had entered and exited Anne's
thigh had closed. Any sign of the bits of fabric the bullet had
driven into her flesh finally vanished.

She began to walk about the bedroom, exercising her leg. Then she began to explore the corridors. In the third week, she asked to be taken to the garden. Walker volunteered to escort her, and Prudence insisted on attending Anne as well. They made their way down countless flights of stairs, through two drawing rooms, and finally out a pair of tall glass-paned doors onto a paved terrace. Anne took a deep breath of the fresh spring air and looked around her.

"I am alive, Miss Watson," she said softly.

"Yes, you are, Lady Blackthorne." The golden-haired young woman never flinched at calling her former maid by this new title, but it annoyed Anne to no end. "I must tell you the truth. I never thought you would live to walk outside again."

"Nor did I." Thankful for life but confused at the turn it had taken, she took the arm of the tall Indian for support. "You saved me, Mr. Walker, and I am grateful. At the same time, I cannot think how I am to go on."

"Breathe air, drink water, sleep at night, find work for your hands. Life cannot be so difficult for the wife of a marquess, can it?"

She sighed. "That is just the problem."

As her need for laudanum had eased during the past three weeks, Anne could no longer deny that she had, indeed, married the marquess. She was now the Marchioness of Blackthorne. Kitchenmaids dipped curtsies when she passed them, and housemaids scurried to tend her before she even requested help. Mrs. Davies, the housekeeper, assigned Anne a lady's maid of her own, and she was bathed, dressed, and perfumed in a manner befitting the aristocracy to which she now belonged.

Anne could hardly keep up with the changes. Not only did the household staff wait on her hand and foot, but seamstresses traveled from London to measure her, milliners came to fit her with bonnets and hats, and shoemakers arrived to design slippers and boots. Prudence Watson considered this turn of events the most delightful experience of her life, and she came out of her gloominess and anxiety altogether. She and Mrs. Davies spent every afternoon instructing Anne on the manners and etiquette befitting a marchioness. Even Mr. Errand came in once or twice to give his new mistress charts of the Chouteau family's ancestry and to explain everyone's titles and how she was to address them.

Her meals could have fed the entire Webster family in Nottingham, who had learned to make do on dark bread, butter, shriveled potatoes, and strong tea. At breakfast Anne faced veal-and-ham pies, mackerel, dried haddock, mutton chops, broiled sheep's kidneys, sausages, bacon, poached eggs, toast, marmalade, butter, and fresh fruit. At luncheon she met with hashed meats, bread, cheese, biscuits, and puddings. At dinner she encountered oxtail soup, crimped salmon, croquettes of chicken, mutton cutlets, roast filet of veal, boiled capon, lobster salad, raspberry jam tartlets, and plum pudding. No wonder the duchess's middle had expanded and the duke puffed when he climbed the stairs.

Since her wedding day, Anne had seen neither of those esteemed noble relations, nor had she laid eyes on the marquess or his brother. In fact, her world continued to be oddly dreamlike, as though she had stepped behind a green baize curtain in a dark corridor and into another existence. Now she could not remember how to get back.

"I feel lost," she said softly. "I do not know where to turn."

"You have been handed the whole world, my lady," Prudence told her. "You remind me of my dear sister Sarah. You know that when her husband and our father died, she was left with a title and a fortune for which she had never been properly prepared. While I urged her to use the money to purchase a lovely country house, you remember what she chose to do with all that money."

Anne smiled. "Yes, I remember it well. She believed that God wished her to give away her fortune."

Prudence sighed. "Can you imagine? She sailed off to the Orient and did her very best to bankrupt herself by funding orphanages and schools for blind girls. Everyone thought her quite mad. But of course, you were working at Trenton House when she returned, and you are well familiar with the astonishing events that led to her marriage to Mr. Charles Locke. Oh, I do miss them both!"

"I long for my family, as well."

"But you can do anything you like now, my lady. You can go anywhere. See anyone. What do you want?"

"Only my family. I have no idea what has become of my father." She touched the white linen of her friend's sleeve. "The marquess never returned my lace, did he?"

"You do not need that scrap of lace," Prudence said. "As his wife, you have all the money you like. Why not send a letter to your mother on the mail coach? In the desk in your bedroom are enough pens, ink, and paper to write a hundred books if you like. Or why not dispatch a footman to inquire at the rectory in Nottingham? You could have your mother, sisters, and brother transported to Tiverton and put up in a good house."

"You say I have money, Prudence. Where is it? Am I to knock on the duke's library door and ask him for a thousand pounds? Am I to go into the duchess's bedroom and rifle through her bags?"

"Inquire of Mr. Errand how you are to get at your fortune. He certainly knows everything else you are meant to do."

Anne tugged her shawl more closely around her shoulders. She might be the Marchioness of Blackthorne, but she still felt like Anne Webster. The thought of demanding anything of the formidable butler sent a knot into her stomach.

If, as Prudence claimed, she could do anything she liked, she wanted to go home. In Nottingham the long hedgerows would be in full bloom—cow parsley, hawthorn, and hogweed dancing with white blossoms. Violets and yellow primroses shyly showing their faces. Ferns beginning to unfurl their green fronds. Kestrels and wood pigeons soaring on cool spring breezes as farmers turned over the rich soil.

In contrast to the wild exuberance of her beloved Midlands, the Slocombe garden was crisscrossed by narrow brick paths, twelve-foot walls covered in ivy, and hedges pruned into sharp boxes or perfect orbs. Roses had been forced over metal arches; daffodils marched in straight, even rows. They looked as confined as she felt.

"I should like to go home," she declared, almost to herself.

Walker stopped in the path. Turning to Anne, he gazed down at her. "You *are* home, Lady Blackthorne. This England, this Devon, this patch of soil near the sea, is your home. It is my home. Forces more powerful than you and I have made it so. Nothing can change that."

"This is not a home, Mr. Walker. It is a prison."

"No, it is only a place. Not so different from any other. If you do not learn to accept it as your home, you will live with anger and regret. You will have no hope. Your faith in God will grow weak."

"My faith in God." Anne hung her head. "I fear in my recent behavior I have given little evidence of my surrender to Christ. I decided that I must pay for my father's defense. I made the lace panel. I entered Sir Alexander's rooms with the purpose of selling my lace. Of course I prayed to God, as I always do. But did I ask His will? Did I submit myself to His leading?"

"Oh, Anne, you are the most faithful woman I know!" Prudence cried, forgetting her friend's elevated status. "You always think of God first. You have taught me how to pray, and your reading of Scripture puts my own study to shame."

"I did not seek God's will in the matter of my father," Anne confessed. "I wanted to free him, and I devised a plan to accomplish that end. Perhaps he is meant to be in prison. From a prison cell, St. Paul led many men to Christ and wrote several of the Epistles we treasure so dearly."

"But your father faces a death penalty, Anne! I cannot believe God would wish that upon His humble servant. No, indeed, you were right to try everything in your power to assist him."

Anne pursed her lips, thinking of the chaos she had created by choosing to follow her own desires. "I did not seek God when I agreed to marry the marquess. Now it is done, and whatever plan God did have for my life is ruined. And meanwhile I must reflect on my wrongdoings from a prison of my own device."

"Maybe one day you will go home," Walker said. "God can do anything."

Anne read the truth in the tall man's dark eyes. During her recovery, as she sat making lace by the window, he had told her about the land of his birth: America. He made it sound wild and beautiful and free. She had heard the longing in his voice, and she knew her own echoed it.

In silence, they walked on down the path. Stopping at a large gate, Anne peered up through the bars at the huge, gray-stone house with its parapets, its countless chimneys, its many-paned windows and heavy iron-and-oak doors. Home? No wonder the marquess had been eager to escape the place.

They had just begun to walk again when Anne glimpsed a man in the grove that edged one side of the garden. He was moving their way, and she felt a sudden fear. She turned around, took Prudence's arm for support, and retreated down the path. But the man, near enough to see them, called out.

"Walker!"

"It is the marquess, Anne," Prudence whispered, clutching her friend's arm. "Oh, dear!"

"Blackthorne." The Indian lifted a hand as the nobleman strode onto the path and approached them. "Where have you been keeping yourself?"

"London, mostly. Good morning, Walker, Lady Blackthorne, Miss Watson." He took off his tall black hat and bowed. "Out for a stroll, are you? Very good. I was told I should find you here."

Anne's legs had turned to wooden boards, and her feet might as well have been nailed to the ground. It was one thing to adjust to her new social status and come to grips with its effect on her life. It was another thing to meet the Marquess of Blackthorne face-to-face and realize he was her husband.

Husband.

She could hardly force breath into her lungs. Her heartbeat hammered in her ears like an infantry drum. *Husband! Husbands mean beds and babies and . . . oh, help!*

Unable to speak a word, she stared at the marquess. He was saying something to Walker about the weather. His black hair curled at the tops of his ears and lay in a ruffle against his high, stiff collar. Beneath his calf-length greatcoat, his shoulders looked enormous. And how prodigiously tall and strong he was!

Mortified, Anne clutched her shawl at her throat. He had said he meant to make use of her. She had thought his statement referred to her lace. It never occurred to her that he had any other purpose in mind. She had expected herself to die and be free of him. But now . . . now!

"And your injury, my lady?" he said, turning to her. "Has Walker healed you, as I expected he would?"

Anne had no choice but to look straight into his gray eyes. His dark brows lifted a little in inquiry, and one corner of his mouth turned up. He leaned toward her, waiting for her reply like a cat toying with its prey.

"I am well," she managed, horribly aware that her voice sounded like a mouse's.

"Capital. Nothing could cheer me more. Then will you do me the honor of accompanying me into the arboretum for a brief tête-à-tête?" He glanced at the other two. "You do not mind, do you, Walker? Miss Watson?"

Prudence glanced at Anne, wide green eyes clearly conveying her panic. She did not want to leave her friend, but what could be done but obey the request of a marquess? "Of course, my lord," Prudence said meekly.

The Indian tipped his head. "I shall return to my smithy."

"No, wait for me in the library, please. There is a fine prospect from the south windows to entertain you. I shall not be long, and I have a great deal to tell you."

Without waiting for his friend's answer, the marquess took Anne's hand, tucked it around the inside of his elbow, and set off toward the tree-filled park near the path. Anne glanced back to see Prudence staring at her, white-faced with trepidation, as she was led away by Walker.

"London is abuzz with news of our wedding," the marquess began when he had walked his wife through the gate into the arboretum. Trees of every species in England filled the walled grove, their shadows darkening the sunlit grass. "Miss Pickworth writes of little else. Her readers are desperate for information. Because this infamous creature chooses to write under a pseudonym, she cannot request an interview with you, but editors at *The Tattler* have been frantically sending me letters in the vain hope that I may address the issue."

"Miss Pickworth, whoever she may be, ought to keep her nose in her own affairs."

"Ah, but what fun is that for Society's gossipmongers? No, indeed, you and I are quite the scandal of the moment."

"I have never been a scandal," Anne said firmly.

"You had better accustom yourself to it. A minister's daughter snaring a marquess . . . it is deliciously appalling. The predators can hardly wait to get their talons into you.

Errand assures me he and Mrs. Davies have trained you well, but you will have to rely on your wits when you enter the lair of Society."

"I have no plan to go to London, Lord Blackthorne."

"No? What do you plan?" He stopped walking and looked down at her.

"I plan to get my lace back from you, Lord Blackthorne," she said and held out one hand. "You made me a promise."

He took her hand, turned it over, and kissed it. "You made me a promise, my dear lady. To love, honor, and obey . . . until death do us part."

Anne snatched her hand away. "I was drugged, and you knew it! I believed I was going to die. Do not tell me you mean to continue this charade. Give me my lace, sir, and let me go back to Nottingham where I belong. I have had more than my fill of roasted pheasant, bowing servants, and ivied walls."

"Good, then you cannot object to embarking on a tour of pleasure. London first, then Belgium and France. We shall stay in all the best houses, dance at the most elegant balls, and eat and drink ourselves into oblivion. You shall have a new gown every day and the latest hats—"

"I have more gowns than I can possibly wear already. And I do not want new hats, sir. I was happy enough with my straw bonnet."

"You were not." He leaned close and took her chin. "You were trying to sell lace to my brother. You wanted more money than the laceman would give you."

Anne clamped her mouth shut. Vile man! He was a rogue.

"You, my dear wife, are enterprising, visionary, and ambitious. You see curly hair where others see foggy windows. You weave silk threads with the skill of a spider. You managed to marry yourself off to a marquess. Do not tell me you are content with a straw bonnet and a dustcloth."

"I am meant to be a maid. That is all." She knotted her hands into fists. "I shall not be played with, sir. I shall not be made sport of by you. I only want . . . I want . . . "

"What is it you want, Anne Chouteau, Marchioness of Blackthorne? Tell me. What are your dreams?"

Anne turned her head away and stared into the top branches of a giant oak tree. Light green leaves rustled in the cool air. What did she want? Her old dreams had grown as tangled as the tree's budding branches. To sell her lace . . . free her father . . . to marry . . . to start a lace school . . . to have children . . .

"I want to do God's will," she said.

"God's will? And what is that, pray tell?"

She swallowed. "I confess, I am not certain. But I do know that despite all your great wealth and prestige and standing in Society, you are powerless to make me happy."

"I shall wager you are dead wrong there." He caught her elbow and turned her toward him. "I would wager my entire fortune that I can make you happy . . . very happy. But then, you are not a gambler, are you? No cards or dice for my little saint who seeks only God's will to make her happy. Tell me, wife, do you intend to read the Bible every night before we retire to our bed?"

Anne gulped down a bubble of air. His fingers on her arm were warm and firm. His dark hair fell in a tumble of curls over his brow. The tendons in his neck bunched, and the small muscle at the side of his jaw flickered as he stared at her.

For an instant, she was captured by the moment—aware of

the man's scent, entranced by the contrast between his black hair and the blue sky behind him, trapped in his gray eyes, bewitched by his mouth. For an instant, she forgot her stolen lace and her imprisoned father and her desire to do God's will. For an instant, she imagined she was melting into this man, enfolded in his strength and pressed against his beating heart. For an instant . . . and then she remembered.

"Stop." The word barely escaped her trembling lips. "Do not mock me."

"Never. I always tell the truth, and I always see the truth. Do not believe you can fool me with the façade you have built around yourself—minister's daughter, lady's maid, faithful Bible reader, common lace stitcher. From the moment we met, I knew you."

"You know nothing of me."

"No?" He slid his fingers down her arm and lifted her hand. Tugging away her glove, he regarded her with a confident smile. He dropped the glove into the grass and laced his fingers through hers. "I know your hands, my lady. Yours are fingers that can weave magic from silk thread. Magic and mystery. I understand how few can work such wonders. In the past three weeks I have been to the lace schools at Honiton, I have spoken with Mr. Heathcoat the lacemaker, and I have watched women bent over their lace pillows. You were quite right in your boast that day in my brother's bedroom. Few can equal the skill with which you work lace; fewer still can prick patterns in parchment with your expertise. None . . . none I saw in my journeys could design with such inspiration as you."

"You are a demon with your bewitching words."

"I know your hands," he went on, as if she had not spoken, "and I know your mouth. Your words made a beggar believe she was a duchess. Your words cowed the vicar of Tiverton. Your words charmed and delighted my father. The duke simply cannot stop talking about you."

"That is not true."

"Indeed, it is." He drew his finger across her lips. "My lady, I know the magic of your mouth."

Anne gasped at the intimate touch. But how could she back away? She belonged to him now. He was her husband. Worse, she found she could not keep her eyes from his.

"I know your hands. I know your mouth." He traced a line across her forehead. "And I know your mind. You view life as you do your lace patterns—as a great weblike maze to be worked through, one which you alone understand. You hold the threads, do you not? It is you who designs the patterns."

"No!"

"Yes, and the more you learn about the world, the more complex your design grows. You have read a few books, now you want to read more. Your father taught you to speak your mind, now you speak to dukes and duchesses. You traveled from Nottingham to Tiverton. Now I think you would very much like to see London . . . and Paris . . . even America."

"I would not!" Anne cried, and even then she was unsure she had spoken the truth.

"You would, and you will. I have ordered your trunks packed, and tomorrow we shall set off on our grand pleasure tour. Miss Watson may accompany you along with your lady's maids, and I shall take Foley and the odd footman.

Walker will go with us, too, and we shall all have a capital time."

"Stop this!" Anne pushed at his chest with both hands until he released her. "Mr. Walker said nothing to me of a pleasure tour on the Continent."

"And why should he? I have not yet informed him of it."

"You expect him to go with you? How little you understand the man you call a friend. Mr. Walker will never leave Devon. Only moments ago, on the pathway, he told me this land has become his home. Your arrogance blinds you, Lord Blackthorne."

As she swung away, her shawl slid to the ground between them. Abandoning it, she took two steps toward the gate before whirling to face him.

"You speak as if indeed I am a spider, spinning webs and manipulating the threads of my own existence. It is you who are the predator, Ruel Chouteau, Marquess of Blackthorne! You chase people into corners. You mock and ridicule the innocent. You force even your friends down paths of your own choosing. What will happen after you have devoured us all? You will be alone, will you not? As alone as you truly are right now in your empty, black soul."

He stared at her, letting his gaze wander down to the hip on which she had set a clenched fist. Then he raised his focus to her eyes. "My empty, black soul does not interest me in the least," he said. "My wife, on the other hand, intrigues me endlessly."

Anne lifted her chin. "My husband does not interest me in the least. Though I shall make it my duty to pray for his empty, black soul."

"Not at bedtime, I hope. I should dislike anything to interrupt us then."

Her cheeks hot, Anne narrowed her eyes at him. "I have no intention of performing conjugal duties for you, sir. Though I lay drugged and injured on our wedding day, I clearly heard you assure your father that in time you mean to terminate the arrangement between us. If you think for one moment that I shall accommodate your physical desires or bear your children, you are sadly mistaken."

"Am I?" He advanced toward her, leaving her glove and shawl on the grass behind him.

"Yes, you are." She took a step forward. "I intend to speak to the vicar and ask his blessing on an annulment of this preposterous situation."

"And then what will you do?"

"I shall go back to Nottingham."

"With what money?"

"You will give me back my lace!"

He stopped less than a foot from her. "I am afraid I left it in London."

"You are the very devil!" She clenched her fist to strike his chest, but he caught her arm.

"Come with me to London and Paris, Anne. Charm the ladies and disarm the men. Make them believe we adore one another, that our tour is nothing less than a grand gallivant to the Continent in celebration of our wedding."

"Make them believe?" She fought the tears that had sprung to her eyes. "This is what you want of me?"

"Not only that. In France, I mean to use Walker's assistance and skill with metalwork in setting up an enterprise."

"Smuggled lace machines."

"Do not make them sound so evil. They are nothing but glorified stocking knitters. All the machines can do is create net. Innocent enough, and all but valueless."

"Unless they are worked over with patterns . . . by hand." A chill washed down Anne's spine. "You cannot do this without me."

He smiled. "We have struck a bargain, have we not?"

"If we did, it is because you need me. You need my skill, my expertise. Without my help, you are doomed to failure. And I can demand of you whatever I choose."

"I shall make a gambler of you yet." He touched her cheek. "What is it you would ask of me, my dear wife?"

Knowledge of her own power sent a tingle of triumph through Anne's veins. Mr. Walker had been right—God could do anything. Perhaps the marriage had not been such a dreadful mistake. Perhaps the Lord would make good come of her willful, thoughtless actions.

"My father," she said quickly. "I wish to engage an attorney to defend his case to the court."

"Already done. While in London last week, I made arrangements with the Chouteau family's personal barrister. He will investigate the matter at once and advise me as to the best course to take."

Anne tried to breathe. He had done it already. Already. He had known what she wanted. He had understood her hopes. She looked into those gray eyes, suddenly afraid he did know her as well as he had claimed.

"Anything else you would request of me, dear lady?" The corner of his mouth tilted up in that now-familiar expression of amused confidence. "Surely hundreds of things come to mind. Jewels? A grand house in London with liveried servants? A country manor? A chaise-and-four?"

Anne shook her head. "I do not care about such things, and you certainly know it."

"Yes, I do." He ran his hand down her arm and took her bare fingers. "Remember, I know you, Lady Anne Blackthorne. You want books to read. You want a garden lush with wild roses, hawthorns, foxgloves, feverfews, and buttercups. You would like a large, sunlit gallery furnished with a mahogany table upon which you can design lace to your heart's content. You want reams of parchment on which to prick elaborate patterns. You want threads in silk, linen, and cotton. You want stuffed lace pillows and steel pins by the thousands. You want twenty skilled young women to whom you can teach your secrets. Am I overlooking anything?"

She wished his fingers were not so large and firm and pressing so hard against her own. She wished he were not looking into her eyes as if he could see straight to her soul. Most of all, she wished her heart would stop beating so fast.

"You paint a bewitching picture," she said, "and one that tempts me. But you are wrong to believe I would ask such things of you. If I agreed to receive them, I should only be chained more tightly to your benevolence. I shall not allow that. You are taking care of my family, almost a fair trade for my assistance in your smuggling venture."

"Almost? What else would you have of me?"

"Distance." She took her hand from his. "Do not come near me again, Lord Blackthorne, or I shall tell the regent himself of your plan. I shall sleep alone and, other than maintaining the pretense of marriage with you in public, I shall not be forced to endure your presence."

"Endure me? Am I so odious?"

She swallowed the urge to confess the unsettling, tantalizing emotions he evoked in her. "Do you not know how I feel about you?" she asked, taking on the mocking tone he so often used with her. "But I thought you knew everything about me, Lord Blackthorne."

"I believed so."

"You said yourself you know my hands, my words, my mind. Before I spoke of it, you knew my plan to save my father. You even guessed at my dreams of a lace school. Surely you know how I feel about you."

"Anne—"

"You will not touch me. Swear it."

He reached out to her.

She stepped away. "Promise me."

"This is a wretched business!" He raked a hand through his hair. "Blast it all, if that is your wish then I shall not touch you."

She rewarded him with a smile. "And I shall help you transform your ugly machine-made net into lace so sumptuous that every French aristocrat will shower you with ducats. But lest you become too confident in our partnership, Lord Blackthorne, do not forget there is one part of me you do not know . . . and never will know."

His gray eyes softened as he watched her drift away from him. "What part of you is that, my lady?"

"My heart."

After giving her husband a little curtsy, she turned and walked through the gate toward the house.

৩ Eight ৩

"Quite impertinent of you, Walker." Ruel crossed his arms over his chest and leaned against the sill of the huge, multi-paned window in the library. "Now is not the time to play the loyal Devonshire blacksmith."

"I do not play at my work." The tall Indian eyed the younger man. "I am a blacksmith. Devon is my home. I shall not leave."

"For years, all you have spoken of is America. You have told me a hundred tales of that land. You are why I traveled there. I had to see the place for myself, and now I have. Missouri is as beautiful as you said, as lush, as green, as populated with deer and bison and wild turkey. Your people are there, Walker."

"*Your* people are there. They have taken the land."

"Not all of it. The Osage still roam the forests and streams of Missouri as they always have. How can you tell me you do not wish to go back to them?"

"I have no people. I no longer remember the Osage tongue. I do not look or behave as they do. I told you, Blackthorne, with my English manners and my blacksmith's skills, I am worth nothing to the Osage."

"Then come with me as far as France."

"Never."

"Are you afraid?"

"Of course I am. In order to ensure Osage obedience in the Louisiana Territory, I was sent to France as a hostage. Thanks to God, I escaped. If I were seen there again, I could be thrown into prison."

"That happened years ago. The Louisiana Territory is greatly altered. Osage land is now part of the Missouri Territory—independent of France, Spain, England, and everyone else who has tried to control it. I expect the Missouri Territory will become one of the United States before long. France certainly has no time to track down an escaped hostage. Napoleon has returned from Elba, and that country is in arms. The truth is, Walker, no one even remembers your journey to France."

"How can you be sure? You know I was not the only one."

Ruel did know. Of course his friend had kept the details from him when he was a child, but in the years since then he had learned the full, appalling story. In 1725 a group of Indians—Osage, Missouria, Illini—had been taken to France to meet the boy king, Louis XV. Like circus clowns, they were driven to the Bois de Boulogne and told to run down a deer. They were dressed in cock hats and coats trimmed in gold. They were ordered to dance at the Italian Theatre and at masked balls. They knew the bedchambers of the French aristocracy. Mighty warriors had been sent to France as play-things for the nobility. One of the Indian hostages was a young Missouria girl. The French named her LaBelle Sauvage and lavished her with diamonds and jewels. The Duchess d'Orleans made herself the girl's godmother, had her baptized in Notre Dame de Paris, and arranged her marriage to a French sergeant. All for the amusement of the aristocracy.

Walker's voice dropped. "You toy with the young lacemaker, Blackthorne. She is an honest woman, and she would make a good wife for some man. She deserves a home, a hearth, children . . . a loving husband. Yet you play with her life, with her heart."

"No more than she plays with mine."

"Truly?"

Ruel frowned, uncomfortable at how much he had revealed. "Listen, Walker, if you think I mean to make use of you for my own pleasure, you are dead wrong. Yes, your skill with metal can help me assemble my lace machine in France. I shall not deny that, and I have stated my intent to pay you handsomely for your services. But I have no purpose in taking you to America other than to restore you to your people."

The Indian gave a snort. "My people. When the Indian delegation was taken away, the Little People said they would mourn for fifteen moons. After that period, if the hostages did not return, they would be counted dead. Fifteen moons. I have been gone twenty-eight years."

Ruel turned away in exasperation. How could Walker so easily dismiss his childhood home? Ruel knew he never could. He gazed out through the library window. The parks, gardens, and woods that stretched for miles around Slocombe

House always had been home to him. He was tied to Slocombe House with bonds that would never let him go. Oh, certainly, his family's imposing edifice on Cranleigh Crescent in London held a great fascination and delight, but this was where he belonged. He could not understand Walker's indifference toward his place of origin, nor his conviction that no one would be waiting for him there. Though Ruel could not imagine leaving England for decades at a time, he knew he would always be welcome no matter when he returned.

He had not expected Walker to be so difficult. Ruel needed the man at his side for a more important purpose than assembling a lace machine, yet he did not know how to persuade the Indian to accompany him. Should he tell the truth? Should he reveal the suspicion that had begun to gnaw on him while he was in America and now seemed to be confirmed—the suspicion that someone meant him bodily harm?

"On August 16, 1787," Walker was saying, his voice trancelike, "Wa-Tcha-Wa-Ha and Arrow-Going-Home were called to Chouteau's Town, St. Louis. The Spanish officials of the territory demanded that some of their chieftains be delivered as hostages to New Orleans. The hostages were to guarantee Osage future good behavior. Of course, the Osage would never turn over their leaders, the Little Old Men, so they sent others—Padouca and Pawnee captives who had learned the Osage language and manners after living so many years with their captors . . . and Osage warriors who could defend themselves. They sent me, Walks-in-the-Night."

Ruel had heard the story of Walker's journey to New Orleans and then to Spain as a hostage of the Spaniards. He knew all about the Treaty of San Ildefonso, signed in 1800, transferring the Louisiana Territory from Spain to France. Many times as a boy, Ruel had listened to Walker tell him how he and the others had been transferred from Madrid to Paris. Walker had become certain he would never return to America, and his desperation had been intense.

Listening to a story he had heard so many times before, Ruel let his focus linger on the scene outside the library window. The pathways, the knot gardens, the parks . . . the arboretum. His heart lurched. A slim figure slipped between the heavy iron gates and into the tree-filled enclosure. Her wisp of a green dress told him it was Anne.

Straightening, he tried to watch her progress through the trees. Just a glimpse. She appeared for a moment in a glade, then vanished again. What was she doing? Why had she returned to the place of their meeting? Did she hope to find him there? Or had she some other assignation . . . a lover?

He had not considered that possibility. Might the woman he had married love another man? A footman or a gardener? Despite her assertions to the contrary, maybe she had attached herself to the gamekeeper. Ruel had been told of the man's pursuit of her. Did she return his affection?

"It was in Paris that I heard again the beloved name of Chouteau," Walker was saying. "Then I knew I had hope. I made arrangements to meet this man, Etienne Chouteau, uncle of Auguste, who is friend to the Little People. Etienne Chouteau is a great man, very wise and very, very old. He had me brought in a carriage from the prison to his grand house on the Champs-Elysées, and there he told me that he had two brothers."

Ruel nodded. Yes, yes, he knew the story. There were three of them—sons of Raoul and Marie Chouteau of France—Etienne, Laurent, and René. Etienne lived in Paris and was a grand patron of the aristocracy. Laurent had traveled to England, where he assumed the family's duchy of Marston, married the Englishwoman Beatrice, and produced five daughters and two sons, the elder of whom was Ruel himself. René had married Marie Therese and journeyed to America to seek his fortune. He became the father of Auguste Chouteau before separating from his wife and fading into anonymity.

The story was as familiar as any nursery rhyme. Ruel was much more interested in the slender woman who had vanished into a copse in the arboretum. Perhaps she was only a commoner, a housemaid, a criminal's daughter—but she was his wife. She certainly owed her husband the pretense of faithfulness. If she were attending a lover's tryst, could she not at least conduct her rendezvous away from the grounds of Slocombe House?

The thought of Anne folded into the arms of another man sent a stab of anger through Ruel's chest. The image of her lips pressed against another man's mouth . . . of someone placing his hands around her waist . . .

"Do not touch me," she had said. *"Promise me."* Of course she could not bear for Ruel to touch her! Of course she denied him the marriage bed. She was in love with someone else. Why had he not seen it?

Because he had been too busy arranging for her father's defense and sending seamstresses and milliners to clothe her in silk and feathers! Too wrapped up in his own plans and too absorbed in investigating the mystery that swirled around in his head, he had missed the truth in front of him.

"It was Etienne Chouteau who helped me escape to his brother Laurent, in England," Walker continued, as if he were speaking to a rapt audience. "Here in Devon, though I knew I would never be welcomed as an equal, I was given a home and a trade and treated as a man. I am grateful to your father for saving me from a life in the prisons of France. That is why I shall never go back to that country. Not even for you."

Ruel scowled at the window. Where had she gone? He had a mind to walk straight down to the arboretum and publicly disgrace her and her ill-bred lover. She was his wife, for heaven's sake. She had promised allegiance. Did he not have the right to expect a degree of faithfulness?

"Did you hear me, Blackthorne?" Walker asked. "I told you I will never go to France."

"Dash it all, Walker, you have to come." Ruel swung around. "Someone is trying to kill me."

The Indian stared at him. "Kill you? Why?"

"Any number of reasons. Wimberley believes himself cheated of his fortune. Barkham blames me for the seduction of his wife. Droughtmoor claims I ruined his sister."

"You loved these women?"

"Of course not. They were mere amusements. Any man in my position can be expected to have engaged in various dalliances."

"But now you are a married man. You will be faithful to your wife, will you not?"

"Well, I . . . I . . ." Ruel glanced out the window. Anne was nowhere to be seen. It had not occurred to him that if he expected faithfulness of her, he would be held to the same exacting standard himself. Could he be loyal to only one woman for the rest of his life? Hard to imagine. Yet the thought of wanting any woman other than Anne . . . that was difficult to imagine also.

But she did not want him. Refused to have him in her private chamber. Would not allow even his hand on hers. *"Do not touch me."*

"If you are settled with a wife and children," Walker said, "why would these enemies pursue you for revenge? Surely what happened was many years ago when you were barely more than a boy. Among the Osage, a peace gift is given to the one wronged. Why not present these three men with a small measure of your wealth, Blackthorne, as we do among my people?"

"Your people!" Ruel took the man's shoulder. "You admit it. The Osage *are* your people, Walker, and they always will be. Come to France and America. Help protect me."

"I cannot."

"You must. On a roadway in Missouri, I was attacked, stabbed, and left for dead. At sea I was beaten senseless and expected to die. Neither time was I robbed. Both incidents were investigated, but no perpetrator was found and no motive revealed. Three weeks ago, someone shot me through the left shoulder, six inches from my heart. When I fell, the marksman vanished. Who was it, Walker?"

"People said it was the gamekeeper, a spurned suitor of Lady Blackthorne."

"William Green was drinking ale at the Boar's Head Tavern in Tiverton at the time of the shooting. A number of reliable witnesses attested to that fact. Who wants me dead so badly he would see me tracked to the ends of the earth by his hired assassins? And if this murderer is so determined and so deceitful that he would send someone to ambush me rather than challenge me to a duel himself, how am I to defend my life? Walker, you have always been loyal. You were the one I came to as a boy when I was frightened, sad, or angry. Indeed, you are the only man I can trust. Help me now. I need you."

The Indian looked away, his expression troubled. "You ask much of me."

"Please, Walker."

His focus on the ground, Walker nodded. "Very well, then. I shall go with you to France."

"It is not for me alone." He glanced out the window. "Anne was almost killed by that ball, Walker. She has no idea I am a marked man, and I shall not have her wounded in this way again."

The Indian lifted his head, surprise written in his brown eyes. "You love her then?"

"Nonsense. Love is for dandies and fluff-brained ladies. I merely want the woman protected . . . for business reasons as much as anything." He put his hand on the Indian's arm and turned him toward the door. "Come now, Walker, you had better shut down the smithy and pack your things. We leave for London in the morning."

As Walker nodded farewell, Ruel stepped to the window again. At that moment the arboretum gate swung open, and Anne slipped out of the shadows onto the path. She wrapped her shawl closely about her shoulders as she hurried toward the house. Ruel wondered if only the evening breeze had chilled her—or if perhaps a man's fiery kisses had made her shiver.

cᴏᴏᴏᴏ

Four carriages emblazoned with the crest of the Duke of Marston drew rows of spectators as they rolled into London. Ragged boys chased after them while little girls in patches waved from the windows of houses. The curious stares made Anne shrink into her seat. The city was enormous, gray with soot, and so very crowded. Though trees had leafed out in small gardens and flowers bloomed in clay pots, dirt lay heaped in corners, soggy newspapers littered the sidewalks, and the smell . . . oh, the smell. She lifted her handkerchief to her nose and drank in the scent of the lavender blossoms in which the linen fabric had been stored.

"Ah, London," Ruel said. "Cesspool of England. Home to harlots, actresses, fishwives, and other countless squashed cabbage leaves."

Anne eyed him. For some reason Ruel was angry, and the closer they drew to town, the darker his mood grew. Now he looked a veritable volcano, smoldering inside his black traveling coat and high, starched collar. His eyes flashed a steely silver gray as he observed the city through the carriage window.

"Armpit of the Thames," he said under his breath. He had spent the journey discussing one thing and another with his brother. They had talked politics, world affairs, business. Though Anne and Miss Prudence Watson were the only others in the coach, they might have been tufts of horsehair protruding from the seat for all the attention the men paid them. At the coaching inns where the travelers stayed each evening, Ruel played cards, wagering and usually winning large sums of money before he retired to a room alone.

She should have been grateful. Clearly her husband was honoring his promise to keep his distance. All the same, the situation grated.

Anne deplored gaming. She disliked bumpy roads. And she was growing to despise her aloof spouse more than ever. She supposed his ill temper had to do with her insistence that he make a vow of restraint. Too bad. The longer she had thought about their conversation in the arboretum, the more thankful she was for having the presence of mind to extract his promise. The fact was, she did not trust herself.

Ever since that afternoon, she had found herself thinking about the marquess, remembering the way he had held her so tightly beneath the trees, recalling the warmth in his eyes and the scent of his breath. She had wanted him to kiss her then. No matter how misguided that desire, she was not capable of preventing it. Worse, she still wanted his kiss, and each night as she fell on her knees in prayer, she thanked God she would never know it.

What would become of her if she allowed the man his spousal rights? She would become pregnant, of course. She would bear a child, outlive her usefulness to Ruel in the lace venture, and be cast into the streets like the poor women he termed "squashed cabbage leaves."

"The house on Cranleigh Crescent should be opened by now, but just barely." His low voice against her ear startled her. Lifting her head, she realized that Sir Alexander and Prudence were deep in conversation—hidden artfully behind her open fan. Having worried about a growing attachment between the two, Anne would have liked to eavesdrop. But Ruel had chosen the moment to confer privately with her.

"The servants should have aired out the rooms and put things right," he remarked. His shoulder pressed against hers, and his warm breath stirred the hair over her ear.

"How nice," she managed.

"For appearances' sake, you will take the suite next to mine."

Anne dipped her head in acknowledgement. If she intended for the marquess to keep his part of their agreement, she must keep hers and pretend to be his loving wife. If they slept in different wings, every footman and maid in the house would know. Gossip in the great houses ran rampant, as Anne well knew, and what a maid from one family whispered to a maid from another was soon common knowledge in Society.

"Miss Watson will be returning to Trenton House, of course," Ruel continued. "I understand her elder sister is expected home at any time from a journey abroad."

"Indeed, as Prudence herself has informed me. Although she has not received a letter from Mr. and Mrs. Locke in several weeks, she learned of her sister's whereabouts in *The Tattler*. My friend and I are among Miss Pickworth's most avid readers, you know. Nothing in Society—whether rumored or factual—escapes our intelligence."

Anne watched Ruel's left eyebrow lift as he regarded her. In truth, she had little use for Prudence's devoted appetite for every tidbit of information dealt out by the mysterious Miss Pickworth. As a minister's daughter brought up in Nottingham, Anne was unfamiliar with the names of London's *ton* and cared not a whit for their intrigues and assignations.

But she had learned to appreciate Miss Pickworth's column in *The Tattler* for another reason. Once the gossip was dispensed, the anonymous writer answered questions put forth by her readers. So impassioned were the queries—and so sensible Miss Pickworth's answers—that Anne had come to eagerly anticipate the arrival of the newspaper each afternoon. Indeed, she had even considered setting her own dreadful situation before Miss Pickworth in hope of some response that might lead to a happy resolution.

"I shall be most disheartened to lose my friend's companionship," Anne said. "Perhaps if your brother had not so hastily engaged himself to a Frenchwoman, Miss Watson might have continued in my presence a great deal longer."

Ruel studied the two whisperers for a moment and then returned his attention to Anne. "As it is a short walk across the green, I imagine you will have ample opportunity to meet with Miss Watson while we are in London. We shall take callers, give dinner parties, and attend balls."

"How delightful."

His expression darkened. "Lady Blackthorne, you will behave as Mrs. Davies instructed you, and your manners will be impeccable. No matter what is said of you, you will hold your head high. You will remember that you are the daughter of a minister, the heiress to a duchy, and the wife of a marquess."

"A man with whom I am deeply in love," she added. "And how long are we to continue our charade before Society, Lord Blackthorne?"

"Until the time is right."

"This pretense is all about France, is it not? You are waiting for something to happen in Paris."

"Insightful, as always."

Anne drew away and fingered the fringed curtain on her window. Then she leaned into him again to whisper her concern. "Do you expect that little emperor to do something to make your lace venture more profitable? Surely he will not permit the aristocracy their fripperies. The common people fought far too hard against such luxury."

"The little emperor's name is Napoleon Bonaparte. You must learn to call him Boney among your new friends."

"Friends? You once called them predators ready to tear me apart with fangs and claws." Anne could not deny how much she dreaded the coming weeks in London, but she dared not allow the marquess to sense any trepidation in her, lest he use it to gain the upper hand. "So, this Boney . . . how can he possibly help you?"

"I am counting on him to blunder into a war with England and Prussia."

"Good heavens," she said aloud. Catching a glance from Sir Alexander, she lowered her voice again. "I cannot cherish the prospect of touring France in the midst of such hostilities."

"There are a great many things about this venture I cannot cherish." He studied her so intently that Anne felt her cheeks grow warm. "I suppose you bade your farewells to everyone at Slocombe House."

"I was sorry to leave Mrs. Davies and Mr. Errand. Even Mrs. Smythe, for all her blustering, was good to me. The kitchen staff, too, became dear friends, many of them."

"And the gamekeeper?"

"William Green? He shot the both of us, you will recall. Why should I be sorry to leave such a man as that?"

"You expect me to believe you were not in love with him?"

"In love with the gamekeeper?" she said. "Upon my honor, sir, that is absurd."

Without speaking, Ruel turned to the window. "Marston House at last. I see Miss Watson's sister is just arriving at Trenton House as well. How fortunate for us all."

"Sarah!" Prudence squealed at the sight of her sister's carriage. "Oh, Sarah is home at last! Look, Anne! She is come!"

Anne grabbed the edge of the leather seat as the carriage slowed. Though Prudence was pulling on her arm and bouncing up and down on the seat, all she could think of was William Green. In love with a man like that? How could Ruel possibly think such a thing? Where had he gotten so ridiculous a notion? But he had said it with such confidence . . . tossed it between them like a gauntlet. She had no weapons with which to duel such a man as the marquess. How could she prove him wrong? For that matter, why did he even care?

Ruel stepped out of the carriage and tugged the tails of his coat into place. Then he held out one gloved hand to Anne. At the sight of his cold eyes and rigid mouth, her dismay changed to anger. She set her hand in his and leaned through the door.

"I rejected the gamekeeper two times," she hissed in his ear as she descended. "That is why he shot me."

"I saw you go into the arboretum—"

"Sarah!" The young woman fairly flew out of the carriage, knocking Anne and Ruel aside in a rush to see her sister.

"Prudence!" The mahogany-haired beauty running across the crescent-shaped sward of green park between Marston

House and Trenton House stole their attention. Picking up her skirts, she hurtled headlong at her sister.

"Oh, my dearest Sarah!" Prudence cried, bursting into tears and sobbing on the other's shoulder as they met in a fond embrace. "You cannot imagine how happy I am to see you! After you and Mr. Locke left me all alone at Trenton House, I became utterly despondent, and thank goodness for the Duke of Marston who invited me to Slocombe in the country to recover my health. Anne Webster was given to me as lady's maid, but she is no longer Anne at all, for she has married the marquess! Oh, Sarah!"

"Prudence, my poor sister." Mrs. Locke made no attempt to muffle emotion. "Oh, Pru, how you must have suffered."

"I feared for your life every day. Dear Sarah, I am so glad you came back!"

"How could I not? Oh, but you are thin! Let me look at you." She held her sister at arm's length, her brown eyes misty and her lips trembling. "Goodness me, you are dreadfully wan." She pressed her fingers to Prudence's cheeks. "What has happened to my little sister? My darling Pru with her golden locks and happy smile . . . my precious, silly girl!"

Prudence sniffled. "Sarah, now that you are home, I shall be myself again."

"Of course you shall! And who is this?" She caught Anne's hands. "My dear friend, are you now a marchioness? Can such a thing be true? But you are a lovely girl and of such a pleasant disposition. Of course, the marquess adores you. I can see it perfectly. What a sweet companionship! Oh, my dear Lady Blackthorne, I am so happy for you!"

Anne could hardly resist the flood of warmth she felt as she was swept into Sarah's embrace. Enveloped in the scent of roses, she slipped her arms around the woman and held her tightly. "Please call me Anne, as you did before. I am not so very different from the lady's maid who once waited upon you."

"Then you must call me Sarah, and we shall consider ourselves equals and friends." She beckoned the handsome gentleman who now strode across the green. "Charles, I have wonderful news. My dear lady's maid has become a bride! She has wed Lord Blackthorne."

"Upon my word, I am pleased to hear this happy news." Mr. Locke removed his hat and gave Anne an elegant bow. "I wish you great joy, my lady. And you, my lord. My heartiest congratulations."

Anne stood to one side as the travelers were caught up in the swirl of coachmen unloading trunks and footmen offering trays of drinks. When the Lockes realized that in Prudence's absence Trenton House had been shut up for several months and would be unready to receive them, Ruel offered rooms in his father's house. Accepting with gratitude, Prudence and Sarah chattered excitedly about their adventures and vowed they must invite their middle sister, Mary, to join them as soon as might be. Amid the hubbub Anne spotted Mr. Walker climbing down from a carriage.

In spite of the marquess's more luxurious vehicle, she realized she gladly would have ridden in the servants' coach. Surely Mr. Walker would never stoop to accuse her on unfounded rumors. The blacksmith, hat pulled low on his head, was starting up the steps into the house when the marquess noticed him.

"Walker! Do come and meet the Lockes." He caught

Anne's arm and urged her into the gathering. "Perhaps you would introduce your friends, my dear wife."

Anne swallowed, uncomfortable at playing such a farce before those she had grown to respect and admire. The Indian kept his eyes to the ground as she made the introductions.

"You live in Tiverton, then, Mr. Walker?" Sarah Locke asked.

"I am a blacksmith."

"How very nice." She glanced at Anne, clearly uncertain as to how a blacksmith and a marquess had formed so close a friendship. "And you hail from America. Lord Blackthorne, I believe you have recently returned from that country. We had heard you might have lost your life in such a savage place."

"St. Louis is hardly uncultured, madam," Ruel informed her. "Indeed, the city is quite as civilized as London. More so, in many ways."

"But of course. How thoughtless of me. And St. Louis is home to your Chouteau relations." She waved her hands in agitation. "How could I have forgotten? Yet, I am so beside myself to see my sister again, and now Anne is wed into the aristocracy—"

"Sarah, you are all aflutter," her husband said gently. "I fear in a moment you'll begin to weep great rivers of tears all over your sister and the marchioness. My lord, may I suggest that we all go inside and retire to the drawing room?"

"Tea. Superb idea," Ruel said. "You will join us, will you not, Walker?"

"Thank you, but I am not in the custom of drinking tea. Excuse me." He gave the company a curt nod and continued up the stairs and into the house.

Still chattering like squirrels, Sarah and her younger sister followed. After giving instructions to his footmen regarding their trunks, Mr. Locke turned to Sir Alexander. The two men had been at school together, Anne knew, and were not only friends but business partners in a tea enterprise. Engrossed in conversation, they climbed the steps to the front door of Marston House.

Anne closed her eyes and lifted up a fervent prayer for forgiveness, fortitude, clarity, and peace. She had relied more on Prudence Watson than she liked to think, and now that Sarah had returned, Anne would not see her friend so often. She would be alone—with Lord Blackthorne—and the thought of it frightened her to the very depths of her heart.

"The arboretum." The word was spoken so close to Anne's ear that she jumped. "I saw you there."

She looked up into a pair of eyes the color of slate. "Of course you did," she whispered back. "You dragged me into the arboretum yourself."

"You returned there after I had gone up to the house." He took her arm and propelled her toward the stairs. "Whom did you meet?"

She tried to think, but his hand gripped her arm so tightly and his shoulder was pressed so hard against hers that it was all she could do to climb the steps without stumbling. "If you were so intent in spying on me, you should know what I did."

"I was not spying. I was talking to Walker in the library when I witnessed your secret assignation." He pulled her through the marble-floored hall and turned her into a small parlor hung with gold and velvet. Kicking the door shut with his foot, he pressed her up against a wall. "If you have a lover, I want to know his name. Tell me."

"You say but little to me for three days in the carriage, and now in the midst of your family and friends you assail me!" She squared her shoulders. "What does it matter to you whom I love?"

His jaw tightened. "You are my wife."

"Do not be absurd, sir. I am a housemaid with a gift for making lace. I am a commoner you need for a business enterprise. I am not your wife!"

His hands on her shoulders tightened. "As long as you wear my name and my title, you will not take lovers."

"Will *you*? Or do we play our game of charades by different rules?"

"Dash it all, woman! Who was in the garden with you?"

"My glove," she snapped. "You had tossed it away, you odious man. I went back to fetch it. And my shawl. Unlike you, I regard my material possessions with respect, and I should never abandon my glove in the arboretum or leave my shawl in the grass . . . or mislay a length of valuable hand-made Honiton lace in London!"

As she spoke, his face lifted, and his mouth tilted into a grin. "Your glove?"

She waved her fingers in front of his face. "My glove. You might have remembered it yourself had you not been so blind with jealousy over some imagined lover."

"Jealous, am I?"

"Are you not?" She narrowed her eyes. "Blind with it. In fact, you are the blindest man I have ever had the misfortune to know. Blind to the beauty of the world around you. Blind to the love of your father. Blind to the selfish greediness of your dreams. Blind to the people who surround you."

He lifted her chin with the crook of his forefinger. "I seem to see you clearly, my hotheaded beauty."

She turned away. "Proof of your blindness. I am no beauty. Your brother declared my hair the brown of a mouse's rump."

"My brother is a fool."

"Anne?" The female voice outside the parlor door echoed through the foyer. "Anne, where are you?"

"It is Mrs. Locke," he whispered, pulling Anne into his arms. "Hold me, quickly," he mouthed against her cheek.

Obedient without forethought, she slid her hands around his back as the door burst open.

"Anne?" Sarah gasped. "Oh, dear!"

Ruel lifted his head. "Good afternoon, Mrs. Locke."

Sarah glanced at Anne and clapped a hand over her mouth. "I do apologize, sir. My sister and I were looking for your wife. Had we but considered that you might . . . Do forgive me, please. I am so sorry."

Mortified, Anne prayed that Sarah could see through the ruse. But the young woman was utterly taken in by what she had witnessed—which was exactly what Ruel had planned, of course. Anne dared not speak as the wicked man let his warm fingers slide down her arm.

"Do not trouble yourself so, Mrs. Locke," he said. "My wife and I have been imprisoned in that frightful carriage for three days. You were a bride not so long ago, I understand."

"Yes, my lord, and certainly Anne is . . . is a lovely and . . . and charming . . ." Her words faltered as a blush crept up her face.

"Thank you, Sarah, you are always too kind." Anne stepped away from Ruel. "I should like to freshen up for tea. Excuse me, please."

"Dearest." His voice stopped her. "I very much hope you will leave your hair loose at tea as you promised. I feel quite determined to enlighten my brother's opinion of its color."

Anne suppressed a glare. How dare he ask her to wear her hair loose like some wanton?

"I shall leave my bonnet in my room, dear husband," she said. "At your pleasure."

He smiled. "Where you are concerned, my pleasure knows no bounds."

She dipped her head at Mrs. Locke and slipped out into the hall. As she fled up the grand staircase, she could hear him chuckling behind her.

∽⊙ *Nine* ⊙∽

To Anne's surprise and dismay, Sir Alexander invited a horde of Society's most esteemed members to Marston House for dinner that evening. Nothing had prepared Anne for the assault that began almost the moment the Marquess of Blackthorne introduced her as his bride. What a "fortuitous marriage," the jeweled matrons murmured. As a woman with such an "unfortunate upbringing," Anne must consider herself very lucky indeed to have caught the eye of such a "handsome and noble" gentleman.

Sarah and Prudence did their best to protect their friend, but their defense had little effect. By marrying Charles Locke, Sarah had lost her title as baroness. Though her fortune allowed her to remain in Society, it afforded her no special rank. Poor Prudence was nothing more than a pretty young lady of no lineage and little means.

Anne tried to hold up her chin, but Mrs. Davies's instruction in manners proved useless beneath the onslaught of snide comments and digging retorts flung at the bride from "friends of the family" who gathered around the long mahogany table in the formal dining room. Mr. Errand's lengthy lists of ancestors, descriptions of coats of arms, and maps of family properties did little to deflect the volleys launched at the newest member of the Chouteau dynasty.

By the time the last pies and puddings had been eaten, Anne's stomach had twisted into a Gordian knot she was certain nothing could untie. Swathed in a hideous gown that Sarah and Prudence had pulled out from some clothier's contribution to her trousseau—a wedding cake of pink silk, pink ribbons, and rows of pink lace at the hem—she felt sure her cheeks matched her dress to perfection. Never in her life, not even when her father had been cast into prison, had she felt so humiliated. The Reverend Webster's stand in support of the Luddites of his parish had held a righteous tone, and his imprisonment made him a hero for their cause. Anne felt like nothing more glorious than a spitted pig, roasted over a fire, slowly carved apart piece by piece.

Fortunately the marquess had been seated at the opposite end of the long table, which released her from having to act as if she adored him through dinner. Unfortunately his distant position prevented his championing his new wife. Sir Alexander had decided to continue his attentions to Prudence, complicating everything and adding to Anne's turmoil. Mr. Walker might have helped her, but he had declined dinner, saying he was stiff from travel and wanted to walk in the gardens.

When the ladies at last retired to the drawing room, leaving the gentlemen to their masculine pursuits, Anne seized the opportunity to escape. She hurried up to her suite of rooms, dug her Bible out of her trunk, and read three chapters in First Corinthians. Sensible words on the qualities of Christian love—patience, kindness, forbearance—strengthened her, and she began to feel that she might return safely to the lion's den below. Perhaps indeed she would be able to resist the temptation to slap the next young lady who made mention of her "poor, poor relations" who must be ecstatic at her "astounding and unexpected connubial state" to the Marquess of Blackthorne.

It was her own fault, Anne realized as she sat miserably on the bed. Had she been as interested in God's will as her own, she might have bothered to ask His advice and assistance earlier. Now she was paying for her sin by suffering ridicule and persecution. Worse, she could see no happy ending to the muddle she had made of her life. Even if her father were freed and her family were cared for financially for the rest of their lives, she could not escape this dreadful marriage. And if the marquess were the blackguard he seemed, then why, oh why, had she enjoyed his embrace this afternoon? Why did she find her attention drawn to him time and again? How could she rid herself of the constant desire to talk with the man, to feel his hand on hers, to know the sweet brush of his kiss?

Somewhat calmed after her time in Scripture reading, Anne returned to the drawing room and realized—to her satisfaction—that tables of cards already had been set up and filled. The pianoforte was occupied, and ladies of varying ages had gathered around the instrument to sing while their husbands discussed the latest doings of that "flagitious tyrant," Napoleon. Spotting a shelf of books, Anne made for it like a magnet to iron. She grabbed the first volume of the history of Russia, found a chair in the corner, sat down, and began to read.

"How are the czars getting on these days?"

She knew the voice without looking up. "Famously, Lord Blackthorne."

"And you?" He knelt beside her and spoke barely above a whisper. "Still in one piece, or have the vultures torn you asunder?"

She set her finger on the page to hold her place and lifted her head. "Sir, I—"

The look on his face stopped her. His eyes had softened to a quiet dove gray, and they searched hers as if reading them were the most important thing in the world. He took her hand and brought it to his lips. As his head bent, she gazed down at the rumple of silky black curls and felt a jolt run through her chest.

"My love, that shade of pink quite lights up your face." His expression was tender, but his mouth lifted slightly at the corners. "You are as enchanting as a new rose this evening."

And then, of course, she remembered. The bargain. She glanced away from him to find every eye in the room turned their way. Fixing her attention on him again, she forced her lips into a smile. "Thank you, dearest. You flatter me most becomingly."

"Did you enjoy your first dinner in your new home, my sweet?" he murmured, just loud enough for everyone present to hear.

"The leg of lamb was exquisite and the filet of veal sumptuous. My compliments to the cook. Oh, Ruel . . ." On an impulse, she reached out and stroked the side of his face with the back of her hand. At the touch of his smooth, taut skin, her heart began to hammer. Willing it to silence, she painted a coy expression on her face. "I missed you dreadfully, my dear. You seemed miles and miles away at the other end of the table."

"Indeed I was." He took her hand and kissed her palm and then her wrist. Taking a deep breath, he shut his eyes. "Lavender. This was the scent you wore when we met."

"Ah, yes, we stood together in that enchanting room filled with mingled scents and succulent treats."

He chuckled at her reference to the sooty kitchen at Slocombe. "You are my succulent treat, beautiful Anne."

"Oh, Ruel, my dearest love . . ." She leaned against him and whispered into his ear. "You are a blackguard."

Throwing back his head, he laughed aloud. "Little minx!"

He slipped an arm around her waist and stood, bringing Anne to her feet. Holding her closely against him, he extended a hand toward the open French doors that led onto a long walk. "A promenade, my love? The air is quite warm, and the moonlight beckons."

She tipped her head. "Indeed it does."

Eyes locked in an eternal gaze, they wandered out onto the flagstone path. A ripple of sighs from the company in the drawing room was followed by the urgent return to gossip and recountings of what had just been witnessed.

ↄ๛ⴲ๛

At the flush of color that had spread up Anne's neck, Ruel found he could hardly resist the charming young woman. Though she had played the part of a blushing bride with the

skill of a London actress, he sensed there might be some
genuine pleasure in her response to his flirtation. Could it
be that she had never heard such words from a man?

He entertained the hope that his reluctant wife might let
down her guard against him, but the moment they stepped into
the shadows of an overhanging swag of ivy, she pulled away.

"I am going to my rooms," she said.

"Not so fast." The marquess caught her and drew her
under his arm again.

"That is quite enough now, sir!"

"Enough for whom?" His grin broadened. "I find I am
enjoying our little drama immensely, my darling wife. Come
stand with me here in this patch of moonlight, and let us give
our guests a bit of a show."

"Whatever can you mean?"

He turned her into his arms and leaned her into the pale,
buttery glow of the moon. The vision that greeted him in
that instant left him momentarily speechless. In his effort to
ignore this woman since their wedding, Ruel had reminded
himself she was a commoner, hardly educated, quite plain,
actually, and of little consequence. In short, she was nothing.

Indeed, he had almost made himself forget the upward tilt
of her eyes and the soft angle of her nose. But now she lifted
her chin and turned her liquid chocolate eyes on him, and he
suddenly remembered why he had been so determined to save
her life and make her his own. Her soft shawl slipped off one
shoulder to reveal delicate bone and alabaster skin. Her long
neck arched upward. Her pink lips parted as she breathed in
rapid, shallow gasps.

She was enticing and enchanting, and he wanted her more

than he had wanted any woman. Yet even now she was dis-
tancing herself, backing away from him, ready to escape like
a wisp of lace caught in an afternoon breeze.

"I cannot tell you how intoxicating I find the scent of your
skin."

"Sir, release me this minute!"

Her voice was a hiss of confused desperation. He found her
dismay amusing . . . amazing . . . and powerfully stimulating.
"Hold me, Anne," he murmured against her ear. "We are
being observed from the drawing room, and we must not let
down our façade for a moment."

"But this is . . . this is—"

"Soft, very soft." His lips caressed her cheek. "Very
fragrant—"

"You promised not to touch me," she sputtered. "You
made me a vow."

"You promised to prove to everyone that we are madly in
love. What better way than this . . . here, in the midst of
those most intimate with my family?" He lifted her chin.
"Do my attentions disturb you, Anne?"

"Of course. I am not accustomed to . . . to this sort of
thing, and you should not . . ."

"I must say, I find your consternation most intriguing."
He pulled her closer, relishing the curve of her waist against
his hand. "You see, were this truly no more than a bargain
between us, and had you nothing but contempt for me, you
would merely perform your role in a perfunctory manner.
Instead, you blush and sigh and avert your eyes in a beguiling
way. And every time I hold you in my arms, you seem to have
the most dreadful time breathing."

"I do not!" she puffed.

"In fact, my dear Anne, I have come to the conclusion that you have never been properly wooed."

"Rubbish. William Green the gamekeeper wooed me."

"That boor?"

"As did a young man in Nottingham." She squared her shoulders. "A man I plan to marry someday."

"A weaver, no doubt."

"A farmer."

"Oh, a farmer. How charming. Tell me, Anne, did your young farmer kiss this particular place on your shoulder?" He drew a line with his fingertip. "Or perhaps here?"

She grabbed his hand. "Beast!"

"Beauty." He took her hand, forced it behind her back, and pulled her close. "Contrary to my original assumption, I do not believe you have ever been loved, Anne Webster Chouteau, Lady Blackthorne, future Duchess of Marston. I doubt you have even been kissed."

Before she could push at him again, he covered her lips with his mouth. Against him she stiffened and took in a deep breath. He softened the kiss, suddenly determined to explore the fascinating shape of those lips that could speak with such vehemence and smile with such radiance.

"Anne," he whispered. "Kiss me."

"Oh, dear." A sigh of pleasure escaped, and then she caught herself. "Lord Blackthorne, I—"

"Ruel."

"I think we have performed quite well enough to convince anyone."

"I am convinced." He kissed her again. "Are you convinced, Anne?"

"That you should not take such liberties again. Yes, I am quite sure of it. And will you please . . ."

He shook his head. "No, I shall not."

The longer he kissed this woman, the more certain he became that he had to have her as his wife in every sense of that word. Never in his life had he felt such desire. She longed for him, too, whether she would admit it or not.

"Anne, come with me." He could hardly force the words out. "Upstairs. We shall hardly be missed."

"No—"

"Yes!" He caught her shoulders. Staring down at her, he could see the longing in her eyes. "There is so much more to learn of each other."

"Ruel, the bargain—"

"Hang the bargain. I want you."

"Blackthorne? Are you out here?" It was his brother. Sir Alexander stood in the doorway, squinting into the darkness. "The guests are going, Blackthorne."

"Wish them off yourself, Alex."

The younger man walked toward them, his face pulled into a frown. "What are you doing? Kissing, is it?"

"She is my wife. I shall do what I like with her."

"Will you sire children with her, then? Jeopardize the duchy?"

Ruel clenched his teeth. "Go back inside the house, Alex. You disturb our reverie."

"Upon my honor, I cannot allow you to do this!"

Anne backed up against a pillar as the marquess grabbed his brother's arm. "This is not your affair, Alex."

"But it is. Do you think I shall stand by while the duchy passes to a child born of you and this . . . this wench?"

"Get out!"

"Swear you will not touch her!" Alex's face went red as he took a step toward Anne. "She is nothing but a housemaid. A conniving little schemer."

"Stand back from her, brother, I warn you."

"Look at this mouse." Alex jerked Anne into the moonlight. "She is common. She is nothing. Dally with every woman from Soho to Belgravia, Ruel, but not her." He shook Anne for emphasis. "Not her."

"Take your hands off my wife." He pushed his brother's chest. "You cannot know what you say, Alex. Let her go."

"You claim to care so much for the duchy that you would wed a lace-making maid in order to restore our fortunes. Prove your loyalty then! Swear to find yourself a noble wife. Promise you will not consummate your union with this common bedbug."

"Your brother has already taken that vow," Anne said, tugging her arm from Sir Alexander's grip. She lowered her voice. "It was my understanding that you have known from the beginning about his plan for the lace industry, sir. I believed you understood the purpose for this journey to London and then to France. Surely you have grasped that your brother's advances toward me are merely an imposture."

"Well, I . . ."

She looked at Ruel. "You made me a vow of celibacy, did you not?"

His eyes narrowed as he realized what she was doing. "I did."

Turning to Sir Alexander, Anne gave him a small smile. "There you have it, quite publicly presented. Your brother will not, as you say, consummate our union."

"You do not want him and the security his child would bring to your family?"

"What I want, Sir Alexander," she said softly, "is of little consequence. It has never mattered to you or your brother what I think or how I feel, but only how I can be of use. If you learn nothing else about me in the short time I shall be your sister, know this one thing, sir: I am not an object to be used."

"How dare you make such a speech to me!"

"Only a warning." She took a deep breath. "The next time you encounter me, you will do so with deference. I am the future duchess. I am also the key to your brother's plans. Moreover, I am beginning to understand certain unhappy qualities of your character. Qualities that would not serve you well were they noted by those presently too blind to see them."

"What?" His head swiveled toward his brother. "What is she blathering about, Ruel?"

"Furthermore," Anne said, taking a step toward Sir Alexander, "you will address me in public with the respect I am due. You impugn your entire family with such insults."

"Do I, now?"

"Indeed." She set her face to the door and lifted her chin. "Excuse me, gentlemen. I shall bid farewell to our guests."

⁂

Eyes burning, Anne hurried back into the drawing room. It was bad enough to be called conniving, to have her unborn children labeled as worthless, to be regarded as a common bedbug . . . but to know that even now she felt breathless from the kisses of a man who toyed with her as a pawn on his chessboard—how awful! How hopeless and weak she was.

As she moved from one powdered face to the next, kissing cheeks and bidding empty farewells to people who disdained and envied her, it was all she could do to hold back tears. Ruel's attentions to her were wrong . . . and right . . . wicked and beautiful. His mouth was so warm, and his lips moved across hers in such a beckoning, tempting . . . oh, dear! The last of the gathering stepped into the hall, and she started for the corridor. To bed, to sleep, to escape.

"Anne!" Sarah Locke caught her hand. "My dear friend, I must tell you how beautiful you looked tonight and how handsomely you answered each question. You charmed everyone in the assembly."

Anne bit her trembling lip. "Thank you, Sarah. How good of you to say so."

Prudence stepped to their side and laid her hand on Anne's arm. Mary Heathhill, the middle sister of the three, joined them. A small woman with sharp features, she had given birth to a baby girl not long before. Though clearly enjoying herself at the dinner, even Mary seemed concerned at the effects of the company's sharp remarks on the new Lady Blackthorne.

"Sharks, they are," Prudence said heatedly. "Those fine ladies and their coy daughters are nothing but a great school of hungry, wicked, biting sharks."

Anne sniffled. "Y-yes. They are."

"Oh, my dear, are you gravely wounded?" Sarah slipped

her arms around the younger woman and clasped her tightly. "I pray not."

"You were magnificent," Mary stated. "Quite astounding in the face of it all, my lady. I do not know how you could be so brave."

"Thank you, Mrs. Heathhill. I pray you will call me Anne."

Prudence pressed a silk handkerchief into her friend's hand. "There now, you must rejoice in your victory. Dry your eyes, and hold high that lovely chin."

Anne dabbed the corner of her eye. "Without you beside me at dinner, I should not have endured. You were all more than kind to speak on my behalf."

Sarah studied the floor for a moment. "Blackthorne is a difficult man. His friends, I fear, are even worse."

"We did not grow up in such company as this," Prudence said, her green eyes filled with compassion. "Our father was in the opium trade, and when he made his fortune, we were moved from Cheapside to Trenton House. Sarah suffered far more than Mary and I. She was forced to wed a horrid old baron before Mr. Locke, and she had to spend all her time in Society. I much prefer the country. Indeed, I am most obliged to the Duke of Marston for inviting me to Slocombe House when Sarah went abroad and I was feeling so dull."

"I do wish Lady Marston had been here tonight," Mary murmured. "The duchess is not a woman to be trifled with. She prefers Sir Alexander to his elder brother, but that is of little consequence in a situation such as this."

"She favors one brother over the other?" Anne asked.

"Indeed," Mary said. "Anyone will tell you the duchess was

displeased at the birth of a dark-haired boy several years after the last of her daughters. For more than a year she confined herself to isolation."

"She makes no secret of her preference for Sir Alexander," Prudence whispered. "She shamelessly dotes on him. He was born with the golden hair and blue eyes of his sisters."

"There are rumors, of course," Mary continued, one eyebrow lifted knowingly. "Certainly the duchess cannot be pleased with her elder son's choice of a wife."

"Mary!" Sarah scowled at her sister.

"I only speak the truth," Mary said. "One can hardly expect the duchess to rejoice at what she would term an inferior connection. All the same, she would have been most perturbed here tonight. She never could have allowed such condescending disregard to be heaped upon her son's wife."

Letting out a breath, Sarah took Anne's hands. "Never mind what the duchess or anyone else thinks. Mary, Prudence, and I are all delighted the marquess was wise enough to have valued your beauty and goodness above all else."

"Before meeting you, he went from one woman to another," Prudence observed. "He fairly leapt from adventure to adventure, making a shallow sport of life itself. But when he is with you, Anne, I see in his eyes true joy. True love."

"Oh, dear Prudence!" Anne exclaimed, wondering whether to laugh or cry.

Sarah kissed Anne's cheek. "Say nothing, dear friend. Merely know how greatly we all esteem and admire you. God has blessed you in marriage, as He blessed Mary and me. I could not be happier than when I am near my beloved

Charles. And Mary adores John and their new baby. Love your husband, Anne. Love him with all your heart."

Anne fought the hard lump in her throat. How could she go on deceiving these generous and kind companions? What would they think of her when the marquess dissolved their union? Oh, it was too horrible.

"Good night, Anne." Mary pressed a soft kiss on her cheek. "I hope we may meet again soon."

"I shall stop in at your rooms shortly," Prudence told Anne, a demure smile on her lips. "But first I must bid someone good night."

⋘⊙⋙

"Tell me about Sir Alexander, Prudence." Still distraught over the evening's events, Anne stood at the door to the sitting room near her bedchamber. "I saw you speaking with him in the corridor just now before you came to me."

"He is engaged to a Frenchwoman, and yet he remains the most determined flirt in the kingdom. That is all one needs to know about the man."

"You were whispering together in the carriage."

"He wanted information about you. I told him the truth. You are wonderful."

"Thank you, Prudence." Anne focused on her true concern. "And what of Mr. Walker? I believe you paid special attention to him on our journey to London. You spoke with him even more than with Sir Alexander."

"Did I?" Prudence went quite pale. After some hesitation, she replied. "The blacksmith has been kind to me since our first meeting at Slocombe. I took my horse to his smithy for

175

shoeing, and of course, you and I walked very often with him in the gardens during your recovery. Through our conversation we have become civil acquaintances."

"Civil acquaintances!" Anne laughed, releasing pent-up tension. "Oh, Prudence, do not patronize me, I beg you. This is Anne Webster you are speaking to, not some marchioness with her nose so high in the air she cannot see what is going on beneath her own chin. You fancy him, and I sense the emotion is mutual."

"Mr. Walker is sensible . . ."

"Prudence, really!" Turning, Anne took her friend's shoulders. "You must tell me the truth. When he looks at you with those great brown eyes of his, you blush as pink as a carnation. Have you fallen in love with him?"

"You should hardly concern yourself with *me*, Anne! I stood near you all evening. The marquess could not keep his eyes from you. Upon my word, I believe he worships you!"

"Prudence, honestly, you do run on!"

"Dear Anne, you must think about what you are going to do about the man. You hardly know him, and he is besotted with you."

"I am glad you believe so."

"My sisters wish the best for you, as do I. But Sarah thinks well of everyone, and Mary can hardly see beyond the privilege of wealth and title with which you are now endowed. I am not so willing to overlook your husband's reputation. Please tell me why you believe the marquess's ardor for you can endure. I must speak plainly, Anne. He is known to be a rake."

"You need not concern yourself, my friend." Anne sat on

a long, velvet-upholstered settee and regarded Prudence's serious expression. "I shall speak plainly, too. The marquess's attentions to me are nothing but a ruse. Before we left Slocombe we agreed to an imposture. Everyone is to believe my husband loves me violently, though of course he does not. I am to fawn over him as though he were King of England."

"You play at marriage?" Prudence appeared dumbfounded. "Anne, I can believe this of him. But why would you stoop to such deception?"

"You must promise to keep this confidence in utmost secrecy."

"But of course!"

"We have made a bargain. In exchange for my father's defense and the welfare of my family, I am to assist the marquess in his plans for the future of the duchy. No one in London must suspect our marriage is a sham. We must always appear to be madly in love."

"I could not believe it more myself."

"Good, and you must never betray the truth about us. You must pretend to believe that the marquess and I truly do adore one another as husband and wife."

Prudence sat down beside Anne and took her hand. "But, dearest Anne, will you be intimate with this man? And what if you should bear his child? What if he should cast you off in such a dire circumstance?"

Anne looked down at the thin fingers of the young woman who had befriended her when she was only a lady's maid. How could she be anything less than honest with Prudence? But what was the truth about Ruel? Remembering the moment when he had held and kissed her, she let her eyes drift shut. Did he truly desire her, as he had said? Or was that part of the imposture, too? Either way, she must do nothing but continue to turn him away.

"Anne?" Prudence squeezed her hand. "Have you been . . . will you be intimate with the marquess?"

"No, of course not." She tried to laugh as though such an idea were beyond silly. "I cannot abide the man. He ridicules and mocks me. He pushes me about and questions my virtue. He is stubborn, demanding, and disputatious. I have warned him not to touch me, or I shall reveal his schemes to the authorities."

"Anne! How very bold of you."

"*Careful* is a better word." She tugged the pins from her hair and let it tumble to her shoulders. "Are you being careful, Prudence?"

"Mr. Walker is . . . wonderful," she said softly. "He is so kind and gentle."

"People do not treat him well."

"That is their loss. I have never heard him speak an ill word of anyone."

"Then you do care for him, Prudence?"

"Yes." She clasped her hands together and shut her eyes. "I adore him, Anne. I love him . . . but nothing will come of it."

"Why do you say that?"

"He is more than twice my age."

"Does it matter?"

"I fear it does." She shook her head. "Mr. Walker has been badly wounded in his life. There is a great emptiness in him, a sorrow so deep I can never touch it."

"The root of his pain is human cruelty."

"But what can overcome that?"

"Abiding love. My father always preached that love has the power to destroy or the power to heal."

"Did he now?" The voice from the doorway drew the attention of both women. "Most ministers I know hold forth on sin and suffering."

Prudence let out a squawk as she leapt to her feet. Anne stood, grabbed her friend's arm, and faced the object of all her greatest fears and hopes.

Lord Blackthorne's face softened into a grin as he strode into the room. "Abiding love, indeed," he said. "I should be pleased for you to enlighten me further on that subject, my dear wife."

～ Ten ～

Ruel studied Anne's face as he walked toward her. Her almond eyes, tilted up at the corners, glittered like onyx in a pool of clear water. Enchanting, delectable creature. Pale and velvety, her fair skin begged for his touch. Her hair, loose from its pins, tumbled around her shoulders like a cascade of dark syrup. Her lips beckoned.

"There is no need for your theatrics here, sir," she said, pursing those pretty lips. "This is not a public room, and Miss Watson is privy to our secrets."

He glanced at the slender young lady, recalling she had been Anne's friend at Slocombe. Prudence Watson had been the one to run to Tiverton for help when they had been shot at on the road, had she not? Flushing bright pink, Miss Watson had backed so far into the settee it was a wonder she did not vanish into it altogether.

Nothing to worry about from that one, he decided. She would not have the temerity to use the secrets of the high-born to her advantage. It was his wife he needed to keep a close eye on.

As he had climbed the stairs to his rooms that evening after the gathering, it occurred to him that he might use Anne's innocence to his advantage. Were she truly a trollop, as his brother had implied, she would never succumb to a severe case of infatuation. Were she accustomed to the easy dalliances of his society, she would not likely believe herself—or him—to be in love.

But his wife was a minister's daughter. Shy. Untouched. Pure. It should be a fairly simple matter to convince Anne that she had fallen deeply in love with her husband. Regardless of his personal feelings for her—which, he wryly admitted, he did not choose to examine too closely—such a development would clearly be to his advantage. A woman in the throes of romantic passion, he had been given to understand, would do anything for her beloved. He could take her wherever he liked and count on her to labor at his lace venture for as long as he wanted. And he would never have to fear her betrayal.

As he approached Anne, a stain of color spread from her neck into her cheeks. It would be more than a little enjoyable to make this woman his. Despite her heartfelt avowals to the contrary, she did admire him. And he admired her.

"You may go," he said, dismissing Miss Watson with a wave.

"Stay, Prudence," Anne countered, holding out a hand to stop her. "We have not concluded our conversation."

The young woman's eyes grew round and frightened as she glanced from her friend to the marquess. Ruel squared his shoulders. "You may go," he repeated. Then he lowered his voice. "Should you wish to retain rooms in my house for yourself and your sister, Miss Watson, I suggest you comply with my wishes."

"Yes, my lord. Of course." Eyes darting to Anne one last time, Prudence grabbed her skirts and fled. As she shut the sitting-room door behind her, Ruel tugged the knot from his cravat.

"Obedient," he said. "I like that in a woman."

"Have you something important to say to me, sir?" Anne gripped her silk shawl tightly and hiked it an inch higher until the knot of fabric was jammed against her throat. "It is late, and I am to call at three houses in the morning. I should very much appreciate my privacy."

"What happy manners you have, my lady. Mrs. Davies certainly taught you well."

"And you poorly. You failed to knock. You did not announce yourself. You rudely drove away my friend. And you have continued to stay when you are not wanted."

"Am I not wanted?"

She glanced away, but only for an instant. "As I told you, I am fatigued. If you have something to tell me, say it quickly and be gone."

Determined to stay until he was satisfied, Ruel walked across the room to a window, drew back the heavy drapes, and peered outside. He had resolved to discover Anne's true feelings toward him—and to see that she acknowledged aloud her growing passion. Equally important, he wanted to determine what it was about this former housemaid that so intrigued him. Was it those brown-gold eyes and that tiny waist of hers? Was it her saucy conversation that amused and challenged him so? Or was it the bright spark of her obvious intelligence that drew him?

"You have a charming prospect of Cranleigh Crescent from this room," he remarked, setting one foot on the window seat and resting his arm on his thigh. "Did you know I used to sleep in this room when I was a boy? These quarters were the nursery in those days. I would sit in this window for hours watching carriages come and go, studying the ladies and gentlemen out for their promenades, spying on housemaids as they flirted with fishmongers and vegetable boys. What do you think of town, Anne?"

When he looked at her again, he noted with dismay that she had managed to pin up her hair and exchange her pink silk shawl for one of thick white wool. Gone was his temptress. She looked chaste. Ethereal. Angelic.

Blast.

He had come into the room intending to make her his conquest. Now she looked like a creature from heaven. A minister's daughter. How could he seduce that?

She glided slowly across the carpeted floor and joined him at the window. Peeking between the drapes, she studied the lamplit street.

"I prefer the wilds of the Midlands," she said in a soft voice. "Through my curtains in our little rectory in Nottingham I watched butterflies dance above yellow primroses and saw hedgehogs scurry through the fern. I memorized the songs of the blue tit, the wood pigeon, and the wren. Bumblebees in the knapweed and ladybirds on the dandelions fascinated and charmed me."

"Bumblebees and ladybirds?"

"I see lace in the commonest things," she said, turning her brown eyes on him. "In the spiral of a cobweb . . . in the white blossom of a hawthorn shrub . . . in the curls of a small green moss on a gray stone. Sometimes I think I am quite mad."

He could not hold back a smile. "You have a gift."

"Not a very useful one . . . except perhaps to a marquess with grand dreams."

"Which I am." He pulled his cravat from his neck. "Do you believe I want only to make use of you, Anne? You implied as much tonight with my brother."

"Have you any other purpose, sir?"

He focused on the window again, remembering his plan to make a conquest of her. More and more often, he was finding it easy to scheme while alone in his chamber—and impossible to carry out his plans in the presence of this woman. She was too good. Too gentle. Too moral.

"No," he said, standing suddenly. "I have no purpose other than the plan we made. Yes, I am using you in my commercial venture, but no more than you have used me to accomplish the release of your father."

"My father," she said, suddenly anxious. "Have you had any report of him?"

"A note from the barrister I engaged. Nothing new."

"I see." She sank down onto the window seat.

Annoyed with himself and with her, he raked a hand through his hair. "Anne, I must apologize for my brother's behavior tonight in the garden. Alex can be quite revolting."

She had tucked her knees beneath her chin and was staring

out the window. Her gown draped in a puddle of pink silk on the floor. "It must be very hard for you to be so unloved."

"Unloved? My dear lady, I have been loved a great deal more ardently than you, I should think. I believe my reputation in that regard preceded my own person into the kitchen on the day we met."

Her focus never left the window. "I do not speak of physical passion. I believe true love has little to do with the body and far more to do with the spirit. The soul is the repository of love, and without love the soul withers and dies."

Religious gibberish. Romantic nonsense. Frowning, Ruel had the sudden urge to take his little zealot straight into his arms and teach her how very much the body did have to do with it. She sat there so smugly virtuous. What did she know about the world?

"I never think about anyone's affections or disaffections toward me," he said, taking a step toward the door.

"Do you not?" She laid her cheek on her arm and watched him. "Then I fear you are more empty inside than Mr. Walker."

"Empty? What gives you that idea?"

"Prudence and I were discussing it."

He rolled his eyes. "Miss Watson hardly knows me. And how on earth do you deduce that Walker's life is empty?"

"Prudence spoke with him at length in Slocombe. And they were together during our rest stops on the journey to London." She narrowed her eyes at him. "Tell me, sir, do you observe nothing?"

"I see important things."

"Aye, your great financial schemes and adventures. What about the people around you?"

"I avoid people when I can. Unfortunately I have been surrounded by them all my life. I endure their mincing and gossiping and preening until I am nearly ill from it. Only in America was I ever able to escape such posturing—and then but briefly. In general, people annoy me, Lady Blackthorne. Especially those who labor on and on in conversation of little consequence."

As though she had not heard him, she continued in her soft, magnetic voice. "There are those around you whose character runs deep. Some of them love you. Others despise you. You would do well to find out which are which."

"Your character runs rather deep, I should think. Tell me, do you love me or despise me?" When she made no answer, he smiled. "Well, Lady Blackthorne, which is it?"

"If by this time you do not know my feelings for you, then you are far more blind than I thought." She stood and faced him, her soft gown swirling at her feet. Lifting that delicate chin, she narrowed her eyes at him. "I pity you. You are friendless and loveless, and your soul is blacker than the night outside this window. I find you self-centered, disagreeable, and immoral. I dislike you very much."

He rested one hand on the back of a chair and studied her. Why could she not be like the other women he knew—moldable and silly, eager for baubles, and as visionary as clams?

"Then you despise me," he said.

"I dislike you . . . but I cannot despise you."

"If you cannot despise me, then you must love me. In your speech moments ago, you left no other option." As he spoke, Ruel walked toward her. The light in her eyes changed from defiance to uncertainty to distress. All her bold words to the contrary, she was afraid of him. Afraid of the emotion he evoked in her. And her fear gave him power.

"In fact, I believe you do love me, Anne," he went on. "You find me intriguing and intelligent. In spite of yourself, you are curious about me. You admire my brashness and my disrespect for Society. You are attracted to my bold tongue, my sense of foresight, and my enterprising nature. It is you who would wish to save me from myself. It is your love that you would have fill my empty, black soul."

He stopped a breath away and stared down at her upturned face. "Am I right?"

"No."

But her eyes said yes. He searched them, awed by the intensity he saw in their depths. This was not a woman he could toy with and then cast easily aside. Her love really might fill his soul . . . fill it up . . . and overflow it . . . and possess him.

"You frighten me, Anne Webster," he whispered. "You frighten me as much as I frighten you."

"Go away, Ruel. Please." Her voice held a note of pleading that transfixed him. "Go now, and leave me in peace."

She took his shoulders and pushed him through the door. When she had shut it, he stared at the blank wood until he heard her singing softly in the next room. It was a hymn.

❧

After reading her Bible and saying her prayers, Anne lay in her bed for nearly an hour watching the moon rise through the open curtains. London. Cranleigh Crescent. A marchioness. What had become of her?

She had not worked at lace in weeks. She had not seen the inside of a kitchen or scrubbed a floor or brushed crumbs from a tablecloth in ever so long. She had traded the chatter of the servants' quarters for the sniping and backstabbing of the upper class. She had exchanged bowls of hot oatmeal and hearty roast beef for hare soup and ragout of duck. She had given up the silly flirtations of vegetable boys and fishmongers for a man whose desire simmered openly in his eyes.

And what of Prudence? If only Anne could relinquish this enormous, overstuffed bed for her narrow cot in an upstairs room with her friend. How cozy that had been, the two young women chatting after dark and giggling over this and that. Happy hours of making lace by the window . . . lighting candles in the corridors . . . arranging bouquets of fresh flowers in the drawing rooms.

Anne sat up in bed and threw her combing gown over her shoulders. Prudence would understand. She had to. Prudence had always listened, and she had far more experience with men than Anne. Maybe she would know what to do about the marquess and his magical kisses.

Aware that the full moon would cast enough light in the corridors for her to see her way to her friend's room, Anne elected not to light a candle. She stepped into a pair of soft slippers, pushed her loose hair over her shoulders, and peeked through the doorway. The corridor was deserted. Shutting the heavy door behind her, she crept down the hall past the marquess's chambers, edged around a corner, and finally tiptoed up a short flight of stairs and through a green baize curtain.

"I came when I found your note in my room."

The male voice was only paces away, and Anne froze in

surprise. A chill washed down her skin. The hour was much too late for anyone to be about.

"Thank you for coming. I felt I had to speak with you."

Prudence! Or was it? Anne backed through the curtain and stood breathless on the other side, certain her heartbeat could be heard a mile away. Was this a tryst? Who was the man?

"It is not wise to meet in secret," he said. "You are an unmarried woman, and I—"

"I know. I am sorry. But I had to see you alone."

Anne leaned against the wall and shut her eyes. It was Mr. Walker. Oh, this was dreadful.

"Are you well?" Prudence's words were soft and fearful.

"Well enough. You?"

"I am all right. It pleases me to see my sisters again."

"Yes. They were kind to me this evening."

"Neither of them would do anything to hurt you. Nor would I. Please understand that. I simply . . . I wanted to talk to you."

"I do understand."

Knowing she should go, Anne found she could do nothing but stay, her back pressed against the wall and her breath shallow. It was wrong for these two to meet in such a way. It was secret and shameful and a terrible sin.

Yet she could hear the longing in the voices of the two, and for some unexplainable reason she responded to their pain.

"I think of you every day," Mr. Walker said in his graveled voice.

The woman sniffled. "And I, you."

"I saw him speaking with you. He gave you his attentions

in the carriage. And tonight at dinner, you were speaking to him."

"He is nothing to me. I swear it!" Prudence was audibly weeping now. "Oh, what shall we do?"

"You have my love. But we are too far apart. You are young. English. Wealthy."

"None of these things matter to me!" Prudence whispered through her tears. "I must tell my sisters. They will give me their blessing. I know they will! My eldest sister gave up her title to marry the man she loved."

Mr. Walker let out a low groan of smothered anguish, and Anne collapsed against the wall. How terrible. How wonderful. How hopeless.

She knew she would never have a love like that, such depth of passion. To think that poor Prudence had given her heart to the blacksmith!

What if Ruel were in love with some woman in such a way? Impossible. He had made it clear he was annoyed by the society of others. Perhaps he was incapable of true love and uninterested in even the pretense of affection. Ruel had felt no serious qualms about marrying—and later divorcing—an impoverished housemaid with no family ranking and no dowry. Anne meant nothing more to him than a means to gain wealth.

"I never think about anyone's affections or disaffections toward me," he had told her. Of course not. Every flirtation was a sham, every sweet word a lie.

"I must go." Mr. Walker pushed back the curtain and stepped into the corridor as Anne pressed against the shadows. He ran through the hall to the stairs. Never looking back, he vanished down the narrow passageway. In a moment, she heard a door shut somewhere below.

⌒⌒⌒

Eyes closed, Anne leaned back against the wall and sighed. Poor Prudence had sobbed softly behind the curtain for some time, but Anne dared not step into her presence and reveal what she had overheard. At last, Prudence had sighed, sniffled one last time, and closed her door.

Anne's legs felt stiff and cold when she finally moved. Her impulse to fling herself into Prudence's arms and pour out her heart to her friend had faded. Clearly her friend had problems of her own, and this was not the time to burden her with Anne's dismal lot in life.

Anne brushed her fingertips over her cheek as she crept down the stairs to her quarters. What a great muddle she had made of her life. What an equally great fool she was. How could she have thought Ruel's kiss in the garden held any real ardor? Worse, how idiotic to have responded to that false passion with feeling of her own.

She had melted into his arms and shivered at his touch. For longer than an eternity she had drifted in rapture. She had actually been deceived by her own charade! How silly!

Not only had Sir Alexander believed his brother was in love with Anne . . . not only had all the company gathered in the drawing room believed it . . . not only had Prudence believed it . . . but Anne had believed it, too! What a buffoon she was.

She stepped into the drawing room of her suite and shut the door behind her. The air felt stuffy and humid, so cloying she thought she might be sick. Stepping out of her slippers, she walked to the window and opened it. As she gazed down onto the green, crescent-shaped park, she thought of Ruel's words to her not long before—the way he had recalled looking down on the grand comings and goings of this great city. He had seemed gentle then, almost like the little boy he had described. But all the while he had been thinking about another woman.

"Sleepless?"

Anne sucked in a breath and whirled around. The man himself reclined on a settee near the fireplace, his great gray eyes luminous in the moonlight.

"Lord Blackthorne! But you . . . I thought you were—"

"Awaiting your return? I was." He cocked his arms behind his head. "Perhaps you might share with me your whereabouts for the past half hour."

"I . . . I went to see Prudence."

"Miss Watson—whatever for?"

"I wanted someone to talk to." She met his bold stare. Despite her recent conclusion that he must have some woman languishing for him, Ruel was not behaving the least bit lovelorn. In fact, he seemed his usual cocksure self.

She sat down on the window seat. "And you, sir? Where were you this past half hour?"

"Here, of course, wondering what my wife was up to," he replied. "I remembered something I had forgotten to tell you. As you know, in less than a fortnight, the Season will be well under way. Everyone will be in town, and we shall have hardly a moment for private conversation. Anyone of significance in the military, most of the peerage, and usually the regent himself spend the evenings attending one or more balls. The most influential gentlemen in England go to these ridiculous dances, and our own presence is crucial. So is our performance."

"Performance?"

"It will be our labor to convince all of Society of our undying love," he said, coming to his feet. "We must be as one. Husband and wife."

Anne held her breath as he walked toward her. Still dressed in his white shirt, sleeves rolled to the elbow and collar loose, he loomed huge and dark in the dimly lit room. His curly black hair spilled over his brow and onto his neck. His eyes never left her face.

"There are things you should know about me," he said.

She nodded. "I understand you have many secrets," she said in an effort to portray sympathy. "Tell me everything."

"Tongue. I loathe it."

"What?"

"Pickled, boiled, garnished with brussels sprouts—no matter how it is prepared, I refuse to eat tongue. Cannot bear the stuff. You should know that about me. Turnips. I never touch them. Head cheese. I find it revolting."

"Head cheese? But . . ."

"Despite what that blasted Miss Pickworth has written about me, I never touch strong drink." He began to pace. "I am partial to gingerbread nuts with my tea—"

"What are you talking about?"

"Me, of course. If we are to convince everyone of our love, we must know about one another. Turkish delight and treacle are particular favorites, and I am fond of trifle. I like my coffee black, my tea the color of caramel, and my toast piping hot. You?"

Anne swallowed. This was not at all what she had expected. All she could think of was Prudence and Mr. Walker in the corridor. The tears . . . the anguish . . . their forbidden love. Anne had convinced herself that Ruel must have some beautiful woman stashed away waiting for him. And now he was speaking of tongue and brussels sprouts!

Worse, he had stopped his pacing and begun walking toward her. His black hair gleamed silver in the moonlight. His gray eyes drank hers. "Anne," he said, "what do you like?"

"Everything," she said quickly.

"Everything? That is unusual."

She gulped down a bubble of air. "Except eels. I despise eels."

"Do you sugar your tea?"

"Two lumps."

"Coffee?"

"I do not drink it."

"Your favorite color is . . . pink."

Remembering the dress she had worn that night, she smiled. "Hardly. Blue."

"Green for me. The color of the Atlantic Ocean off the coast of Florida. My favorite book is Chaucer's *Canterbury Tales*. Yours is—"

"The Bible." Their words overlapped, and he chuckled.

"Of course it is. Tell me, Anne, have you ever read Solomon's Song?"

"I heard a sermon on it once. My father says that book is a dramatic interpretation of Christ's love for the church. Christ is the bridegroom, and the church is the bride."

"'Let him kiss me with the kisses of his mouth,'" Ruel murmured in a low voice. "'His left hand is under my head, and his right hand doth embrace me.'"

"It is meant to be symbolic."

"Symbolic? I should like to hear your father interpret this: 'Behold, thou art fair, my love; behold, thou art fair; thou hast doves' eyes within thy locks. . . . Thy lips are like a thread of scarlet, and thy speech is comely. . . . Thou hast ravished my heart—'"

"Stop!" She put out her hand. "You are hovering close to sacrilege."

"I am only reciting what I read as I waited for you." He gestured to her Bible on the nearby table as he sat down beside her on the window seat. "It quite mesmerized me to think of you reading such poetry, my dear. 'Thy neck is like a tower of ivory,'" he resumed quoting. "'Thine eyes like the fishpools in Heshbon . . .'"

Ruel reached out and gently stroked her neck with the side of his thumb. Anne shivered, paralyzed with confusion. How could he? How could a man so much in love with one woman be able to woo another with such ease? He was a rogue. With his warm breath, magic fingers, and silken words, he wove his evil spells, and she fell under them like a sailor hearing a siren's song.

"'How fair and how pleasant art thou, O love,'" he whispered, taking her hand and laying it across his palm. "'Thy stature is like to a palm tree . . . and the smell of thy nose like apples; and the roof of thy mouth like the best wine.'"

His lips covered hers, and what could she do? Anne had

thought of nothing but his mouth all evening . . . nothing but the brush of his rough cheek against hers.

"Wicked man!" She shoved him back and turned away from him on the window seat. "You wicked, wicked man. You vowed never to touch me, but you come into my private quarters and attempt the most boldfaced seduction. You misspeak the very Scriptures in your unholy aim! Have you no conscience? You use and abuse every poor woman who falls prey to your charms. You are horrid! Leave me at once."

"Anne—"

"Do not talk to me, sir. I feel disgust at the sound of your voice."

"Anne, I spoke the Scriptures as they were written. I cannot believe those words are some high symbolic portrayal of a holy bond between Christ and the church, no matter what your father preached. Those words are words of love from a man to his bride."

He left the seat, knelt beside her, and took her hands away from her eyes. "Wanting the man you married is not wrong. It is no sin to desire your own husband, Anne. Passion and ardor—if one can believe Solomon's Song—are sacred."

"Passion and ardor! Yet, as you said yourself, your reputation with women preceded you on the day we met. That sort of passion is not sacred! It is sinful!"

"I cannot deny my past. But I never took anything that was not offered."

"You are disgraceful."

"Anne, look at me."

"I cannot. You repulse me."

"I entice you."

"You are repugnant."

"Tempting."

"Lies!" She grabbed the shirt fabric on his shoulders and squeezed it into fists. "Lies!"

"Truth." He leaned forward, taking her mouth again, pressing her against the window. "Love me, Anne, I beg you. Love me."

His fingers slid into her hair even as tears squeezed from the outer corners of her eyes. She let him kiss her and hated herself for it.

"Anne, I have desired you from the moment I heard your voice," he murmured. "The way you wove that magic tale for the little girl in the kitchen. A duchess, you called that child. I wanted to make you my own duchess. I wanted to know the touch of fingers that could make lace as you make it. Please, Anne, do not be frightened of me. I am your husband."

It was true, she realized. Horribly true, and if she had not been so willful, she might have prevented it. But now she was a wife and this man her husband. And oh, why did his kisses stir her so?

"Tell me you want me," he whispered. "Say the words, Anne. I will not take you unwilling. You must desire me as much as I—" He stopped and kissed her temple again. "Your hair is damp. You are crying."

"Oh, Ruel," she said, shaking her head.

He pulled away abruptly. "I have made you weep."

She let out a breath. "And more."

❧ *Eleven* ❧

"Why are you crying?" Ruel studied Anne's face in the moon-light. Beautiful and good and far too pure, she was beyond him. He had assumed he might seduce her if he wished. She had responded . . . and would respond to his touch until he had won her. But suddenly he realized he no longer wanted her. Not that way.

"The women," she whispered, brushing her cheek where a tear still clung. "I thought about you and . . . all those poor women who have loved you . . . might love you even now."

"You weep for me because of my past—my black soul, as you put it? Yes, I have been a cad, but . . ."

How could he explain that those encounters had meant noth-ing? Youthful gallivants, no more. And nothing to feel proud of, especially when he looked into Anne's deep brown eyes.

"To make a woman believe you care for her," she was saying, "to convince her she is the only creature you desire . . . that your heart belongs to her alone . . . and then to . . . to . . ."

"But you are the only woman—"

"No, I am not."

"No, indeed." Ruel jumped to his feet, sweat breaking out across his brow. "You are quite right about that. I cannot think why I said it. Upon my honor, I hardly know what has come over me."

He swiped a handkerchief across his forehead. Had he lost his mind? Almost telling her she was the only one in his life. Insane. He had gone insane. Three years without the company of a woman would do that to a man. Three years was a long time. Too long. But his travels had hardly left time for liaisons, and on the journey he had met no one he cared to woo. No wonder he was acting the fool over this creature with her white gown and brown eyes.

"Please, sir," she whispered. "You must not play with women's hearts. If she loves you truly, a woman will be loyal to you no matter what happens. She will hold the candle of her passion for you through separation and obstacle and the passage of countless years. Nothing will snuff it out. Nothing."

"I do not want that." He turned away, unable to face her. His words were a lie. For the first time in his life, he did want that. He craved a woman's passion, her commitment, her faith in him through a lifetime. He wanted someone to weep over him and laugh with him. He wanted it all. And he wanted it with Anne.

"Listen to me." He swung on her, finger outstretched. "You will make lace, and you will pose as my wife, and that is all. Do you understand?"

"Of course."

"You will not talk to me about watching hedgehogs from

your bedroom window or dreaming of moss on gray stones. You will not gaze at me with those brown eyes and lecture me about passion and love. And if I am called upon to woo you in public, you will not respond with anything but sham emotion. Do you understand me?"

"I understand perfectly." She stood and set her hands on her hips. "And should I discover you slipping into my private quarters and kissing me, how am I to respond then, Lord Blackthorne?"

"I assure you, such a thing will not happen again."

"I am greatly relieved to hear it. Then will you do me the favor of leaving my presence so that I may restore my dishabille?"

"Gladly."

He walked to the door that joined their suites. Feeling her eyes on him, he sensed he was being assessed by someone whose character was far too close to that of God Himself. Anne reviled him. The ache that spread through his chest at the realization hurt so deeply he clutched his arms tightly around himself.

Go away, Ruel, he could almost hear her saying. *You are a rake and a libertine, a liar and a tormentor.*

He tried to rid himself of the thought. Even if there had been no other women, this one was only a temporary bride. Only a housemaid. One day he would be a duke. Even if all the other things that separated them were to vanish, that alone would hold them apart forever.

"Good night, Lady Blackthorne," he said, turning in the open doorway.

She lifted her head. "I am only Anne."

He leaned a shoulder against the frame. "Good night, then, Anne. My lady."

Their eyes held until the door shut between them.

⁓◌◔◌⁓

Prudence's squawk dragged Anne out of the depths of sleep. She squinted at the sunlight pouring through the open curtain. What time was it? And what on earth was Prudence screeching about?

"The marquess was here! In your quarters!" she cried, staring in horror at Anne. She held out an armful of rumpled clothing. "Look! His cravat and his coat were in the sitting room. And his own bed was still made this morning. My lady's maid whispered to me that it was unrumpled and perfectly flat! All the servants can talk of nothing else, wondering when the first little heir will make his appearance. Oh, Anne, your ruse is at an end, and I fear you are utterly ruined!"

"What are you going on about, Prudence?" Anne edged up on her elbows and stared at her friend.

"You ought to have resisted him, for now you must surely be cast out into the streets! No one will care for you unless I can persuade my sister Sarah to have pity. I certainly cannot afford to take you in, for I have only just enough to live on! What future will you have? You must not suppose the marquess will keep you as his wife simply because you have borne him a child. Men such as he do not. They cast their mistresses aside like so much dirty laundry. Oh, Anne!"

"Prudence, stop it at once, I beg you." She swung her legs over the side of the bed and slid to the carpet. "It is not at all what you imagine. The marquess was waiting for me when I—"

"Waiting for you! Oh, then it is true. We must get you away from London at once. We shall ask my sister Mary for a carriage to take you back to Nottingham. You can hurry home and pray you have not conceived a child by him. And if by some miracle—"

"Do be quiet, Prudence, if you possibly can." Anne tucked the coat and cravat under her arm. "The marquess wanted to speak with me last night, and he waited for me in my sitting room. He was reading the Bible."

"Oh, Anne, you cannot expect anyone to believe—"

"I speak the truth," she retorted. "Nothing happened between us, Prudence, believe me. You have let your imagination run away with you. All the same, you must allow people to go on thinking the marquess and I live as husband and wife, and you must let them speculate about an heir. It can only be good for his enterprise. In the meantime, have no trepidation on my behalf. I would never give myself to such an untrustworthy man as the marquess, and I should hope you would have more faith in me than that."

"But he sent me out of the room to be alone with you . . . and I saw the way he was looking at you all night . . . the way he follows you with his eyes and how he was kissing you in the garden—"

"It was a charade! I told you that already. Really, Prudence, what must I do to convince you?"

"I am frightened that you will accidentally be seduced by him. He is fearfully handsome and such a favorite with all the ladies. Their flirtations with him last night were shocking, and he is to be a duke one day. How can you resist him?"

"Easily. The marquess is a cad. He holds no appeal for me. Thus my virtue is secure. It is *your* reputation that concerns me far more." Anne laid a hand on Prudence's shoulder. "Late last night after the house fell silent, I heard someone in the corridor near your room. It was Mr. Walker."

"Oh!"

"I heard someone else there, also. It was a woman. They were unchaperoned."

"Oh, dear!" Prudence gasped, her eyes wide.

"I have considered confronting this young lady about her behavior, for she will be startled to learn that I heard her and Mr. Walker speaking together in the darkness."

Prudence swallowed. "Did you hear the subject of the conversation between the lady and Mr. Walker?"

"I did, and I believe she is in much greater danger of falling in love than I shall ever be."

Knitting her fingers together, Prudence stared across the bedroom to the open window. "I believe that Mr. Walker would be most unhappy . . . most distraught . . . to know he had been overheard."

"He will never know. Yet, my concern is greater for the woman. Their parting was most pathetic."

"Perhaps they realize that their situations in life must prevent their ever being together." Prudence's eyes filled with tears. "Perhaps they are most violently in love and yet their ages, their society, their conditions of upbringing cannot allow them to marry."

"Prudence," Anne said softly, "with how many men have you been violently in love?"

The young lady flushed a bright pink. "I do not know. Several, I suppose. But Mr. Walker is not the same as most men."

"I shall not deny that." She thought for a moment. "But what of Sir Alexander? He was paying you a great deal of attention at dinner. Is he the same or different from most men?"

"Sir Alexander is engaged to the daughter of the Comte de la Roche."

"True. And yet the Season approaches. I imagine you will soon have any number of 'different' men interested in you."

"As will you, Anne." She lifted her chin. "You must not be so naïve as to suppose that you and your sham husband are immune to Society's games. All summer long, these lords and ladies play at their affairs of the heart. They are hardly better in their country houses in winter. Men will pursue you. The marquess will pursue you. And if you do not wish to end up selling yourself on the corner of Tottenham Court Road, you would do well to keep your bedroom door locked." Prudence let out a breath before continuing. "But we have both spoken more boldly than we should. You are my dear friend, and I wish only the best for you."

"Thank you, Prudence. I see that our feelings are the same."

"I shall speak to you again at breakfast, then." Prudence stepped toward the door, but she caught herself and turned back. "Your carriage is waiting to take you on your morning calls. You must never forget who you are now, Anne. And I pray you will not forget what you might become if you are not careful."

Anne watched the door shut behind the young woman. She studied the rumple of clothing in her arms. Why had Ruel not slept in his own room last night? Had he been with another woman after Anne refused him?

Oh, it was all so confusing. As she crossed to her dressing room, Anne wondered what she should do with Ruel's things. The faint whiff of spiced lemon and cedar drifted under her nose. Burying her face in the folds of rough, tweedy fabric, she drank in the scent.

"How much better is thy love than wine! and the smell of thine ointments than all spices!" The words of Solomon's Song of Songs—words she had read for so many hours last night alone in her room—came back to her. *"Thy lips, O my spouse, drop as the honeycomb: honey and milk are under thy tongue; and the smell of thy garments is like the smell of Lebanon. . . . Make haste, my beloved, and be thou like to a roe or to a young hart upon the mountains of spices."*

⁓⊙⊙⌇⌇

"Two lumps as always, my dear?" Ruel held the silver sugar tongs over Anne's teacup.

"Thank you, darling."

He watched her struggling to keep her hand from shaking as she stirred her tea. It was the first time they had been together among so few people since that first night at Marston House. Two weeks had passed—two weeks of paying calls and receiving calls, of going to parties and giving parties, of gossip and innuendo and slander. All the things he most despised about his rank.

Now Anne's mother had come to call on her daughter and

new son at Marston House on Cranleigh Crescent. In the past week, Mrs. Webster, the children, and all their belongings had been transported from the rectory in Nottingham to a large, quiet house in London. The house, of course, was owned by the Chouteau family, and the Websters were provided for with funds delivered by a footman promptly at nine each Monday morning.

Their previous patron, the baroness Lady de Winter, had not abandoned the Webster family. Indeed, she insisted on spending the first week in town helping the parson's wife settle into her new quarters.

The four of them were seated beside a large window in the drawing room, a prospect of sunlit summer gardens stretching out before them. The round table had been laden with scones, clotted cream, strawberry jam, and all manner of tiny sandwiches and tarts. The baroness, adrift in the scent of rose water, rustled with purple silk and countless rows of Nottingham lace. Mrs. Webster, small and timid in such grand surroundings, perched like a little brown wren on the edge of her chair.

"Thank you, Anne," she peeped when her daughter offered her a petit four. "Lady Blackthorne, I mean to say."

Anne smiled, her face pale. "You are quite welcome. Lady de Winter? A petit four?"

"Thank you, my dear. Ah, delicious!" The baroness continued to speak between bites of the small iced cake. "I must tell you, when I first received intelligence of the love match between darling little Anne Webster and the handsome Marquess of Blackthorne, I could hardly believe such happy tidings. To see you risen from such dire, dire circumstances to this grand a height of opulence is most rewarding to me, my dear. How pleased I am to have played but a small part in your happiness."

"Lady de Winter," Anne said quickly, "your role has been anything but small. I shall never forget that you preferred my father to the parish before anyone ever dreamed the ensuing events might lead me to such a station in life as this."

"Quite true." The elderly lady's face folded into lines of pleasure. "Such happy, happy events."

Ruel studied Anne, wondering if she would be able to maintain her composure in front of her mother. She appeared ready to throw herself into the woman's arms and confess the entire contrivance. A dire event indeed, were it to occur.

Moments before entering the drawing room with Anne that afternoon, Ruel had reminded her that the baroness was a formidable force in the handmade lace industry of the Midlands, and that she would oppose his scheme. She had directed her employees in smuggling ventures undertaken with great derring-do. These had included exporting her contraband wares to France in coffins, their lifeless contents luxuriantly swathed like lacy Egyptian mummies. The baroness had even sent dogs wrapped in lace across the forested border from Belgium into France, where the smuggled wares were removed and sold to the aristocracy. Lady de Winter's coffers boasted the rich results of her success.

With fervor, he had warned Anne not to mention his own plans for smuggling lace-making machinery into France. Further, he had cautioned her that the impression she made on the baroness—more than on any other person in Society—would count toward his success or failure. No matter that her own mother would be in the room, Anne was not to drop for a second her facade of true love for the marquess.

"You may recall," Anne was saying now, "it was you, Lady de Winter, who sent a letter of recommendation to Trenton House on my behalf. Without your backing, I should never have earned the friendship of Mrs. Locke and her two dear sisters. Nor would I then have traveled to Slocombe House, where I met the Duke of Marston and his charming . . . gallant . . . generous son."

Ruel let out a breath of relief and took one of Anne's hands in his. "Indeed, we are eternally grateful to you, Lady de Winter. My marriage to this beautiful woman has made me the happiest of men."

"And you, Anne . . . Lady Blackthorne," Mrs. Webster asked softly. "Are you happy?"

"My goodness . . . well, of course."

She tried to smile as she looked into her mother's brown eyes, a mirror of her own. At the sight, Ruel knew another rush of alarm. Clearly his wife was a terrible liar, and her every emotion was written plainly on her face.

"Your daughter and I have a great deal in common, Mrs. Webster," he spoke up quickly. "Though it is true we come from different stations in life, we immediately discovered threads of similarity in our interests and avocations. Did we not, my dear?"

"Yes," she fumbled. "Of course."

"Really?" Mrs. Webster was staring at her daughter. "I cannot imagine that. What sorts of things do you have in common?"

When Anne failed to respond, Ruel filled in. "We are both

fond of the out-of-doors. Anne has told me of the quaint prospect from her window in Nottingham. Hedgehogs scurrying through the knapweed. Wood pigeons and blue tits in the hawthorn tree. Curly moss on that . . . that . . ."

"On that gray stone. You know the one, Mother?"

"Near the oak tree?"

"The very one!" Ruel said with a triumphant grin. "The gray stone near the oak tree."

Mrs. Webster laughed in relief. "I almost feel as if you have been there, Lord Blackthorne."

"As do I. Your daughter has such a way with words."

"And what else?" Anne's mother asked. Ruel shifted in his chair. Did the woman's eyes appear to narrow as she questioned him? "Do tell us the other things you enjoy in common."

Ruel frantically searched his mind. "Food," he blurted out. "We have similar culinary likes and dislikes. Neither of us can bear eels."

"Eels?"

"And . . . and two lumps of sugar in our tea. We both like that, though Anne will not drink coffee, and I never go without it in the morning. She prefers blue, and I like green, but what of that? They are only colors, are they not?"

Mrs. Webster stared at her daughter. "You both like the out-of-doors and despise eels. Anne, have you made a marriage on nothing more substantial than this?"

"Not only those things, Mother." She squeezed Ruel's hand. "My darling husband and I both adore . . ."

"The Bible," he said.

"The Bible!" The baroness dropped her spoon. "Lord Blackthorne?"

"I have become an avid reader."

"He can quote entire passages," Anne put in.

Ruel looked up with what he hoped was a humble expression. "I flatter myself, I have become quite the scholar."

"I am happy to know that." Mrs. Webster stirred her tea. "Anne's father will be more than pleased when I write to him. My husband has been most . . . most distressed at the turn of events."

"Distressed? Mrs. Webster, my wife is a marchioness, a ranking of no little power, wealth, prestige. What better circumstance could you and your husband wish upon your daughter?"

"We are grateful, of course, for your assistance in all our affairs. But you must understand that our daughter's happiness is of utmost importance. Our Anne is . . . well, Anne is special." Mrs. Webster lifted her chin in exactly the manner of her daughter. "Lord Blackthorne, if I may be so bold as to ask . . . do you know anything of my daughter's talents in the design and making of lace?"

"Anne is a genius. I am deeply in awe of her skill and artistry."

"Is that so?"

"Indeed. You might like to know that I carry a bit of her work with me at all times." Ruel slipped his hand into his pocket and drew out the panel of lace Anne had hoped to sell to his brother. "Can you see the family crest in the center? My wife designed this as a gift for our wedding."

Anne sucked in a breath as he turned the lace this way and that. The delicate scrap shivered as she reached for it. "My dear husband, may I see that?"

He gave her a quick kiss on the cheek and tucked the lace back into his pocket. "Anne is always thinking how she might rework it. But I consider this lace a masterpiece, and one cannot improve on perfection."

"How lovely," the baroness said, beaming. "How very sentimental and charming of you, Lord Blackthorne."

"I hope you will not try to keep Anne from her dreams," Mrs. Webster said softly, "as you keep her from that lace. You do share Anne's dreams, do you not?"

"Some of my dreams have changed, Mama." Anne removed her hand from Ruel's and leaned toward her mother. "Things are very different for me now. You must try to understand."

"But you always had so many dreams—a head filled with them! You dreamed of a lace school of your own. You wanted to teach others your patterns and your techniques. You spoke so often of marrying a man you could love forever, as I love your father. You wanted to live with him in a small stone house with a fireplace where you could sit and make your lace. Dear Anne, have you given up those dreams for grand palaces and ornate furniture?"

"Oh, Mama, I—"

"And what of children, Anne? Has that hope changed, too? Do you no longer ache for little ones dancing across the hillsides, playing in the primroses, and picking pails of blackberries? You wanted them to run in bare feet . . . swim in a farm pond . . . stand under a thatched roof in the rain . . ."

Mrs. Webster wiped her eyes. Her voice was a throaty whisper when she spoke again. "Oh, Anne, did you give it all up? Did you make this marriage . . . for the sake of your father?"

"Nonsense!" the baroness pronounced. "Lady Blackthorne can have anything she likes. As her husband said, she is a marchioness now and one day she will be a duchess. What woman would want barefoot children and lace schools when she can have silk slippers and private tutors?"

"Anne did."

"Mama, please try to understand. I am very, very happy with Lord Blackthorne. I admire my husband so much. Our future is . . . is . . ."

"Bright and wonderful." Ruel took her arm and pulled her back until he had her securely tucked against him. "We shall have handfuls of children, and they may all run as barefoot as they like. Dear Mrs. Webster, please be assured of my undying devotion to your daughter and all her dreams."

"Anne?" the woman asked, her eyes on her daughter.

"My wife's happiness is my entire focus," Ruel said. Concerned that the tea party would end up with both Webster women dissolved in tears and all his plans exposed before the baroness, Ruel rose. He kept Anne's arm pressed firmly under his as he gestured at the table. "Would you like another cup of tea, Mrs. Webster?"

Sniffling, Anne's mother gathered up her reticule, stood, and shook out her skirts. "Thank you so much, my lord. I must be getting home."

"Indeed," the baroness added, rising. "Mrs. Webster's furnishings arrived yesterday morning, and things are at sixes and sevens."

"We do appreciate the house, Lord Blackthorne," Anne's mother said, "and all your efforts on behalf of our dear daughter."

After interminable farewells, the baroness and Mrs. Webster were seen from the drawing room by a waiting footman. The moment the door shut behind them, Anne flung herself at Ruel.

"Give me my lace this instant, you beast!"

∽ఇ $\mathcal{T}$welve ఇ∽

Anne reached for Ruel's pocket. "I want my lace, and you have no right to it. Give it to me!"

He grabbed her wrists and braced his feet to hold her back. "And have you racing back to Nottingham so you can buy a little stone house and marry some farmer who will give you lots of barefoot children? Not a chance."

"What do you care how I live?" She lunged at him, barely missing his face with her nails. "Your little ruse is never going to work! The baroness saw through you instantly. The Bible!"

"Eels!" he scoffed, pushing her down onto the settee.

"Hedgehogs in the knapweed."

"Stop fighting me!"

"Give me my lace!"

"Never. What else do I have to hold you?"

"You have *me*. I am your prisoner! Bound to do as you tell me, or you will throw my family to the dogs and let my father be executed or sent away on a convict ship."

"Bound to do as I tell you? But you are failing miserably at that! You cannot bring yourself even to pretend to like me." He pressed her down into the cushions as he mocked her voice. "'I am very, very happy with Lord Blackthorne.' You might as well have told her I am torturing you on the rack."

"You are!"

"How?" he exploded, straightening and setting his hands at his hips. "Any other woman would be ecstatic to be married to a marquess—to have countless properties, the prospect of Seasons in London and winters in the country, the finest gowns from the best seamstresses, shoes and jewels and scores of bonnets. What do you want?"

Her brown eyes darkened, but she said nothing.

"Do you want stone houses?" he demanded in frustration. "I have stone houses enough for ten wives. This is a stone house, blast it! Slocombe is a stone house. You can have them both. They are yours. You want to make lace? I shall import two thousand bales of silk thread to keep you and fifty lace schools busy for a hundred years. Why can you not be happy? What do you want?"

"What do you care if I am happy or not?"

"I care. I need you, Anne." He caught himself, aware he had said far more than he meant . . . more than he should. He took a chair across from her. "I need your help. And if you are miserable, you are likely to go racing back to Nottingham or blurting my plans to Lady de Winter. You are important to the success of this entire venture. You are . . . you are an ingredient in the recipe. A cog in the wheel, so to speak. Why is it so difficult to pretend to care for me?"

"Because I do not know you."

"This again? What do you want—a recitation? I loathe tongue, I like the color green—"

"Those things are not you. Any number of men might recite the same litany." Her eyes searched his face. "How am I to go on pretending to adore you when it is clear to everyone that we share nothing of the heart? The things that matter in a marriage are not a taste for the same foods or an affinity for the same colors. What counts is a common purpose in life, shared dreams and hopes, a united faith in God."

"That is romantic nonsense, my dear lady. My parents have been married for forty-two years, and they share few interests beyond entertaining acquaintances and playing whist. They have no common purpose other than getting through life in the most comfortable fashion possible. As to shared dreams and hopes . . . I cannot think they have spoken together long enough at one time to address the subject."

"Do they love each other?"

He paused for a moment, pondering. "What difference does it make? Love has nothing to do with the reality of marriage."

"Does it not?" Her expression softened. "My parents taught me by example that when two people are anchored in Christ, and when they sacrificially place their love for each other above all worldly concerns, they do far more than get through life in the most comfortable fashion possible. They have a deep and abiding love, an unending enchantment, a bond that nothing can sever."

Ruel looked into Anne's depthless eyes as she spoke, and he knew she believed completely in what she said. She had witnessed such true love. She possessed utter faith in the reality of such love. And she had committed herself to sharing that love someday with a man.

He felt suddenly at a loss. He had no idea how to achieve such a pinnacle in life—nor even how to pretend he had. Worse, a curl of envy gripped his chest as he thought of the man who one day would capture this woman's heart and share her faith, her passion . . . her love.

"You told me you want everyone to believe I adore you," Anne said softly. "Then you must wish for us to feign a marriage of love, as my parents truly have. I cannot go on pretending—especially not in the face of my own mother—unless I know something of the depths of your heart. You heard my dreams. What are yours?"

"I have told you already. My dreams are neither romantic nor ethereal. I have only practical goals, those I can achieve through physical effort and the application of my own intellect. I want to save the Chouteau dynasty from financial ruin. I want to establish a mercantile trade with America and France."

"Then you wish to make something from nothing. As do I." To his surprise, she reached across and touched a curl that had fallen onto his forehead. "Commerce from bankruptcy. Lace from silk thread. Something from nothing."

As her fingers brushed the lock into place, a shock of desire shot through Ruel's chest. But it was not merely a physical yearning. With the depth of her understanding, Anne had touched his heart.

"Something from nothing," he echoed, suddenly finding it difficult even to speak. "There, my Lady Blackthorne, we have discovered what we have in common."

"But I abhor your lace machines." Drawing away, she sat up straight, her shoulders squared. "Your scheme is a wicked one, sir, and it will harm those I care for most deeply."

Reality descended again. He gritted his teeth. "You despise my scheme only because you view life in too narrow a manner. You must open your eyes wide and look ahead. The world is on the threshold of great things. There is power in steam—power we have barely begun to harness. I believe that one day London will grow into an enormous city with factories and commerce at its hub. England perches on the verge of world dominance. Our nation has the potential to become a mighty empire."

"England? I trust you jest with me now, sir. England is nothing more than a tiny, foggy island populated by shepherds and fishmongers."

"Anne, the world waits at our doorstep. America . . . you should see the untouched treasures there. France . . . and India . . . and China. Even Africa! One day, they will all be woven together by the threads of commerce. I want to be a part of that."

"You want to make a lace out of the whole world." Her face broke into a smile. She spread wide her arms as though holding a length of the finest Honiton. "Here is England with her roses and misty moors. Here is China with little footbridges and peonies. India with mysterious temples and twining cobras. Africa with coconut palms and jewels. And America—"

"Wildflowers and oak trees and mighty rivers."

"Threads twine and swirl from each continent all meeting at one central motif: the crest of the Chouteau family."

He grinned. "A bit grandiose, is it?"

"Grand, not grandiose. I hope your dream comes true for you." She touched his arm. "But, Lord Blackthorne—"

"Ruel."

"Ruel . . . when you have harnessed the world with your threads of commerce and woven your empire with machines of steam, I pray you will not forget all the common people who can dream of nothing but the next loaf of black bread they hope to eat."

"People who live in small stone houses and teach at lace schools?"

"All who survive by the labor of their hands. Those whose livelihood is threatened by your machines."

Unable to resist her, he stroked his thumb down the side of her cheek. "I shall never forget you, Anne Webster. I cannot think how you came to haunt me in the first place."

"You stole my lace."

No, he wanted to tell her. *You stole my heart.*

But such a thing could not be true, could it? Ruel had never believed he possessed enough heart to matter one way or another. He had never received much love in his life, and he knew he had precious little to give away. So why did this common creature with her almond-shaped eyes and her saucy mouth fill his thoughts night and day? Why did it tie his stomach in knots to contemplate the reality of someday releasing her into the arms of a Nottingham farmer?

"I must go now, Lord Blackthorne," she said softly. "Our tea is completed, and I cannot speak with you in peace. You stole my lace, and I fear you did little to allay my poor mother's fears. You dream of the whole world, whilst I dream only of a home and a family of my own. What you want, I cannot give you. And what I want, you cannot give me."

"Is that true?"

"It is. And what is worse, the longer you stare into my eyes, the more I begin to forget how very much I dislike you." She stood. "The more I forget how truly abominable you are, the more I want you to kiss me again as you did in the garden. And the more I want you to kiss me again, the more hopeless my future becomes."

"Anne!" He rose and caught her around the waist.

"Good afternoon, Lord Blackthorne," she whispered, pulling away and running toward the door.

⌒⌒⌒

To Anne's utter surprise, one Tuesday morning Miss Pickworth reported the most monstrous lie ever printed in *The Tattler*. A terrible falsehood about the Marchioness of Blackthorne and her new husband—yet it was the exact plan Ruel had whispered to Anne only three nights before as she made her way along the corridor to her bedroom. How news of this stratagem had come into Miss Pickworth's hands, she could only guess, for she had told no one but Prudence Watson and her two sisters.

Anne knew that *The Tattler* was avidly read by everyone in London who could afford to purchase it. The newspaper was then taken in hand by the household staff, who secretly perused each word before carrying it to the dustbin. And finally the vegetable and fishmongers plucked the printed pages from the refuse and used them to pack their wares—but not before eagerly gathering around someone who could read

to them all the secrets the aristocracy would least want anyone
to know.

Miss Pickworth, the anonymous columnist who reported
the affairs of Society and answered heartfelt petitions from her
faithful readers, penned the most enthusiastically devoured
words in the entire newspaper. No woman worth her salt
would set out in her carriage for Hyde Park unless she knew
what Miss Pickworth had reported about her neighbors that
morning. No man would step foot into his gentlemen's club
without the knowledge of who had done what and with
whom in London that week. This doyenne of civilization's
real name was anyone's guess and everyone's speculation.
Miss Pickworth was feared and reviled and fervently
embraced by one and all.

Prudence Watson, living once again with Sarah and her
husband at Trenton House, raced across the green park of
Cranleigh Crescent that Tuesday morning and slapped a copy
of *The Tattler* on the tea table in front of Anne.

"Look at this!" she cried. "See what Miss Pickworth has
written about you! How did she know? Who could have told
her, for I promise you that neither my sisters nor I breathed
a word to anyone!"

Anne picked up the newspaper, but before she could begin
reading, Prudence snatched it away again. "'By all accounts
merry as well as married,'" Prudence read aloud Miss Pickworth's alliterative prose, "'the Marquess and Marchioness of
Blackthorne mean to depart our Society at the summit of the
Season. In an enchanted European excursion they will enjoy
dining along the Danube, ascending the Alps, and sunning on
the seacoasts of southern Spain.'"

Anne set her spoon on her saucer. "*He* must have put out the information. The marquess."

"'Beginning in Brussels,'" Prudence continued reading, "'the contented couple will favor fashionable Flanders with their esteem and elegance. But will they flee in favor of farther shores, or will they choose to commingle with their comrades in an effort to encounter England's most enigmatic and elusive enemy?'"

"What does Miss Pickworth mean by that?" Anne asked. "What enemy of England could be considered an enigma?"

"She is talking of Napoleon!" Prudence cried, dropping onto a chair and taking her fan from her reticule. "Anne, have you not taken note? This year's Season is quickly disintegrating as more and more members of the *ton* book passage for Europe. And now you will join them."

Anne took a sip of tea before responding. She knew Ruel had not shared the full scope of his scheme with her, and this new information concerned her deeply. "Why is everyone rushing off to the Continent?"

"Because that is where all the excitement is happening! Napoleon was declared an outlaw two months ago, and as you know, all the sovereigns of the Continent have agreed to join forces against him. No one in our Society wants to miss out on the possibility of a thrilling campaign."

"Aristocratic London wishes to participate in a French war?"

"Not participate, silly goose. Observe! Everyone is talking of how gripping it will be if Napoleon throws his army against us!"

Gripping? Anne could hardly believe Prudence's words to

be true, and yet she had heard such whispered rumors herself more than once. It was a fact that she and Ruel were not the only couple making plans to depart England for France. Even his parents, the Duke and Duchess of Marston, were expected to journey there eventually. In early September, Sir Alexander was scheduled to wed Gabrielle Duchesne, daughter of the Comte de la Roche. The duke and duchess would travel to Paris for the happy nuptials, and then all the family would return to England together for the start of winter and the foxhunt season.

"Do you not want to see our men in action?" Prudence asked. "All the officers in their handsome red coats! Oh, it will be simply too magnificent!"

"But, Prudence, you are talking of battles and bloodshed." Anne shook her head. "I cannot think why anyone would hope to witness such violent conflict."

"I should wager you dread encountering our Society more than the French soldiers." Prudence fanned herself. "But you must take comfort on that account, Anne. Sarah commented to me how brilliantly you have deflected the wicked barbs aimed in your direction and reduced them to brief snide remarks. And Mary says you have befriended several of the young wives who have not yet skipped away to the Continent."

"It is impossible for anyone to say I have friends in London," Anne said. "You and your sisters are my only true confidantes. Oh, Prudence, I dread the thought of separating from you."

"Then you may set your mind at ease." Folding her fan, the young woman smiled coyly. "I am to accompany you to France!"

"Truly? But you have said nothing to me of this."

"Sarah and I discussed the situation at length, and of course Mary gave her opinion. We all agree it would be unwise for you to be abandoned to the company of your husband and his companions with no one to defend you. You are too naïve to maneuver through the traps and obstacles the *ton* may lay in your path while in France. And you are still very much in danger from the marquess. Sarah wrote to him yesterday, and he sent a message by return post. He has welcomed me to join your party."

"You will come? Oh, Prudence!" Anne threw her arms around her friend. "Then God has indeed answered my most heartfelt prayers. If you and I are together, nothing can overtake us."

⁂

Shortly before the marquess and his companions were to depart for Brussels, Anne returned from a round of paying calls to discover a note on her dressing table. Picking up the letter, she recognized the dark, bold script at once. It was dated that morning and had been left unsealed.

"My darling Anne," Ruel had written. *"I shall be visiting several of my properties in the country during the next two days, as I told you last night. How dreadfully I shall miss you!"*

Anne frowned. Properties in the country? The marquess had not mentioned anything of the sort the night before. In fact, they had dined at opposite ends of an enormous table in a long, mirrored hall at the home of Lord and Lady Something-or- other. Later, she had been compelled to dance with so many different men she had hardly laid eyes on her husband. This letter was clearly not intended to be private. The marquess expected its contents to have been read and spread about by the household staff. She studied the note again.

"In preparation for our journey to the Continent," he continued, *"I have had your trunks sent out to various clothiers. I hope you do not mind, dearest. I took the liberty of ordering a substantial number of new items for your wardrobe. I am sure you must be pleased."*

Pleased? Anne hardly needed new clothes. She already had more gowns than she could wear in a year. What on earth could this mean?

"Your trunks will be returned to you locked, but please do not fret. I do so wish to see the surprise on your lovely face when you discover what I have selected for you. The thought of the light in your eyes will keep my heart in eager anticipation of the moment when I shall hold you in my arms once again. Until then, do think of me often and remember how very much I adore you. Your loving husband—B."

Anne stared out the window. Properties in the country. Clothiers. Locked trunks. It must have something to do with his scheme. But what?

Determined to discover at once the meaning of the letter, she debated whom to approach. Sir Alexander, of course, would know everything his brother had planned. But the thought of meeting privately with the young man held no satisfaction whatsoever. Anne knew she could expect insult from him at the very least, for his demeanor toward her had not changed since their encounter in the garden at Marston House. Sir Alexander considered his brother's wife nothing better than a conniving little bedbug, and she knew she could never trust him.

Mr. Walker would know Ruel's plans, as well. Anne decided she must find him at once and ask the meaning of the message. If anyone could be depended upon to speak the truth, it was the Indian. Anne drew a blue muslin pelisse over her white morning dress and hurried out into the corridor and down two flights of stairs to the library.

From that room she knew it was possible to see all the back garden, the kitchen garden, and part of the drive. If Mr. Walker were anywhere about the property, she probably could spot him through the library windows.

Anne pushed open the door and stepped into the room. Instantly she realized the window draperies had been drawn apart no more than half a foot, and a slender, silhouetted figure stood peering between them.

"Excuse me?" she said softly.

"Oh!" Prudence whirled around and dropped the curtains. She flushed bright red, as though she were a child caught with a finger in the pudding. "Anne, is it you?"

"Prudence? What are you doing at Marston House? Why was I not told of your arrival?"

The young woman exhaled. "I . . . I was simply . . . you see, I spoke with Sarah at breakfast this morning just before she went away in her carriage to make the rounds at Hyde Park. I told her . . . I said I thought I might stroll across the green to see . . . to speak to you."

"Ah." Anne studied the blushing girl and the hastily drawn curtains. "But somehow you were distracted from your mission?"

"I was indeed. The prospect from this window is very fine."

"Yes, it is." Anne walked toward the window. "I was just coming down to speak with someone myself. Have you seen Mr. Walker today?"

"The blacksmith? Perhaps he went away with the marquess to tour the country properties."

Did everyone know *everything* about her personal business? Anne wondered. She had barely had time to read the note herself, yet Prudence already knew of its contents.

"I doubt Mr. Walker journeyed with my husband. A companion was not mentioned in a note to me." Anne stepped to Prudence's side. "Lord Blackthorne has written a most puzzling message. I should like you to read it, Prudence, but it is too dim in here to make out the words."

As she took hold of the curtain, Anne suddenly realized she might find someone hiding behind it. Someone her friend very much did not want her to see. Someone tall and dark. Someone who had spoken of love in a corridor and had held a weeping woman in his arms.

It was too late for hesitation.

She grasped the curtain and pushed it aside. No one stood behind it.

Anne let out a breath of relief. What if Mr. Walker had been there? How dreadful to discover such a thing and then to be forced to confront the two of them. She must learn to be more circumspect.

Prudence scanned the note. "It appears quite sensible to me."

"Aye, but what of the locked trunks and the mysterious clothing orders? And why does he write to me so lovingly when I have hardly had a kind word from him of late? I should very much like to speak to Mr. Walker, for I am sure he would know the meaning of it all. Perhaps he went for a stroll. My husband tells me he is partial to daily meanderings along the Serpentine."

"Indeed, for Mr. Walker says the summer green of Hyde Park and the beauty of the river put him in mind of America," Prudence said. "He grew up along the . . . oh!"

Catching herself, she clapped her hand over her mouth. Anne gazed into the olive green eyes and shook her head.

"Prudence, what have you been doing?"

"Mr. Walker speaks often of his homeland. I think he wishes to return there."

"You are seeing him in secret," Anne said. "You are going to France with our party because you wish to be near Mr. Walker, and you have . . ."

A sniffle stopped Anne's words. Prudence had begun dabbing her eyes. A wisp of golden hair had escaped her bun and lay on her shoulder in disarray. Her shawl, a lovely scrap of lace with long fringes, dropped to the floor at her feet.

"Oh, Prudence." Anne stepped forward and took her friend's hands. "I should not have spoken to you so boldly. The affections between you and Mr. Walker are no business of mine. Please believe I never meant to cause you unhappiness."

"You must not mind me." Attempting a smile, Prudence tucked her handkerchief inside the hem of her sleeve. "I find things . . . difficult these days. So very difficult."

"Have you and Mr. Walker formed an attachment?"

"No," she said, shaking her head. "He . . . he . . ." Her face crumpled again. "He will not have me. I feel I have finally found the only man I can ever love, and he is determined not to see me."

"He is right to dissuade you, dearest. He is too old, too different, too many things that are very wrong for you."

"Aye, and now . . . now he will go off with you and the marquess and . . ." She pulled out her handkerchief and blotted her cheeks. ". . . and Sir Alexander and pay me no heed. It is a great deal for me to bear."

"You should stay in London, Prudence. Play with Mary's baby girl and take tea with your sisters." Anne squeezed the poor woman's hands, all the while knowing exactly what Prudence intended to do. Her friend could no more turn away from the man she loved than Anne could prevent herself from thinking about Ruel day and night. But it would be a mistake for Prudence to join the party. Mr. Walker could never marry her, and they were smuggling lace machinery—

Lace machinery! That is what was in her trunks. Of course. How could she not have known at once? But how appalling to carry the disassembled loom in her own luggage! What if the parts were discovered by the authorities? Anne herself would be accused, of course. She would take all the blame.

But that must be the very reason she was to carry the equipment. The marquess would never risk allowing himself or his brother to be discovered smuggling. Were his common, ill-bred wife to be caught, Anne could fall to her doom with little discomfort to anyone. After all, her father was already in prison. Such intelligence could be put about Society as a perfect excuse for Anne's illicit activity. *Her father is a common criminal, you know,"* she could hear them whispering. The marquess could cast her off as easily as a snake sheds its skin.

"You have gone quite pale, Anne," Prudence said, touching her arm. "Do sit down and let me ring for tea. I am afraid I have upset you with my tears."

"No, it is something I have just realized. Something . . . dreadful."

"Has it to do with my accompanying you on your tour?" Prudence seated Anne in the leather sofa near the window and sat beside her. "I must go with you, you know. I have no reason to stay at home. Sarah and Mr. Locke are so much in love, and they have their tea enterprise and charitable ventures to oversee. Mary and Mr. Heathhill are besotted over their daughter and hardly talk of anything else. And I . . . well, I have nothing here. I must go with you. I know I can never truly have him, and I shall . . . I shall let him go." She bit her lower lip and dabbed at her eyes. "I shall let him go, as I must. But not yet, Anne. Please, not yet."

Anne watched in a daze as the sobbing woman did her best to dam the river of tears pouring down her cheeks. Prudence truly believed herself in love with Mr. Walker, though Anne was a bit skeptical. Prudence had always enjoyed scores of admirers, and Anne felt certain she would recover her senses in time. Anne had known her far too long to doubt it. Yes, Prudence was miserable, but Anne knew no one could possibly feel as terrible as she did at this moment. No passing affection for the latest in Prudence's long line of beaux could compare to the reality that Ruel Chouteau, Marquess of Blackthorne, was perfectly willing to betray his own wife.

"I must go back to Trenton House," Prudence whispered. "I should not have come here today."

Anne put out her hand. "Are you well?"

"I am all right. And I shall behave myself on our journey. That is a promise." She tucked her handkerchief away once again. "Thank you, Anne."

As Prudence walked across the carpeted floor, slipped out of the library, and shut the tall door behind her, Anne lifted her eyes to the window. Rising, she leaned against the glass and studied the long rows of clipped hedges in the garden outside. Ruel really was the scoundrel Prudence insisted he was, and Anne must never forget it. Never mind his hypnotic kisses and teasing words. Never mind his warm hands and tender looks. He was a rogue with no more scruples than a common criminal—a man who would use his own wife to smuggle goods and then let her take the consequences if discovered.

Prudence, Sarah, and Mary would nod knowingly if they were ever to understand how correct they had been all along. Anne shook her head, then she stiffened in surprise when she saw her friend step out from behind a hedge onto a patch of green lawn in the garden beyond. The next instant she was joined by none other than Mr. Walker.

"Oh, Prudence!" Anne gasped.

Bonnet cast aside, Prudence threw back her head and laughed. Her hair of pale gold shimmered in the bright sunshine. She stretched out her arms to the blacksmith, beckoning, welcoming. After only a moment's hesitation, he took both her hands. She swung backward, lifting her face to the sky.

Anne had never seen anyone so radiant. The young woman glowed. Her cheeks had blossomed into pink roses, and her eyes sparkled in her bright, lively face.

Anne leaned forward on the windowsill, entranced. The blacksmith said something to Prudence. She laughed and whirled away from him, lifting her skirts in her hands and spinning in giddy circles. His own face transfixed, Mr. Walker set his hands on his hips and watched the young woman, a smile softening his dark, craggy features.

"Prudence!" Anne whispered. "Oh, Prudence, what have you done?"

Golden hair flying, the young woman skipped across the grass toward the blacksmith again and flung her arms around him. With a look that somehow mingled both sadness and joy, he caught her up, swung her around, and kissed her gently.

"Prudence, you are truly in love," Anne murmured. "And Mr. Walker is in love with you."

As Anne let the curtains fall together, she discovered she was crying. She drew a handkerchief from her sleeve and buried her face in it, understanding at last why her friend had wept.

What could be more hopeless than the certainty that a love so rich and true must never be? What could be more numbing than to exist, as Ruel had said of his parents, in a marriage with no common purpose other than getting through life in the most comfortable fashion possible?

Anne pressed her handkerchief into the corner of her eye and stared down at her lap. Existence as the wife of the Marquess of Blackthorne offered at its best nothing better than routine and getting through life. At its worst, it might bring her a prison sentence.

There was only one thing to be done. She must put all romantic nonsense of her husband into the rubbish heap where it belonged, do her best to maneuver through the coming few weeks without becoming trapped like a spider in the marquess's web of intrigue, and then hope . . . wish . . . pray that somewhere, somehow she might find a true love who would lift her up, swing her around in his arms, and kiss her gently on the lips.

❧⊙❧⊙❧

Though fear nearly paralyzed her breath at dockside on the Thames, Anne watched her baggage loaded into the ship's cargo hold without incident. Of course, it hardly mattered if she arrived in Flanders with a lace machine in her trunks. It was not there but in France that both the lace and the looms had been prohibited.

Barely in time to board the same ship transporting his party to the Continent, the marquess arrived from the purported inspection of his properties. By that time, everyone in the group had settled into their rooms. Too angry to confront him about her trunks, Anne avoided her husband at every turn.

The group sailed the short distance across the North Sea from England to Flanders. They then traveled by carriage to Brussels, where they put up in the Gothic fifteenth-century Hotel de Ville near the center of the city. Anne took a large suite next to her husband's rooms, but she could not bring herself even to dine with the man. Though she would have no choice but to accompany him to balls and parties each evening, she refused to consider spending time with him alone. Instead, she ordered all her meals sent up to her, and she watched the city through her long, open windows.

Brussels. Anne could not have been more filled with wonder had she been escorted into heaven itself. Flanders was the birthplace of lace. Each city's artisans had developed their own special techniques and decorative styles. Antwerp lace, known for its vase-and-lilies motif, was called pot lace. It symbolized the Annunciation, for lilies in a pot were shown often in early illustrations of the visit of the Angel Gabriel to the Virgin Mary. At Bruges, the very best lace cravats were made, and no English gentleman of an aristocratic bent would be without one. The marquess himself owned five, though Anne felt humbly certain that her own length of Honiton far surpassed them. Beautiful lace also was made at Ghent, Mechlin, and Ypres. Anne had heard of a parasol cover once made in Ypres using eight thousand bobbins.

But Brussels . . . ah, Brussels! The best of all Flanders lace always had been made in Brussels. Lacemakers in that city used exceptionally fine thread to work the most delicate creations Anne had ever seen. Indeed, she had been privileged to witness such lace only twice in her lifetime. The webbing was so fine that it was easily discolored by a worker's hands. To overcome this, each airy bit of handwork was powdered with either white lead or lime.

Anne treasured the hope of visiting lace schools in Flanders, or at the very least speaking with some of the designers and pattern prickers. She mentioned her desire on their second evening, as she and the marquess were returning to the hotel after a particularly late ball. He informed her that what little lace still was being made in Flanders was created by nuns in closed religious communities.

"Abandon your interest in lace for the time being," he whispered to Anne, leaning against her shoulder as they entered the hotel foyer. "The less you are associated with the subject in people's minds, the better."

"Shall I deny the essential quality of my character for your enterprise?" she snapped in return, annoyed that he must always look so handsome and smell so intriguing when she wanted nothing more than to despise him. "You jeopardize my person with your illicit activities. Will you also jeopardize my very soul?"

Turning on her heel, she started up the stairs. He caught up and took her elbow. "Anne, what are you talking about?"

"I am speaking of the lace machine, of course."

"Shh!"

"I assumed we would depart as all proper smugglers do from Devon—that we should leave from Mount Pleasant Inn in the Warren or from Sladnor House near Torquay. I imagined us slipping away from England into France with our cargo secreted on some small boat. Instead we sailed gallantly away from London as though we had no other purpose than a pleasure tour. We are smugglers, are we not, Lord Blackthorne? Villains whose true mission is to transport a lace machine?"

"*Will* you be quiet?" He opened her door and shoved her roughly into the room. "Do you want the whole of Brussels to know our plan?"

"*Your* plan."

"Your own life is at stake in this, Anne."

"Thanks to you." She tore off her gloves and flung them on a side table. "Where is the loom?"

"It is better that you not know the exact location."

"And why is that? So I may be properly shocked when the authorities in France open my trunks and discover your machine neatly packed away among my possessions?"

"Lower your voice, please." He stripped off his coat and tugged his cravat loose. "What leads you to believe the loom is in your luggage?"

"Is it not?" She walked over to the stacked metal-and-wood boxes and gave the bottom one a swift kick. "Locked, are they? Filled with a brand-new wardrobe for your darling wife, are they?"

"Did you not believe my letter to you?"

"Not a word of it."

"Of course not." He drew a set of keys from his pocket, pulled one from the chain, and tossed it atop the nearest trunk. "Open it, then."

Anne stared at him. Could she have been wrong? He had not truly bought her new gowns, had he? Of course not.

"Open it," he repeated. "Go on, Anne. Open the trunk."

✍ Thirteen ✍

"Have a look at the glorious machine I hid in your trunks," Ruel said, gesturing at the locked chests.

Suddenly unsure, Anne eyed them warily. Pandora's boxes? Would she open them to find beauty and delight in the form of a hundred new gowns—or all the evils of the modern age worked in the shape of hard, cold machinery? All at once she was not certain she wanted to see what was inside at all.

"If the loom is not in my baggage," she asked the man who stood so cocksure before her, "where is it?"

"As I told you, it is better for you not to know." He took a step toward her and slipped his hand behind her neck. Warm fingers pressed against her skin. "Are you frightened, Anne?"

She clenched her jaw against an unbidden shortness of breath. "I prefer to know what is to befall me."

"What is to befall you is nothing more than the Duchess of Richmond's ball. It takes place tomorrow night, the fifteenth day of June, 1815, and it will be attended by some two hundred persons. I feel certain you will look magnificent in one of your many new gowns."

"And after the ball?"

"Another ball. And then, perhaps another."

"I cannot bear this game of endless waiting!" She jerked off her headdress of ostrich plumes and diamonds. "I am suffocating in feathers and silk. When will we go to France?"

"When the time is right. As the daughter of a minister, Anne, you should know better than anyone how little control we have over our lives. No one can really determine his own fate." He tilted her jaw upward with his thumb, forcing her to meet his eyes. "We shall go to France when the situation there warrants."

"Are you to be the judge of that?"

"I am doing what I believe to be right and prudent. Please trust me."

"Have I any choice? You claim we have no control over our lives, yet you control everything about me. You say where I may go and when. You predetermine how I must behave and what I must say. You regulate everything about my existence from what I do each day to how I dress. You even lock my trunks to keep my own clothing from me! I feel as if I am hemmed in by walls of your construction—a prisoner to your every whim."

"Far from it." His mouth fell into a grim line. "Far from it. Though you may feel confined by our present situation, I am no more able to capture you than a man can capture a hummingbird."

"You speak in riddles."

"Hummingbirds are found in America. They are small,

very bright, totally entrancing. Their wings move so quickly they cannot even be seen as the little birds hover to sip nectar from red and orange flowers. A man is free to observe them and to be both enchanted and mystified. But to make a hummingbird a prisoner? Impossible."

Disturbed by his words, Anne found she could no longer meet his eyes. She turned away and went to the window. Was it possible her husband was as tormented as she by this impossible marriage they had made?

Opening the curtains, she looked down on the tree-shaded boulevards and imposing monuments that characterized the city. She had hardly admitted to herself the torture of endless hours in his presence—unable to touch him, hardly able even to look at him. She felt as though she were burning up inside, like a volcano on the verge of eruption.

How could she endure another ball? He would take her in his arms and hold her tightly. She would smell that maddening scent of cedar and spice that clung to his skin and clothing. She would hear the rumble of his deep voice inside his chest, feel the warmth of his breath against her ear, and look into eyes whose messages of desire belied every glib and careless word of his mouth.

Everything about the man was familiar now—as common to her as her own reflection in a mirror. She knew the exact breadth of his shoulders, knew the solid ripple of the muscle in his arm, knew the curl of his hair at the back of his neck. She knew what made him laugh and what made him angry. She had memorized the shape of his hands with their long fingers—large, strong, and far too brown to be fashionable. She was intimate with the ridge of toughened skin on the middle of his palm where he had labored at some task in America of which he would not speak. The veins that coursed down his arms like narrow blue ropes had held her spellbound. Even the crop of short black whiskers that he daily shaved away were as familiar to her as old friends.

"You asked if I were frightened," she said softly. "Indeed, I am. I am terrified."

"Why?"

Could she tell him? Dare she admit that her own feelings for him disturbed her beyond words? Could she let him know how deeply it had hurt to believe he might have meant to betray her if the authorities discovered his detestable machine? Could she tell him how she ached at the things that separated them—their conflicting beliefs, their values, their backgrounds? Of course not. She could reveal nothing. She must go on playing their game of charades until he finished what he had to do and could cast her aside.

"Anne?" he asked, touching her arm. "What frightens you? You must tell me."

She swung around, replacing her anguish with anger. "You and your friends continue to play at silly balls and parties as though the arena of war were nothing more than a picnic ground. Everyone in your elegant Society has come to Brussels as they would flock to a cricket match or a game of croquet. Are they so completely ignorant of the potential for violence here?"

When he said nothing, she forced herself to meet his gaze. "I do not believe you have known violence, Lord Blackthorne," she said in a low voice. "But I have."

He frowned. "You?"

"You must not forget my father is a Luddite. I observed the

secret meetings of his fellows, heard their plans, witnessed the fire of righteous indignation burning in their eyes. I saw those men take their hammers and their axes and rush to the factories. And I saw them when they returned—bloodied, injured, ultimately defeated."

She held her folded hands to her lips, lost in memory.

He laid a hand on her shoulder. "Anne, I shall protect you, whatever we may encounter."

"So you say. But you must understand that the passion to right wrongs stirs deeply within my own blood. I know what sort of ardor leads to war. I myself feel convictions so strong I would fight to the death to defend them." She lifted her head. "I cannot believe that the forces of Napoleon in France and the companies of English and Prussian troops stationed here in Flanders are willing to lay down their lives for a cause so unworthy as to be made a spectacle of by the aristocracy. For those soldiers and for the people they defend, the issues at stake have nothing to do with balls and parties. These are men who would kill and die for what they believe. We are wrong to treat their cause so lightly."

"Do you understand their cause, Anne?"

"I do not, nor do I care to. I only know that to dance blindly into the midst of their war as though waltzing through a ballroom is a mistake. To believe we can transport ourselves and our great load of lace machinery across a battleground is foolish. If we undertake an outing into the open country—me garbed in a silk pelisse and satin gown, Sir Alexander in his cossacks and vest, you in your tall hat and polished boots, and Prudence with her silly . . . oh, we shall be cut to pieces, and we shall deserve it."

Ruel pushed his hands into the pockets of his trousers and began to pace. "You are right, of course. Again, I have failed to give your wisdom and insight the credit they deserve. No matter how my Society might wish to view the wife of a marquess, I know you are no giddy debutante. Like the hummingbird, you are aggressive and fearless in the face of attack."

"I have witnessed violence," she said in a low voice. "I understand it. I shall never passively allow myself—or anyone else— to be injured senselessly."

"I made you a vow on our wedding day," Ruel said, turning and taking her shoulders. "I swore to protect you, Anne, and I shall."

"You have made me far too many vows—few of which you have kept."

"What promise have I broken?"

"You swore if I married you, you would return my lace. You have not done so."

Letting out a breath, he turned away and stalked to the trunk. "If you will not unlock it, I shall." He inserted the iron key, gave it a turn, and stepped back. "Open the trunk, Anne."

She drifted to his side, curiosity conquering her uncertainties for the moment. Bending, she grasped the heavy lid and lifted. The moment she saw what was inside, she gasped. A gown of fragile blue satin lay draped across a length of white silk. Like nothing she had ever seen, the garment shimmered in the lamplit room. Its low neckline had been edged with delicate white lace, and the puffed sleeves were trimmed in a pale gold fringe. From the short gathered waist, a divided overskirt of blue crepe cascaded down in luxurious folds. And carefully stitched to the very center of the satin slip, in prominent view, lay . . .

"My lace!" She caught up the dress and hugged it to her bosom, her dark mood suddenly vanished. "Oh, this is the most beautiful gown I have ever seen!"

"I am pleased you like it."

"So I do!" She laughed in spellbound disbelief. "You had my lace worked into the gown! I can hardly believe it!"

"I could not very well go traipsing into France with a panel of elegant Honiton in my pocket, now could I?" He grinned. "Besides, it is your lace, and I promised to return it to you."

Immeasurably relieved, Anne skipped across the room to a tall gilt-framed mirror in the corner. "This is splendid. Magnificent." She laughed again, turning this way and that with the gown held in front of her. "And it is a soft sky blue! My favorite shade. Oh, sir—"

"Ruel." He crossed his arms, as if forcing himself to keep from taking hold of her again. "My name is Ruel."

"Just see how the fabric sets off the lace. It is perfect! I might have created it for this very gown." Aglow with delight, she smiled at him. "Thank you. Thank you for the gown, and thank you for keeping your vow to me. I felt sure you would never return this lace. I thought you meant to keep it forever. After all, it does bear your crest."

"And yours."

"Yes," she whispered. "Mine, too."

⚬⚬⚬

Ruel watched Anne as she laid the new gown across the trunk again. He was pleased at her happiness over his gift. At the same time, this woman he had bargained into a sham marriage confused him to no end.

When confronted by his brother about Anne's nerve and stamina, Ruel had defended her with utmost confidence. The closer they came to the moment of adventure, he had predicted to Alexander, the more alive and fiery she would become. Anne would plunge into her role with relish and would be a key to the success of their lace manufacturing venture.

Instead, she had grown almost fragile. With candlelight now silvering her face, Anne had transformed again into an angel. Her brown hair, caught up in rosebuds and ringlets, tumbled down her back. Her gown, a wisp of pale violet crepe over a satin slip, draped softly to her ankles.

Ruel tried to convince himself that he was impervious to regarding this woman with anything but courtesy and respect. But as he observed her, he again took note of the feminine form that had mesmerized him all evening at the ball. She was soft and gently curved, and the constant urge to hold her tormented him.

If he came too near, he would hear her words, smell the scent of lavender on her skin, and want to touch her. Want it too much. Did she want him?

"I believed that you had put the loom into my trunks," she was saying.

"Why did you suppose such a thing?" he asked, stepping toward her despite the warnings in his head.

"I believed that if the trunks were opened and the machinery discovered, I should be forced to take the blame. I believed you would betray me into the hands of the authorities with little compunction. Now I feel as if I have betrayed you."

Without thinking, he drew two fingers down the length of her arm. "Anne, I must ask you to trust me without question in the days to come." He took her hand and wove his fingers through hers. "When the moment comes for us to leave Brussels, things may happen very swiftly, and not at all as you expect. I cannot predict each event and its consequence. If I tell you everything I plan, you may fall into danger yourself. There are those who . . ."

"Who what?" she asked softly.

"You are no fool, Anne. You are aware I have enemies who would rejoice in my downfall and would think nothing of using you to bring it about. It is for your own protection that I must keep you innocent of certain things. And protect you I shall, no matter the cost. But I must have your trust."

Anne looked into his eyes. "You have kept your vows," she replied. "That is certainly a start."

"I have not kept them all, and you well know it." He fingered a ringlet that curled down to her shoulder. "Resisting the temptation to touch you is quite impossible. I find your eyes alluring and your lips far too sweet. Can you release me from that promise, Anne?"

She held her breath as he trailed the tips of his fingers up the side of her neck. "To what end?"

"I should like to kiss you again. This time away from the eyes of family and friends." He took another step, bringing her lightly against him. "Anne, may I?"

"Yes," she said quickly. "I mean *no*. It is . . ."

Her protest faded as he slipped his arms around her and

247

pulled her close. His hands tilted back her head, her eyes drifted shut, and he kissed her. Pure bliss.

She slipped her hands over the rigid muscles in his arms. "Yes," she murmured. "Oh, yes."

"Dearest Anne, you are magnificent!" Ruel found he could no longer speak in riddles or tease her with meaningless tripe. The fortifications in their civil war—the ritual, the formal talk, the polite nothings—had been breached.

"Anne . . ." He spoke against her cheek. "Anne, this pretense between us is maddening. Touching you, holding you . . . I am the one who has lived imprisoned."

"No more than I."

"You are my wife . . . my desire . . . and I cannot heed the consequences of it."

As he kissed her again, he tried to remember what those consequences were. He could see his brother's angry face . . . the shocked expression of Prudence Watson . . . his mother's dismay. . . . He knew it must be a mistake to care so deeply for this woman.

But the only real consequence of his kiss was utter wonder at this beautiful creature trembling in his arms. A delightful consequence. A magical consequence.

His heart slammed against his ribs as he felt her sigh against his neck. Would she allow him to take her as his wife? He hardly dared to hope.

"Anne," Ruel said, "I have never . . . never in my life . . . desired a woman as I desire you."

He could hardly believe he had said such words, and yet they were true. The way she melted into him had torn every scrap of logic from his mind. Reluctantly he drew his mouth from Anne's and traced the horizon of her shoulder with his lips. Her skin felt like pure silk.

"Ruel." She gasped, clutching his hand. "I cannot bear it. I can hardly breathe."

"Do not try." He tilted her chin with the curve of his index finger. "Stay with me, Anne. You are my wife. That I desire you cannot be wrong. That I touch your flesh can only be right. . . ."

"I am a maiden," she whispered.

He looked into her honeyed brown eyes and understood for the first time what those words meant to such a woman as she. A maiden. Untouched. She had never cast herself lightly into any man's bed. That she would even consider giving that gift to him tore at his heart.

"Anne," he ground out, "I will never take what you cannot freely give."

"I find it impossible to reason," she managed. "My mind has completely ceased to function."

"Dearest, most beautiful wife." He smiled as he kissed her. "Anne, look at me. Look into my eyes. Know what you possess and who dares ask for such a gift."

"I know." She smoothed her hands over his shoulders. "I know you, Ruel Chouteau, and I cannot think beyond the heaven of your kisses and the silver in your eyes. Yet, how dare I pay more heed to my own desires than to reason? Until our wedding was sealed, I had failed to seek God's will. But now I have prayed mightily about you . . . about us. I dread to think that anything we do might bring harm."

"You speak of a child. Could an heir to my family line be regarded as anything but precious?"

"I fear for the future of such a child. Yet, my father taught me that all things work together for the good of those who love the Lord and are called according to His purpose. I have been heedless and headstrong in the past, but the Lord has not forsaken me. Indeed, He has forgiven me and will do so again and again. No matter how many times I fail Him, He will never fail me. How can I believe that anything less than good will come of our union?"

Ruel shook his head as he gazed at her. "You paralyze me, woman. One moment you dizzy me with desire . . . in the next breath you quote Scripture. You are some sort of inexplicable, unexpected miracle. Perhaps you are right. Perhaps there is a God after all. And perhaps He has planned something good even for such a man as I."

"Of course He has," Anne said softly.

"Come, then."

He took her in his arms. As her head fell backward and her arms tightened around him, he realized she had given him her answer. Yes, she wanted him, would have him at any cost.

Sweeping her into his arms, he let out a sigh of joy. "Anne, my Anne."

A sudden sharp rapping on the door interrupted their embrace. Ruel flung it open to reveal a footman. "Begging your pardon, Lord Blackthorne. Your brother bade me summon you at once."

∽ *Fourteen* ∽

Perhaps what had happened the preceding night had been but a dream. Anne rose from her bed, lifted the gown she had worn at the ball, and breathed in the scent of the man who had held her. Until Ruel was called away abruptly, it had been wonderful. His words of passion had led her to believe he truly cared for her. She had expected him to return to her room. But he had not.

Had Ruel changed his mind about her? In his brother's company, had he been forced to see Anne as Sir Alexander did—a conniving bedbug? Had the possibility of a baby suddenly become real to him? a child with all the consequences an heir might bring? Or had something happened to his plans for the lace machine?

Hearing in her mind the echoed refrain of his words of commitment and desire, Anne moved numbly through her day. She bathed. Dressed. Ate. Made three calls. Changed clothes again. Received two calls. And then it was time to dress for the Duchess of Richmond's ball. In all that time, she neither saw her husband nor was told what had become of him.

Anne put on the blue lace-trimmed gown and sat while her lady's maid arranged her hair in curls and ringlets. During the day she had turned over in her mind what she might say to Ruel when she saw him that evening. "Let us pretend we never spoke last night." "Do not worry. We shall not be alone again." Nothing sounded right.

And then word came that the carriages had arrived, and Anne was awaited. As she carried her skirts down the long staircase to the foyer below, she could see Ruel engaged in conversation with his brother. His face intense, almost angry, the marquess hammered his palm with a fist. Anne's stomach twisted in unhappy anticipation of the moment she must face him again.

In the midst of Sir Alexander's equally agitated response, Ruel suddenly lifted his head, and his eyes focused on Anne. His grim mouth went slack, the gray in his eyes deepening to charcoal. He pushed past his brother and strode to the bottom of the staircase as he regarded the approaching woman.

Palms damp inside her gloves, Anne managed the last few steps without tottering. "Good evening, Lord Blackthorne." It was all she could say in spite of her hours of rehearsal. He looked unbearably handsome. Single-breasted black coat with gold buttons, white waistcoat, starched cravat, black breeches, black stockings, and black gold-buckled shoes—he might have been a king, for all Anne knew. With his black hair and searching gray eyes, he cut a figure like that of Sir Lancelot who had entranced fair Guinevere.

But Blackthorne was no knight in shining armor. He was an angry marquess who doubtless regretted his lowborn wife. She must not forget it.

"My lady," he said, removing his tall hat and taking her hand. Before she could descend the final step, he bent and kissed her fingers. "I have never seen you more radiant." He lowered his voice and spoke against her ear as he escorted her across the hotel foyer. "Only once have I seen you so beautiful. Last night."

"Ruel, I—"

"Where is that redskin?" Sir Alexander growled. "The ball began more than an hour ago. Ruel, have you seen the fellow?"

"Lady Blackthorne," Ruel said, handing Anne to his brother, "Alex will escort you to the carriage. I must see what delays our reluctant Mr. Walker."

Before Anne could respond, Sir Alexander was escorting her out into the cool evening, where a line of carriages stood to receive ball guests. It would be a night like all the others, she knew, yet somehow everything felt different. Ruel had been much too polite. The normally bustling streets were silent, as if everyone had paused in anticipation of something. Hotel guests moved in purposeful solemnity toward their carriages. The air seemed to crackle around Anne's ears.

"You have bewitched him," Sir Alexander spat as he hustled her down the walk. "Do not lie to me. Everyone says it is true. My brother has bedded you, has he not?"

Flushing, Anne tried to pull her arm free. "If your brother wishes you to know his business, sir, he will tell you himself."

"You cannot deny it, can you? Then it is true! Blast it all!" He pushed her up the carriage step and through the door.

Shoving her against the seat, he uttered a string of vile curses. "You seduced him, you little wench!"

Anne recoiled. "I have never seduced anyone."

"Bah! That is utter rubbish!" he hissed into her face as he sat down beside her, crushing the blue gown. "You intend for your own son to inherit the duchy. Are you with child? Tell me!"

He grabbed her shoulder and wrenched it until she cried aloud. "I shall thank you to ask Lord Blackthorne what it is you wish to know! I am nothing in this but a pawn, as you well know, and I shall not—"

"Lady Blackthorne?" The blacksmith stepped up into the carriage. Seeing Anne's face, he paused. "Are you well?"

"Mr. Walker." Anne flicked open her fan. Stirring the air around her face, she tried to catch her breath. "Do take a seat, sir. How fine you look this evening."

Regarding her curiously as he folded his tall body into the carriage, the older man ran a finger around the inside of his stiff cravat. "I prefer my collarless shirt and leather breeches." He leaned toward her. "Are you feeling all right? The injury to your leg . . . does it trouble you?"

"No, I am . . . I am well enough."

"Walker, a fine evening for a ride, eh?" Ruel entered the carriage. "Anne and Alex, you must be especially good to our American friend tonight. He has come only at my sternest insistence, and I am afraid he is feeling rather more foreign among us than usual."

Sir Alexander moved to the seat opposite Anne, but his eyes never left her face. As the horses drew the visiting aristocracy down the streets of Brussels, Ruel took Anne's hand. She stared at their twined fingers, well aware that such action meant her husband was returning them to their charade. He would feign adoration all evening. She must smile and laugh and swoon against his shoulder. All the while, she would know how deeply he must regret the turn his life had taken.

The house rented by the Duke and Duchess of Richmond was a grand structure, large and somber on the outside but inside a gilded masterpiece of marble columns, crystal chandeliers, and statues. Nearly every member of London's upper class and what must be half the officers in the British military gathered in the large ballroom with its rose-and-trellis-patterned wallpaper.

Uniformed gentlemen mingled with feather-bedecked and diamond-spangled ladies around long tables on which silver platters held enough food to fill everyone twice over. Rising above the comestibles, gold statues of Grecian women lifted trays laden with grapes, quinces, figs, cherries, and strawberries. Swags of roses and ivy draped from the elbow of one statue to the elbow of another. Fountains gurgled. Above all, saturating the very air, swam the strains of waltzes played by a large, liveried orchestra.

When Ruel began to greet acquaintances, he slipped an arm around Anne's waist. "This is my wife," he introduced her. Then again, "My wife, the Marchioness of Blackthorne." And again, "My wife."

Cringing inside, Anne pasted on the best smile she could muster. *"My wife."* For a few moments the night before, she had almost dared to believe his words. Yet they were merely a rote recitation from this same drama he had played with her so many times. She had been a fool to think his avowals held any essence of truth. Like his brother, he must detest the very idea that his rash marriage might threaten the family legacy.

Despite Anne's unease, she had no choice but to join Ruel as they strolled through the ballroom, meeting colleagues they had recently seen in London and enduring introductions to countless members of the Brussels elite. Royalty fairly infested the place. The Duke and Duchess of Richmond chatted with the Duke of Brunswick, who bounced the little Prince de Ligne on his knee all the while. Talk of Napoleon mingled with inquiries about health and holiday plans.

The arrival of the Duke of Wellington, commander of the allied armies, produced an excited stir. With his patrician nose and strong jaw, the duke cut an imposing figure as he strode into the ballroom a good two hours late. Anne noticed that Mr. Walker took advantage of the hubbub to fill a plate with bread and fruit and escape through a pair of long, glassed doors. She would have traded her title to do the same. Prudence, she noted, was nowhere to be seen inside the crowded room.

Ruel moved to Anne's side as people gathered around the Duke of Wellington to fawn over the handsome military leader. In his uniform adorned with jeweled medals, bright sashes, and loops of gold cording, he seemed to carry all of England's majesty with him. Having led his troops to victories in India, Hannover, Portugal, and Denmark, he was considered a masterful soldier. His success in the recent Peninsular War against Napoleon had earned him the gratitude of the regent, along with large estates, cash awards, and the title of Duke of Wellington. Now that Napoleon had escaped

Elba and returned to France, Wellington's powerful presence in Brussels captivated everyone in the *ton*.

When the dancing began anew, Ruel guided Anne across the crowded floor. "I must speak with you alone for a moment," he said in a low voice. "Walker told me he witnessed my brother treating you roughly in the carriage tonight. Can that be true?"

"Sir Alexander . . . he questioned me." She glanced up, but the look in Ruel's eyes made her turn away quickly.

How dare he gaze at her with feigned adoration? She could never take lightly what had happened between them, and he knew it. She had been willing to surrender herself completely, irreparably. Did that mean so little to him? His easy ability to slip into the role of doting husband infuriated her.

"Alex questioned you about what?" He took her elbow and turned her toward an alcove near the long windows. "Anne, you have no obligation to speak to my brother about anything. What occurs between you and me is none of his affair."

"Ruel, people are beginning to stare at us."

"Let them." He slipped his hands behind her head and tipped her chin up, forcing her to meet his eyes. "Last night I found him drunken and angry and filled with foundless accusations. I do not care what he thinks. Nothing matters but—"

"Someone is coming." She looked over his shoulder at the three men approaching the alcove. "Ruel, please. Talking can only make things worse between us. I acknowledge my own responsibility in what occurred last night, and you may rest assured it will never happen again."

"Never hap—?"

"Blackthorne." One of the three men tapped him on the shoulder.

His dark brow furrowed, Ruel swung around. "What?" Seeing who stood there, he let out a breath. "Droughtmoor, Wimberley, Barkham. Good evening, gentlemen."

"We have come to speak with you, sir."

"As you can see, I am busy at the moment."

"This is a matter of utmost urgency. We can wait no longer."

"No longer? I returned from America three full months ago, yet you choose to address me only now?" He lifted one eyebrow. "Ah, yes, I forget myself. You have been absent from Society in London these past months, Lord Drought- moor. How we all have regretted the absence of your charm- ing company."

"Enough of your nonsense, Blackthorne," Droughtmoor said. "We have an item of business to attend."

"In such a place as this? Sirs, you will forgive my bluntness, but this is a pleasure ball. I have only lately arrived with my bride, and I intend to spend the evening dancing with her. Matters of business are not on my agenda."

He made as if to lead Anne away, but Droughtmoor grabbed his arm. "You know very well why we have come, Blackthorne, and if you think you will escape our mission this time, you are sorely mistaken. You have besmirched each of us in a method most unforgivable, and we require recompense."

"Besmirched you, have I?" Ruel squared his shoulders. "Droughtmoor, your inability to resist the bottle has black- ened your name far more effectively than I ever could. Barkham, your dalliances with ladies dwelling in the West End of London are far more condemning than any indiscretions your wife may have committed before her marriage to you."

"Upon my word!" Barkham exploded.

"And Wimberley," Ruel continued. "Dear old Wimberley. Your fondness for gaming surpasses my own. Unfortunately, you are famous only for your outstanding losses. Equally unfortunate, you failed to abandon your fondness for cards when it became clear they were ruining you, while I have had the good sense to relinquish gambling to the faded recesses of my past."

"Now then, Blackthorne—," Wimberley began.

"Gentlemen, far be it from me to take credit for besmirching your honorable names. You have succeeded admirably without my assistance."

Ruel took Anne's hand, but before he could lead her out of the alcove, Droughtmoor stepped in front of him again.

"Vile man," he spat. "Do not think your fine words will release you from your debt. This time you cannot flee to America. I am calling you out."

Ruel turned, a slow-burning anger suffusing his face. "Anne, perhaps you would like to go and speak with the Duchess of Richmond's daughter for a moment. I understand Lady Georgianna has been eager to make your acquaintance."

Handed the opportunity for escape, Anne suddenly knew she could not take it. Ruel had been called out. A duel. She studied the hard angle of his jaw and understood at once the gravity of the matter. If he were to retain his honor, he could not decline.

"Excuse me," she said in a low voice. Leaving the alcove, she headed straight for the long French doors.

Were Ruel to face Droughtmoor in a duel, he might be killed. The thought of it ripped through her stomach like a knife. No! She could never let it happen. Spotting the black-smith alone at the far end of the walkway, she lifted her skirts and ran to him.

"Mr. Walker, you must come inside at once!"

"Lady Blackthorne?"

"Three men are confronting Ruel in the ballroom. One has called him out and means to kill him! You must stop them, I beg you!"

"I shall do what I can."

In moments, Anne had directed Walker to the knot of men gathered in the alcove. She knew she should stand aside. But how could she? Ruel was her husband. No matter in what way he cared for her, she cared for him. More than that. She had given her heart to him. She loved him.

"Dear Lord, help!" she whispered in prayer as she started toward the men. She had to do something. Had to stop this madness.

"Tomorrow morning, then." Droughtmoor nodded at Ruel. "Pistols."

"At first daylight."

"No!" Anne cried. "No, Ruel, you must not—"

Her words were drowned by a shout. "War! A message has come. Napoleon has crossed the Sambre. He has taken Charleroi by storm and is now marching toward Brussels!"

"War!" A cacophony of shrieks and screams erupted. Music faltered. The dancing stopped. Disorder broke out at the long tables. A lady swooned. Another collapsed into the arms of her partner.

As the room erupted into chaos, Anne clutched her fan and stood on tiptoe, searching for Ruel among the swarm of men. The Duke of Brunswick leapt to his feet, dropping the toddler prince to the floor. The Duchess of Richmond clutched her throat. Soldiers dashed to gather around the Duke of Wellington, who stood in earnest conversation with the messenger who had brought the news. Through the open windows, the roll of drums began to thunder through the night air. Trumpets called out from every part of the city.

"Anne!" Ruel caught her around the waist. "Stay near me."

"Oh Ruel, will Napoleon really come to Brussels?"

"Brussels and then Vienna, if he has his way. Wellington will oppose him."

"But Miss Pickworth says Napoleon has amassed two hundred thousand troops. Wellington has far fewer men—and less than a third of them are British."

"Hang Miss Pickworth. What does a Society maven know of war? The Russians are on their way through Poland to assist him. Austrian troops will join Wellington, as well."

"The Austrians are needed in Italy!"

"Never underestimate the Prussians. Field Marshal Blücher is a canny man."

As he spoke, a second courier arrived. People made way to allow a caped soldier to approach Wellington. The man presented the duke with a leather packet, and the Englishman opened it. He scanned the documents enclosed, then lifted his head.

"Napoleon has attacked Field Marshal Blücher," Wellington announced. "Due to the considerable force of the enemy, the battle has become serious. As reported earlier, the French have captured Charleroi. Now I am told they have gained some advantage over the Prussians." He paused, looking around at his officers. "The English will march in support of our allies. Gentlemen, prepare to depart the city at once."

Amid gasps and cries, Wellington strode out of the ballroom. Most of the uniformed men went with him. A few stayed behind to take a hasty leave of their wives. Women hurried to help their husbands, fathers, or brothers gather their belongings. In confusion, half the orchestra remained and began to play some frantic little tune. The other half rushed to join the departing troops.

"Droughtmoor!" Ruel spotted his accuser as he and Anne joined the throng pouring through the doors. "What of your challenge?"

"Tomorrow at dawn!"

"Impossible. We are leaving the city tonight."

"I shall have my revenge, Blackthorne!" Droughtmoor vanished into the corridor and was lost to them in a flood of pushing, shoving people.

Ruel wrapped his arm around Anne's shoulders and pulled her close. "We must return to the hotel at once." He spoke against her ear so she could hear above the tumult. "Our plan begins immediately. A plain gown, black shawl, and bonnet lie in a paper-wrapped box inside your trunk. Put them on, pull the shawl over your head, and go downstairs. Miss Watson will join you, but explain nothing to her. No one must recognize either of you. Walker, Alex, and I will carry down the baggage. A vegetable cart will arrive at the back door of the hotel. Get in and pay the driver with this money. Do you understand?"

"Yes." She nodded as she took the wallet he handed her.

"After the driver has taken you to safety, send him away and wait with Miss Watson until we come. Have you seen Walker?"

"He is over there." Anne lifted her hand to point out the tall man in the throng, but the blacksmith was already pushing toward them, his eyes wide and his mouth open in a cry of desperation.

"No!" he shouted. "No!"

Anne smelled black powder just as Ruel crumpled onto her. She heard nothing but the roar of the crowd, saw nothing but the spurt of crimson blood that burst before her eyes, felt nothing but the weight of the man dragging her down to the hard marble floor.

"Blackthorne!" Walker bellowed as he threw himself across his fallen friend.

Anne lay pinned beneath the marquess, unable to move. A foot stepped into her hair. Another tangled in her dress, tore the fabric, hurried on. Someone leapt over them. She tried to breathe, tried to speak, and found she could not.

"Lady Blackthorne?" The weight lifted off of her, and a hand slid under her neck. "Are you injured?"

"No," she said with a gasp. "Ruel?"

"He has been shot in the face," Walker said. "Blackthorne, lie down. You are bleeding."

"Anne! Where is she? I cannot see. Someone find my wife."

"I am here." She pushed out from under him, wiping at the blood that dampened her own face. "Ruel . . . oh, dear Lord, please help us!"

"Are you hurt, Anne?" He grabbed her shoulders hard. "Did the ball strike you?"

She stared into his face. His right cheek had been slashed open, ripped downward into a gaping flap of skin. Blood poured from the wound, covering his white cravat and waistcoat.

"Walker!" she screamed. "Walker, you must help him!"

As she cried out, the blacksmith was tearing the cravat from around his own neck. "We must find a physician," he said, pressing the white cloth against Ruel's wounded face. "This will need to be stitched."

"Ruel? Good heavens, what happened?" Sir Alexander dashed up and crouched at his brother's side. "A saber?"

"A coat pistol," Walker barked. "Fetch a doctor, sir, I implore you."

"They will all be leaving with Wellington. Walker, who did this? Was it Droughtmoor? Did you see?"

"I saw only the pistol. A moment before it was fired." The Indian scooped Ruel into his arms. "We must return to the hotel."

"I shall sew him myself," Anne said. "The Lord has given me skill with a needle."

Dabbing tears and blood from her cheeks, she followed the men down the steps to the waiting carriage. Prudence emerged through the crowd and caught Anne's hand as all around them the city continued to erupt. Bugles sounded. Drums thundered. Horses clattered through the streets. Men loaded baggage wagons, and soldiers harnessed artillery trains. Officers rode toward the Palace Royale while foot soldiers marched along with knapsacks on their backs and rifles on their shoulders. Flags went up, and children cried.

⌒⌒⌒

"Bleed him," Sir Alexander commanded. "If you do not bleed him, he will die."

Walker settled Ruel in the back of the open cart and wrapped a blanket around the semiconscious man. "He can lose no more blood, or he surely will die."

Seated beside Prudence, Anne tucked the frayed and blood-spattered blue silk gown around her legs and lifted Ruel's head into her lap. At the hotel, she had not had time to put on anything except the black shawl, and she hardly cared. Sir Alexander had spent the hour there dosing Ruel with laudanum. Mr. Walker tried to stanch the flow of blood while Anne carefully stitched the terrible wound in his face.

She had worked in spite of her horror. The ball had entered from the front, just to the side of Ruel's nose, and had torn its path of destruction all the way to his ear. Though the cheekbone had just been nicked, the flesh had been sliced raggedly all the way to the teeth. Had the pistol been aimed an inch to the left, Ruel would be dead.

"Mr. Walker speaks the truth, Sir Alexander," she said firmly. "You must trust your brother's treatment to the blacksmith now. He knows how to keep the wound clean and prevent infection. Ruel has lost far too much blood already. A bleeding would kill him."

"You think this redskin can save his life?"

"He saved mine."

"And we are very grateful for that." With a snort, Sir Alexander slapped the side of the wagon. "Go on, then, all three of you. Take my brother to France. I shall meet you in Valenciennes, as we planned. Two days."

"Give us three." Walker climbed onto the wagon's seat and took the reins. "We may have trouble."

"Does Ruel know any mode of existence other than causing trouble? Gaming, smuggling, being shot by angry assassins bent on revenge?" He shook his head. "Be at the fountain in Valenciennes in three days, or I shall ride for Paris."

"Paris?" Anne stared at him. "You would not search for us? But you know we travel directly toward the French border just behind Wellington's troops. Anything may happen."

"How do you suppose I shall get to Valenciennes myself? Fly?"

"You are armed and on horseback, sir. We have nothing to protect us but this old cart filled with half-rotted vegetables."

"At least you will have something to eat." Still wearing his evening clothes, Sir Alexander slipped his foot into the stirrup and swung onto his horse.

"Why will you abandon us, my lord?" Prudence cried out suddenly. "Your brother needs you."

"I merely follow Ruel's own command to me. In fact, Mr. Walker and I were originally scheduled to journey together. My brother wished to travel separately to arouse the least amount of suspicion toward your trunks there."

Anne stared at the baggage in the cart. "But . . . is the lace machine in my trunks?"

"Of course. Where did you suppose it was?" With a flick of the reins, Sir Alexander spurred his horse. "Three days, Walker, or I am off to Paris and the arms of my fiancée. Gabrielle Duchesne has been waiting far too long."

Anne stared at the man's back as he vanished down the alley. Then she turned to the trunks lying amid piles of cab-

bages and baskets of green peas, strawberries, and early potatoes. "Mr. Walker," she whispered, "is the loom truly in these
trunks?"

The Indian jostled the reins and set the two horses to pulling the cart toward the sunrise. "Yes, Lady Blackthorne. Not
many days before we left London, Ruel returned to Tiverton
and packed Mr. Heathcoat's unassembled lace-making
machine inside the trunks. It has been with us all along."

"With *me*, you mean." She let her focus drift down to the
man whose head lay on her lap. Sleeping from the laudanum,
Ruel looked nothing like the devil she knew him to be. A
tangle of dark curls fell over his pale brow. Thick black lashes
lay like twin fans on his cheeks. The lips that tilted so easily
into a cynical curl had softened. Only the wound that slashed
across his cheek reminded her that this man was scarred both
outwardly on his flesh and in the depths of his black heart.

He had lied to her. Dared her to open the trunks. Counted
on her to trust him. Counted on her to believe his every word
and not to use the iron key he had tossed so casually onto the
trunk lid. She had trusted him, of course, especially when she
saw the blue gown packed at the top. She had trusted him,
fallen into his arms, loved him.

The cart rolled out onto the main road, and Walker steered
the horses toward a little town called Waterloo.

⤜ॐ Fifteen ॐ⤛

They had traveled fewer than five miles when English soldiers
put a halt to the journey. Camped along high ground near the
main road into Brussels, the troops wanted no interference
from wandering vegetable sellers. Seeing the wounded man in
the cart, they sent the four sojourners to wait out the expected
confrontation with the French in the stone barn of a land-
owner named Hougoumont, whose château had been con-
verted to an English stronghold.

While Walker tended Ruel, Anne and Prudence climbed to
a window in the top of the barn and studied the French troops
camped fourteen hundred yards away on the opposite ridge, a
place they had called La Belle Alliance. Hearts hammering and
palms clammy with helplessness, Anne and her friend witnessed two horrific battles that day. Both times, Napoleon's
men forced their enemies to retreat. Even though the French
fell short of a complete victory, the allied troops suffered
countless casualties. Gradually the barn filled with wounded

men, and the two young women went down to help Walker and the military physicians who arrived to treat the victims.

All the following day, the seventeenth of June, rain poured, turning the hard ground to deep, sucking mud. Lightning slashed across roiling gray skies while thunder shook the barn's thick rock walls. Wellington's men assured Anne that this was a wonderful omen. Every one of the duke's peninsular victories, they told her, had been preceded by violent storms. This hardly encouraged a woman who put her faith in God and not in atmospheric portents.

Inside the barn, soldiers sat in clusters, talking, playing at cards, singing. Others helped tend the wounded. Plans for engaging the enemy in battle were abandoned, for the rain made fusils, cannons, and most of the other weapons useless.

When night fell, Anne sank onto a pile of dank hay beside the vegetable cart. Mr. Walker and Prudence sat in the hay together, the woman lying half asleep on the older man's shoulder.

"So . . . how is he?" Anne asked.

"Who?" the blacksmith returned.

"The marquess, of course."

"I am surprised you care. You have not visited your husband's side a single time today."

Anne closed her eyes and let out a breath. "As you and Prudence both know very well, Lord Blackthorne is my husband in name only."

"He would not agree."

"How little you understand him, then."

"I know him better than I know any man. In you, Lady Blackthorne, he believes he has found the healing of his heart."

"Only God can heal a man so villainous as my husband." Anne let out a bitter laugh. "Healed, indeed. This is a man who elected to store contraband in his wife's baggage. A rogue who would see her turned over to the authorities and thrown in prison should her trunks be opened and the lace machine discovered."

Walker sat up, his dark eyes piercing. "Is this what you believe?"

"How can I think otherwise?"

"Have you looked at the trunks since we began our journey from Brussels, madam?"

"No." Anne glanced at Prudence, whose pale face shone in the darkness of the barn. "I have been tending the wounded."

"Your name was painted over, Anne," Prudence whispered. "I thought you knew. A new name and direction were inscribed on the trunks."

Her pulse racing, Anne scrambled to her feet and took hold of the iron spokes of one of the cart's wheels. Pulling herself on tiptoe, she peered into the wagon bed. Lying on a pallet of rough blankets, the Marquess of Blackthorne turned his head to gaze at her.

"Mr. Hezekiah Cutts," he said in a low voice. "Tailor."

Anne's focus darted to the trunk. The name Ruel had spoken was newly inscribed. "Tailor?"

"Tailor." His mouth twisted into a pained grin.

When he spoke, she could see how difficult it was for him to form the words, yet she stifled any feelings of compassion. She intended to hear how he would explain himself. "Who is this Mr. Cutts? Where is he?"

"He is right here before you, lying in a vegetable cart with his face half peeled away by an assassin's ball. I am the tailor, Anne, although you are much handier with a needle. After Droughtmoor shot me, I had no time to tell you about the disguises we were to take on. I am Hezekiah Cutts, a poor tailor traveling from village to village, and these trunks contain my wares—gowns of every size and hue."

"Gowns." Her voice held disgust.

"Gowns," he repeated. Then he dropped his voice. "False-bottomed trunks are the smuggler's stock-in-trade, you know."

Anne frowned. "And Mr. Walker?"

"Walker is our friendly village vegetable seller. Prudence is his wife. And you, I trust, are still mine."

Anne tightened her fingers on the wheel spoke. "Why did you lie to me?"

"I have never lied to you. You asked me that night in Brussels if the machine was in the trunks. I gave you the key to open them and discover the truth for yourself. You chose not to." He shifted on the hard-plank wagon bed, a grimace contorting his face as pain shot through him. Touching the bloodied bandage on his cheek, he lay still for a moment, breathing hard.

Then he turned his gray eyes on her. "I wanted you that night, Anne. I knew if I told you about the loom you would be angry with me on too many counts. I am well aware you despise my intended industry, and you disdain my machine and all it stands for. I also understand you feared I might betray you if it were discovered. But far more important to me, I knew your safety depended on your ignorance. It still does. I cannot forgive my brother for telling you about the trunks' contents. It was not his place to do so. The machine is my responsibility, and I alone intend to bear the consequences of my deeds."

Confused, unwilling to believe he told the truth now when she had been so certain he was a liar, Anne studied the vivid discoloration showing at the edges of Ruel's bandage. "You already suffer the consequences of your deeds, my lord."

"What do you mean?" He bolted up, staring at her for a moment, then suddenly grabbed her hand. "Will you now abandon me?"

"I speak of your wounded face." She pulled away. "Lie down. Your exertions may cause you to bleed again."

He slumped back onto the pallet. "Send Walker to me, will you please? I need something for the pain."

Anne stayed at his side for a moment, watching the agony write shadows and lines across his face. How dare her heart ache for him? How dare her heart beckon her to crawl into the cart and curl up against him and lend him her warmth? This was a man who relied on no one but himself—his own wisdom and his own strength. In that, he was too much like her for any good to come of their union. But at least she *tried* to pray. Impetuous and sinful though she was, she made an effort to be obedient to God. Her father had spoken of the changes the Holy Spirit brought about in the life of one who submitted to Christ, of how a person's old sinful nature was destroyed and a new creation took its place.

Anne believed with her whole heart that she truly had given herself to God in this way. But she could not deny that her stubborn, impulsive will too often asserted itself. How many times must she confess her failings, only to turn around and sin all over again? She could comfort herself only with the knowledge that St. Paul himself had endured similar struggles. He had admitted to the Christians in Rome that while he really wanted to do what was right, he did not do it. Instead, he did the very thing he hated, because he was still sinful and rotten inside.

As bad as she was, Anne always reminded herself that she must try to live as Christ commanded. His power—and not her own—freed her from the holy wrath she deserved. But Ruel never even made an effort to behave in a Christian manner. He simply did whatever he wanted. He was a man others tried to kill, a man who thought nothing of breaking laws for his personal gain, a man who easily might betray those who loved him most.

Loved him? Yes, it was true. Terribly true, and Anne loathed herself for it. Mr. Walker said she had made Ruel a new man. In fact, Walker insisted she had brought Ruel a healing of the heart. Without doubt, Anne believed that through Christ's love, lives could be changed, sinful creatures born again, black hearts washed as white as snow. But could one lowborn woman—admittedly stubborn, impatient, and far too selfish—actually aid the Almighty in healing a man's heart? Was there hope for such a transformation in a man like Ruel Chouteau, the Marquess of Blackthorne?

"Hezekiah," she said softly. "Do you know the meaning of the name you have chosen?"

Ruel's eyes fluttered open. "No."

"Jehovah strengthens." She reached out and gently laid her hand over the wound on his face. "Be strong in the Lord."

Dawn of June 18 brought new trepidation to the band of travelers as the sun emerged on the horizon and the rain stopped. Ruel lay dazed, helpless, and increasingly frustrated in the back of the cart as Walker called out news from the window of the old stone barn filled with wounded soldiers. On the opposite ridge, the highly trained French troops had begun to assemble and prepare their artillery. Far outnumbering the seventy thousand English soldiers, Napoleon's two hundred thousand men were openly contemptuous of their rivals. They shouted insults, taunting the English that any battle between them would be no more difficult than eating breakfast.

Ruel sensed growing trepidation in the two women. Prudence Watson whispered to Anne that she believed the French taunts. Anne tried to calm her friend. Just as Prudence was insisting she wanted to go home to Trenton House and see her sisters and read Miss Pickworth's latest advice on the proper way to eat peas, the enemy attacked.

Walker cried out that Napoleon's brother, Jerome, led the assault down from La Belle Alliance, across the valley, and up toward the château of Hougoumont. Four full regiments—highly trained and brilliant in their tactical skills—charged Wellington's fusiliers. They stormed the stone houses and steadily fought all the way up to the courtyard of the farm.

As the French burst through the old iron gates, Prudence shrieked in terror and ran into the blacksmith's arms. While the enemy poured into the courtyard, Walker beckoned Anne, and the three of them climbed into the old vegetable cart with Ruel. If the barn itself were taken, he had told them earlier, they stood little chance of surviving the assault.

Around them soldiers fell and cannonballs exploded. Clods of dirt flew into the air as men cried out in pain. Bullets rang against the barn's walls and shattered the stone into bursts of razor-sharp shards. The four travelers huddled together, clutching each other. Prudence wept. Anne prayed. Walker hovered over Ruel, tried to protect the women, and darted to the window to check on the status of the battle.

At noon, Walker cried out that a miracle had occurred. The defending British somehow had managed to repel the better-armed French. But the rally was short-lived. Wellington's men had hardly taken time to regroup when a thunderous cannonade announced the second advance of the French infantry. The ground shook, and the air around Ruel's ears vibrated. Covering her head, Anne could no longer hold back the trembling that overtook her.

"Dear God, please save us," Prudence sobbed. "We shall all die! We can never hold them back this time!"

Anne squeezed her friend's hand. "Take courage, Prudence. Death is hardly the worst thing that can happen."

"Oh, Anne! How can you be so calm?"

"My wife is quite prepared to die," Ruel uttered from his pallet. "She spoke those words to me once, and I have never forgotten them." He inched up onto his elbows and attempted a wink. "Mrs. Cutts, would you care to accompany me upstairs to the loft? I believe our party shall find greater refuge there than here."

With effort, he rolled to a sitting position, took out his ring of keys, and unlocked one of the trunks. He lifted out a small firearm and pulled it to half cock. Then he handed it to Anne. "This is a coat pistol. It is loaded; aim well before you pull the trigger."

He removed three more weapons and a powder flask from the trunk before locking it again. "Another coat pistol for Miss Watson, also ready to shoot, a blunderbuss for Walker, and a German Jaeger rifle for me. Shall we go up?"

"Blackthorne, the laudanum dulls your thinking," Walker said gruffly. "You should stay here."

"Walker, you know as well as I what the coming hours may bring. The night Droughtmoor shot me, I vowed it was the last time I would meet any foe unprepared." He forced a lighter note to his voice. "Come along, ladies. Let us secure our own little fortress against the storm."

Walker grudgingly helped Ruel climb down from the cart, and with the ground shaking beneath them, they all made their way up the stone steps to the barn's loft. In an alcove near the window, Walker and Ruel built a rough barricade of hay bales and feed sacks. Gripping her weapon, Anne helped Prudence nestle into the protected corner. Walker knelt beside her, his eyes trained on the stairway for any sign of invaders.

Ruel had no intention of hiding. He had led these people into the midst of this nightmare, and he would not sit by and allow them all to be killed—no matter how prepared Anne was to meet her Maker. He propped one shoulder against the window frame and looked out on the battle.

"You must not overexert yourself." The soft voice at his side was unexpected. "You lost more blood the night you were shot than I knew flowed through any man's veins."

"Did you believe I would die?" he asked, turning. When he looked into Anne's face, he saw that the pink had washed from her cheeks in fear, but the light of determination burned brightly in her brown eyes.

"Yes," she said.

"Did you care?"

"Yes," she said again, then looked away for a moment. "As I recall, you were unwilling that I should perish of my leg wound. You brought Mr. Walker to take care of me. As the recipient of your benevolence, how could I wish for you to die?"

"Tit for tat, then."

"If you wish to believe I would press your flesh together with my bare hands, stanch your blood, and pierce your skin with a needle merely from a sense of obligation, I can offer nothing to counter your opinion." She lifted her chin. "By the same token, if you wish to believe I would willingly ride into the thick of battle simply because I bear your title, or covet your inheritance, or long for more gowns and jewels, I can say little to sway you. And if you think I would have given away my innocence for nothing more than a night of pleasure, how can I convince you otherwise? If I have learned one thing about you, Lord Blackthorne, it is that you will believe as you please, think as you wish, and do exactly as you see fit."

"Is that so?" He reached out and fingered the tattered gold fringe on her sleeve. "Then you believe yourself powerless where I am concerned? How very wrong you are."

As she looked into his eyes, Ruel realized for the first time that his desire for this woman went beyond comprehension.

And what a place of misery he had brought her into. Her lustrous hair hung limp and tangled against the rough black shawl around her shoulders. The blue gown bore splatters of blood—his own blood. While expecting betrayal at her husband's hands, Anne nevertheless had sewed up his wounds and followed him into the unknown.

"What manner of creature are you?" he asked in a low voice.

"You know exactly who I am." Her eyes narrowed, and she set her hands on her hips. "Ruel, you must come behind the barricade. You are not well, and I fear you will—"

"Anne, listen to yourself!" Overwhelmed that she would continue to place his welfare above her own, he took her into his arms. "Dear lady, if you should die . . . if I have led you to this . . ."

"Shhh," she whispered, laying her cheek on the rough fabric of his coat. "Please do not distress yourself."

He knew he should release her. Christian charity could have motivated her ministrations to him, but how could she feel anything in her heart for him beyond animosity? Her words to him in all the weeks of their marriage had held little but repugnance. She had instructed him not to touch her, told him she disliked him, accused him of betrayal, and repeatedly referred to his black heart.

Why then did he want nothing more in life than to hold this woman? Hold her forever . . . smell her hair against his nose, stroke the smooth skin of her arms, enjoy the musical lilt of her voice, taste the sweetness of her lips . . .

"Anne, I beg you to forgive me for bringing you to this," he choked out. "Were it within my power, I should see you taken far away from here. Back to Nottingham, if you like. I should grant you that stone house of which you dream. A lace school. Hedgehogs in the brush and gray stone with curling moss."

He stroked his hands over her thin shoulders, memorized the feel of her skin. He could not bring himself to wish her a farmer or a weaver for a husband. No matter how deep her distaste for him, he wanted her as his wife. He loved her. He loved her, and he would tell her, no matter the damage to his already battered pride.

"Anne—"

"Dear God in heaven, have mercy upon us!" Crying out a desperate prayer, she pulled from his arms and dropped onto the stone sill. "Look out, Ruel. They come!"

"Get back!" He pushed her away from the window and grabbed his rifle. "Walker, take Anne! Guard the women."

Leaning against the window, Ruel looked out onto the sight that had terrified Anne. Sixteen thousand infantrymen, rifles shouldered and sabers flashing in the sunlight, swept down from La Belle Alliance and rushed across the valley toward Wellington's fusiliers. Despite Wellington's brave defense, the French surrounded the second of the two farms occupied by the British.

"Napoleon has stormed La Haye Sainte," he called out. "Wellington sends his own infantry against them."

He watched as the two armies clashed and men fell. The acrid scent of gunpowder drifted through the air as shouts and screams of pain mingled with the report of rifles. Minutes ticked by, and neither side made headway.

"What now, Blackthorne?" Walker called.

"Wellington is sending out the cavalry."

"Who rides?"

"I can just make out the Scots Greys and Life Guards . . . and there charge Inniskillings and the King's Dragoons." He paused, taking in the incredible sight of the huge British warhorses straining forward and whinnying as they galloped against the enemy. "Wellington is forcing back the French! . . . Yes, Napoleon's men are retreating . . . fleeing across the valley! Wellington is pursuing. He has captured two of their standards and several guns!"

"Thank God!" Anne cried. "Ruel, should we take the cart and escape this place?"

"Impossible. There are far too many soldiers in the fields. Wellington's cavalry is still chasing the French." He paused, his breath hanging in his chest while the horses thundered up the hill toward La Belle Alliance. "Dash it all! Can they not see they must turn back? Sound the retreat! Napoleon will call in his reserves!"

Ruel stared in helpless frustration as the giant horses churned the mud across the cornfields, their riders crying out, "For England!" and "Scotland Forever!" The trumpeters called the retreat again and again, but the dragoons rode on. Ruel watched in horror as his fears were realized—Napoleon's reserve troops turned on the British.

"Too late!" he cried out. "Too late to turn back. Napoleon's men and horses are fresh. The French lances are far longer than our short swords. Our cavalry is doomed!"

The minutes slipped into hours as Ruel called the agonizing news of the battle to the others in the alcove. "Their cannons are slaughtering us . . . blowing our men to pieces.

The Lancers are mowing us down, unhorsing and mutilating us! . . . Killing our men as they try to crawl away."

"How many are dead?" Anne asked.

"Three hundred Greys at least. I count only a few dozen riding to safety."

"Where is Wellington in all this?"

"He rides among them, here and there, rallying the Brunswickers, leading the cavalry back into position. He is magnificent. But the devastation is too great."

"Are we wholly defeated?"

"The British center holds, but only just."

"And the Prussians? Where is Blücher?"

Though it had seemed impossible that Wellington's allies could reach the battleground in time to lend their assistance, Ruel finally spotted the Prussians advancing down the road from a great distance.

"Blücher is coming." He glanced at the others. "I can just make him out."

"He is too far," Walker said. "To hope for victory would be preposterous."

"I fear as much. The French are better trained, and their guns are superior. Now . . . now Napoleon comes at us again! Upon my word, I recognize Marshal Ney himself! His cavalry is charging La Haye Sainte again. Look, he rides straight into our guns! What a fool! I cannot believe it!"

Unable to stay in hiding any longer, Anne joined Ruel at the window. He drew out his pocket watch. It was six o'clock in the evening and drawing toward dusk, but the orange light revealed the enormity of Ney's error as his light cavalry rode directly into a wall of British musket fire. As the Frenchmen were mowed down by their much underarmed foes, Ruel made his decision.

"The fields are blanketed with smoke and fog," he told Walker quietly. "Mud disguises nearly everything. Every able-bodied man left in this barn is using the chaos to make an escape. We must join them."

With Prudence protesting and Anne half numbed with the horror of what she had witnessed, the men urged the women down the stairs and into the wagon. "You and I shall guard either side of the cart," Ruel instructed Walker. "Shoot any man who comes at us. Anne, you and Prudence must lie down in the midst of the wall of trunks. They will barricade you from the bullets."

"Who will lead the horses?" Anne asked. "You will never be able to shield us and guide the cart through the sticky mud at the same time. I shall take the reins. No, do not even attempt to argue with me, Ruel. There is no choice in this matter. You know as well as I that the horses will never go willingly into such conditions."

She pulled her shawl around her head and clutched the leather reins. "Shall we go?"

Ruel breathed the first prayer he had prayed in twenty years. "Dear Lord, I have failed You in many ways. But now I beg You to protect us. Please guard this woman I love so dearly. And if You can accept me, allow us to have a life together." Lifting his rifle against one shoulder, he fought the pain in his cheek. "Lead out," he said as he urged the horses through the barn doorway.

The horses pulled the cart across the courtyard littered with bodies, and into the battlefield. Coughing in the smoke, Anne jerked on the reins, attempting to guide the cart toward shelter in the nearby forest. The two horses tossed their heads in fear. Walking wounded staggered toward safety. Riderless horses, crazed with terror, galloped aimlessly, colliding with the onrushing cavalry. Scattered corpses blocked the path, and Ruel fought to keep the cart moving.

"Walker!" he shouted as a steaming horse bolted from nowhere and across their path. His voice was lost in the explosion of a cannonball not ten yards away. Clods of wet dirt splattered over him. Prudence lifted her head in an agonized scream. Deafened by the cannonade, Ruel heard nothing.

He looked up at Anne. Chin set, she flicked the reins across the horses' backs. Her loose hair streamed behind her. Mud peppered her face and gown. Glancing down at him, she nodded encouragement. "It's all right," her mouth seemed to say, forming words he could not hear.

"Anne!" He wanted to tell her, had to tell her of his love for her. As he spoke, another missile exploded directly in front of the cart. The horses shied, threw back their heads, bolted. "Anne!"

He struggled to hold the harness, but the horses tore it from his hands, pulled away, and thundered straight toward the battle lines. Sprinting through the fog, Ruel could just make out the cart lurching toward the line of Wellington's fusiliers, who somehow still held the French forces at bay from fewer than two hundred yards.

"Anne!" he bellowed. He plunged through a cloud of smoke, chasing the runaway horses, leaping over fallen men, sloshing through mud. Walker ran at Ruel's side two paces away, his expression stoic.

"Anne!" Ruel shouted her name until he was hoarse. She never turned. In the hazy twilight he could just make out Prudence clambering onto the seat beside Anne, grabbing at the reins, attempting to control the horses.

A cannonball exploded in front of the two men. They both fell, lay stunned for a moment by the shock waves, then scrambled to their feet and continued to run. Bouncing, jolting over ruts, the cart again vanished behind a wall of smoke as another ball exploded, then another.

Ruel looked to his side. Walker had disappeared. He ran on toward the front line. Anne. Had to get to her. Had to save her. A bullet zinged past his ear. Another knocked the hat from his head. A soldier tumbled from a horse and fell to the ground at Ruel's feet. Ruel leapt over him and ran on.

"Anne!" He spotted the cart through a clearing in the smoke. It had stopped, tilted crazily to one side. No! Lungs burning, he jumped across a ditch and fell to his knees against a wheel. The two horses lay dead, mangled by a cannonball's explosion. Ruel pulled himself to his feet and reached over the edge of the wagon for the seat. His hand closed on soft blue fabric.

"Come, Ruel!" Walker's voice shouted into his ear, and the Indian appeared at his side. "Nothing can be done here."

As Walker tugged his friend's hands from the cart, Ruel looked into the wagon. Both women lay sprawled across the seat, their faces, hair, gowns spattered with in blood. Breathless, lifeless, they hung like limp mannequins, arms dangling and mouths opened in wordless screams.

"Anne!" Ruel howled her name again and again as Walker dragged him away from the cart, across the muddied fields, and finally into the safe haven of the woods.

Crumpling, Ruel sobbed against the ground as he clutched handfuls of damp earth. He had killed her. Led Anne to her death. Failed the woman he loved, the only woman he would ever love.

"We must get out of this place," Walker urged. "The French are coming."

"I cannot leave her."

"She is gone, Ruel. They both are. You saw them."

"I want to bury her."

"Impossible. It will be done with dignity. Nothing you can do will bring her back, Ruel. We must save ourselves now. Come."

"No." He grabbed the Indian's shirt and twisted it in his fist. "I love her. I love her."

Speaking into Ruel's face, Walker enunciated each word. "Anne . . . is . . . dead. *Dead.*"

"God help me!"

"Yes, God will help us both. He will watch your woman now . . . and mine. But we have been spared. And we have work to do. We must go to Valenciennes and meet your brother. Sir Alexander may yet be waiting."

"No. I shall not go to France." Ruel gritted his teeth.

"To England, then. We can return to England. Your father will rejoice at your safe return."

Ruel shook his head. "I cannot go back to London. London, where she lived . . . the house . . . the gardens . . . the rooms where I loved her . . ."

Walker laid a hand on his friend's arm. In the distance, Ruel could see the Prussian troops arriving to bolster Wellington's forces. Would they be enough? It hardly seemed possible. The French pressed on, driving the English lines back closer and closer to the forest.

"We must go," Walker said. "We must find a place of refuge."

"Refuge?" Ruel lifted his head. *Refuge.* Yes, that was what he needed. Home. "I can think of only one place for my heart to find peace."

"Where?"

Rising unsteadily to his feet, the younger man replied, "Slocombe. I must go home to Slocombe."

∽ *Sixteen* ∾

Spilled sugar. It lay scattered across the tablecloth, a grand mess to be cleaned up before Mrs. Smythe would notice. The sugar sparkled and glittered in the firelight from the cooking hearth. The tea cloth, a smooth expanse of lustrous black velvet, stretched on and on along the huge table. Sugar . . . endless, endless sugar . . . like stars in a deep, ebony night . . .

Stars. Anne sat up. A breath of fog whispered past her face. She shivered. Where was Mrs. Smythe? And the sugar . . .

"Prudence?" she called, but her voice made no sound. Her friend would be near, for Prudence nearly always was seated with her sisters when tea was served. "Sarah? Mary?"

But this was not the drawing room at Trenton House after all, was it? Nor was it the kitchen at Slocombe. Anne looked around her, searching for signs of the familiar fireplace, the long worktables, the black-and-white-tiled floor. Instead of the massive stone hearth and blazing logs, she saw lights in the distance, the flash of swords glinting in the starlight.

Rather than basking in the smell of baking cinnamon and roasting duck, she choked on the smoke. Black, cloying smoke with the scent of gunpowder. In the place of the laughter and fuss of the kitchenmaids, she heard . . . nothing. She heard nothing!

"Prudence?" Her own voice made no sound. She had gone deaf. Panic gripped Anne's heart. This was not the kitchen at Slocombe. This was the battlefield. Waterloo.

"Ruel?" she cried out. Again, she heard nothing, not even the word she had shouted at the top of her lungs.

Frantic, she felt around her, groping, touching. Her fingers fell on something soft. A hand gripped hers, and she screamed. Again, nothing. No sound.

Prudence's moonlit face formed in front of Anne's, a mask of terror. Prudence's lips moved, forming words, but saying nothing. Panic widening her eyes, the young woman covered her ears and shook her head violently at her own inability to hear. Prudence clutched Anne's arms, tears running down her cheeks.

Oh, Prudence! Anne threw her arms around her friend. They must be deaf, both of them. Deafened by the cannonade. The men . . . where was Ruel? And Walker? And look at the poor horses. Dead!

They had to get away from this field of destruction. In the distance, the battle continued. It hardly seemed possible that men were still fighting in the darkness.

No matter what the outcome of the battle at Waterloo, Anne knew she and Prudence had to find Ruel and Mr. Walker. Oh, she could hardly think. If the men were alive, they would be nearby. Or might they have gone on to Valenciennes? And were they alive? Or dead?

No. Anne could not reason beyond her unbearable thirst and the ringing in her ears. Not dead. Ruel was not dead. Impossible.

She set Prudence away from her and pointed toward the forest and safety. Prudence nodded, seeming to understand. Hoisting her skirts around her knees, Anne climbed down from the cart and began to unharness the horses. It was hard, unpleasant work, but determination to escape drove her. Too many times in the past days, she had witnessed near victory, only to see it followed by another onslaught of Napoleon's forces. Though it looked as if the French were retreating and the Prussians and British were racing after them, slaughtering their enemies without mercy, Anne dared not trust her eyes.

Gesturing and mouthing silent words, she indicated to Prudence that they each must capture another horse from those wandering loose on the battlefield. They must take the cart with them into France.

Coming out of her shock, Prudence slipped down to the ground. Together the women trudged around the clusters of dead soldiers until they found two horses calm enough to approach. They led them to the cart, harnessed them, and climbed back onto the wooden seat.

Anne pointed toward the west. "France?" she mouthed.

Prudence's lower lip trembled as she nodded. Anne knew it might be easier to return to Brussels and take refuge there. Even if Napoleon took the city, there would be food to eat, water to drink, and hope for passage back to England. But Anne had no doubt where her heart belonged. They must find the men.

The horses slowly pulled the cart across the gruesome farmland that had become a killing field. Anne shut her eyes, allowing the team to take the lead until she could bear to look again. Her thoughts drifted as she tried to make sense of her situation.

What had happened to Prudence and her in the passing hours? The last thing she recalled, a cannonball had exploded near the cart, and the horses had bolted in fear. Anne remembered Ruel clinging to the harness, running alongside the cart, trying to stop the frightened animals until he could hold on no longer. Though she had fought for control, the cart had bounced and jolted directly toward the front line. Men had been shouting, mud flying, hooves pounding. And then . . .

Oh, then a runaway horse had galloped toward the women. The frenzied beast had crashed full force into the cart just as a second cannonball flew whistling toward them. Falling. Falling.

Anne remembered nothing after that. Not the ball hitting the earth. Not the explosion. Not the cart slamming into the pit created by the blast. Nothing. Where was Ruel during all that time? Had he been killed? Surely not.

Yes. Anne squeezed her eyes more tightly shut against the reality. If he had been alive, Ruel would have come and found her and Prudence. Anne had doubted much about her husband, but this one thing she knew for certain. Alive, he never would have abandoned them on that battlefield.

Glancing at Prudence, Anne saw that her friend must have come to the same conclusion. Prudence sobbed into her skirt, shoulders shaking in sorrow. The men were dead. Ruel, Anne's husband. Walker, Prudence's love. Gone forever.

The moonlit night brought little comfort. The two horses pulled the cart along muddy lanes and byways, westward away from the battlefield and toward France. Anne took turns with Prudence driving the wagon and sleeping in the back amid the trunks. Neither woman could hear the other, but it hardly mattered. Lost in their grief, they had nothing to say.

⋅⋅⋅

Two full days and nights passed before Anne and Prudence crossed the border into France and drove their little cart into the city of Valenciennes. After leaving the carnage behind, they had stopped along a riverbank, slaked their thirst, and washed themselves. The horses also drank deeply and grazed in the tall grass at the water's edge. Though Ruel had taken the keys to the trunks, Anne used a stone to break the lock on one.

The women dressed in two of the simple gowns they found inside—pale cotton garments and soft woven shawls. As they traveled the highway, passing through an occasional village, their hearing slowly returned. Neither Anne nor Prudence spoke French well, and they had no way of understanding the news of the battle. Was Napoleon defeated or victorious? And how would either result affect them—two young English-women in France?

"The fountain," Anne spoke up, tugging on a rein to turn the horses down a street in Valenciennes. "That is where Ruel agreed to meet his brother."

"Sir Alexander gave us but three days to travel from Brussels, and many more than that have gone by, Anne. You know he will have gone to Paris to stay with his fiancée's family."

"Then I shall write him a letter and beg him to come to our rescue."

Prudence studied her gloveless hands. "Oh, what is to become of us, Anne? I cannot have such faith as you that Sir Alexander or . . . or the other men . . . or anyone will be waiting for us."

"I have little faith in it myself. I only know it was Ruel's plan for everyone to meet in Valenciennes. If we have any hope of help, we must find that fountain."

"What then? Do you mean for us to stay here in this enemy land? What shall we do with ourselves in France? We know no one here, and we cannot speak the language. I want to go home. I want to sit with my sisters at tea. I long to see Mary's baby again, and listen to Sarah's calming words. Oh, dear . . ."

"We have little money, Prudence, and we cannot leave until we have made certain whether the men came here or not." Anne surveyed the town with its bustling market, narrow streets, and crowded, half-timbered houses. "Ruel must have planned to meet a person other than his brother in France. He surely had planned that someone here would set up the machine."

"In this small town? It is hardly a commercial center. I presumed he would be going to Paris eventually to join Sir Alexander." Prudence fingered her shawl as she scanned the streets, her eyes brimming with hope. "Anne . . . do you think Lord Blackthorne and Walker are here already? Could they be waiting for us?"

Even as Prudence spoke the words, Anne knew they were impossible. Not only would the men not be here, but she and

Prudence already were in jeopardy. The two women had driven a cart full of contraband lace machinery into a country where the people spoke no English and most were loyal to Napoleon Bonaparte.

"I only know we must find the fountain," Anne said softly. "Perhaps someone will help us there."

As she guided the horses toward the center of the little town, she considered what she and Prudence must do after the reality of their situation became inescapable. It was foolish to believe Ruel and Walker could be there. Sir Alexander would not be there either. No one but God could help them.

They might sell the horses and cart, sell the gowns in the trunks . . . even sell the lace loom. With the money, they would have some hope of returning to England. But what awaited them there? Anne thought of her father languishing in prison. His case depended on the goodwill of the Marquess of Blackthorne.

Without him . . . without Ruel . . .

"There it is!" Prudence cried, pointing. "I see the fountain."

Anne flicked the reins and sent the tired horses the last few yards toward the trickling cascade. Surrounding the fountain, small booths with colorful canopies offered cheeses, fresh strawberries, wooden clogs, and iron pots for sale. Ladies filled shopping baskets with goods while children played in their mothers' skirts. It was a scene that brought Nottingham to Anne's mind, and for the first time in weeks she felt the tension begin to slide out of her body.

"It reminds me of home," she said softly as she pulled the horses to a stop and set the brake. "The houses. The gardens. The market."

"But no one is here. No one awaits us."

"No, indeed." Anne drew her shawl from her shoulders and folded it into her lap. In the quiet of the morning, she could hear birds twittering in the trees overhead. A child laughed.

"Ruel wished this for me, Prudence," Anne whispered, suddenly unable to keep back the tears. "We stood in the barn window at Waterloo watching the battle, and his words took me far away from those fields of slaughter. He told me he wanted me to have a stone house and a lace school and . . . and hedgehogs. Oh, Prudence, I would trade a hundred lace schools to see Ruel again!"

"Anne." Prudence folded her friend into her arms. "He loved you, Anne. He loved you so."

"I cannot believe you," she wept. "How could he have cared for me? I was awful to him! I was mulish and impertinent. I could hardly bear the society of his acquaintances, and he knew it. I learned Society's proper manners and decorous speech, but I never belonged in his world. Worse than my own incompetence was my harsh tongue. I accused Ruel of having a black heart, and I told him I found him stubborn, disputatious, and difficult. I was never anything but trouble to him."

"But he loved you all the same."

"No, Prudence."

"Mr. Walker insisted it was so. He told me of the events that occurred one night at Marston House in London. Do you recall the first evening of our stay there? After dinner, the marquess held you in his arms in the garden outside the drawing room. You said the embrace had meant nothing. You insisted Lord Blackthorne was merely acting out a drama for the benefit of visitors to the house. But much later that night, after Walker had . . . after he had spoken with someone in the corridor . . ."

"With you, Prudence."

"It hardly matters now, Anne. After that encounter, Walker was distressed. He went downstairs to Lord Black- thorne's bedroom. The marquess, too, was distraught. Lord Blackthorne told Walker he was ready to abandon all his dreams for the future if only he could make you truly his wife. Yet he was convinced you loathed him. He believed he could never win you over."

"He said I loathed him? But I did not. I struggled to con- trol my affection for him."

"Walker said he believed the marquess began to love you at that moment in the garden. Already Lord Blackthorne was an altered man, you see. Altered by his acquaintance with you. But not until the garden did he truly love you. From that time onward, though the marquess would not allow himself to acknowledge it, his heart belonged to you and you alone."

Anne shook her head as the marketplace bustled around her. "Oh, Prudence, I never had faith in Ruel's constancy. I believed he toyed with me for his personal gain."

"You were wrong, Anne. Walker knew Lord Blackthorne better than anyone did. He had loved the marquess himself since Blackthorne was but a small, lonely boy loitering out- side the blacksmith forge in Tiverton."

"Madame? *Bonjour.*"

At the heavily accented voice, Anne looked down from the cart to discover a short, wiry man smiling up at her. With a pair of gleaming spectacles perched on his large, hooked nose, he looked to Anne like one of the fairy-tale shoe-maker's elves.

"I am sorry," she said, "I cannot speak French."

"No, no. I have a little English. I see the . . . how you say? . . . the boxes here in your cart. The name is Cutts, and I am waiting for you many days. Hezekiah Cutts? He is with you?"

"No, he is . . . he was . . ." She gestured down the road. "We were separated at Waterloo."

"Waterloo?" The man frowned. "He is killed?"

Anne bit her lower lip. "I fear it may be so."

The man lowered his head and slowly removed his beret. "*C'est la guerre*. Very sad news. Very sad. His brother will grieve."

"Is his brother here?"

"In Paris. He waits for Monsieur Cutts there."

"He waits in vain." Anne studied the little man for a moment. "May I ask your name, sir?"

"I am Monsieur Pierre Robidoux. And you?"

"I am Lady . . . Mrs. Cutts. Anne."

"Your lovely *compagnon de voyage*?"

"I am Miss Prudence Watson." The slender young woman held out her hand. "Pleased to meet you, Mr. Robidoux. Can you tell us, sir, how you know of Mr. Cutts? Were you his friend?"

"*Oui*. His friend and business acquaintance. Perhaps you come to my house? We talk? Eat?"

Anne glanced at Prudence. Clearly charmed by the French-man, Prudence would have leapt at the chance for a glass of fresh water and a loaf of fresh bread. Anne had no such confidence in him. All she could think of were the trunks in the back of the cart and the danger they represented.

"Thank you, but we must find lodging in Valenciennes," she replied before Prudence could protest. "We shall wait here for a few days in the hope that my husband may arrive."

The man nodded slowly; then he spoke in a low voice. "Douai is a better place to wait, Madame Cutts. Your husband sent a letter instructing me to prepare a small house and also a place for your . . . for the boxes in the cart." He regarded her for a moment. "It was his plan."

"How shall I trust your words are true, Monsieur Robidoux? We have only just met."

"Monsieur Cutts told me you were *la belle dame d'esprit.* The beautiful lady of wit." Robidoux favored her with another warm smile. "I tell you this. The name of your new house is the Black Thorn. *Oui?*"

She shrugged. "A good name."

"You are not convinced. Then I tell you this of which I know. I am the finest weaver of stockings in the whole of Nord-Pas-de-Calais. My looms are in the town of Douai near Valenciennes. Mr. Walker, I believe, is the finest blacksmith in all of southern England. And you, *madame*, I am told are the finest lacemaker in all of Nottingham."

Anne clapped her hand over his to stop him from saying more. "Enough. Take us to Douai."

"I shall drive the cart," Robidoux announced as he climbed onto the seat beside the women. "You must think what your husband would wish to happen to his plans now."

"What do you mean?"

The cart turned into a narrow alley. "I mean this, Lady

Blackthorne," Robidoux whispered. "Napoleon was defeated by Wellington at Waterloo. The general was expected to arrive in Paris this morning. There will be an uproar in that city."

"Civil war?"

"But Sir Alexander is there!" Prudence exclaimed.

"Not war." Robidoux shook a finger. "The Chamber will argue about what to do, and perhaps Napoleon will abdicate to his son, Napoleon II. But Fouché, who was Napoleon's servant, also wishes to seize power. Of course, England and her allies wish to put King Louis XVIII onto the throne of France. The struggle for power will be fierce, but it cannot last for many days. A week or two at the most."

"What does this have to do with us?"

"We have only a short time to make our decisions and act on our plans. I believe King Louis will be returned to France by the English within a month or two. By that time our machine must be assembled and prepared to operate. We must be the first to weave lace with the new English machine. We must obtain French patents for the loom. Everything must be done in order, or others will take our place at the front of this new industry."

"But how can we do all that ourselves? Lord Blackthorne is . . . I think he must be dead."

"Even so, you are his wife. Sir Alexander supports us, and he will inherit the duchy in England. Things do not change so greatly, do they?"

"Everything is changed! I have no husband. I have nothing."

"You have all you need, madame. You have the name, the title, the inheritance, and most important, the skill. If you are able to design patterns as beautiful as Blackthorne promised, you and I can develop the most important lace center in all of France here in the region of Calais. We may rival Nottingham itself one day. We have the machines. We have the buildings. We even have the funds your husband established here to begin the work."

"But we do not have him. Lord Blackthorne's vision was behind this plan. It was his dream, not mine."

"Then do this for him. Make his dream come true." He looked into her eyes and gave a solemn nod. "Do this for the man you love."

For a long time Anne rode without speaking. Fear urged her to leave the cursed machine with the little Frenchman and hurry back to England and her mother's arms. If nothing else, she could take another position as a housemaid or a kitchenmaid.

She had not been brought up to smuggle contraband or apply for a patent or manage a business or establish a lace industry. She had no desire to rival Nottingham's lace dynasty, and she could not imagine living in a country that teetered on the brink of revolution. She certainly had not been raised to promote the very machines her father was imprisoned for destroying. Reason told her to leave. Common sense insisted that she abandon the machine and return to safety.

But her heart . . .

She shut her eyes and allowed the jostling cart to rock her body with its rhythm. In her mind's eye she pictured him then. Ruel. His gray eyes beckoned her. The curls of his black hair seemed nearly within reach. She could almost see that familiar grin on his face, one corner of his mouth turned up and his lips twitching with suppressed laughter.

Was he truly dead? The thought of him lying on that grisly battlefield was too much. If he had died, he had lost his life trying to save hers. If that was not a sign of love, what was?

Perhaps . . . perhaps in spite of everything she had said to him and everything lowborn she had brought to their marriage . . . perhaps Prudence had spoken the truth. Perhaps in his own way Ruel had loved her.

If so, what right had she to abandon his dream? Monsieur Robidoux was right. Ruel had given her his name, his titles, his wealth. He had trusted her to be his partner. And he had given his life for her.

Until now, Anne had chosen to act on impulse. She had created the lace with the Chouteau medallion, wed a man she hardly knew, and allowed that man to claim her heart. All without consulting God or seeking His will. She had told Ruel that she believed the Lord could make all things work together for the good of those who love Him. Was this the good that God had brought her to do? To prosper and refill the coffers of the Chouteau family while seeing to her own father's safety? How could she think otherwise?

"I shall stay," she said softly. "Until my husband's goals are achieved and my father is freed from prison, I shall stay in France and help you."

Prudence took Anne's hand. "I mean to stay with you. I have neither the funds nor the courage to get back to England on my own. I am your friend, Anne, and I cannot leave you."

"Very well then," Anne said. "We shall build a lace

machine, and in the name of his son, we shall do our best to restore the fortunes of the Duke of Marston."

Monsieur Robidoux patted her arm. "*La belle dame d'esprit.* Your husband knew you well."

⁓⊙⊙⊙⁓

Ruel leaned over the ship's rail and looked down into the gray-green water swirling below. Beside him, Walker reclined with his back against the rail, his eyes searching the vivid blue sky.

"My life runs in a circle, like the flight of those weary seagulls who follow our ship," the Indian said. "My existence is one of endless repetition. Everything I have loved has been taken from me. My family. My home. The woman."

"I did not know you cared so much for Miss Watson," Ruel said.

"I speak of days long ago."

"You were once in love?"

"More than once. I lost everything then. Now I have lost my world again. When Miss Watson entered my life, I began to believe something good might come to me after all. The woman had such faith in the Creator."

"As did my Anne."

Walker nodded. "Prudence was young and full of hope. So pale and beautiful. You know, she did not care about the color of my skin. She told me I was handsome."

Ruel glanced at his friend. A wry smile was written on the older man's face. Ruel smiled in return.

"You *are* handsome, Walker. You are tall and strong. I suppose in a way you are rather striking."

"I have the face of a buzzard." He gave a rueful laugh and then let out a shuddering sigh. "I loved her, Ruel. Even though I knew she was too young, that her heart would change, that we could never marry . . . I loved her deeply."

"I had no idea your feelings were so strong. I am sorry." Ruel shut his eyes against the recurring image of the two women sprawled on the wagon bench. "At least Prudence knew of your love for her. I never told Anne. Unable to admit it to myself, let alone say the words to her. I had no idea I was even capable of such emotion. I imagined love was a pastime for dandies and women. Romantic nonsense, I always maintained. To me, marriage was an arrangement for social benefit and the procreation of children. Secret liaisons took care of the rest. That was it. All I thought life had to offer. Love? I never believed I had it in me."

"The day you came to see me at the smithy in Tiverton I knew you loved that woman. The look in your eyes was one of terror. She might die, you said. 'You have to save her, Walker.' So I did."

"A lot of good it did her. I led Anne from one catastrophe to the next. Shot through the leg. Tricked into transporting contraband across land and sea. Forced to carry contemptible lace machine parts in her baggage. Obliged to drive a cart through a bloody battlefield. She spent her days as my wife either fending off barbs from those in my Society or ducking lead balls being fired by someone trying to assassinate me. Oh, I did well as a husband, Walker. Very well indeed."

The Indian rested silently against the rail for a long time. His eyes combed the clouds as though he might read answers in them. "All the same," he said finally, "you cannot flee from your responsibility."

"I should let Alex have the duchy of Marston and all that goes with it. He is more comfortable in that world than I have ever been."

"You know Sir Alexander would squander his position. The family wealth will run through his fingers as flour through a sieve."

Ruel studied the waves slapping against the side of the ship. Overhead the masts creaked and the sails snapped. The scent of saltwater stung his nostrils, easing in his chest the agony that had weighed on him like a millstone.

"I shall never relinquish my title," he said in a low voice. "I have lost the lace machine, but I must manage our properties. Believe me, my brother's hands will not hold the purse strings. When I am back in England, I shall again see to my responsibilities there."

"You are wise."

"I am a fool. I had everything, and I could not see it. Now I have nothing. Nothing."

"You are young. Intelligent. Not without means. You have enough."

Ruel slammed his palm on the rail and turned away. Striding down the deck toward the ship's stern, he fought the black mist of hopelessness. What good was youth if he had no one with whom to enjoy the long years to come? What use was intelligence if there was no one to match wits with? Of what benefit was wealth in an empty bed in the middle of a cold night?

Yes, he would go back to England and continue to try to

save the duchy from financial ruin. He came to a standstill on the slick wooden planks and lifted his head to the billowing white sails. But what good was it? What good was anything without her?

⨏ *Seventeen* ⨏

Anne and Prudence moved into a small house in the town of
Douai on the border of France. Like many other homes in the
region of Calais, this one had been built of stone, its walls
plastered white and its steep roof heavily thatched. The two
women slept upstairs in a bedroom with a view of the River
Somme. Anne wrote a letter to the Duke of Marston and
Prudence wrote to her sisters, but with France in a state of
chaos, they could not be sure whether their messages would
reach London.

Using funds previously deposited by the Marquess of
Blackthorne and managed by Monsieur Robidoux, Anne
purchased pots and pans for the cozy kitchen. She furnished
the small living area and bought a table and four chairs for the
dining room. She hired a cook, planted a vegetable garden, and
employed a tutor to teach her and Prudence to speak French.

As the days passed, Anne again learned that though some
might have called her husband a wastrel, he had not earned

that label. Ruel had been no fool. His plan to enrich the duchy of Marston had been a good one, and his trust in Monsieur Robidoux was well founded. The Frenchman was a master stockinger with a profitable weaving business, and a leader in the town. He told Anne he had met Ruel many years before, but their partnership in the lace business had been undertaken solely through letters. Anne felt certain that had he lived, Ruel would have made his enterprise successful.

After settling the women into their house, Monsieur Robidoux had driven the cart into one of his large warehouses on the outskirts of town, opened the trunks, and removed the machinery. He and his employees labored day and night to assemble the equipment. Though the English-made machine had been adapted from a common stocking loom, Robidoux was challenged to figure out its workings and its quirks, learn how to thread it, and, finally, begin to operate it. When the first inch of lace net rolled off the loom, even Anne felt a measure of satisfaction.

While struggling with grief and the very effort of survival in a foreign land, Anne and Prudence eagerly waited for each tidbit of information Monsieur Robidoux brought them from the outside world. Shortly after Napoleon's defeat at Waterloo, their host told them, the emperor abdicated in favor of his son, Napoleon II. But the Chambers denied the young man recognition. As Wellington and Blücher advanced, Napoleon fled the country by sea on July 8, the same day the English escorted King Louis XVIII into Paris.

Though Wellington wanted Napoleon handed over to the King of France, the man managed to board the ship *Bellerophon* and sail for England, where he hoped to solicit mercy from the regent. On July 20, buckling to allied pressure, eight hundred French generals and senior officers surrendered in Paris. Everyone from Napoleon's former regime—his son, brothers, members of the Chambers, and even his foe, Fouché—was expelled from the country. Napoleon's defeat was complete. Four days later, the *Bellerophon* arrived in England near Torbay.

To the surprise and delight of Anne and Prudence, Monsieur Robidoux pointed out to them one day that Miss Pickworth's column of rumor and advice from *The Tattler* was translated each week into French and placed prominently in the local newspaper. Miss Pickworth's reports about Napoleon's lifestyle in English territory appalled Anne. Rather than living in shame, he was treated by London Society as the celebrated emperor he once had been.

"Sightseers in boats surround the *Bellerophon*," Miss Pickworth wrote. "Napoleon's avid admirers call to the elegantly exiled emperor every time he parades on deck. In recent days, he has been moved to Plymouth, where nearly ten thousand gawkers gather around his ship to gaze at him and exclaim on his fine features and magnificent manners. Indeed, Napoleon has charmed everyone in England and is beloved beyond belief."

Magnificent manners, Anne fumed. *Murderer* would be a better description of the despicable man. If not for the French people's fawning admiration of English citizens, she and Prudence would have been mortified to let their nationality be known. Everywhere in France, Napoleon was vilified, while Parisians cheered as British troops marched in parade down the Champs-Elysées.

With the monarchy restored, Hezekiah Cutts's smuggled machine went to work. The sudden voracious demand for lace by everyone from the wealthy aristocracy to the humblest peasants took even Monsieur Robidoux by surprise.

"Lace," Miss Pickworth reported one day, "has enthralled everyone across the Continent."

She was correct.

Anne hardly had time to breathe, and the spectacled little weaver became positively frenetic as they worked to keep the lace machine running constantly. Prudence took it upon herself to become fluent in every aspect of French fashion. Anne was relieved that the dark malaise which once had compelled her friend to leave London in search of solace in the countryside at Slocombe did not return. Despite Prudence's longing for London and her sisters, and though she continued to mourn the loss of Mr. Walker, the young woman fairly threw herself into the tasks of browsing shops, scouring newspapers, and even consorting with French Society in an effort to assist in the new enterprise.

Prudence informed Anne that the war was beginning to influence even the simplest of designs. Within two weeks after Waterloo, men began wearing full-skirted frock coats modeled after military wear. The single-breasted coats featured distinctive Prussian collars without lapels. Wellington's name was given to every type of clothing from coats to pantaloons to boots.

The end of hostilities also brought a tide of new fashions for women. Straight-edged lace went suddenly out of fashion. Blonde lace began appearing on everything from dresses to aprons.

In a headlong rush to escape her memories, Anne flung herself into making Ruel's dream a success. Aware that many of the elderly laceworkers in Calais had abandoned their techniques, and no young women knew the methods, she thought about starting a lace school. She could begin by teaching her students how to embroider the muslin and net that rolled off the machine in Monsieur Robidoux's warehouse. And there might come a day when the more talented employees could begin enriching parts of the white embroideries with sumptuous fancy fillings in needlepoint stitches.

A month after arriving in France, neither Anne nor Prudence had heard a word from London. Anne had expected nothing from the house of Marston. After all, there was no doubt the Chouteau family preferred to pretend that a brown-haired housemaid named Anne Webster had never existed. But Prudence began to grow alarmed. What if something dreadful had happened to Sarah or Mary? What if Trenton House had burned or Mary's baby had fallen ill or Mr. Locke had taken them all to China to grow tea?

Sir Alexander had failed to answer Anne's letter to him in Paris, nor had she received any word from her mother. Miss Pickworth made no mention of the Duke and Duchess of Marston. Indeed, it was as if England and Anne's life there had vanished the moment a cannonball exploded near her cart on the battlefield at Waterloo.

One glowing pink evening just at sunset, Monsieur Robidoux knocked on the door of the house where Anne and Prudence were staying.

"Information regarding the Duke of Marston," the Frenchman said as he presented her a copy of the evening newspaper.

"The family is in London. The duke's son, Sir Alexander, is to marry Gabrielle Duchesne, daughter of the Comte de la Roche, there at the end of the month. Will you go to this wedding?"

Anne glanced up in surprise at his tone. He sounded resentful, almost angry, that she might leave. "I do not know, sir," she replied. "I have not been invited to the wedding, and I suppose . . . I suppose I may not be welcome. Not everyone in my husband's family was pleased by our marriage."

The gentleman took a step closer to her and lowered his voice. "If the duke disavows his responsibility to you, madame, have no fear. I believe our industry here in Calais will grow beyond our dreams. You may be assured of financial comfort, and it is possible that together we may grow wealthy."

"*Merci*, Monsieur Robidoux." Anne dipped a curtsy. How could she explain to him that she had never wanted wealth or security? Her father's health and freedom had been uppermost in her heart for so many years that she had hardly been able to think beyond it. Anne would never be content until she was certain that her family was together and safe. But even then, she knew she could never wish for material possessions. She had tasted the joy of human communion, and she could never forget the man who had held her in his arms. More than that, she had learned the dire consequences of heedless action. God asked for submission, and Anne now longed to be as compliant as a wisp of lace thread woven into something beautiful by His loving workmanship.

"I am an honorable man, madame," Robidoux continued, tugging at his lapels. "I will see to your care. No matter the contents of this letter, you have no need for concern."

"*Bien entendu. Merci beaucoup, monsieur,*" she said softly. As the Frenchman walked down the lane to his carriage, Anne scanned Miss Pickworth's column. Though translated into French, the words were clear enough. Anne shut the door behind her and slipped to a chair beside the fire. "Sir Alexander is to be married in London," she said. "As his brother's widow, I should go."

Prudence took the newspaper and scowled as she tried to make out the information. "It is true!" she said. "A wedding. Oh, London at last!"

"But I cannot go."

"Whyever not? Monsieur Robidoux will not deny us the money for our travel. I want to go home, and you must be at the wedding."

"Alexander Chouteau will not want me there, and seeing his father will only remind me of Ruel. I shall have to answer a thousand questions and try to explain what we were doing at Waterloo. I shall be forced to relive everything. I cannot bear it."

"You must go, Anne. You have no choice. You must represent your husband at his brother's marriage. If you do not attend, everyone will believe you have something to be ashamed of, hiding away here in France."

"I am not hiding!"

"Are you not? You go nowhere but to the warehouse and the lace school. You wear nothing but black dresses day after day. You never attend teas or receptions, though you have been invited to go with me many times. You will not pay calls, and you are reluctant to receive visitors. You might as well be invisible, for all the lightness you display."

"I cannot deny my lack of liveliness, Prudence. These past weeks have been difficult. You lost a friend, but you know what Ruel and I . . . you know we had become more deeply attached toward the end. We were more than partners in a marriage bargain. More even than companions. When Ruel died, I lost my husband."

"Then go to London and sit in the chapel with the Duke of Marston and his wife. Take your place in the family, or they will cut you out of everything you are owed."

"I am owed nothing, Prudence, and you know it. Ruel and I were hardly married under normal circumstances. Everyone hoped I would die soon after the wedding, and when I failed to do so, I was little more than an embarrassment to the family."

"All the same, you must attend the wedding, Anne. It is time for us both to go home to London."

Dropping into her chair, Anne stared at the fire. "Do you want to know something strange, Prudence? At this very moment, I have everything I believed I might have wanted in life. I possess my faith in God. I can take enough money to ensure the release of my father in England. Even this house . . . a little stone house. Do you know . . ." She stopped, struggling against tears. "Do you know, I always wanted a lace school . . . and now I have one. I even . . . I believe Monsieur Robidoux wishes to marry me."

"Marry you? Anne, I am all astonishment!"

She gave a laugh that was half a sob. "He informed me yesterday at the warehouse that he has been thinking we should wed. Oh, Prudence, I shall have my stone house and my lace school and even . . . even my weaver."

"You make it sound like a death sentence. But perhaps

such a future for you is not so bad. You could go to London, reestablish your valuable connections in Society there, and then return to marry Monsieur Robidoux. He can hardly be called handsome, but he is a good man. He treats you fairly, and he respects your skills. Why not marry him?"

"I do not love him."

"Nor does he love you. But look what love brought us, Anne. You are the widow of a man who left you nothing but memories. And I . . . I am utterly bereft."

Prudence stood and tossed her knitting into her chair. The ball of yarn tumbled to the floor and rolled toward the hearth.

"Better to marry for security and comfort than for love," she went on. "Wed Monsieur Robidoux, Anne. You will have a home of your own and a husband who will not go plunging across bloody battlefields and getting himself killed. That should be happiness enough. Surely it is a wiser course than the one I chose."

Anne brushed a tear to keep it from rolling down her cheek. "I am sorry, Prudence. I know your grieving for Mr. Walker is very great."

"Everyone says that I am silly, and now I see how right they are. I had to fall in love with Mr. Walker, had to sink into his arms, had to melt at the sound of his voice. I thought him magical, and he was. He was so magical, he vanished. My sisters would laugh at my foolishness."

"Oh, Prudence," Anne rose from her chair and embraced her friend. "Prudence, never say such a thing again. Your sisters adore you, and they want only your happiness. Had they any idea of the depth of your feeling for Mr. Walker, I am sure they would have supported you."

Tears trickled down Prudence's cheeks. "I adored him, Anne."

"I know you did." Unable to hold back her own sorrow, Anne held her friend close. "I loved Ruel so much, and I shall never see him again. I love him still—and I am angry with him, too, for dying and leaving me alone. That night in Brussels, when I knew beyond all doubt that I wanted to be his wife, I believed my life had just begun. I had never known such happiness. Such peace. And then . . . oh, Prudence, how can I go on without him? What shall I do?"

"We are truly undone!"

Anne lifted her head and stared at the bare white ceiling. Hearing her own despair echoed in Prudence's sobs, she suddenly saw a path laid out before her. As clearly as she could picture the proper placement for every one of a thousand pins on a parchment pattern of bobbin lace, she understood how it must be.

"We shall travel to London together, Prudence." She drew in a deep breath. "Before the wedding, I shall request a tête-à-tête with the Duke of Marston. I shall put my affairs in order with the Chouteau family and ask that I be given some recompense for my title. I believe the duke may settle as much as four or five thousand pounds on me."

"Four or five thousand pounds? But that is nothing! How could you agree to such a small amount?"

"Quite easily. I need only enough to ensure my father's freedom and my family's welfare. As the wife of Monsieur Robidoux, I shall be quite comfortable. When I return from London, I shall marry the weaver."

"Anne, you cannot marry Monsieur Robidoux! Truly, I did

not mean what I said before about him." Prudence's eyes filled with tears again. "He is far too old for you, and he is hardly as tall as your shoulder. You cannot possibly learn to love him, no matter how decent and respectable he is. Be his partner in business, but not his wife."

"Now you *are* being silly, Prudence. Men form partnerships only with other men. Monsieur Robidoux respects my talents, but he will never view me as an equal with him in the lace business. I must marry him to safeguard my interests."

"But, Anne, you are perfectly good and kind, and your way with lace is pure genius."

"How little you know. My value to Monsieur Robidoux cannot last forever. The women of Calais have lace-making talents as laudable as the most skilled in Nottingham. Yesterday, one of the elderly ladies showed me a length of magnificent *point d' Alençon* she had helped to make, and I was truly astonished at its complexity. The blonde laces from Chantilly are superb, and even the Lille and Arras laces evidence great skill."

"Perhaps other women can create fine patterns, but it was you who smuggled in the loom. And it was you who set up a school to teach the women how to turn Robidoux's dull machine-made net into beautiful lace. You are invaluable not only to him but to the entire lace industry in France."

"Prudence, your loyalty touches my heart, but you must learn to face the facts. Now that the king rules again, it will not be many months before other Englishmen arrive in France with lace machines of their own. Others will set up lace schools, and the competition for skilled labor will be fierce. Calais promises one day to be the center of French lace manufacturing."

"And Monsieur Robidoux its emperor."

"Shall I not be his empress?"

"Oh, Anne, you have never wanted fame or fortune."

"No, but I mean to ensure security for my family. With the settlement I receive from the duke, I shall have enough money to pay the barrister Ruel engaged to free my father. But, Prudence, he will never again be allowed to minister in a church. You know that as well as I. His association with the Luddites and his imprisonment have ruined his reputation forever. No, I must bring my parents to France and make certain they never endure the ignominy of poverty."

"You would marry Monsieur Robidoux for your family?"

"I married Lord Blackthorne for them," Anne replied. "I believed that was by far the worst thing I possibly could do. But God permitted me moments of great happiness despite my rash behavior. Will He not reward me even more for an action much more sensible?"

"But you will never love the weaver as you loved Lord Blackthorne."

"No." Anne shook her head. Before she could start to cry again, she touched her friend's arm. "Now, pick up your knitting wool before it rolls into the fire. You had better start packing those French bonnets you purchased, or you will never get them all back to London."

"London! Oh, joy!"

With a shriek of delight, Prudence flew upstairs as Anne walked to the window. The last fingers of sunset threaded through the trees on the hillside. A wisp of black smoke drifted across the evening, and once again she knew the ache of memory.

Perhaps it was only her gift of seeing patterns where others viewed only the common objects of life. Perhaps it was her tendency to envision lace where others saw nothing. All the same, she was certain she saw in that breath of smoke the curl of a man's black hair.

In the rustle of leaves against the windowpane in the evening breeze, she heard the whisper of his voice. In the dark pearl of the sky, she saw the gray of his eyes. And she was quite sure, at that moment, he was looking into her soul.

❧❦❧

"'The wedding of the Duke of Marston's younger son to the daughter of the Comte de la Roche promises to be everything his elder brother's should have been.'" With a snort of disgust at what she had just read aloud, Prudence dropped *The Tattler* into her lap.

Flanked by her sisters, she studied Anne, who sat across the afternoon tea table at Trenton House. The two friends had been back in England for only three days, enjoying the comfort and warmth of the home that Sarah and Charles Locke's happy marriage had created. Upon arrival, Anne had sent a message to the duke, but she had heard nothing in reply— clearly a social snub, as Prudence had helpfully pointed out. Anne preferred to think the family were consumed with wedding preparations and would acknowledge her in time.

"What does Miss Pickworth know of anything?" Prudence asked. "She did not witness your wedding, and she has no idea how lovely you looked despite your wounded leg and pale complexion."

Anne had to smile. "My wedding had nothing of the pomp

319

and pageantry now taking place across Cranleigh Crescent at Marston House."

"One would think France had invaded England!" Mary exclaimed. More harried than usual, she had joined her sisters only for an hour. Her dear husband, Mr. John Heathhill, was ill with influenza. She fanned herself as she spoke. "It appears as though the French aristocracy view this marriage as a symbol of their happy alliance with England, and thus they all have descended upon us."

"We *did* restore their beloved monarchy," Sarah reminded her. "Why should they not make Sir Alexander's wedding a cause for celebration?"

Mary gave a sniff of distaste. "The ceremony should be English at its essence. The Comte de la Roche and his French friends are using it as a grand opportunity to display everything they had stashed away during the years of war, to unfurl every yard of lace that had been hidden, to flaunt every diamond and emerald in the realm. Shocking!"

"The shock is our dear friend's sad demeanor," Sarah said, reaching to lay her hand on Anne's. "You wear black as though certain of your husband's death at Waterloo. But in England, we hear he may not have perished. Miss Pickworth reports sightings of your husband in Brighton and in Devon."

"Miss Pickworth is an idiot!" Prudence declared. "Anne and I were on that battlefield, and the men would never have abandoned us in such a desperate place. They are dead, both of them, and Anne is right to wear black."

In sharp contrast to the finery of her friends, Anne dressed in crepe mourning gowns decorated with nothing more than black bugle beads, black roses, black velvet Vandykes, or

black chenille. She wore no jewelry but a jet brooch at her
neck, and she carried a black silk handkerchief in her reticule.
It was the least she could do in Ruel's memory.

"If Ruel Chouteau is dead," Mary said, "his brother is now
Marquess of Blackthorne. But we have had no such intelli-
gence from the family. I believe Miss Pickworth is correct,
Anne. Your husband lives."

"If he were alive, would he not be at Marston House for
the wedding?" Sarah asked gently. "No, Mary. I fear that Pru
and Anne are correct. The two men who took them to France
perished at Waterloo."

Mary's eyebrows lifted. "If his brother is dead, Sir Alexander shows not the slightest trace of mourning. He struts from
tea party to ballroom arrayed in the very finest French fashions, outshining even his fiancée—though she is hardly to
be missed. The perfume! One can find Gabrielle Duchesne
simply by sniffing her out in a crowd."

Prudence giggled. "Is she that bad?"

"No worse than the duchess. Sir Alexander's mother
parades about as though she were the Queen of Sheba. With
her ample figure swathed in lace and satin, she fairly billows
like a ship asail as she tacks from one event to another."

"Oh, Mary, do not be unkind!" Sarah exclaimed, though
she was hard-pressed to hide her smile.

"I should think Her Grace, the Duchess of Marston, would
recognize what bad form she displays," Anne stated. "The
duke should wear a black armband in mourning his son's
death. And the duchess should wear nothing but the darkest
colors."

Though she and Prudence had been told the rumors about

Ruel and Mr. Walker, Anne could give them no credence. Miss Pickworth reported each tidbit of information that reached her anonymous ears, and she had no compunction about presenting them as truth. Of course people wanted to believe the Marquess of Blackthorne was still alive, but Anne knew it could not be so. Though he might have left an unwanted wife on the battlefield, he would not have abandoned his lace machine. He had too many plans. Too many dreams. He had risked his life to take that machine into France, and if alive, he would have returned for it and taken it to Calais. Monsieur Robidoux had heard nothing from Ruel.

No, Anne's hopes—and fears—about Ruel were unfounded. The man was gone, and with him any thought of their future together.

"In my opinion," Prudence said, setting her teacup in its saucer, "the duchess is vain and shallow. She has not one drop of the character Anne's husband displayed, and nothing of his wit and charm."

"Character?" Mary retorted. "The marquess was a rake. Frankly, I am a bit surprised at our dear Anne's sorrow."

"Mary!" Sarah chastised her. "He was her husband!"

"But everyone knew the sort of man he was. Women, strong drink, cards—"

"He had changed," Prudence cut in. "You did not see him after he truly began to love Anne."

"Love her?"

Mary's question hung in the air as a footman gave a polite cough while entering the room with a silver tray. The sealed letter upon it was for Anne.

"It is from the Duke of Marston," she told the others.

Suddenly out of breath, she broke the seal and scanned the contents. Then she looked up at her friends. "My presence is required at Marston House immediately."

"Required?" Mary sat up straight. "Not requested?"

"The Duke of Marston requires my presence," Anne repeated. "At once."

Without hesitating a moment longer, Anne stood and made for the foyer. Prudence and her sisters followed, handing Anne a pair of gloves, tossing a shawl around her shoulders, and urging her to be brave as she followed the footman toward the door.

"Prudence, please pray for me," she said, turning and taking her friend's hands. "You know my mission. You know my dread. When I see the duke, I shall think of . . . of him . . . and I shall . . ."

"You are the dowager Marchioness of Blackthorne, and he owes you money," Prudence said firmly. "Think of nothing else!"

Anne nodded as she pulled away and hurried down the steps.

⌘

A liveried footman announced Anne's presence to the Duke of Marston and his wife, and she stepped into a large drawing room. At once, she could see that something profound had taken place. The duke hardly looked up at her. The duchess reclined on a settee as her lady's maid fanned her ashen face. Sir Alexander was nowhere to be seen.

When Anne had been seated, the duke stood, balanced himself on his cane, and fitted his monocle to his eye. "An event of great import has occurred," he intoned. "I have had a letter from my elder son."

"Ruel!" Anne gulped down a cry of shock.

The duchess closed her eyes and emitted a loud moan.

Trembling, hardly able to breathe, Anne watched as the duke shook out the folds of a sheet of white paper and began to read. "'My dear father, as I pen this letter, I am fast at sea on a ship bound for England. My traveling companion and friend, Mr. Walker, previously employed as a blacksmith in Tiverton, accompanies me. After making port in Brighton, I shall make my way to Slocombe House.'"

"He is in Devon?" Anne cried out. "Alive?"

"We are as astonished as you," the duke told her. "This letter was written more than a month ago, and we had given up all hope of him."

"Read on!" the duchess urged. "Why did he not come to us? Why has he left us in this state of dire confusion?"

The duke held the letter to his monocled eye and began reading aloud again. "'On leaving Brussels, the Marchioness of Blackthorne and I were held siege in a barn during the battle at Waterloo between the forces of Wellington and Napoleon. During the conflict, we attempted to escape. My wife was killed.'"

"Killed?" Anne jumped to her feet. "But I was not killed! There was a cannonball, you see." She sucked in a sob. "Oh, sir, is my husband truly alive?"

"Sit down, Lady Blackthorne, if you please," the duke ordered her. "I have endured histrionics enough for one day. I shall continue the epistle."

Shaking with disbelief, Anne sank into her chair.

"'My wife was killed,'" the duke repeated. "'Of that event, I am able to write nothing further, nor can I bring myself to speak of it even to Mr. Walker. On our escaping to safety, I made the immediate decision to return to England without delay and to take up residence at Slocombe House. I trust you will respect my desire to spend a time of mourning in a place of quiet and solitude.'"

"Why did he not write to us from Slocombe?" the duchess wailed. "Why was his letter so long delayed? Poor Alexander!"

"Poor Alexander, indeed," the duke scoffed. "That boy has merely lost a title he did not merit in the first place. I believed I had lost a son! I hardly know whether to rejoice that Ruel is alive or to reprimand him for keeping us in suspense all these weeks."

The duke allowed his monocle to drop from his eye. He turned to Anne. "My elder son is alive and believes you dead. But I am told you have been living in France. Making machine lace, spending money that rightfully belongs to the duchy of Marston, and consorting with a certain Monsieur Robidoux. Madam, what do you have to say about that?"

⁓ *Eighteen* ⁓

"I know nothing, Your Grace," Anne informed the duke. "As I wrote to you, an explosion rendered me unconscious on the battlefield at Waterloo. When I became sensible again, night had fallen, and I discovered myself to be alone with my friend, Miss Prudence Watson. I could see little in the moonlight save the countless thousands of dead around me. I had no doubt my husband was among them."

"Did you search for my son's body?" the duke asked.

"Your Grace, the battle continued all around us. Miss Watson and I were in great jeopardy. We unharnessed the dead horses, captured two others we found wandering loose on the field, and fled into the forest. We both firmly believed that if my husband and Mr. Walker had still been alive, they would have taken us to safety themselves."

"The last you saw of my son he was living?"

"Yes, Your Grace. Lord Blackthorne was attempting to restrain the runaway horses. We were separated, and I never

saw him again. I was certain he had died. I had no doubt
of it. Even though I have heard you read his letter, I cannot
believe that if Ruel were uninjured he would have left me
alone and unconscious on that battlefield."

"Why not? He believed you dead."

"But I was alive!"

"You were dead enough for him," the duchess said suddenly, rising from her couch like a sounding whale. "Clearly
he saw little point in rescuing you, dead or alive. He left you
there to die, young lady, and he counted on you to do so. But
once again you failed us, did you not? You wrote to us that
he was dead, and then you made your merry way to France,
where you spent the marquess's money investing in the manufacture of lace. Then you, the Marchioness of Blackthorne and
illegitimate bearer of our family's proud name, proceeded to
find yourself a Frenchman to wed. And a merchant at that!"

"I believed my husband dead, madam."

"You wished him dead and yourself the richer for it," the
duchess snapped. "But now he is alive, and Alexander has
gone to Slocombe to fetch him back."

"But the wedding . . ."

"Postponed." The duchess shook her handkerchief at
Anne. "Ruel is alive, Alex is gone, the wedding is delayed,
and it is all your fault! Your fault, you shameless creature!
You have spoiled everything."

"Spoiled everything?" Anne slowly rose. "Your son is alive.
Alive. My husband lives! And Mr. Walker, too! Oh, I must
tell Prudence. I must beg your leave at once. I cannot see why
anyone could be anything but happy."

"Can you not?" the duchess barked. "Tell her, then,

Laurent. Inform this common upstart of her position in our family."

"Enough, Beatrice! I shall do the talking here!" The duke hammered his cane into the floor. "Lady Blackthorne, today I have received two letters. Not only have I heard from my son, but also from a Pierre Robidoux. He wrote to inquire about you, and he informed me of your agreement to marry him. I now wish to settle on you the sum of ten thousand pounds in exchange for your promise to wed this Frenchman and never trouble us again."

The duchess eyed Anne. "We consider your relationship with our family at an end."

Anne stared back. "Then you err, madam."

"What did I tell you, Laurent?" the duchess burst out. "Now that she sees she can sink her claws into us again, humiliating us before everyone, she leaps at the opportunity."

Anne turned on the older woman. "I shall say again as I have said before. Everything I did—from my journey to France to my association with the man who has asked for my hand—stemmed from the belief that I was a widow. No, madam, despite the fact that I am despised and rejected by you, I shall not walk out of this family. I care nothing for titles or wealth, but I view my marriage as a blessing not to be forsaken so lightly. Perhaps I undertook it for the wrong reasons, but God used it for good. He may still have some purpose in such a mismatched union. Madam, in the months I knew your son, I grew to love him. I love him still."

"Love, love, love," the duchess spat. "Run to your beloved husband, then. See how happy he is to take you back after

Alexander informs him you promised your hand to another man within three months of his supposed death."

"No!" Anne gasped. "Sir Alexander has gone to tell Ruel that?"

"And to bring him back to London," the duke cut in. "Before they arrive, let us settle this matter once and for all. Lady Blackthorne, I propose you leave for France at once and carry out your plan to wed the Frenchman. You will remarry under the mistaken assumption that Ruel is dead. By the time news of his welcome return reaches you in Calais, everything will be cleanly resolved."

"Resolved?" Anne cried. "Upon my honor, I shall do no such thing. I know now he is alive, and I mean to welcome him home as a dearly loved husband!"

"He is not your husband!" the duchess shouted. "He is not, you vile creature! You are nothing but a housemaid like . . . like—"

"Be quiet, Beatrice." The duke pounded his cane. "Be quiet and sit down!"

"I wish him dead," the duchess shrieked. "His birth obliterated all my happiness, and now he has besmirched our name with his shameless marriage. He ought to have perished in France and taken away all the misery he has caused me through the years. Now he has ruined Alexander's hope of inheriting the duchy. Oh, that wicked boy has destroyed my life!"

"As you destroyed his." Anne glared at the woman. "Ruel has perceived your rejection, madam. Your senseless hatred of him. You planted every seed of bitterness in his life. You nurtured every root of unhappiness. You watered what animosity

you could create between your sons by adoring the younger
and despising the elder. You never taught Ruel the blessing
of home and hearth. What he has been for too many years is
thanks to you. What he can become rests only in the hands
of God."

Unable to face them any longer, Anne turned and ran from
the drawing room. Ruel was alive. It was all she knew. Ruel
was alive, and Sir Alexander was going to him to tell him she
did not love him.

As she lifted her skirts and took the stairs two at a time, she
at last understood exactly what God willed for her life. She
must go to Devon and be a wife to her husband.

⌒⌒⌒

"You were at the marquess's side the night of the Duchess
of Richmond's ball," Charles Locke said to Anne as they
bumped along in the carriage on the road to Slocombe
House. Sarah's husband had kindly agreed to accompany
Anne and Prudence on the long journey south. "Did you see
Droughtmoor fire the pistol?"

Anne tried to sort through her memories of that event. So
much had whirled past her in the evening hours following the
revelation of Ruel's letter to his father. On hearing that Mr.
Walker was alive, Prudence immediately had decided that
she, too, would travel to Slocombe House. Sarah had volunteered her husband's assistance and protection.

As Sarah sent for Charles to return from his offices at
Locke & Son Tea Company, Anne and Prudence had hurried
to pack their trunks. Mary Heathhill had begged the two
women to delay their journey until the next morning, for

everyone knew the danger of traveling England's roadways at night.

They had reluctantly agreed, but with daylight came the dreadful news that Mr. Heathhill's health had worsened. While Sarah rushed to her sister's side, Prudence made the difficult decision to leave them. She would go with Charles Locke and Anne to Devon, assure herself of Mr. Walker's safety, and then return immediately to London.

Anne could hardly endure the endless carriage ride. She longed to see Ruel, yet she dreaded his reaction to the news Sir Alexander must be telling him even now—that his wife was alive, but she intended to marry someone else. Unable to sleep the night before, Anne had written to Monsieur Robidoux to inform him of the situation and to sever any personal connection between them.

"I can hardly remember how Ruel was shot that night in Brussels," she told Mr. Locke. "At the news of Napoleon taking Charleroi, everyone began rushing through the corridors of Richmond's house, out the doors, and into the streets. I recall Mr. Walker shouting something—a warning, I suppose. I smelled black powder. And then Ruel fell to the floor."

"Did you actually see Droughtmoor?" Charles asked.

"Not in the crowd, but I have no doubt he was the assassin. Earlier that evening, I heard him challenge Ruel to a duel. When news of the war broke out, Ruel told him their assignation the following morning would be impossible, and Droughtmoor vowed to have his revenge. The next thing I knew, Ruel lay bleeding in my arms."

Charles clenched his teeth for a moment. "Lady Black-

thorne, I must inform you that the assassin was not Droughtmoor."

"How can you be certain?"

"The newspaper accounts were clear. More than one witness vouched for his innocence. Barkham, Wimberley—"

"Droughtmoor's accomplices. Of course they defended
him! You must have had your information from Miss
Pickworth, sir, for it is clearly prejudicial."

"Miss Pickworth's version of the event is reliable. The
Duke of Richmond bore witness on behalf of Lord Droughtmoor, as well. The duke was given intelligence of a hostile
exchange between the men. He followed Droughtmoor outside to have a word with him, meaning to forestall any duel of
honor on foreign soil. The duke was speaking with Droughtmoor in the roadway when word of Blackthorne's shooting
came."

"Then it must have been Barkham or Wimberley."

"Both were with the duke." Charles shook his head as he
regarded her. "Someone else shot your husband, Lady
Blackthorne. He has been fired at more than once, as you well
know. Have you any idea who might want him dead?"

A sickening chill surged through Anne as she remembered
the earlier incident involving Ruel. Everyone had assumed the
spurned gamekeeper wanted to kill Anne. But that man, too,
had an alibi. Then she thought of the family meeting when
the Duchess of Marston had reviled Ruel and voiced her wish
that he had perished at Waterloo.

"The duchess?" she whispered. "Could his own mother
have hired an assassin?"

Charles lifted his eyebrows. "She minces no words concerning her dislike for her older son."

"No," Prudence spoke up. "It was not the duchess."

"How can you be certain?" Anne asked.

"I shall speak plainly," Prudence said. "I never wanted to tell you this information, for it is only rumor. I know you revile gossip, but now I must be frank. It is said that the Duchess of Marston is not the mother of the marquess. When the duke's wife failed to bear him an heir, he took a mistress. Ruel is reportedly the son of a housemaid who died at his birth."

"A housemaid?" Anne murmured, recalling the duchess's angry denouncement of her. "No wonder she despised me."

"When Sir Alexander was born to the duchess," Prudence went on, "his mother doted upon him."

"But this rumor only enhances my suspicion that she may have paid someone to shoot Ruel!"

"No, she would never harm the marquess. The duchess disdains her husband's older son, but she has tolerated him as heir apparent for too many years. If she had wanted him dead, she would have seen to it long ago."

Anne nodded. "The man who shot Ruel is someone else. Someone who stands to gain by my husband's death."

Prudence stared at her. "Can you be thinking—"

"Sir Alexander," Anne said.

"Surely not," Charles protested. "I have heard Sir Alexander express nothing but the deepest affection for his brother. He rushed to Devon the moment he heard Ruel was alive."

"Sir Alexander is a cruel man and not to be trusted," Anne declared as dread drained the blood from her face. "His mother's favoritism poisoned him. The news that Ruel was alive infuriated the duchess. I saw her—heard her words of rage. She was livid that her younger son had lost the title and fortune she wished for him."

"Angry enough to urge Alex to murder Ruel?"

"I believe Sir Alexander is capable of such evil even without a push from his mother. Mr. Locke, you and your Society witnessed only his public facade. In private, I saw his true character too many times to believe him incapable of such action. He had the motive and the opportunity."

"Lady Blackthorne," Charles said in a low voice. "Sir Alexander will arrive at Slocombe House long before us. If Ruel believes his brother loves him . . ."

"Sir Alexander will kill him." She swallowed. "For all his impenetrable exterior, Ruel is a gentle, kind man at heart. Lacking his mother's love, he has become both hardened and vulnerable at the same time. No one knows the chinks in Ruel's armor better than his brother." Her fingers tightened on her shawl as she thought about what might happen. "Even if I arrive in time to caution him, he may not believe what I tell him."

Charles Locke regarded her for a moment without speaking. Then he took her hand. "Lady Blackthorne, do you love your husband as you vowed you did?"

"At first the marriage was nothing more than an arrangement between us. I thought of it as another of his games. He called it a bargain." She looked away. "I learned to love Ruel. These past months . . . thinking him dead . . . have been unbearable. The truth is, I care nothing about where we live or what his properties and connections in the *ton* may be. I love him. I love Ruel, and if . . . if I lose him again—"

"You must make him believe in your love," Prudence said. "Anne, he will trust you."

"I agree with Miss Watson," Charles said. "Nothing but the most profound assurance of your own devotion may convince him of his brother's evil wishes."

⁓⊙⊙⊙⁓

By the time the carriage arrived at Tiverton in Devon, Anne had completely restored the panel of lace she had removed from her bloodied blue gown. Prudence had changed her mind a hundred times—glad she had chosen to accompany Anne to Devon, and then despising herself for abandoning her sisters when Mary's husband had grown so ill.

Prudence peppered Anne with questions that had no answers. Would Mr. Walker be glad to see her? Might he want to continue working at his smithy in Tiverton for the rest of his life? Could she possibly live so far from her dear sisters? Would he be willing to move to London to be near her? Did Anne believe he would consider marrying Prudence despite her youth? Ought she to set her sights on some other man instead?

Anne knew little beyond her own fear and constant preoccupation with prayer for Ruel's safety. As the carriage horses were watered at an inn in Tiverton, Charles Locke learned that Alexander Chouteau had passed through only hours before.

Carriages were prone to breaking down, Anne knew, and horses sometimed pulled up lame or lost a shoe. Might she catch up to Sir Alexander? Might she stop him? She brushed aside Prudence's suggestion that they stop at the blacksmith's cottage. The smithy appeared deserted as they drove past it on their way through Tiverton.

Never had Anne known such apprehension. Prudence twisted her gloves until they began to shred, and even Mr. Locke could not stop drumming his fingers on the carriage seat.

"Do you think they will both be here, Anne?" Prudence asked. "Your husband *and* Mr. Walker, I mean?"

Anne took Prudence's gloves away and dropped them into her own reticule. "It is the presence of Sir Alexander that troubles me the most," she said. "We shall know everything soon enough."

The carriage finally drew up to the front of the imposing stone house. Mr. Locke helped Anne and Prudence step down while the footman unloaded their trunks. In moments, they were standing at the door.

"Yes, sir?" The servant who answered their knock ignored Anne and Prudence and looked questioningly at Mr. Locke.

"The Marquess of Blackthorne?" Charles asked. "Is he here?"

"And Mr. Walker?" Prudence put in. "Where are they?"

"Have you a calling card, sir?" He continued to address Charles.

"Tell the marquess that his wife, the Marchioness of Blackthorne, has just arrived."

The footman finally noticed Anne, and his eyes widened. "I beg your pardon. Will you not come in?" He stepped aside and ushered the women into the cool entry hall before starting up the long staircase.

Anne's heart leapt for the first time since she had heard the duke read from Ruel's letter. She was not too late! He was here! Would he want her? Would he recognize her? Oh, she looked terrible.

"Prudence, my hair. Is it—"

"Anne?"

She looked to the top of the stairs. He stood outlined in the morning sun, tall, raven-haired, magnificent. White shirt, black trousers. Leather boots. A pen dropped from his fingers to the carpeted landing.

"Anne?" he repeated.

All these hours, and she had not planned what to say. Had not imagined how it would be to actually see him again.

"I am here, Ruel," she said. "I have come from France."

Nostrils flaring, he gripped the banister as he started down the stairs. His gray eyes burned silver. "Anne, is it really you?"

She left Prudence's side. "I thought you had died at Waterloo—"

"But it was you—"

"No, I was alive. I . . . we went to France and—"

"You are not dead?"

"No, but I thought you were until the duke—"

"Thank God!" He leapt down the last five steps, tore across the hall, caught her up in his arms, and swung her around and around. "This is a miracle! Anne! Dear Lord, You have brought her to me!"

Laughing, crying, she clung to him. "I cannot believe it! You are alive!"

"God has given you back to me! A second chance!"

"Ruel, I was certain I should never see you again. So many weeks—"

"An eternity." He let her slide down until her feet touched the floor. Searching her eyes, he shook his head. "You are beautiful."

She thought of the miles she had come, the wrinkles in her dress and tangles in her hair, and none of it mattered. To him she was beautiful. Beautiful!

"I believed I could never hold you in my arms again," he murmured. "I saw you dead on that battlefield. Your blue dress was drenched in blood. You lay lifeless, as did your friend. The horses were mangled and the cart badly damaged. How many times I have recalled the scene in my mind. Your mouth open . . . your eyes rolled back. . . . You were dead, Anne."

She shook her head. "Prudence and I lay unconscious for many hours. It was night when we became sensible again, and the battle still raged. Our ears had been deafened by the blast of the cannonball, but we could see the fallen men lying all around us. We had no doubt you and Mr. Walker were among the dead at Waterloo."

"You were mistaken. After finding your bodies there on the front line, we knew we had no choice but to flee the battle-ground. Walker insisted we run. He said otherwise we would be killed, too." He gripped her shoulders. "Anne, I have grieved you more than you can know."

"And I you. Prudence and I concluded that you and Mr. Walker had been killed, for we thought surely you would not have abandoned us." She turned, seeking her friend.

"Where is Mr. Walker?" Prudence asked as she stepped forward.

"He has been living in Tiverton at his cottage," Ruel said.

"He has forgotten me. Oh, Anne, I knew it!"

Anne gathered her friend close. "Ruel, I beg you to send for Mr. Walker. He must be told that Prudence lives."

Nodding, Ruel summoned a footman. As he gave instructions for a rider to take a message to the blacksmith in Tiverton, he paused and turned to gaze at Anne.

Her arms around Prudence, Anne looked into his eyes and saw what she had never imagined possible. He loved her. Wholly, without the slightest hint of hesitancy, he loved her. And how very dearly she loved him, too.

⁓⊙⊙⊙⌇

Still in a daze of disbelief, Ruel followed the footman to the front door. A horse was brought quickly from the stable and a rider dispatched with a message Ruel had scrawled out. As he watched the horse's hooves send up a line of dust along the road, his mind still struggled with the realization. Anne! Anne had come back from the dead. She was inside the house. How could that be?

He had been haunted by her memory. Though certain that he loved her, he had failed to tell her at Waterloo. Then she had been killed on the battlefield. Killed. He had been so sure of it. Every mile he had crossed in his journey back to England had been etched with his agony. Regret. Anger. Disbelief. Sorrow. Self-contempt. Fury. Rage. Tears.

How many tears had he wept over her? When he thought back on his life, he could not recall shedding a single tear about anything. Ever. Grieving Anne had torn the edges of his heart.

Once in Devon, he had hidden himself away at Slocombe

House. Feeling dead inside, despairing of hope, he had found his only comfort in God. There were no cathedrals or abbeys like the ones he had known in London, so he sought strength in the Bible he found in the library. But Ruel could hardly accept that God's grace, His free gift of love, could reach down and touch his own life so profoundly. The most undeserving of men, he had been remiss in too many ways. As the dark days passed, Ruel had repented, vowed to change his life, surrendered his own will to God's leading. Yet he could not break free from the sorrow and regret that had held him in chains of anguish.

But now God had brought Anne to him. Feeling like a young colt set free in a spring pasture, he bounded back across the foyer.

"My wife," he said proudly to the footman. In a clear breach of every rule of etiquette, he slipped his arm around Anne and drew her close. With a laugh, he kissed her cheek.

"So pleased to meet you, Lady Blackthorne." The footman made a deep bow. "We were given to believe you had perished."

"And we are all happily wrong." Ruel turned to Anne. "You must be exhausted from your journey. I shall take you to our chambers at once, and Mr. Locke and Miss Watson must be shown to the guest rooms as well. Simmons, see that hot water is sent upstairs directly. And the trunks, of course. Let us plan to gather for tea at four o'clock in the drawing room."

"I welcome the opportunity to refresh myself," Anne said softly. "But first I must request a tête-à-tête with Sir Alexander."

"Alex?" Ruel said. "Alex is not here. He prepares his wedding in London."

"But he was ahead of us."

"Alex is coming to Slocombe?"

"Your family had no idea you were alive, sir," Charles Locke spoke up. "Your letter from France arrived at Marston House only two days ago."

"Two days? Impossible! I sent it weeks ago."

"It is true," Anne confirmed. "Your parents summoned me the moment they received the news, for of course I had written to tell them you were dead. The moment Sir Alexander heard you were alive, he abandoned his wedding plans to come to you at once. He arrived in Tiverton last night. Surely he is here already."

"Evidently you outpaced him." Ruel's grin broadened. "But this is excellent news! My brother is on his way. Alex is coming. What a splendid reunion we shall have!"

∾ Nineteen ∾

Teatime came but Anne could not tear herself from the bliss of Ruel's arms. As the party sat together in the drawing room, the sun drifted down toward the horizon casting lacy shadows from the oak trees outside the window. Anne tried to think about important things. Prudence. The duchess. Sir Alexander.

All she knew was this man whose warm embrace folded her in security and love. He was just as she had remembered him. And different, too. The scar on his cheek made a fitting emblem for the new man. His pain was more open now, more easily revealed. But so was his love. He had been wounded by loss. But she sensed that he had healed into a more compassionate human being.

Ruel had not moved from Anne's side, and even now he kept one arm firmly around her shoulder as if he could not bear to be separated from her for even a moment.

"Calais," he said to her as a maid poured tea into empty

cups. "I can scarcely believe that you and Miss Watson were there all the time."

Anne shifted at the mention of France. "Ruel, I must tell you what became of your lace machine."

"Never mind the loom. I am now considering an offer my brother made to me some time ago. Mr. Locke, I understand that you have had a letter from Henry Carlyle, your partner with Sir Alexander in Locke & Son Tea Company."

"Several letters, in fact," Charles replied. "Henry Carlyle, Lord Delacroix, writes to say he is safely arrived in China, and he is successfully negotiating a large shipment of the finest tea that country has to offer. Locke & Son may expect to turn a handsome profit when he returns to England. Lord Blackthorne, you are more than welcome to join your brother, Lord Delacroix, and me in this venture. Indeed, I am sure we should all be most grateful for your influence."

"I thank you, sir. Like my brother, I am deeply committed to the financial well-being of the duchy of Marston. I should very much like to learn more about the tea trade."

"But what about lace?" Anne spoke up. "Monsieur Robidoux is doing so well in Calais."

Ruel turned to her. "Robidoux? You know him?"

She glanced at Prudence for reassurance before continuing. "Prudence and I took your machine into France, and Monsieur Robidoux met us at Douai. Hezekiah Cutts has been a great success. You are the owner of a growing lace industry in Calais—with a lace school and a clever manager. Monsieur Robidoux is a most competent businessman."

Throwing his head back, Ruel laughed heartily. "*You* took my machine to France? *You* set it up? My little Luddite?"

"How could I not, sir?" she asked softly. "It was your dream."

Sobering, he shook his head. "Thank you, Anne. I know it was a great sacrifice. Your father—"

"I trust you will continue to work toward his freedom."

"Of course. Your mother and the others are well, I am sure, for I commissioned my steward to take the best possible care of them."

"You are too good." Embarrassed at the public exchange of emotion between herself and Ruel, Anne knew she must move quickly to other matters. "I must address an issue of great import. It has to do with the attempt on your life in Brussels."

"Give Droughtmoor no thought, I beg you. The man is of little consequence and—"

"But I speak of Sir Alexander," she cut in. "He may have been the assailant."

Ruel scowled. "My brother?"

"Sir, you stand between him and the duchy." She sucked in a breath, trying to force herself to tell him what had occurred when the duke had read aloud his letter. "Upon hearing news of your presence in Devon, your brother departed London at once, leaving his bride-to-be in the lurch. The duchess was . . . distraught."

"In a snit, no doubt. I long ago heard the rumor that she is not my true mother—though I assure you no one in the family gave credit to such vile gossip. All the same, I have ruined her plans more than once. Anne, you must understand how the duchess views her life. I am not the first child whose mother rejected him in favor of a sibling, nor shall I be the last." He paused, searching her face. "My mother, Drought-moor, Society—nothing in the past can have importance now. But you do. Will you stay with me, dear lady? Can you make Slocombe and Marston your home?"

Forgetting all about Sir Alexander, Anne slipped her arms around his neck. "Oh, Ruel, I am at home already."

"My home is in your heart," he whispered.

"Ahem!" The footman cleared his throat. "I beg your pardon, Lord Blackthorne. Mr. Walker is here at your request."

As the tall figure slipped into the room, Prudence gasped and leapt to her feet. "Mr. Walker!"

Before she could rush to him, the man stiffened. "Miss Watson? I . . . but we thought—"

"Excuse me," the footman interrupted again. "Alexander Chouteau has arrived. May I present your brother?"

"Of course!" Ruel stood. "Show him in at once."

Sir Alexander strode into the room. "Ruel, how surprised I was to learn you are alive and well," he began. "I bring warm greetings from our parents."

"Alex, upon my word, I cannot credit the notion that you thought me dead!" Ruel crossed the room to embrace his brother. "I wrote to you from France. I told you all I was coming here to Slocombe."

"Your letter was waylaid, and in the meantime, Lady Blackthorne gave us to believe that you had perished in France." Sir Alexander spotted Anne, and his face darkened. "Are you aware, brother, that your wife betrothed herself to a wealthy French merchant—merely weeks from our parting at Waterloo?"

Her heart hammering, Anne gripped the arm of the settee

and pushed herself to her feet. "Sir Alexander, this is a private matter, and I have not had time to speak to my husband about it."

"Anne?" Ruel turned from his brother. "Is this true?"

"Monsieur Robidoux can hardly be considered wealthy."

"Robidoux?" Ruel's face softened. "Do you speak of Pierre Robidoux of Douai?"

Anne relaxed a little at the quizzical smile that tipped one corner of his mouth. The short Frenchman with his large nose was something less than a romantic rival. Ruel knew that, and so did Anne. But Alex clearly did not.

"Believing you had been killed at Waterloo," Anne told her husband, "Monsieur Robidoux asked for my hand. He had come to consider me an asset to the lace industry in Calais. I knew I could not rely upon the largesse of the Chouteau family, for they had ignored my communications."

"Lies!" Sir Alexander burst out. "She cannot claim we ignored her. For all we knew, she was dead, too."

"Sir, it is quite impossible that none of my letters reached you in Paris. You never troubled yourself to respond. And your parents knew of my situation. As you just stated, they received the letter I wrote to inform them that I believed their son had perished."

"Never mind that, Anne." Ruel took her hand. "Do you hold any affection for Robidoux?"

"Nothing more than a business arrangement ever passed between us. Prudence can attest to that, as will Monsieur Robidoux himself. Ruel, please, you must believe me."

Pulling Anne protectively against him, he made no answer. Instead, he faced his brother. "Alex, why have you come to Devon? What brings you to Slocombe House when all London is abuzz with preparations for your wedding?"

Alexander paled. "To prove to myself you were alive, of course," he blustered. Pointing at Anne, he added, "Why do you suppose *she* came?"

"Anne is my wife. We made a vow to spend our lives together. Alex, you knew I was alive. My letter proved it. Why have you come?"

"Upon my word, Ruel, I am astonished at such a question. I have been on the road for two days. My carriage lost a wheel and nearly overturned. My best horse has gone lame. Is this the sort of greeting I deserve?" Alex gave his brother a disarming grin. "Now, then, have I missed teatime entirely?"

Ruel's shoulders relaxed. "Come then, let us sit down together, all of us. You may have more adventures to relate than anyone else."

Clapping his brother on the back, Ruel started across the foyer with Alex. Anne stood for a moment. Her mind told her all was well, but her heart still pounded in alarm.

"Sir Alexander, you never answered Ruel's question," she said.

The men stopped and looked back at her.

"You came to Slocombe House at your mother's bidding, did you not?" She squared her shoulders. "Or was it your own idea?"

"Anne, what are you talking about?" Ruel asked. "Alex has come to wish us well."

Trying to breathe normally, Anne faced down her brother-in-law. "You should go back to London, sir. Go back to Gabrielle Duchesne and make a good husband of yourself.

Tend to your affairs, and allow your brother to resume his position in the family."

"What affairs?" His face reddening, Alexander took a step toward Anne. "You have taken everything. You got your claws into my brother, and I have no doubt you mean to bear him an heir."

"Alex!" Ruel cut in. "You will not insult my wife!"

"You know nothing about this wicked creature, Ruel." Alexander's voice rose. "She is nothing more than a devious housemaid! She believes she can weasel her way back into your life and into our money. Well, it should be my money, do you hear? Just as the title ought to be mine!"

"Alex, the title is mine by birthright." Gathering anger darkened Ruel's features. "You know I am heir apparent."

"Mother would have *me* inherit," his brother exploded. "You have done nothing with your life—women and dice and roaming about the world spending money on your foolish schemes. Lace! Lace, for heaven's sake!"

"Alex, you are raving."

Ruel reached to try to calm his brother, but Alex leapt backward. Suddenly drawing a small pistol from his pocket, he pointed it at his brother. Anne saw at once he carried it on the half cock.

"Alex, stop!" she cried out.

"You are not to be the heir. I am." He leveled the weapon at Ruel's heart. His voice dropped. "You hear me right, dear brother. After you left for America, Mother told me that the rumor of your parentage is true. You were born of our father's mistress—a housemaid. No wonder you were so eager to wed Anne Webster. Like her, you are a commoner. A nobody!

I am the legitimate son of our parents, not you. Mother always preferred me, and when we heard you were dead, we rejoiced. Even Father was relieved, for you have never been anything but trouble to him. Now you have spoiled all our plans."

"Alex, what are you saying?" Ruel looked from his brother to his wife. "Anne?"

"No matter what the truth of his elder son's parentage may be, the duke has always considered Ruel his heir," she told Alex. "Ruel was brought up for the duchy, and he is meant to have it. Sir, I beg you to put down the pistol—"

"Never! I have spent years of my life trying to see this useless brother of mine dead. I sent assassins after him to America. They failed to kill him. I shot at him myself from the roadway near Tiverton. Do not look so shocked, Ruel. I wore my hunting greens into the forest and followed you from the churchyard out onto the road. Had you seen the weapon aimed your way, you would have noted it was a fine German Jaeger rifle."

"Dash it all, Alex!"

"I tried again in Brussels. Thought I had you that time. All the confusion. The crowds. I knew you had been with your scheming little wife by that time, knew you would try to produce an heir to work me completely out of the picture. Clever boy."

"Alex, do not be preposterous."

"I missed again. But not this time. Not this time." He pulled back on the metal hammer, setting it at full cock. "Think I will not do it? Pity, Ruel."

"Alex, no!" As his brother pulled the trigger, Ruel reached for a pistol from his own coat, but Anne knew he was too late. She screamed. Alexander's ball tore past his brother's left shoulder and splintered into the wooden front door. As it did, Alex stiffened, his eyes blank with disbelief.

As he fell forward, Anne saw a hatchet buried in his back, its blade severing his spine. In shock, she looked beyond the fallen man. Near the doorway stood Walker, one hand still outstretched toward his target.

With a cry of anguish, Ruel crouched beside his fallen brother. "Oh, Alex . . ." he murmured, stroking the golden hair of the dead man. "Nothing was worth this."

Anne knelt near him. "Ruel, your brother would have killed you. His aim was true."

Brushing a tear from his cheek, Ruel looked up at the man who approached. "Walker, you threw him off. You saved my life."

"As you saved mine." The Indian laid a hand on his friend's shoulder. "All these years in England, I have lived because of one thing, Ruel. I lived because your friendship gave me hope. Despite the words of your brother and the disfavor of your mother, you are a man of honor. You always treated me well. You were the son I could never have. The brother I had lost so many years before in America."

"I am not so good as you claim," Ruel said through clenched teeth. He stood, shaking his head. "My own brother would have killed me for my title and properties. My mother wished me dead. My father—"

"Your father loves you dearly," Anne spoke up. "I was in the drawing room when he read your letter aloud. Never once did the duke back away from his devotion to you. He called you his son, his heir. He has always believed in you, and you have not disappointed him."

"Excuse me, please." Pulling away from them, Ruel strode across the drawing room. Anne heard his footfalls as he ran down a long corridor. Somewhere in the distance, a door to the outside swung open and then slammed shut.

⚬⚭⚬

Anne straightened from the washstand and allowed the fragrant, steaming water to run down her neck before she toweled herself dry. She had given Ruel nearly an hour to walk alone in the garden. Mr. Walker and Prudence remained below, giving an account of the incident to the authorities who came from Tiverton to deal with the dreadful occurrence at Slocombe House.

Having chosen to retreat to her room, Anne reflected on the part she had played in the tragedy. In France, she had been certain Sir Alexander meant harm to his brother. The duchess's words only confirmed that her younger son had wanted the duchy of Marston for himself. There could be no doubt about that.

But to kill his own brother? Common sense argued against it. Alex had always been loving toward Ruel. Yet his dislike of Anne could hardly be termed irrational. In the eyes of Society, she was the lowly housemaid who had entrapped the grand marquess. She might bear a child who would become a duke.

If, indeed, Ruel's own mother had been the duke's mistress—a commoner used to sire an heir to the duchy—it was no wonder the duchess resented the older boy. The birth of her own son not long after the duke had declared Ruel his heir must have driven a knife through her heart. The entirety of the situation was enough to infuriate any blue blood.

Anne laid the towel on the washstand. She realized she could destroy her sanity in the attempt to understand exactly how Alex had become his own brother's worst enemy. The most important thing now was not to focus on death but to be thankful for life. She must convince Ruel of her love for him. Nothing mattered more than their future.

She splashed the scent of lavender on her wrists and elbows and then went to her trunk. Lifting the lid, Anne took out a new blue gown. Would Ruel understand what she intended by wearing this copy of the one he had given her? Would he know the significance of the Honiton lace panel she had mended? She could only pray he would.

⌘

Ruel's gray eyes burned as Anne walked toward him across the grass in the rose garden. Her heart stumbled and began to thud. They had been quick to embrace each other on first meeting again, but now she felt shy. Awkward. He was taller than she remembered, broader of shoulder, his hair blacker. The faded scar trailed in a curve across his cheek, and she remembered the night a lead ball had nearly taken his life.

"Walker spoke to me a few minutes ago," he said. "He is not to be charged with Alex's death."

Anne clutched the edges of her shawl. "I am glad. Prudence will be . . ." She stammered as his hand reached out to her. "Prudence is so very . . ."

"Anne, I am not the least bit interested in Miss Watson at the moment." He slipped his fingers into her hair, cupping the back of her head as she drifted toward him. "I still can hardly believe you are here. Walking in the garden, I began to doubt my own senses. Perhaps you had not really come. Perhaps Alex was still alive."

She rubbed her cheek against his hand. "I might have prevented everything. Had I been able to make you see—"

"Alex was poisoned by my mother—" he paused—"by the duchess . . . while I was in America. He was no longer the brother and friend I believed him to be. He would have killed me."

"He tried many times."

"Until this moment, I have understood so little. I existed in a sort of trance, unable to see truth. Unwilling to weed out the wrong and embrace the right. I placed value on worthless things and failed to honor everything significant. I did not understand God as I do now, nor did I allow Him the rightful place in my life."

"I, too, have made great errors in judgment."

"But, Anne, you are the one who brought me to my senses. The moment I first laid eyes on you, I began to awaken. The moment I heard your voice. The moment I listened to you weave a spell around that little urchin in the kitchen." He folded her into his embrace. "Anne, you have brought me such joy, such purpose . . . such love."

Slipping her arms around him, she laid her head on his chest. "We are quite a pair. We have played at charades, danced around each other, argued incessantly—"

"I stole your lace just to annoy you."

"Did you?"

"You are the only woman who ever verbally fenced with me.

And you parried my every move." He traced his finger over the outline of her lips. "You are a wily creature, Anne Webster."

"Am I?" She smiled. "You are the man who turned Solomon's Song into a lyric of seduction."

"Is it not?" He stroked the pad of his thumb down her cheek. "Can you deny it is the love song of a man to his wife?"

"Perhaps not." She sighed. "Oh, Ruel, I can hardly believe you are real. After that last night in Brussels, I wanted nothing but you. And then I lost you."

"Never again."

She looked up into his eyes, marveling at the depth of love in their gray pools. "Kiss me, Ruel," she begged. "I have ached for this moment."

"No." He swallowed and gritted his teeth. Taking her shoulders, he set her a little away from him. "I have something to say to you, and I refuse to speak the words in the heat of passion."

A momentary fear gripped her. "What is it?"

He took her arms, forcing her to meet his eyes. "Anne, I love you."

"Ruel . . ."

"I love you, Anne. You must hear it, and hear it again. This is not a charade, not a game, not a ruse. I say it not for the benefit of Society and not to manipulate you in any way. Our bargain is ended, and our real marriage is begun. Standing before God, with Christ as my witness, and in the truth of the Holy Spirit I swear this vow. I love you, Anne. I always shall."

She bit her lip to hold back the tears and nodded.

"I felt it from the moment we met," he went on, "but not until Waterloo did I truly know how deeply I loved you. I meant to say the words. And then I lost you. I have lived with that pain until it has nearly broken me."

"Oh, Ruel." She threw her arms around him and buried her face in his neck. "I felt your love, or I would not have come to Devon in the hope of finding it again. Ruel, I love you. I love you."

"My wife," he murmured, pressing his lips to hers at last. "My dearest . . . only . . . forever love."

Miss Pickworth's Ponderings

After reading the tale of the bachelor's bargain, please peruse Miss Pickworth's ponderings. She has a quantity of questions, and she wonders if you, dear reader, may come to any clever conclusions.

1. Was Anne Webster right or wrong to take matters into her own hands to save her family? What bargain did she make with Ruel Chouteau, Lord Blackthorne? How did this bargain promise to benefit each of them? What effect did the bargain end up having on them?

2. Can you see the very great differences between the upper and lower classes during the Regency? What are some of these differences?

3. How was Anne, a lower-class serving girl, able to converse so intelligently with the Duke of Marston and his two sons?

4. Prudence slipped into depression after her sister Sarah went on a sea journey and her sister Mary became preoccupied with the coming birth of her baby. Do you think Prudence is a Christian? Can Christians become depressed? What was done for Prudence during this dark time? What can Christians do to deal with depression?

5. What do you think of Mr. Walker's life story? Why did the blacksmith stay in England instead of returning to America? What is his primary characteristic?

6. Why did Anne fear becoming a real wife to Ruel by allowing him into her bed? What would the consequences be for her? for her family?

7. What sort of man is Lord Blackthorne at the start of *The Bachelor's Bargain*? Is he different at the end? If so, what has changed him?

8. What was Anne's attitude toward God at the beginning of the book? Was her behavior consistent with her attitude? Is she different at the end? If so, what has changed her?

9. Does God promise to give Christians an easy life if they obey Him? What will He do if His followers disobey Him? Can God still love believers and use them if they make terrible mistakes? What if these wrong things are not mistakes but are outright, purposeful sins—can God forgive them? Does God's forgiveness mean that believers have permission to do whatever they want?

10. Read Romans 7:14–8:2 to meet someone who struggled with disobedience. You might be very surprised!

The trouble is not with the law, for it is spiritual and good. The trouble is with me, for I am all too human, a slave to sin. I don't really understand myself, for I want to do what is right, but I don't do it. Instead, I do what I hate. But if I know that what I am doing is wrong, this shows that I agree that the law is good. So I am not the one doing wrong; it is sin living in me that does it.

And I know that nothing good lives in me, that is, in my sinful nature. I want to do what is right, but I can't. I want to do what is good, but I don't. I don't want to do what is wrong, but I do it anyway. But if I do what I don't want to do, I am not really the one doing wrong; it is sin living in me that does it.

I have discovered this principle of life—that when I want to do what is right, I inevitably do what is wrong. I love God's law with all my heart. But there is another power within me that is at war with my mind. This power makes me a slave to the sin that is still within me. Oh, what a miserable person I am! Who will free me from this life that is dominated by sin and death? Thank God! The answer is in Jesus Christ our Lord. So you see how it is: In my mind I really want to obey God's law, but because of my sinful nature I am a slave to sin.

So now there is no condemnation for those who belong to Christ Jesus. And because you belong to him, the power of the life-giving Spirit has freed you from the power of sin that leads to death.

11. Here are several Bible passages that speak about obedience and disobedience. Read them and decide what you believe God is trying to say to you about this subject.

Now, Israel, listen carefully to these decrees and regulations that I am about to teach you. Obey them so that you may live, so you may enter and occupy the land that the LORD, the God of your ancestors, is giving you. (Deuteronomy 4:1)

I lavish unfailing love for a thousand generations on those who love me and obey my commands. (Deuteronomy 5:10)

O LORD, God of Israel, there is no God like you in all of heaven and earth. You keep your covenant and show unfailing love to all who walk before you in wholehearted devotion. (2 Chronicles 6:14)

Will those who do evil never learn? They eat up my people like bread and wouldn't think of praying to the LORD. Terror will grip them, for God is with those who obey him. The wicked frustrate the plans of the oppressed, but the LORD will protect his people. (Psalm 14:4-6)

Joyful are people of integrity, who follow the instructions of the LORD. Joyful are those who obey his laws and search for him with all their hearts. They do not compromise with evil, and they walk only in his paths. (Psalm 119:1-3)

[Jesus said,] "Not everyone who calls out to me, 'Lord! Lord!' will enter the Kingdom of Heaven. Only those who actually do the will of my Father in heaven will enter." (Matthew 7:21)

Jesus came and told his disciples, "I have been given all authority in heaven and on earth. Therefore, go and make disciples of all the nations, baptizing them in the name of the Father and the Son and the Holy Spirit. Teach these new disciples to obey all the commands I have given you. And be sure of this: I am with you always, even to the end of the age." (Matthew 28:18-20)

[Jesus said,] "Why do you keep calling me 'Lord, Lord!' when you don't do what I say? I will show you what it's like when someone comes to me, listens to my teaching, and then follows it. It is like a person building a house who digs deep and lays the foundation on solid rock. When the floodwaters rise and

break against the house, it stands firm because it is well built. But anyone who hears and doesn't obey is like a person who builds a house without a foundation. When the floods sweep down against that house, it will collapse into a heap of ruins." (Luke 6:46-49)

12. How are these verses different from Romans 8:28?

Anyone who believes in God's Son has eternal life. Anyone who doesn't obey the Son will never experience eternal life but remains under God's angry judgment. (John 3:36)

[Jesus said,] "If you love me, obey my commandments." (John 14:15)

When you obey my commandments, you remain in my love, just as I obey my Father's commandments and remain in his love. (John 15:10)

You used to live in sin, just like the rest of the world, obeying the devil—the commander of the powers in the unseen world. He is the spirit at work in the hearts of those who refuse to obey God. All of us used to live that way, following the passionate desires and inclinations of our sinful nature. By our very nature we were subject to God's anger, just like everyone else.

But God is so rich in mercy, and he loved us so much, that even though we were dead because of our sins, he gave us life when he raised Christ from the dead. (It is only by God's grace that you have been saved!) (Ephesians 2:2-5)

Get rid of all the filth and evil in your lives, and humbly accept the word God has planted in your hearts, for it has the power to save your souls.

But don't just listen to God's word. You must do what it

says. Otherwise, you are only fooling yourselves. For if you listen to the word and don't obey, it is like glancing at your face in a mirror. You see yourself, walk away, and forget what you look like. But if you look carefully into the perfect law that sets you free, and if you do what it says and don't forget what you heard, then God will bless you for doing it. (James 1:21-25)

Don't be fooled by those who try to excuse these sins, for the anger of God will fall on all who disobey him. Don't participate in the things these people do. For once you were full of darkness, but now you have light from the Lord. So live as people of light! (Ephesians 5:6-8)

Oh, what joy for those whose disobedience is forgiven, whose sins are put out of sight. Yes, what joy for those whose record the LORD has cleared of sin. (Romans 4:7-8)

There are many more teachings in the Bible about obedience. Do you think you are obedient—as God wants you to be? If not, why don't you ask God to forgive you right now, and then to help you follow Him more closely. That's what obedience is all about!

Miss Pickworth Poses Problems

Regular readers may recall that trifling tidbits need to be tidied:

Can Anne and Ruel confound the sniping and simpering Society which so besets them? Will they live in London or set up housekeeping at Slocombe?

What is to befall our pretty Prudence? Will she wed Walker, or leap into the arms of a new love?

What of maternal Mary and her sickly spouse? Will he get well? And what of their wee one?

Sarah and Charles, happily home at last! But what awaits the Lockes when their shipment of tea arrives in London . . . or doesn't?

Dear dapper Delacroix . . . still sailing the seas in search of tea. Will he return safe and sound? Or will storms, shipwrecks, and savages undo him?

The Duke and Duchess of Marston, such a powerful pair! What will the dire death of their second son mean to them, and will they still favor their first with both title and wealth?

Charles Locke's father, James . . . young Danny Martin, the ship's boy . . . Mr. Walker, the blacksmith . . . Ruel's birth mother . . . a cast of characters currently left languishing.

Miss Pickworth urges faithful readers to familiarize themselves with another group of Regency friends whose lives are soon to interact with those who live at Cranleigh Crescent. Please read *Wild Heather* and *Sweet Violet*. And take special note of one particular gentleman, William Sherbourne, whose languid life is soon to take a tumultuous turn!

After you have read those books, do please join Miss Pickworth as she observes a most confounding conundrum in *The Courteous Cad* (available summer 2007).

A Note from the Author

Dear Friend,

Lace, tea, and a good book. What else could any woman want? As it turns out, we ladies require much more to keep us functioning—and fulfilled. Though I live beside a sleepy lake in a small resort community, I watch women all around me cram their days to the brim with husbands, children, jobs, manicures, shopping sprees, trips to the grocery store, luncheons, gardening, quilting, cooking, transporting kids from one event to another, and many other activities. Sometimes it wears me out just thinking about all the "stuff" we women do.

But how often do we stop and take time to listen to the way *God* wants us to spend our time, money, and energy? If you're like me, you make lists and then plunge forward into the day with the fervent hope that you can accomplish everything on your schedule. I wonder if the Lord gets awfully tired of watching *me* do *my* thing on *my* time.

What does our heavenly Father really want of His children? When was the last time you asked? Are the activities that fill your day done in obedience to His will? Or are you planning your own life . . . and then counting on Him to mop up the mess you've made by acting willfully?

Isn't it wonderful that in Psalm 37, God promises that even

when we stumble—and, like Anne in *The Bachelor's Bargain*, we certainly will—we will not be hurled headlong off the cliff of self-righteousness? The Lord is holding our hand. Praise Him!

Several years ago, the Holy Spirit opened my eyes to the possibility of writing novels with a Regency setting. I've always loved that period in England (1811–1820), when chaos reigned among England's royalty, Napoleon was wreaking havoc on land and sea, and the writer Jane Austen— delightfully oblivious to the pandemonium—was penning her charming books.

You may be wondering what the Regency period was all about and why it fascinates me so. Please visit my Web site at catherinepalmer.com to step further into this wonderful world of lords and ladies, tea parties and pirates, grand manor houses and wee cottages, and of course, true love!

This series features my favorite character, Miss Pickworth, London Society's witty tattler and advice dispenser. Who is this cleverly cunning columnist? Well, my dear friend, you'll just have to keep reading to find out!

Blessings,

Catherine Palmer

cx/cy — *About the Author* — cx/cy

Catherine Palmer's first book was published in 1988, and since then she has published more than forty books. There are more than two million copies of her books in print.

In 2005, Catherine was awarded the Career Achievement Award for Inspirational Romance by *Romantic Times Bookclub* magazine. Catherine's novels *Sunrise Song, The Happy Room*, and *A Dangerous Silence* are CBA best-sellers. Her book *A Touch of Betrayal* won the 2001 Christy Award for Romance, and *Wild Heather* was a finalist for the 2005 Christy Award. Her novella "Under His Wings," which appears in the anthology *A Victorian Christmas Cottage*, was named Northern Lights Best Novella of 1999, historical category, by Midwest Fiction Writers.

Catherine lives in Missouri with her husband, Tim, and sons, Geoffrey and Andrei. She has degrees from Baylor University and Southwest Baptist University.

Four Seasons...

a new fiction series based on
The Four Seasons of Marriage by
best-selling author Gary Chapman.

DON'T MISS
CATHERINE PALMER'S
NEXT BOOK

the
Courteous
Cad

AVAILABLE SUMMER 2007

Lord Delacroix and William Sherbourne vie for the
hand—and the large fortune—of Miss Prudence Watson.
Can either of these cads charm her, or does her heart
belong to another man entirely?

Dating Mr. Darcy

BY BEST-SELLING AUTHOR SARAH ARTHUR

Practical dating advice from the
world of Jane Austen

HELP THE TEEN GIRL IN
YOUR LIFE DETERMINE HER
GUY'S DARCY-POTENTIAL.

BEST-SELLING AUTHOR of *Walking with Frodo* Sarah Arthur

Dating
Mr. Darcy

*The smart girl's guide
to sensible romance*

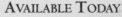

AVAILABLE TODAY

BOOKS BY BEST-SELLING AUTHOR CATHERINE PALMER

WOMEN'S FICTION

The Happy Room

A Victorian Rose

ROMANCE

The Affectionate Adversary

The Bachelor's Bargain

The Courteous Cad (Coming Summer 2007)

Sweet Violet

Wild Heather

English Ivy

Cowboy Christmas

Sunrise Song

Love's Proof

Hide & Seek

Finders Keepers

Fatal Harvest

A Dangerous Silence

A Touch of Betrayal

A Whisper of Danger

A Kiss of Adventure

Prairie Storm

Prairie Fire

Prairie Rose

A Victorian Christmas Cottage

A Victorian Christmas Quilt

A Victorian Christmas Tea

have you visited tyndalefiction.com *lately?*

Only there can you find:

- books hot off the press
- first chapter excerpts
- inside scoops on your favorite authors
- author interviews
- contests
- fun facts
- and much more!

Sign up for your **free** newsletter!

Visit us today at: tyndalefiction.com

Tyndale fiction does more than entertain.

- *It touches the heart.*
- *It stirs the soul.*
- *It changes lives.*

That's why Tyndale is so committed to being first in fiction!

TYNDALE® FICTION